The Real People
Book Eight

THE PEACE CHIEF

Also by Robert J. Conley

The Rattlesnake Band and Other Stories
Back to Malachi
The Actor
The Witch of Goingsnake and Other Stories
Wilder and Wilder
Killing Time
Colfax
Quitting Time
The Saga of Henry Starr
Go-Ahead Rider
Ned Christie's War
Strange Company
Border Line
The Long Trail North
Nickajack
Mountain Windsong
Crazy Snake

The Real People

The Way of the Priests
The Dark Way
The White Path
The Way South
The Long Way Home
The Dark Island
The War Trail North
The Peace Chief
War Woman
Cherokee Dragon

The Peace Chief

A Novel of the Real People

ROBERT J. CONLEY

UNIVERSITY OF OKLAHOMA PRESS
Norman

Library of Congress Cataloging-in-Publication Data

Conley, Robert J.
    The peace chief : a novel of the Real People / Robert J. Conley.
        p. cm.
    ISBN 978-0-8061-3368-3 (paper)
    1. Cherokee Indians—Fiction.   2. Seneca Indians—Fiction.
I. Title.

PS3553.O494 P4 2001
813'.54—dc21

                                                              2001027564

The paper in this book meets the guidelines for permanence and dur-
ability of the Committee on Production Guidelines for Book Longevity
of the Council on Library Resources, Inc. ∞

To Keith and Mikel

Author's Note

The details of the ceremonies depicted in this novel are based, for the most part, on the descriptions given in the John Howard Payne manuscripts. Payne spent several weeks in 1832 as a guest of Chief John Ross, was arrested with Chief Ross by the Georgia Guard and spent some time in jail. In 1840, following the Cherokee Removal over what has become known as the Trail of Tears, Payne was again a guest at the Ross home in what is now Park Hill, Oklahoma. This time he stayed four months. During Payne's time with Ross, he interviewed several Cherokee elders to learn the details of ceremonials which were already being lost at that time.

THE PEACE CHIEF

PART ONE

The New Life

I

Young Puppy of the town of Stikoyi of Ani-yun-wiya, the Real People, had killed another Real Person. That was just about the worst thing a Real Person could possibly do. A member of Ani-Gilahi, the Long Hair Clan, he had killed a man of Ani-Waya, the Wolf Clan. The victim, Asquani, or Spaniard, had been an adopted Wolf, and he had been a good friend to Young Puppy. The killing had been done by accident, or by mistake. Young Puppy, thinking that he alone was fighting several enemy Ofos, had turned and struck when he sensed that someone had come up behind him. He did not know until it was too late that it was his friend, Asquani, coming to his aid.

The blow had been struck. Asquani was dead. And in the end that was all that mattered. It made no difference whatsoever that Asquani had not been born into the Wolf Clan, that neither of his parents had even been born Real People. The fact that Asquani had been Young Puppy's friend, and that Young Puppy grieved for him as much as any other did not count either. Nor was it of any concern that the killing had been an accident. Only one thing really mattered.

A man of the Long Hair Clan had killed a man of the Wolf Clan. That meant that things were out of balance between the two clans, and balance was everything to the Real People. The crucial balance had to be restored, and the usual way of restoring balance upset by a killing was for members of the injured clan to retaliate in kind. A Wolf should kill Young Puppy. Or a Wolf should kill a Long Hair. Any Long Hair. It really didn't matter all that much. With the death of a Long Hair, the balance would be restored. All would be well. That was the usual way.

But the leaders of the Wolf Clan were not unreasonable, and since this particular killing had not been deliberate, the Wolves had not chosen to act on that clan prerogative. Still, they would have killed Young Puppy out of a sense of obligation to their notions of balance. They would have done that. They would have killed him immediately, without giving it a second thought, just as soon as they found out what he had done, but for one thing.

When the discovery had been made, Young Puppy was already inside the protective walls of the town of Kituwah, and no one could be killed in Kituwah. There were no exceptions to that rule. Kituwah was a Mother Town and it was a sanctuary town. Everyone among the Real People respected its special and sacred status.

So the Wolves could only wait and watch for their opportunity. When Young Puppy came out of Kituwah, if he should come out, they could kill him. On the other hand, if he could manage to stay inside Kituwah until the time of the new year, the problem would no longer exist, for at that time, among the Real People, all grudges, all faults, all offenses, all crimes, all animosities of any kind from the entire year just past—were erased from memory. That was a time of cleansing, a time of purification, a time of renewal.

So Young Puppy was safe in Kituwah, and it seemed at least for the time being, that his brothers in the Long Hair Clan were also safe from any retaliation. It seemed that the Wolves had chosen not to kill a substitute. If they had decided to do that, Young Puppy would have given himself up to them. He would not think of letting another die in his place. He was not that kind of coward.

But it did seem that the Wolves were not even seriously considering the possibility of killing a substitute, so all Young Puppy had to do was bide his time and wait for the arrival of the new year. That was all, and it sounded so easy. But the beginning of a new year had only just been celebrated, and so Young Puppy would have an entire year to survive, an entire year to wait out within the confines of Kituwah, if he wanted to secure his life in that manner. It would be a long wait for anyone, especially long for a young man full of energy and hungry for excitement in his life.

And though Young Puppy was not afraid of death, he had no desire to rush into it needlessly and prematurely. He had many reasons to live. He was a young man, who had not yet earned a man's name for himself. Death would not be so bad, he thought, if one had already done something with one's life, if one knew that after he had gone on to the spirit world in the Darkening Land on the other side of the great Sky Vault, others would tell tales about his bravery, and his memory would live on in the hearts and minds of the Real People. He wanted to accomplish things yet with his life.

Then, of course, there was the beautiful Guwisti. He loved her. He had planned to marry her, and she was willing. He believed both clans, his Long Hair People and her Bird People, Ani-Tsisqua, would be willing as well, had not his life suddenly taken on this new and ponderous burden.

And there had been the strange, unwelcome prediction of Uyona, the Horn, the old woman to whom Diguhsgi, the mother of Guwisti, had gone for advice, just as the Real People always did before a marriage. When Diguhsgi had told the old woman of the marriage which was under consideration, Uyona had told her that it was too soon. She had said that they must wait. They must wait for an entire year. They must wait for Young Puppy to die and be reborn.

Young Puppy had been furious at the old woman and at his future mother-in-law for having consulted her. He did not want to wait. He could see no reason for waiting. He especially did not want to wait to be reborn, a concept that made no sense to him whatever. Reborn? How could he be reborn? Would he then be an infant? How then could he marry Guwisti? He had left Kituwah in a rage.

Then he had killed Asquani. Then he had found himself in Kituwah with a year to wait through to keep from being killed in retaliation. Uyona had told them to wait for a year before the marriage. That much of what she had said had suddenly made perverse sense. Had she known that he would kill Asquani? Young Puppy wondered if the rest of her prediction would eventually prove to make as much sense, but he didn't see how it could. How could he be reborn? Such a thing was not easy to believe. It was not even easy to imagine.

It had not taken Young Puppy much time at all to become terribly bored with his dreary life in the sanctuary town. Almost immediately after he had made his decision to remain there for his own safety, he felt not so much like he was being protected, but more like he was a captive, held against his will. Each day was just like every other day. Everything stayed the same. Suddenly he could think of all kinds of places he wanted to go, all manner of things he needed to be doing, and all of them were somewhere outside the walls of Kituwah, out in the vast world beyond his reach.

It did not make his enforced idleness any easier to endure, knowing that he was the once proud owner of one of the few *sogwilis* among the Real People, knowing that he could climb onto the back of the big animal brought to his country by white men and ride fast and free like the wind. No. Thinking about his *sogwili* did not make his waiting any easier.

High on a rocky, tree-covered ridge overlooking a mountain pass that led into the country of the Real People from the east, a group of Wolf People sat in solemn conference. They had met there on the ridge because of their sworn duty to guard the mountain passes and keep out any outsiders who might attempt to enter their country uninvited.

The Real People had made that almost unprecedented decision, following news of the bloody invasion of the monstrous Spaniard de Soto. They had decided to keep all foreigners out of their country—all foreigners of any kind—and the Wolf Clan had taken on full responsibility for putting that decision into actual practice. From their positions on the mountain passes, they would first warn strangers away. If the strangers persisted, they would kill them.

Ordinarily three or four men watched the pass, but on this occasion there were seven. They were not all there to watch. They were conducting a meeting, and they had chosen to meet on top of the ridge because Trotting Wolf was there taking his turn at the watch. They could not meet on any important matter without Trotting Wolf's presence.

"I thought this had all been decided already," Trotting Wolf was saying. "Why do you want to discuss this matter again?"

"Perhaps it was, but I don't think that it was a right decision we made that time," said one known as the Howler. "Young Puppy killed a Wolf, and now he's lurking around down there in Kituwah, so we can't touch him. I think that we should kill another one from his clan, if he won't come out of there."

"That's the law," said Trotting Wolf. "We all know that, but we know some other things as well. The law does not tell us that we have to kill in a case like this. It tells us that we may."

"But I think that we should," said the Howler.

"Then who should we kill?" asked Trotting Wolf. "Who would you select?"

"Anyone from the Long Hair Clan," said the Howler. "It doesn't matter."

"It doesn't matter if we kill a good man who has done no harm? If we kill a man who might do great things for the Real People sometime in the future?"

"We have to restore the balance," said the Howler. "I would kill the first Long Hair that I see."

Some of the other men murmured and nodded as if in agreement with the Howler.

"There are other things to think about," Trotting Wolf went on, as if the

Howler had not interrupted him. "Young Puppy did not intentionally kill Asquani. It was in the heat of battle, and he thought an Ofo had come up behind him."

"That's true. He was as sad about it as are we," said Dangerous Man, "probably more than we. They were very close, those two. Asquani had become like an older brother to Young Puppy."

"And," said Trotting Wolf, "we wouldn't even know what had happened if Young Puppy had not told the tale. No one was there to see what happened. He could have kept quiet about it. He could have told a lie.

"But he chose to tell the truth, even though he knew that the telling would put his own life in danger. He's a young man, and he can yet do much with his life. He's honest, he's brave, and he's becoming a good fighter. He'll likely prove to be a valuable person in the future. It would be a shame to waste his life."

"Then take another Long Hair," said the Howler, "like I said before. I have no objection to that course of action. Take someone else."

"I would argue against that," said Trotting Wolf, "for this reason. Though we adopted him, and he was a Wolf, Asquani was not born into our clan. His mother was not even a Real Person until we adopted her, and his father was an unknown 'Squani. We should weigh all that against the life of a Real Person, no matter what his clan and no matter what has happened."

"When we adopted Asquani and his mother," said the Howler, "they became Real People, and they became Wolf People."

"There is yet another thing to consider," said Trotting Wolf. "If Young Puppy had run away or was hiding from us, then perhaps we could take another member of his clan. But he has not done either of those things. He told us what he did, and we know where he is. He's in Kituwah, the sanctuary town. Under those circumstances, would it be right for us to take another in his place? If we should do so, would we violate the sanctuary? That's something to think about."

"I don't need to think about that," said the Howler. "No one outside Kituwah has the benefit of its sanctuary. There's no reason we can't kill another of his clan."

"I think," said Dangerous Man, "that if we were to let it be known that we intended to kill another, Young Puppy would come out and give himself to us."

"I think so, too," said Trotting Wolf. "I don't believe that he would let another die in his place. And so, we don't really have that option. We either kill Young Puppy, or we kill no one."

When the Howler realized that he was the only one arguing for the killing of a substitute, he decided that it was time for him to back down. It was not good form to keep arguing alone.

"Howa," he said. "I concede. No substitute will be killed, but if Young Puppy dares one time to step outside the walls of Kituwah, I'll be waiting there to kill him. I won't ask anyone what he thinks. I have that right. I have that obligation. It's the law."

Grudgingly, the others nodded their assent. There was no way to argue with him on that. Without the protection of the walls of Kituwah, Young Puppy was certainly fair game for the retaliation of any Wolf. The matter having been more or less resolved, the Howler, feeling somehow more defeated than otherwise, got up and stalked away without another word.

"He's quick to anger," said Trotting Wolf.

"Yes," said Dangerous Man. "I think he wants to kill someone, and he doesn't really care who it might be."

"Perhaps you're right," said Trotting Wolf, and he took out his pipe and tobacco pouch to have a smoke.

The Howler walked back along the ridge to a spot overlooking the walled town of Kituwah, and he looked down upon it with a scowl. Never before had he felt anger toward the town itself, but now he did. What right had it, a town built by the hands of Real People, to keep him from doing what needed to be done? He felt like tearing down its walls. Short of that, he felt like walking boldly into town and killing Young Puppy.

What would happen to him, he asked himself, if he should do such a thing? There was no way to know, for never had the sanctity of Kituwah been so violated. No one would even think of doing such a thing. And, of course, he knew that he would not really be the one to do it. He felt foolish, being angry at a town, and he felt guilty even thinking about violating the sanctity of Kituwah.

Gradually his anger returned to its original object, Young Puppy, the killer of Asquani. A coward, to hide within the sanctuary walls, he thought. But the Ripe Corn Feast was nearly a year away, he realized, and to go free and be forgiven for his deed, Young Puppy would have to stay patiently inside the walls until that time was up.

The Howler had never heard of any man who had managed to stay inside Kituwah for such a long time. Any normal man, he thought, would grow restless and impatient. When other men went out to hunt, would not he want to go? When war parties went out to venture into the country of the enemies of the Real People, would he want to sit at home with the women and old men to be mocked and laughed at? How could any man endure such an existence?

After thinking it over, the Howler decided that Young Puppy would be almost certain to come out before the time was up. No man could stay confined inside the walls of a town for that long. And so the Howler would simply have to wait and watch and be there when Young Puppy had taken all that he could stand and at last came rushing out to seek his freedom. When that time at last came around, the Howler told himself, Young Puppy would find his death instead. A smirk twisted itself across his lips.

But then, he realized, he was condemning himself to the same fate as that of Young Puppy. To be sure to catch him, the Howler would have to stay just hidden outside the town and watch until Young Puppy came out and Young Puppy could decide to come out at any time of day or night, at any time within the span of the entire year ahead.

The Howler would have to find some like-minded friends to help him keep watch. He knew already that he couldn't count on Trotting Wolf or Dangerous Man or the others who had attended the meeting on the ridge. He would have to find someone else. Well, he thought, there must be someone somewhere.

But then he had another unpleasant thought. He realized there was another problem. What if, he asked himself, the man should prove himself to be such a coward that he actually would stay cooped up inside Kituwah's walls until the year is up? What then? He's free, of course. Everything must be forgiven.

Trotting Wolf and the others had already smugly decided that there would be no killing of a substitute, and so, if the killing of Asquani was to be balanced, it must be by the death of Young Puppy. Young Puppy must be gotten out of Kituwah some way.

Might there, the Howler asked himself, be some way of luring him out? That would be his second task. He would find some allies to help him watch the town in case Young Puppy should come out, but he would also try to think of some way to draw his intended victim out. That would be the thing to do.

2

For the first time in the short life of Young Puppy, time had become a burden for him. He tried almost desperately to find ways in which to occupy his surplus time. Sometimes he could isolate himself from others and practice the writing that he had been taught by Asquani. That seemed to him like a particularly worthwhile way to busy himself, for Asquani had told him how important the writing was. He had also emphasized the necessity for keeping it a secret, so Young Puppy had to be careful where and when he practiced.

The writing accomplished two other and more personal purposes for Young Puppy. It made him feel less cowardly for staying in Kituwah to preserve his own life, for, of course, he had not yet passed the secret knowledge of the writing to anyone else. It had not seemed pressing before to do so, for he himself was so young. He had thought that he would have plenty of time ahead of him for that. Besides, he had no idea as yet to whom he would teach it. That meant that his possible premature death would also bring about the loss of the writing, and such a catastrophe would only add to his own burden of guilt concerning the death of Asquani.

The writing had been important to Asquani, so Young Puppy felt obligated to preserve his own life in order to preserve the writing. He would have to live at least long enough to select someone else and to teach that person to write. He owed that to his friend, that and much more. It also seemed a way of keeping the spirit of Asquani with him, and when he practiced, he wrote messages in the dirt for Asquani's spirit to read.

He had become so proficient with the symbols that he could write out anything he could say, and he could do it very quickly. But he could not take up all his time in such a way. At times he could not manage to isolate himself from others, no matter how he tried, and there were times when he just could not keep his mind on the writing. No matter how important the writing, there were, after all, other things in life.

At first he talked to Guwisti a great deal, but he found that it was almost more than he could stand just to be around her, to be close to her knowing that he could not make her his wife for almost another whole year. She had been told by the old woman, Horn, to keep in her house alone for that time, and though both of them, Young Puppy and Guwisti, at times scoffed at the old woman, deep inside, each one was afraid to go openly against the warnings of the widely respected and feared Uyona.

So Young Puppy saw less and less of Guwist' as the days went slowly by, but he did not, therefore, think about her any less. If anything, he thought about her more often than before. It seemed that she was always on his mind. And he thought that the year which lay ahead of him would last forever.

He could not marry. He could not go out and hunt. He could not go out against the enemies of the Real People. He could not even go home to Stikoyi to visit his mother and father. He could do nothing. It was the worst kind of torture. He was walking around among the people of Kituwah, but it was as if he were—

Dead.

As if he were dead. And with that thought, a sudden, new realization came into his mind. The old woman had said that he must die. Perhaps this was what she had meant. Could it be? he wondered. And if it were, then he would be reborn. Yes, he thought. This must be the meaning of her strange words. And after I have suffered this long year of death, I will be reborn. I'll be free to marry. I'll be free to leave the walls of this town. I will have been reborn.

He felt better, having thus, as he thought, at last correctly interpreted the mysterious words of old Uyona, and he wanted to share the news and that resulting feeling of joy with Guwisti.

He went directly to her house, the new one she had built with the help of her clan aunts and sisters of the Bird People in preparation for her marriage, but she was not there. He wasn't surprised at that. She was required by the old woman to live there alone, so during the days, he knew, rather than sit by herself in an empty house, she spent much of her time visiting at her mother's house or at the home of some other relative, some other woman of the Bird Clan.

He walked on to her mother's house, and there he saw Diguhsgi outside, adding some sticks to a small fire. He held back, knowing that he could not speak to Diguhsgi. If things went according to plan, she would be his mother-in-law, and for that reason, he was forbidden to speak to her. He stopped a good distance away and stood in the road, pretending to have no interest in Diguhsgi or her house or anyone who might be there, pretending to be interested instead in a scolding huhu, the yellow bird that mimics others' voices.

Diguhsgi had seen Young Puppy too, and she hastily finished what she had been doing and, ducking low through the doorway, walked into her house. Guwisti was in there, sitting on a bench and weaving a split-cane basket. She looked up as her mother came in.

"That young man you like is out there in the road," said Diguhsgi. "He looks like he's lost. I thought you'd want to know."

Guwisti stood up and walked toward the door. She stopped and turned back to face her mother.

"*Wado,*" she said. "I'll just go out and see if he wants to visit with me."

"Or if he needs directions or something," said Diguhsgi.

Guwisti went outside and saw Young Puppy standing there alone in the middle of the road. She almost laughed, because, just as her mother had said, he looked lost. When he saw her, he started walking toward her, and she hurried to meet him halfway.

" '*Siyo,* Young Puppy," she said, and she smiled, doing her best to appear to be cheerful in spite of their frustrating and uncomfortable circumstances.

" '*Siyo,* Guwist'," he said, looking down at the ground. "I'm glad you came out. I want to tell you something. It's something important that just came to me. Would you like to walk?"

"Yes," she said. "For a little while."

They walked along the road in silence for a time, going toward the wall at the far side of the village, and she wondered what it was that was so important, and if it was so important, why was he taking so long to get it said?

"I'm worried about my *sogwil'*," he said at last. "You know, I left it outside the wall, and now I can't go back out there to look after it."

"Is there something I can do?" asked Guwisti. Was that, she asked herself, all that he had in mind? Of course, the *sogwili* was important. She could understand that.

"Yes," he said, "there is, if you don't mind."

"Of course not," she said. "I can always use some more activities to take my mind off this waiting. Tell me what to do for the *sogwil'*."

"Well, you should make sure there's plenty of grass for it to eat. Move it around from one place to another as it eats the grass."

"All right."

"And you should ride it every day. You know how to ride it. I showed you how, and after that, you rode it very well."

"I don't know if I can put the *gayahulo* on its back though," she said.

Young Puppy wrinkled his brow and thought deeply for a moment.

"Bring the *gayahulo* and the *sogwil'* inside," he said, "and I'll teach you how to put it on."

She smiled at the prospect. No one had ever before brought a horse into the town of Kituwah, although at just this time there were a number of the big animals just outside the walls. There was Young Puppy's mare, and there was the stallion that had belonged to Asquani. It belonged to Osa, his widow, now that he was gone. And there were all the *sogwilis* that belonged to all the Frenchmen who were staying in Kituwah as guests, the same white men who had given the two *sogwilis* to Asquani and Young Puppy in the first place.

They had accompanied Young Puppy home, following his last ill-advised trip north, bringing along with them the body of Asquani. Then Trotting Wolf, the leader of the men of the Wolf Clan, had held a special council to ask permission to let them come into the town and stay as guests. It had been a long argument, but Trotting Wolf had finally won the point, and the Frenchmen had been allowed to come into Kituwah.

It had been quite an occasion when the white men had come in. For a long time now, the country of the Real People had been closed absolutely to outsiders. But the initial excitement of the presence of the white men had died down some, and Guwisti was enthusiastic over the prospect of bringing the *sogwil'* inside Kituwah's walls and of learning how to saddle it up for herself so that she could go out riding alone.

Some of the men and women of Kituwah were learning to ride from the Frenchmen, but, of course, they were riding only with the permission of the white men, and they were riding on the white men's horses and with the white men right there watching them closely.

She, however, would be able to go out anytime she chose, without asking anyone's permission. Everyone would be jealous of her. She knew that, and she enjoyed the thought.

"I'll go out and get her right now," she said.

"First let me tell you something else," said Young Puppy. "A thought just came to me today. A good thought. I was thinking that, since I'm forced to stay inside these walls, and I can't go out, and I can't do anything, that I'm just like a dead man."

A pained expression darkened Guwisti's face, and she opened her mouth as if to speak, but Young Puppy covered her lips with the palm of his hand.

"Wait," he said. "And then I thought that maybe this, and only this, is what the old woman meant when she said that I must die."

Guwisti's face brightened again, and she put her hands on Young Puppy's shoulders.

"Yes," she said. "Of course. That must be what she meant, and then you'll be reborn."

"At the end of the year," said Young Puppy, "following the next Ripe Corn Feast, when I can go outside this town again."

"That's right," she said. "Everything will be forgiven. Everything will be renewed. And you will be reborn. Oh, Young Puppy, that must be what she meant. I know it is."

"Of course," he said, with a shrug, "that's still a year away, almost, but somehow still just that thought made me feel better today."

"Me too," she said. "It makes me feel better too, and I'm glad you told it to me."

She looked so happy and so beautiful, smiling, looking into his eyes, that he wanted desperately to hold her. He put his hands on her shoulders, and he felt a thrill run through his whole body at the touch. Suddenly he pulled his hands back, as if he had touched flame. Then he took hold of her wrists and gently, though almost painfully, pulled her hands away from him.

"Maybe you should go now," he said.

"I'll go get your *sogwili*," she said.

"No," he said. "Not mine. She belongs to you now. I give her to you."

She turned and ran as only a happy and excited young girl can run, and he stood and watched her go, the yearning in his heart causing his whole body to ache with desire.

3

Oliga, of Kituwah, hated Young Puppy. He hated the very sight of him. Every time he saw Young Puppy, he desperately wanted to thrash him into near unconsciousness. It had all started the day that Olig' had asked to ride Young Puppy's *sogwili*. Others had been allowed to ride the animal, and Olig' had only wanted to have his turn.

But that day, Young Puppy, who had just come to Kituwah with his family from their home at Stikoyi, had claimed that the beast was tired and needed to rest. But Olig' had kept asking, insisting even. He would not accept Young Puppy's answer or his excuse for it. He had been determined to have his ride.

At last, Young Puppy had given in. He had said that Oliga could ride the animal after all, and put the *gayahulo* on its back, but when Olig' had mounted it, the *sogwili* had begun to jump around, and it had tossed Olig' clear over its own head. Everyone had laughed at Olig' and said that it had been his own fault for insisting on the ride.

But Olig' was convinced that Young Puppy had somehow caused the animal to throw him. Others had ridden on its back, even the girl Guwist', and it had never thrown anyone else. Only Olig' had been made to bite the earth. Young Puppy must have caused it to happen. He must have done it deliberately, for he knew well how to control the beast. Olig' hated him.

Besides all that, Olig' now knew that he could actually ride on the back of a *sogwili*, for one of the white men had let him ride on his. It was not even all that difficult. He had learned quickly. He had ridden around in a big circle, and he had not been thrown up into the air. The white man had treated Olig'

better than had Young Puppy, one of his own people. Young Puppy made Olig'
sick with disgust.

Now, Young Puppy was living in Oliga's own town of Kituwah, and in order
to keep the Wolves from killing him, he had to stay within the walls constantly.
Because of the time of year, he would have to stay there for an entire year,
and Olig' would have to see him every day. It was too much. Olig' was not at
all sure that he could bear it much longer. It was almost like a personal
affront—the very presence of the man irritated him. If only something would
draw Young Puppy outside the wall, Olig' would show him then what it meant
to be humiliated. He would hurt him. He would pound on him. He would
leave him lying in the dust, bloody from Oliga's blows. He would make Young
Puppy eat dirt, the way Olig' had done. He would put several fistfuls of dirt
into Young Puppy's mouth right in front of everyone.

Olig' was lounging in front of the council house when he saw Guwisti
walking toward the passageway that led out of town. He wondered what she
might be up to, where she might be going. He knew that Young Puppy and
Guwisti planned to marry. Everyone in Kituwah knew their story. Olig' had
begun to hate her almost as much as he hated Young Puppy. She was a
beautiful young woman, very desirable, and as far as Olig' was concerned, that
only made matters worse. He wanted to ravish her. Perhaps he would. He
would enjoy that, and, he fancied, she would too. What young woman would
not enjoy Olig' in that way? Perhaps she would even change her foolish mind
about becoming the wife of Young Puppy. He laughed out loud with lecherous
pleasure at the thought.

Slyly, he watched her until she had reached the place where the walls
overlap to form the passageway. Then he jumped up and ran to one of the
long notched poles that was leaning up against the inside of the wall to allow
sentries to watch for approaching enemies. He climbed the pole, hoping that
no one noticed him, and looked out over the top of the wall.

He saw her gather up the *gayahulo* out there, and the blanket, and all the
various straps that went with it. She tossed the blanket on the back of the
sogwili, and taking the reins, she started to go back inside, leading the *sogwili*
along with her by holding in her right hand the lines that came from its head.
In her left hand she lugged the *gayahulo* along.

She's bringing it into town, he thought with sudden amazement. She has
no right to do that. No one has ever done anything like that before. He thought
about running to stop her, and then he thought about complaining to someone
about her behavior, but he realized that, of course, there was no law or rule
against bringing a *sogwili* inside the walls of Kituwah.

There had never before been such a thing as a *sogwili* around to cause anyone to make such a rule. He decided that he would propose one at the next council meeting. It certainly should not be allowed. He climbed down from the pole and walked over to a nearby tree to lean casually against it and watch. She came back inside, and the hated Young Puppy met her just there where she emerged from the passageway.

Young Puppy adjusted the blanket on the animal's back, then put the *gayahulo* up there. Would he ride? Olig' wondered. Would he risk his life for a ride out of Kituwah? Oliga's heart thrilled inside his chest at the prospect of a chance at Young Puppy. Oh, he thought, if only he would ride.

But then, his fond hopes were dashed. It looked as if Young Puppy might only be instructing Guwisti about how to prepare the *sogwili* for riding. And sure enough, once the task had been completed, it was she, not he, who climbed onto the animal's back. She turned it around and rode it through the passageway back outside the walls, and Young Puppy was still safe inside. He looked so smug.

Olig' seethed in quiet rage. He thought about running out after Guwisti, but he knew that if he did that, he would be seen, and he knew that he would not be able to catch her anyway, not while she was riding on the back of the fast-running *sogwili*. Then he thought about climbing up on the pole again to watch her over the wall, but if he did that, Young Puppy would see him and know what he was doing, and he would feel foolish. He did not want to be made to appear foolish in front of Young Puppy again. That was the last thing he wanted. So he just stood there, leaning against the tree, sulking. He would wait. His time would come.

Young Puppy walked through the passageway stopping just before he would have been outside. He stood there watching Guwisti ride until she was out of sight. His heart thrilled. She was lovely, and she rode the *sogwili* well. He was proud of her, proud of her beauty, proud of her abilities, proud that she wanted him for her man.

When she was gone, he was left staring out at the world outside Kituwah, a world of freedoms denied him. For a moment he found himself actually feeling jealous of Guwisti, and he felt both foolish and guilty at the realization. Then he looked toward Stikoyi, his home, and he thought of his mother. Another direction would take him to Turkey Town, near where he had killed his enemy.

And, of course, there was the way north. He knew that too. He recalled with longing all his past travels, and his lost freedom was like a heavy weight on his chest. He sucked deeply of the outside air, and he thought that it had a different taste from that inside the wall. Sighing, he turned and walked back into town. Having no real destination in mind, he wandered past the council house. Some Frenchmen were lounging there, as well as some of the Real People. Out on the *gatayusti* playing field two young men were practicing with their stone discs and spears.

" '*Siyo, mon ami*," said Jacques Tournier, in a curious mixture of the language of the Real People and that of the Frenchmen. Tournier and his ever-present interpreter, the Catawba, Little Black Bear, were sitting on a bench just beside the entrance to the council house.

" '*Siyo*," said Young Puppy. "*Tohiju?*"

"I am well," said Tournier. "And you?"

"I am all right," said Young Puppy.

"Come and sit with us," said Tournier, making a sweeping gesture with his arm. He spoke French, so Young Puppy did not understand the words, but he did understand the motion of the arm correctly. He walked over to the bench. "Sit down, *s'il vous plaît*," said Tournier. Little Black Bear interpreted, and Young Puppy sat.

"What are they doing over there," asked Tournier, "the two young men?"

Little Black Bear repeated the question for Young Puppy.

"Oh," said Young Puppy. "They're just practicing, I think. If they were really playing, there would be other players, and a big crowd would be gathered here to watch. People would be making bets."

"What is the object of the game?" Tournier asked, after the translations had been made.

"A player rolls the stone," said Young Puppy, "then throws his spear after it. When the stone stops rolling, and the spear has fallen to the ground, the two should be touching."

"*Mon dieu*," said Tournier, in response to Little Black Bear's interpretation. "A difficult game, I would think."

Young Puppy shrugged.

"If you practice all the time like Striker and Woyi there, you should be able to play it pretty well," he said.

"Well," said Tournier, "I suppose."

"Are you being treated well here?" Young Puppy asked the interpreter.

"Very well," said Little Black Bear. "Your people are good hosts."

Tournier asked Little Black Bear what was being said, and the interpreter told him.

"Eh, *bien*," said the Frenchman. "Just small talk. *Bon. Bon.* But ask him how he is doing. That is the question. He is the one with the enforced confinement and idleness. He is the prisoner here. We are happy and contented guests."

Little Black Bear turned to Young Puppy.

"He asks how you are doing," he said. "How are you taking your confinement here?"

Young Puppy shrugged.

"I'm just here," he said. "I wish I could be somewhere else. My family is in Stikoyi. The woman I'll marry is here, but I cannot live with her. Not yet. Many of the young men are out hunting, and I cannot go with them. I have almost a year of this ahead of me. It's not an easy life."

"But, *mon ami*," said Tournier, when he had heard the interpretation, "you are alive. Don't forget that. When it seems unbearable, remind yourself: you're alive. And the time will pass."

"Yes," said Young Puppy. "The time will pass."

Behind a boulder on the slope of a mountain just outside Kituwah, the Howler watched as Guwisti rode past him on the trail below. She rode swiftly on the *sogwili* that he knew belonged to Young Puppy, the man he was sworn to kill. He knew that Guwisti was promised to Young Puppy, if he should survive the year. The Howler meant to see that the wedding would never take place. He watched as Guwisti disappeared on down the road, leaving behind her a trail of dust.

Casually he wondered where she might be going. She was headed toward Stikoyi. That was where Young Puppy's family lived. Perhaps she was going to visit them. Then he had a thought.

What if someone were to capture Guwisti outside the walls of Kituwah? What if Young Puppy was watching and thought that she was being threatened? Would he come running out to save her, in spite of the danger to himself? That might be the only way to get him out, the Howler thought.

The problem would be how to forcibly detain Guwisti without actually harming her, and thereby incurring the wrath of the Bird People, her clan. He would have to think about it. He couldn't tell yet just how it could be done, but it was a possibility worth considering. If he couldn't think of some way to accomplish it on his own, and if Young Puppy failed to come out before much longer, then the Howler would tell some of the like-minded Wolves about this new idea. Among them, they could surely think of a way to seem to threaten Guwisti without making themselves liable to the Bird Clan, a way that would draw Young Puppy out of his safe haven.

Osa lay on her back in her house with her hands on her belly. She was thinking of the new life that was growing in there, inside of her, a life that had been started by Asquani, her husband who was no more.

She thought of the dangers and the adventures that she and Asquani had gone through together, had survived together in spite of incredible odds against them. Together they had fought the vicious Spaniards and won. Then for him to be struck down and killed by mistake by one of his own people, a friend, a young man he had been teaching—the irony was almost too much to stand.

Yet she did not hate Young Puppy. She could not. Asquani had liked him very much, he had even died because he had gone to rescue Young Puppy, and Young Puppy certainly had not killed Asquani deliberately. It was just something that had happened, and there was no one on whom to place the blame.

She tried not to dwell on her loss. She had already cried a river of tears, and her time of mourning was just about done. She had her growing *usdi* to think about. Boy or girl, it would be a part of Asquani, and therefore, he would still be with her, in a way.

So it was vital to Osa that this baby live and be healthy. She decided that it was time for her to get up and go out among people again. It was time for her to consult an older and wiser woman about her condition, about her behavior, and about the future of her child.

She could go to any of the Bird women, for she had been adopted into their clan, but she didn't want to go to them. She did not want to share her secrets and her worries and her hopes with anyone with whom she would be apt to come into daily contact. She didn't want the women of Kituwah talking among themselves about her problems and her condition.

She had heard them talk about the Horn, Uyona, an old woman who lived off by herself and was usually shunned because she was greatly feared. But she was also much sought-after, because of her powers. Osa decided that she would look for Uyona and ask for her advice.

She did not know where the old woman lived, and she did not want to ask any of the women for that information. If she did, they'd know what she was up to, and that wasn't any of their concern. She wasn't sure just how she was going to go about it, but she thought that she'd just go out of the town and start looking. The old woman's house couldn't be too far away, she thought.

She stood up and started looking for something to take to Uyona as a gift. She didn't have much. Looking around the room, her eyes lit on the Spanish sword that had belonged to her husband. She had no use for it, but it must be valuable, she thought. There was no other like it among the Real People, at least not in Kituwah. Its uniqueness alone should make it worth something. She picked it up, ducked her head and stepped outside. There was Young Puppy. He stopped, as surprised as she.

" *'Siyo,*" she said. "*Tohiju?*"

"*Tohigwu,*" said Young Puppy. "*Nihina?*"

"I'm all right," she said. "*Wado.*"

"I was just coming to see you," said Young Puppy. "Is it all right?"

"Yes," she said. "I was just leaving, but I can wait." She pointed with the sword to a stool there in front of her house. "Sit down," she said. Young Puppy sat on the stool, and Osa sat beside the door on a bench. They were both uncomfortable. Both felt awkward. After all, he had killed her husband.

"I haven't spoken to you since—well, since I returned to Kituwah—that last time," said Young Puppy.

Osa nodded her head in silence. She knew what he meant. She knew that he was referring to the time he had come back with the Frenchmen, bringing the body of her husband.

"Maybe you'd rather not see me at all," he said. "Maybe I should leave."

"I don't mind," she said. "It's all right."

"*Wado,*" he said. "I wouldn't blame you if you told me to go away."

"You were my husband's friend," she said. "What you did—well, you didn't mean it. The Ofos caused it, I think, or maybe it just happened. I don't know. But I don't hate you, and I don't blame you for what happened."

"No," he said, and his head was ducked low, his chin almost on his chest. "I didn't mean it. I feel very badly. More than I can say." He decided to change the subject. "You know that I can't leave Kituwah until after the next Ripe Corn."

"I know."

"That means that until then, I'm not much good for anything," he continued. "But if you'll let me, when I'm able, I want to provide for you."

"I'm going to have his child," she said.

Young Puppy looked up, surprised.

"I'm glad," he said. "That is, if you are. Are you glad about it?"

"Yes," she said. "I want it very much. It's all that I'll have left of him."

"Then I want to provide for you and your child. I want that responsibility. Will you let me have it?"

"You'll have your own wife after the next Ripe Corn," she said.

"Yes. I will."

"You'll have to hunt twice as much. It would be like having two families to support."

"Yes," he said. "I know. I'm a good hunter. Will you let me do it?"

"Yes."

"Wado," he said. He stood up. "Now I'll be going."

"Wait," said Osa, rising from her seat. Young Puppy stopped and turned to face her.

"Yes?"

"There's a place I want to go. I don't know how to get there, and I don't want anyone to know I'm going. I don't want anyone to know my business. Can I trust you?"

"Yes," said Young Puppy. "Ask me for anything. If it's in my power, I'll provide it."

"Can you tell me how to find the home of Uyona?"

He smiled and nodded.

"Of course I can."

4

Osa, following the directions that Young Puppy had given her, found the home of Uyona without any trouble. It stood alone in a small clearing deep in the woods, and Osa's first thought when she arrived there was that it looked like a house that had been long abandoned. The wood, where it was exposed, looked to be very old, almost rotten, and large chunks of the dried-mud plaster had fallen off the walls here and there, so that one could actually look through the holes and see inside the house. One could have seen, that is, had the interior of the house not been so dark. The roof of the house as well as that of the small arbor which stood beside it desperately needed new thatching.

Pieces of broken pots, old worn-out baskets, scraps of woven mats and broken sticks were strewn carelessly about, and the only indication of current life about the place was a small pile of black but smoldering ash just a few paces in front of the door. As she approached the house, Osa walked more slowly and stepped carefully, as if she were afraid that she might step into a trap.

Her heart pounded in her chest, and she gave a start—visibly, she was sure—when she saw the stern and wrinkled old face staring at her from the dark doorway. The eyes seemed to glow. She stopped and stood still.

" 'Siyo," said the old woman. "Gado dejado'?"

Osa took a deep breath and tried to regain her composure. She moved in a few short steps closer to the house, and she noticed that her legs were shaking.

"I'm called Osa," she said. "The white men gave me the name. The white men called Ani-'Squani."

The old woman gave a grunt and stepped out of the house. She appeared to be annoyed at the bother of an unexpected and unwelcome guest, and Osa felt awkward and embarrassed—and a little afraid.

Uyona stuck a short clay pipe into her wrinkled lips, bent over the dark ashes and poked around in them with a bony finger. Then she brought out from under the black ashes a small glowing ember. Holding it between her thumb and forefinger, she dropped it into the bowl of her pipe and sucked. Soon clouds of blue-gray smoke billowed around her head.

With a casual nod, she walked toward the arbor, and Osa followed her. Under the dry, ragged roof, they both sat down on crude old log benches. Uyona puffed her pipe, sending smoke up through the roof and on into the heavens above.

"Osa," she said to herself, almost grumbling. "Osa." She looked up quickly. "You're not a Real Person."

"Only by adoption," said Osa. "I came here with my husband, Asquani, and the Bird People made me one of them. I have a house there in Kituwah with the Ani-tsisqua."

"Asquani," muttered Uyona. "Yes. I know him. He was a Wolf, and he was killed by Young Puppy, who thought he was an Ofo coming up behind him." Osa ducked her head and looked at the ground, and Uyona shot a glance at her face, then looked quickly away again. "I've lost men," said the old woman, glancing at the bright sword which dangled from Osa's left hand. "Six of them, I think. Life goes on. Why have you come here to see me today?"

"I'm going to have his child," said Osa. "I don't want to lose it. I want it to be healthy and handsome and strong, like its father."

"Why did you come to me?"

"I don't know," said Osa. "I didn't want to go to anyone in Kituwah. They're all afraid of you. I—I don't know."

"Well," said Uyona, "I can tell you some things, if you want to hear them."

"Yes," said Osa. "I do."

"Well, then," said the old woman, "eat no *saloli*, or the little one will go up instead of coming down, and it may lie in your belly humped up like a squirrel and cause you problems when it's time for it come out. Eat no *duhdisdi* or it will not live. *Guhli* will cause it to have the *gowanigusti* sickness, and *atja* will give it black spots all over its little face and make you bleed excessively during the birth.

"If you eat the flesh of *jisdu*, the child will have large round eyes, and maybe it will even sleep with its eyes wide open. And the meat of *jisduh* will make it go backwards instead of coming out when it should.

"Eat nothing that has been killed by bloodshed, but only eat the flesh of animals that have been snared or stunned. And the nuts of *seti* will cause the *usdi* to have a big, black, ugly nose. Use no salt.

"Stay away from other women when they are in their bleeding time of month, and don't hang around doorways. When you go in or out, do so quickly and get out away from the door. If you hesitate in doorways, so might your *usdi* when it's time for it to come out. Go to the water every morning as soon as you wake up, and wash your hands and face and feet.

"Do not comb your hair backwards or the little one's hair will stick out all over its head. And don't wear anything tied around your neck or waist. This could cause the cord to wrap around the *usdi*'s neck and strangle it to death. And try not to look at any *adutluhdodi*, lest the little one be born with the ugly face that you have seen."

Osa thought that she could remember all the things she was supposed to avoid, except for the various meats she should not eat. She had already forgotten most of them, there were so many. But she told herself that it didn't really matter. She would just avoid eating meat altogether if she couldn't remember for sure. She would take no chances with this child of Asquani's, this fruit of their love.

"Go on home now," said Uyona, "and when first you feel the little one move inside you, come right away out here to see me again."

Osa stood.

"*Wado,*" she said. She held the handle of the Spanish sword out toward the old woman. "I brought you this. It belonged to my husband. He got it from the white men, the Ani-Asquani. From one he killed, I think."

Uyona stood up with her eyes wide. She reached out and took the sword by its handle, and when Osa released it, the unexpected weight of the thing pulled the old woman's arm downward. She recovered quickly though and lifted it up.

"I'll see you again," she said, and Osa turned and left.

Alone the old woman hefted the heavy sword. She grinned. She swung it this way and that and chuckled. Then she swung it wildly, as if she were hacking at her enemies, and she was a little too wild with her swing. She chopped the front corner post of her arbor nearest the house, splitting it in half, and the roof collapsed with a crash and a cloud of dust and debris, sagging on that one corner almost to the ground.

"Ah," she shouted and jumped back, startled, and then, recovered from the fright she had given herself, she dropped back down on her bench, looking at the wreck she had made, and she laughed out loud uproariously.

His name was Ahuli, or Drum, and it was his job to plan, prepare for and lead the ceremonial life of Kituwah. He had only enjoyed a brief rest since the conclusion of the Ripe Corn Feast, and now it was time already to begin the preparations for Ela talegi, the Bush Feast Ceremony.

The people of Kituwah all knew that it was about time for Ela talegi, for it took place at about the same time every year. But Ahuli would tell them when the precise time had arrived. He knew by watching the moon.

But when the time was really close, Ahuli told them, for they all had to make certain preparations, and a few chosen ones had to prepare even more than the rest. Everyone had to obtain a quantity of *tsola gayunli*, the sacred tobacco and a green bough from *notsi*, a white pine tree.

Six men were required to construct large hoops with crossed sticks in their centers. On the end of each stick, a feather from *tskwayi*, the great white heron, had to be attached.

Jacques Tournier saw these preparations taking place, and he became curious. He turned to Little Black Bear.

"*Mon ami,*" he said, speaking French, "what is going on around us here? Why are all these people collecting pine boughs?"

"I don't know exactly why, *Capitaine,*" said Little Black Bear, "but they are preparing for some kind of ceremony. I heard them call it 'bush.' "

" 'Bush'?" said Tournier.

"Bush," repeated the interpreter.

Later in the day, Tournier took a small notebook, a quill and some ink, and made a note.

Septembre, late. The Cheraques are preparing for a feast they call Buisson. They're cutting boughs from le pin. I don't know for what purpose, and neither does my Indien interpreter.

Tournier was not the only one taking a special interest in the preparations for the Bush Feast. Young Puppy was watching with particular interest, because he had so little else to do with his time. He, of course, had watched the ceremonies all his life, had even taken part in them, but he realized that he had not always paid that much attention to what was going on, beyond what he himself had to know in order to play his part.

Now the fire of his curiosity was fanned by enforced inactivity and its resulting deadly boredom. Without making himself too obvious, he tried to observe the actions of Ahuli, and, of course, like everyone else in town, he checked his own supply of ancient tobacco, and he had Guwisti to obtain for him his green bough of pine.

But Ahuli was secretive, and the only thing that Young Puppy was able to tell about his behavior was that the old man was watching the moon each night very closely. Beyond that, he was keeping much to himself.

Olig' went out of town to get his bough for the ceremony, and as he was returning to Kituwah, he came across the Howler lurking behind some brush on the side of the mountain. At first he thought that he'd pretend he hadn't seen the man, for it was obvious to him that the Howler had meant to be hiding, but then he changed his mind.

" 'Siyo, Howler," he said. "Are you hiding in there? I haven't seen you around here now for several days."

The Howler grumbled something low and unintelligible. He was upset at having been discovered. He had been lurking there, hoping to catch Young Puppy coming out of town. But there was no use now ignoring Olig'. Olig' had seen him already and had spoken to him. He sat there on the ground and leaned back on his elbows, trying to appear casual and nonchalant. Olig' walked over and sat beside him.

"I went out to get this," he said, waving the bough, "for the Bush Feast coming up."

The Howler grunted and nodded. He was still irritated at having been discovered, and he did not feel like engaging in casual conversation. Besides, he knew Olig', and he did not particularly like him.

"Have you gotten yours yet?" Olig' asked.

"No," said the Howler, "I don't think that I'll attend this year," and then it came to him that everyone was supposed to get a pine bough for the ceremony. Everyone. He sat up straight and looked eagerly at Olig'.

"Has Young Puppy gotten his bough yet?"

A scowl darkened the ugly face of Olig', and he looked hard at the ground.

"His woman went out and got one for him, I think," he said. "He didn't go out of town. He's afraid to. I wish he had, though."

"What?" said the Howler. "You wish he would go outside the wall?"

"Yes. I'd like to beat him, but I can't do it as long as he stays in Kituwah. I don't think that she should be allowed to get his bough for him. Do you?"

"My friend," said the Howler, moving close to Olig' and speaking low and conspiratorially, "I want to kill him. That's why I'm watching here."

Oliga's face brightened some at those words. He felt as if he'd suddenly and unexpectedly found a new and trusted companion, someone with whom he could finally talk about this all-consuming hatred.

"You want to kill Young Puppy?" he said.

"Yes."

"You're a Wolf?"

"Yes."

"But the Wolves have said that they'll leave him alone as long as he stays in Kituwah," said Olig'. "And Trotting Wolf said that they won't kill another Long Hair in his place. I thought they meant to let him get away with what he had done."

"That's all true," said the Howler, "and I agreed to all of that at our meeting. We won't kill another Long Hair in his place, and, of course, we won't kill Young Puppy while he's in Kituwah. We can't do that. But do you think that he'll be able to stay inside the wall for all that time? Do you think he has that much patience?"

"I—I don't know," said Olig'. "He might get restless, I suppose. I know I would."

"Or something might happen to make him come outside," said the Howler, "and if he comes out, I'll be waiting here."

"But what could make him leave the town?" asked Olig'. "He knows that he could be killed out here."

The Howler gave a casual shrug of his massive shoulders.

"Who knows?" he said. "That girl Guwisti is riding almost every day on the back of his *sogwil'*."

"It's her *sogwili* now," said Olig' with a scowl. "He gave it to her."

The Howler shrugged again.

"Who cares about that?" he said. "But what if something were to happen to her out here? And he would see it happen? Or hear her scream for help? Do you think that he'd just stay in town and watch and listen? Would he cover up his eyes or look the other way? Or do you think that he'd come running to her rescue? Or what if something happened to his mother in Stikoyi? It seems to me that many things might happen that could make him come outside. What do you think?"

"Yes," said Olig', a broad smile spreading slowly across his face. "Many things could happen. And he might come out. And you'll be—"

"I'll be waiting for him here."

5

A huli met in the council house with seven carefully selected councilors, one from each clan, and after the meeting, they called in seven women, also one from each clan. The people of Kituwah, of course, observed what was taking place and knew that the time for Ela talegi was upon them at last.

Then an official announcement was made. Word was sent out to nearby towns with invitations to everyone to attend. Some would and others would not. Some would be performing their own versions of the ceremony.

"Do you mean to say," Tournier asked his interpreter, "that some of the towns have the ceremony and some do not? Is the ceremonial life of these people so haphazard as that?"

"From what I have been able to learn," said Little Black Bear, "these Cheraques used to have a priesthood that controlled all of the ceremonies. Some generations back, the priests had become too powerful, and they were abusing their powers.

"They say that a man came home from a hunt, and he couldn't find his wife. He asked his friends and neighbors about her. One finally told him that while he was gone, the priests had come and taken her away. The man got his friends together, and they decided that they had taken enough from the priests. The priests had finally gone too far.

"And so the people rose up and killed them all—all but one or two. With the priests gone, of course, the ceremonies have suffered. The one or two priests who were not killed showed the ceremonies to some people, I guess, and I guess some old ones remembered on their own how the ceremonies went before. So each town does what it can, and if a town doesn't have anyone who can lead, then they go to another town for the ceremonies."

"I see," said Tournier. He tried to imagine an uprising in France where all of the Catholic priests would be slaughtered, but the people, *les français*, still religious in their hearts and souls, would try to conduct mass for themselves. He found such a situation almost impossible to imagine.

The women from the seven clans went out from their meeting with Ahuli and the seven men went to the other women of their respective clans to organize the preparation of the meals for the ceremony. There would have to be enough for all who would attend.

Jacques Tournier watched all he could, and he asked questions of Little Black Bear almost constantly, but the interpreter, being of a different people, could not always answer them. He did his best though, and whenever he saw an opportunity, he would ask Young Puppy to tell him what was going on, so he could relay the information on to the curious Frenchman. But here he found himself somewhat frustrated, for often Young Puppy did not seem to know much more than did the interpreter.

It occurred to Little Black Bear that if someone, perhaps Ahuli himself, remembered how the ceremony had gone, however perfectly or imperfectly, he might not remember, or might not have ever known, the reasons for all of the actions. And if Ahuli, the leader of the ceremony, did not know, how could Young Puppy know? Or anyone else for that matter?

Tactfully, the Catawba kept that thought to himself. It was just a thought, based on what little he had heard about the revolt against the priests. It would not be good to express it out loud to any of the Real People, or to the Frenchmen, especially not to the Frenchmen. It was none of Little Black Bear's business, and it was certainly none of Tournier's.

The next few days, people came into Kituwah from several of the neighboring towns, places that lacked people with the knowledge to lead the ceremony. Young Puppy watched anxiously as people from his own town of Stikoyi began to arrive, and sure enough, at last he saw Lolo, his mother, and Yona Hawiya, or Bear Meat, his father. As they came inside the wall, he ran to greet them.

"How are you, my son?" asked Lolo.

"I'm well," said Young Puppy, "but I'm so bored in this town. I've been wanting to go home to visit you. I want to go hunt. It's making me crazy. I hope that I can stand it here for the rest of the time."

"You must," said Lolo.

Young Puppy ducked his head and looked at the ground.

"Yes," he said. "I know."

"Son," said Lolo, "Bear Meat and I, we've been talking about moving over here to Kituwah."

"What?" said Young Puppy, almost afraid to believe what he had heard. "You mean—you would live here?"

"Yes," said Bear Meat. "Your mother will build a new house for herself here in Kituwah, and we'll come over here to live."

"At least until your time here is done," Lolo added quickly. "Would you like that?"

"Yes," said Young Puppy, smiling widely. "I'd like that very much."

"Good," said Lolo. "We'll talk some more about it later."

The excitement of visitors in town helped to make the days pass more quickly for everyone, even the Frenchmen, and at last Young Puppy told Little Black Bear that the ceremony was scheduled to begin early the next morning.

Men appointed for the task by Ahuli had reshaped and renewed the altar in the center of the sacred dance ground. They built it of earth and fashioned it in the shape of a cone. When they had just the height they wanted, about halfway between their waists and shoulders, they flattened the top and drew a circle there on the flat surface.

Inside the circle, they carefully placed the inner bark of seven different trees: *tsusga*, the white oak; *tsusga guhnage*, the black oak; *nodu*, the black jack; *tilia*, bass wood; *unagina*, the chestnut; *wanei*, the hickory; and *notsi*, the white pine. Sticks and small logs from the same seven trees were stacked carefully over the bark. An ample supply of logs of the same seven trees was stacked nearby so that the fire could be kept burning.

Ahuli then kindled the fire and said a prayer, and the women of Kituwah began to sing and dance. They were soon joined by the women from the visiting towns. Lolo danced with them. The dance was not elaborate. The women moved around the circle going from east to north to west to south and back again to the east. They moved with short, almost shuffling steps. In spite of his initial curiosity, Tournier found himself getting bored with the monotony of it after a while. Still he stayed. He did not want to risk offending his hosts. Eventually it ended, and people began leaving the area.

"What is happening?" asked Tournier. "The ceremony is not over?"

"I don't think so," said Little Black Bear. "Not so soon." He found Young Puppy and repeated the Frenchman's question.

"No," said Young Puppy. "The ceremony begins in the morning. This was only a friendship dance. It happens the night before the ceremony begins."

"Is there to be nothing more tonight then?"

"No, nothing more. We are all going home to sleep."

Just before he turned to go back to Tournier's side, Little Black Bear noticed Young Puppy cast a doleful glance in the direction of Guwisti. The two young lovers exchanged a brief look, then walked off slowly in different directions.

The next morning a crier's voice awakened the entire town, calling all of the people out to go to the water. At the river's edge, the Frenchmen joined the Real People in plunging into the cold water naked or nearly so. Tournier had once again severely warned his men to be on their best behavior. With the people all in the water, Ahuli stood on the bank and prayed.

Jacques Tournier was astonished to learn that nothing more would happen until that evening.

These are people of very strange habits, he wrote in his notebook that day.

It was almost dark that night when the people once again gathered around the dance ground. Then Ahuli appeared, carrying in both hands a box which he held out in front of his chest. He shouted a phrase out twice to get everyone's attention, and the crowd quieted. Then he began to sing.

As he sang, he moved into the dance area, dancing in the same direction around the fire as had the women the night before. As he moved around the circle, the people gathered around, each tossed some tobacco into his box. He went around four times, then moved out of the circle and vanished.

Then two men carrying the hoops with crossed sticks and feathers moved into the circle. Staying abreast, they began to move around the fire. They were followed by two women carrying green boughs of white pine, then two more men with hoops, two more women with pine boughs, and finally two more men with hoops.

They sang as they danced, and seven times they circled the fire. As they finished their last circle, the women laid their pine boughs across the top of the box carried by Ahuli, who had managed to reappear for that purpose at just the right time.

The ceremonial business was thus concluded for that day, and Tournier reckoned that it had stopped at just about midnight. The crowd broke up, and the people all began going to their homes for the night.

"What will happen tomorrow?" Little Black Bear asked Young Puppy.

"The same, I think," was all the answer he got.

They went to the water again the next morning, and then they visited or slept or went about their daily chores. Young Puppy lounged against the out-side wall of the town house visiting with his father.

"Your mother has been worrying about you," said Bear Meat.

"I'm all right," said Young Puppy. "What can happen to me in Kituwah?"

"Nothing, I guess," said Bear Meat. "As long as you stay inside."

"I'm trying. I have so far."

"Yes. Your mother is afraid that you'll lose your patience and go out too soon."

"No," said Young Puppy. "I won't. I may go crazy, but I won't leave until the time comes. I want to marry Guwisti. I want— Well, I'm just not ready yet to die. That's all."

"Well," said Bear Meat, "I'm sure that Lolo will feel much better once she has her house here and can watch you all the time."

Young Puppy ducked his head and smiled, and just then Oliga came walking down the road. He saw Young Puppy standing there with Bear Meat, and he walked closer to the building, looking away, as if absentminded. When he was just about to pass by, he swept the legs out from under Young Puppy with one of his own. Young Puppy slid on his back down the rough wall of the town house and landed hard on his backside.

"Ah."

Olig' looked down at him, an expression of mock concern on his face. Young Puppy thought that he could see the delight in the man's eyes.

"Oh, Young Puppy, is it? Our fugitive guest," said Olig'. "I didn't see you standing there. I'm so clumsy. Are you hurt?"

Young Puppy stood up with a groan, dusting the back of his breechcloth.

"It's all right," he said. "No harm's done."

Olig' walked on, strutting pompously.

"I believe that he did that on purpose," said Bear Meat, staring hard after the retreating Olig'.

"Yes," said Young Puppy. "Of course he did. He doesn't like me. He'd fight with me if we were outside these walls."

"He's not a Wolf?" said Bear Meat.

"No," said Young Puppy. "He just doesn't like me. That's all."

As Young Puppy had said, the second day of Ela talegi was the same as the first, and so was the third. On the fourth night, however, just after the sun had vanished under the western edge of the Sky Vault, a great feast was laid out around the edge of the dance ground and everyone was invited and en-couraged to partake. All of the Real People, of course, were used to the food, but Tournier and the other Frenchmen were amazed at the variety of delicious dishes they found laid out before them: venison, bear meat, rabbit, squirrel, turkey, fish, several varieties each of squash and beans, corn prepared in different ways.

It was around midnight again, according to Tournier's estimate, when Ahuli appeared at the edge of the dance ground and yelled. The people quieted down and looked in his direction. He was again holding the box, and he started to sing. After a couple of lines of his song, he moved into the dance ground and started to circle around the fire as before.

"*U hu ni du du, a ni hu le ya,*" he sang.

He circled around the fire four times, and as he did, the people reached into the box and took out some tobacco. His four circles completed, Ahuli stopped just outside the dance area and produced from somewhere the pine boughs he had collected before.

The crowd started to move then, but in a remarkably orderly fashion, and each person, as he or she walked by Ahuli, took out of the box a sprig of the pine. They then crushed the pine in their hands and mixed it with the tobacco.

Ahuli sang again and moved to the altar fire, and the crowd moved in around him, forming a circle around the fire. Each person then reached out as if to throw his handful of pine and tobacco into the fire.

"*Yuuuu,*" they sang, their voices rising and falling as they extended the vowel sound.

"*Yuuuu.*"

But each time they reached forward, they drew back their hands, quickly, almost as if burnt by the fire, or, Tournier thought, as if they did not really want to sacrifice the precious mixture in their hands. At last, on a final note from Ahuli, they all, at once, flung their mixtures into the fire. The flames leaped and hissed and popped, and sparks flew high into the dark night air. When the fire was calm again, Ela talegi, the Ceremony of the Bush, was over.

6

It was the beginning of Gola, the cold part of the year. Council meetings, when they were called, took place inside the townhouse. Men were busy hunting, primarily for *awi*, the deer, and the women went out into the woods to gather nuts. The Frenchmen even joined in on the hunts. Poor Young Puppy felt totally useless. His mother had built a new house for herself in Kituwah, and Young Puppy was once again living with his mother and father. But Bear Meat was hunting most of the time, and Lolo was gathering. Guwisti was gathering too.

Of course, Young Puppy was not left entirely alone in town. Hunters went out at different times, not all at once, and not all in one group. The same was true of the women. And there were old men and old women who did not go out at all. Children ran playing around the streets all the time. Young Puppy greatly resented being left in town with the very old and the very young, but, of course, there was nothing that could be done about it.

It was the male time of year, and the healthy men of Kituwah and of all the other towns of the Real People were out doing what men are supposed to do, hunting for meat to feed the people. All but Young Puppy. Of the young and healthy, Young Puppy alone sat idle.

It was the time of the Eagle, Awohali, the great sacred bird, the bird who flew higher in the sky than any other, the bird no Real Person was allowed to kill, no one except the Eagle Killer, Awohalidihi, the one with the special training and knowledge. Young Puppy looked high up into the sky and thought of the eagle flying there and envied him his freedom.

The nights especially were beginning to be cold, and Jacques Tournier knew that he and his men were going to have a long stay in Kituwah. With winter approaching, he was glad to have had the invitation. He wondered how cold and hard the winter would be in this country of the Cheraques, and he wondered how long it would last. When would he be able to begin his trip to the north country to report to the Senikas the success of his peace mission? It was October, and he knew that it would be several months yet. He only hoped that the Senikas would not change their minds in that time.

Uyona, like other women of the Real People, was gathering nuts. She did not wander too far from her little hovel, but then, she did not have to. The thick woods surrounding her house were rich with nut-bearing trees, and the mast was deep on the ground, over her ankles and rich with chestnuts as well as a few other varieties.

The old woman carried a basket woven from honeysuckle vines, and she groaned or grumbled as she bent or squatted to fill it. Times like this she wondered why she had bothered to outlive all her children. An old woman should have children to gather nuts for her at the beginning of Gola, she thought.

She did not really have to gather the nuts, but she had always done so, and old habits are hard to break. Besides that, she couldn't stand the idea of so many nuts lying around and going to waste. And, of course, she had to have something to do to occupy her time, such as was left to her.

But she did not really have to worry about having a good store of food laid in for the winter. Her storehouse was always full. She did not even know exactly who kept her so well supplied, but there was always plenty out there. Sometimes she could hear them going in and out of the small storage house which stood up on stilts just back of the house she lived in. She never bothered to go out and try to catch a glimpse of whoever it was. Obviously they did not want to be seen.

She also kept a small garden plot near her house where she grew some of her own corn and beans and squash, but she wasn't able, at her advanced age, to grow enough to keep her supplied throughout the year. So she planted, when the time was right, and she gathered, when the time was right, and someone or several someones, she did not know, kept putting things into her storehouse.

Gathering her chestnuts, she thought about the people she was concerned with in Kituwah. She wondered how Young Puppy was getting along. She had been consulted by Diguhsgi, the mother of Guwisti, regarding the contemplated marriage of Guwisti to Young Puppy.

She knew that the young lovers had not liked what she had to say. She had told them to wait for a year and then the marriage would prosper. But young people hate to be told to wait. She knew that. It had been a long time since she had been young, but she could remember the hot blood of youth.

Guwisti would whine and pine and whimper, but she would be all right. Young Puppy was a different matter. He was the one confined to the interior of Kituwah. He was the one who would be killed if, in his impulsiveness, he dared to venture outside the wall. The ashes in the fire, the beads, the stick in the water, even her precious *ulunsuti*, the divining crystal from the forehead of the great *uk'ten'*, could not tell her everything.

They could give her warnings, which she could then pass on to others. Wait for a year until you can be reborn, she had told Young Puppy, and if he did not have the patience and the will to do as she had told him, then there was nothing more that she could say or do. She had looked and read the signs and the rest was up to him.

Yet she worried about him. She liked that young man—he made her think about her first husband. He had been about that age when they had moved into her house together. Ah, he had been young and handsome and strong and brave. And such a lover. He had been her first, and none of those who followed had been as good.

Then she thought about the others, all the husbands she had outlived. Most of them had been killed in battle, one by falling off the edge of a steep mountain during a hunt for *yansa*. And the sons and grandsons, she had outlived them all. Ah, how old was she? she wondered. She didn't even know. She thought for a moment that she had lived too long, and that she ought to do the decent thing and just go off somewhere to lie down and die.

But there was Young Puppy and Guwisti. She would like to see how that all turned out before making her final trip. And there was Osa and her coming *usdi*. That was another obligation she had taken on. She decided that she'd just have to wait a little longer before she could go away.

Carrier and Potmaker had mourned the loss of their oldest son, and so they went on with their lives. They were a little sadder, and they felt much older. The loss would stay with them, though the mourning was done. Asquani had been a child born of violence, the assault of a Spaniard on Potmaker.

A Timucua, she had been made a captive of the brutal Spaniards, called

Ani-Asquani by the Real People, when Carrier had gone south to trade. He had rescued her from the white men, and then he had taken her home with him to be his wife. And he had accepted the child as his own. Now that child was dead.

Carrier and Potmaker consoled themselves with the knowledge of a coming grandchild, the son of Asquani, so called because of the Spanish blood that ran through his veins, and his lovely Catawba wife, Osa. The death of Asquani had brought his parents and his wife even closer together than before. All three waited anxiously for the time of birth.

And they had their daughter, a beautiful girl, the child of their love. They had her to live for. They would watch her grow and become a young woman and marry. Maybe they would live long enough to see her children. Yes. The loss was great, but life goes on, and Carrier and Potmaker, even in their grief, knew that they still had much to live for.

But Carrier had within him another worry, one that he could not even share with his wife. When he had been just a boy, still known as Gnat, his uncle, Dancing Rabbit, the former Like-a-Pumpkin, former Kutani, had shared with him an important and dangerous secret. Dancing Rabbit had taught little Gnat the symbols used by the Kutani scribes to write the language. At the same time, he had sworn him to secrecy, for the Real People had only recently killed all of the Ani-Kutani, all but three who had gone west on a mission and had been assumed dead.

Then Dancing Rabbit had returned, and he had been spared. The blood lust was gone from the people but Dancing Rabbit had been afraid that it could return at any time. He feared that knowledge of the existence of the writing might cause them to try to wipe out the last vestige of the hated priests. Yet he had wanted to save the writing. It was sacred.

"Someday," he had said, "the Ani-Kutani will be forgotten. Then whoever knows the writing will be able to give it out to all of the Real People. For now, we must preserve it in secrecy."

He had gone on to instruct Gnat, now Carrier, to select another young man someday for him to pass the writing on to with the same instructions, the same warnings and precautions, and the same sense of sacred trust. Carrier had taught the system to Asquani, and now Asquani was dead. He thought about his beautiful daughter, whom they still called only "Usdi." Perhaps, he thought, she will be the one.

Osa still kept to herself as much as she could. She knew that it was not good form to mourn too long over the loss of her husband, and so she stayed to herself. She would not let them see her in her private grief. No one, she thought, could ever begin to know what he had meant to her, what they had gone through together—how, if not for their coming child, she would not remain any longer on earth without him.

She often thought about Asquani, waiting for her patiently on the other side of the Sky Vault, and she was anxious to go there and join him. But she could not. She was going to have his child. She was longing for the first movement in her belly, the first real sign of new life. That would also be the time for her to go back to see Uyona. The old woman would tell her more at that time, she was sure.

Guwisti went outside the wall to where her *sogwil'* grazed. She carried with her the *gayahulo*, the straps that went with it and the blanket. She was going for a ride. She had come to look forward to her almost daily rides on the magnificent *sogwili*, and she fancied that the animal also anticipated them with some joy. As she walked through the narrow passageway, in her delight and excitement, she did not even notice the vengeful Olig' lurking in the shadows behind her.

7

Ahuli had rested for several days since the Bush Ceremony, and it was time for him to be thinking about and planning for Nuwadi equa, the Great Moon Ceremony. His was a tremendous burden, but it was one he had embraced when it had been thrust at him. He had been a child when the people had risen up against the Ani-Kutani, but he remembered his father's words of caution and fear.

"The Ani-Kutani are the keepers of our ceremonies, the watchers of the heavens and the caretakers of Elohi, this Earth, the Mother of All. To strike them down will mean the end of the world."

Ahuli had never forgotten his father's words about the importance of the sacred ceremonies, and from the time of the early plans to attack Men's Town, the headquarters of the Ani-Kutani, he had started to go over in his mind all of the ceremonies. Somehow, even as a boy, he had realized the importance of remembering them.

He had not remembered everything, and, of course, he had not ever seen the ceremonies performed again. But what he could recall, he went over in his mind again and again, determined to keep the details there. And then Dancing Rabbit had come home, and Edohi, the man who had led the revolt, had convinced the last surviving Kutani to lead the ceremonies once again to keep them alive.

It hadn't been easy. Dancing Rabbit had been very cautious, afraid that being seen again in the role of a priest, he would rekindle the anger of the people and be killed. But somehow Edohi had talked him into it, and Ahuli had taken full advantage of the renewed ceremonies, watching and listening to every detail. He knew that it had to be done. He knew that someone had to assume the awesome responsibility.

It was a heavy burden, this business of keeping the ceremonies, but it was important. It was all important. It was everything, for it meant keeping the people alive. It meant that there would be future generations of Real People and it meant that the world would not end, at least not prematurely.

Ahuli spent much of his time in watching the sky and in counting the days since the waning of the previous moon. He also watched closely the leaves on the trees, studying their gradually changing colors and paying attention to which of them first began to fall. He had to know ahead of time just when the new moon would appear, and he had to have a variety of ways of knowing, for the sky was often cloudy this time of year.

This was the time of the creation, the time of year in which the world had been made way back in the beginning of time. This new moon was the first moon of all new moons. Ahuli had to be ready for it. He could not afford to miss its coming out. He was required to call together the seven councilors exactly seven days before the appearance of the new moon. All of his time was therefore occupied with his observations.

Olig' managed to sneak himself out of town without being seen by Guwisti. At least, he thought that he had not been seen. In order to avoid detection, he ran around a longer distance than would otherwise have been necessary to get to the place were the Howler watched and waited. He had the time to do all this, because it would take Guwisti some time to get the *gayahulo* strapped onto the back of the *sogwili*. Olig' knew that. He had watched carefully for several days, taking note of all the details: how long the preparations took, which directions she would ride off in, how long she was usually gone and which way she would come riding back. But he did have to hurry. He found the Howler in his usual hiding place.

"She's coming," he said. "She's riding the *sogwili*."

"Guwisti?" asked the Howler.

"Yes," said Olig'. "I'm talking about Guwisti. She'll ride right by here, I think."

"She has done so several times now," said the Howler, admitting the probability of Oliga's statement. "But there have also been times when she went another way. We'll just have to wait and see."

"Do you want to take her this time?"

"She may not come this way," said the Howler.

"If she does."

"I don't know," said the Howler. "I'm not sure after all that it's such a good idea."

"What do you mean?" said Olig'. "Why not? It's a way to draw Young Puppy out of town."

"It could be a way of involving a third clan," said the Howler. "Right now, it's just between the Wolves and the Long Hairs."

"We talked about all this already," said Olig', frustrated now with the hesitation of the Wolf person. "We agreed."

"I don't want to offend her clan," said the Howler. "We have this problem with the Long Hairs. It would be foolish to add one with Ani-Tsisqua."

"Then I'll take the woman myself," said Olig'. "You Ani-Waya won't have any trouble with the Birds if I take her."

"Even so, how will we make sure that Young Puppy knows that she's in trouble out here? What if you grab her, and he doesn't know anything about it? He won't come out, and we will have accomplished nothing."

Olig' began to seethe. He had considered this action for a long time now, and the Howler was backing out. He couldn't admit to the Wolf that he had become as anxious to seek vengeance on Guwisti as he was to seek it on Young Puppy. The Wolf had only one thing in mind, and that was the death of Young Puppy. His justification was the killing of Asquani. An attack on Guwisti for its own sake meant nothing to him.

But to Olig', it meant a kind of revenge on Young Puppy, and it meant a degree of pleasure for Olig'. He decided that he would attack her no matter what the Howler thought about it. Still, he would like to have the Howler's help.

"Often," he said, "Young Puppy watches her ride. He climbs a pole and looks out over the wall."

"Is he watching today?"

"I'm not sure. But he might be."

"Wait until another day," said the Howler. "When you see her come out to ride and you know that he's watching, then tell me, and we'll stop her. Then he'll probably come running out to her aid, and we'll get him."

"Not today?" said Olig', almost whining.

"No," said the Howler. "Not today."

Olig' looked toward the town, and he saw Guwisti, mounted up, turn the *sogwili* almost toward him and start to ride. He could see a chance for revenge slipping past him, and he wanted to cry out his anger. He crouched there beside the procrastinating Howler, trembling in his silent rage.

She rode closer. He knew what she would do, for he had watched her often enough. It was almost always the same. She would ride straight away from the wall toward the mountain, staying on the road. When she reached a point almost at the foot of the mountain, she would turn sharply, with the road, toward Stikoyi. Then she would ride on down the road and vanish.

After some time, she would return by the same route. He did not know how far she rode on these occasions, for he only saw her leave and then return. But her pattern was usually the same. Once or twice, she had gone a different way.

She came closer, and he realized that he was poised to strike. He would not be able to restrain himself, he could tell. He wondered just for an instant what the Howler would say or do when he went into action, but the thought was quickly dismissed. It no longer mattered to him what the Howler thought. It would be none of the Howler's business what he did. He would do it on his own.

She was almost at the point where she would turn the animal's head toward Stikoyi, and Olig' leaped up from his hiding place with a hideous shriek. Arms outstretched, waving wildly, he bounded down the side of the mountain and into the road.

The frightened horse stood up on its hind legs and neighed its protest. Olig', seeing the hard hoofs waving there over his head, screamed in sudden terror and started to back up. He tripped and fell over, landing hard on his back in the middle of the road.

Guwisti fought to maintain control of the *sogwili* and to keep herself from being dumped or thrown from its back, and the Howler stood up, revealing his hiding place, to better see what was going on.

The *sogwili* came down again, its forefeet stamping the ground hard, and Olig', fearing for his life, scooted backwards like *jisduh*, the crawdad. The animal reared a second time, then came down again, and Guwisti was still safe on its back. It pranced first this way and then that, and Olig' was afraid to stand.

He watched the huge animal with the sharp hoofs as it danced frighteningly close to him on one side, then around to the other. He held one arm across his face as if to ward off some blow that might be coming at him.

"Olig'," said Guwisti, finally more or less in control again, "what do you think you're doing?"

"I—I—"

"I might have killed you," she said, and she kicked her heels into the sides of the *sogwili* and skillfully rode around Olig' and on toward Stikoyi, leaving her embarrassed would-be attacker lying there on the ground in a heavy cloud of dust.

Olig' coughed, choked on the dust, and through his own coughing, he heard from the direction of the base of the mountain, a loud, raucous burst of laughter. It kept going. It wouldn't stop. When Oliga's coughing subsided enough to allow him to do so, he looked toward the insulting noise, and there he saw the Howler, his mouth opened wide, tears running down his cheeks, holding his sides and shaking as peals of laughter continued to rise up from deep inside his bowels.

Even before Guwisti had returned to Kituwah from her ride, the story was all over the town. Everyone had heard it. People were telling it and retelling it to each other, and laughing at it again and again. But no one had seen Oliga.

It seemed that, as soon as Guwisti had ridden past him, Olig' had jumped up and run into the woods. The Howler had seen him go, but even he had not seen him again after that. Then the Wolf Person had continued laughing until he had almost collapsed from weakness.

At that point, his mood inappropriate, his hiding place having been revealed and his body weak from laughing loud and long, he had given up his vigil and gone down and into Kituwah, where he had told the tale.

"He scooted backwards," he told them all, "like *jisduh*."

And picturing it, he laughed again, and his listeners joined him in the laughing. Soon Guwisti returned, and it wasn't long before she learned that the recounting of the incident on the road had become the latest entertainment in Kituwah. Everyone she met wanted to hear her version of the encounter.

And each time the tale was told, when the teller got to the part where Olig' scooted backward on the ground, one of the listeners would call out the next line.

"Just like *jisduh*."

A roar of laughter would rise up from the crowd. It didn't seem to matter how many times the tale had already been told. Someone would tell the tale through, and as soon as the laughter had died down enough, another would begin again, and it was just as funny as it had been the time before.

"He scooted backwards."

"Just like *jisduh*."

Then at some point in the day, when the story was retold, it was no longer Olig' who jumped out in front of the *sogwili* and screamed in fright and fell down in the road. It was Jisduh.

"Has anyone seen Jisduh yet since he ran away into the woods?" someone asked.

"No," said another. "I don't think Jisduh has come back home yet."

"Likely Jisduh won't ever come home again," said a third, and at that, another burst of laughter rumbled through the town.

"If he does," said another, "he'll be coming in backwards."

The laughter filled the air. Streams of tears ran down almost every cheek. Sides and bellies ached from shaking from the laughter.

The Howler was a part of the joyous crowd, as was Young Puppy. Young Puppy had been filled with anger when he had first heard the story. What, he wondered with some horror, had Oliga's intentions been? But very quickly he joined in the spirit of the crowd, and then he laughed as hard as any other. Underneath the laughter, he was very proud of Guwisti, and he was anxious for a quiet time when he could tell her so.

It was well after dark when Olig', by now known to one and all in the town of Kituwah as Jisduh, the crawdad, slipped back inside the town. Stealing along the inside of the wall, he made his way toward his mother's house. He could hear the sounds of laughter coming from the interior of the townhouse, and he wondered what was going on in there, so he ran over to press his ear against the outside of the building.

"The *sogwili* stood up," he heard, "and Jisduh fell over on his back."

He had heard more than enough. He skulked his way to his mother's house, and he was greatly relieved when he found no one at home. Whatever was happening back there, even his own family must be involved in it, he thought. They were there with everyone else in town, laughing at his misfortune.

Quickly, he ducked into the house and gathered up his things. Then as stealthily as he had come in, he left the town, determined to go out for a long hunting trip, long enough to let them all forget.

8

Oliga walked into the night with no destination in mind. His only thought was to get as far away from Kituwah as he could as quickly as he could. He had made a fool of himself, and the whole town knew the story and was laughing at him. In the dark, alone, away from the town, away from any other human beings, he still felt the skin of his face burning red with humiliation.

The loud, hateful laughter still seemed to ring in his ears, and he could not stop his traitorous mind from repeating over and over the hateful phrase, "Just like a crawdad."

He had made a big fool of himself, trying to attack a young woman, still a girl really, and then falling down in front of her frightened beast and scooting backwards, screaming. Walking away from Kituwah in the dark, he had ample opportunity for reflection. Of course they were laughing at him, and it was his own fault for having behaved like a fool. He was surprised to discover that his hatred for Guwisti and, yes, even for Young Puppy, was diminishing, even as his shame and embarrassment increased.

They had not made a fool of him, he realized. He had done it to himself, and he had no one else to blame. Even the Howler had told him not to take any action that day. Why had he not listened? Why had he been so stubborn? What was it, he asked himself, that had caused him to be so foolish?

He found himself thinking back to the beginning of this trouble with Young Puppy, and he admitted to himself that it had been his own stubbornness all along that had been the cause. When Young Puppy had asked him to wait to ride the *sogwili,* he should have accepted that response to his request.

It had been, after all, Young Puppy's *sogwili,* and it had been well within Young Puppy's rights to refuse. And Young Puppy had not said that Olig' could not ride the beast. He had only said, "Not now." Yet Olig' had insisted. Some of his friends had even chastised him at the time for his rude and selfish behavior.

As a result he had been unceremoniously dumped on the ground, and he had been laughed at. He should have shrugged it off, he knew, for that had been nothing compared to the way he was being laughed at now.

Eventually he wore himself out with walking and worrying, and he dropped down to the ground to sleep, but his sleep was fitful. It was troubled by horrid images of neighing horses and flailing sharp hoofs. It was tormented by the sound of laughter.

When he woke up the following morning, he decided that he would hunt. He needed some activity to take his mind off his troubles. He thought about hunting deer, but then he realized that he would have no use for so much meat. He did not plan to return to Kituwah anytime soon. He settled in his mind on something smaller, a meal for himself, *saloli* or *jisdu.* Of the two, he preferred the taste of the rabbit. He decided that would be his prey.

Osa had been visited that morning by the parents of her lost husband, and she knew they meant well, but she would rather have been left alone. Seeing them only made her pain that much worse. Everyone told her that time would heal her wounds, but it seemed to Osa that she only missed Asquani the more as more time passed.

She wondered if she would be able to stand it even long enough to let her *usdi* come into the world. She caught herself thinking very seriously about ending her own life, about making her journey to the other side of the Sky Vault to look for him, and she was suddenly terribly afraid that she would actually do it.

Desperate, she got up and left her house. She walked out of town and made her way through the woods to the home of Uyona. She found the old woman sitting under her arbor, the sagging roof of which was propped up on only three poles.

" '*Siyo,* daughter," said the Horn. "What is it that brings you out here to see me? You can't have felt it move inside you yet?"

"No," said Osa. "Not yet."

"What then?" said the old woman.

"I—I need to talk to you."

"Come in and sit down."

Osa ducked her head to walk under the drooping roof of the arbor, and she found a stump on which to sit. Uyona looked at her, trying to read the long face, the sagging shoulders and the heavy steps. Such profound sadness in one so young, she thought.

"Tell me, daughter," said Uyona, and she realized that twice she had called the young woman that. And then she thought, almost with embarrassment, that she was actually feeling that way toward the girl. She had thought that such feelings had left her long ago. But there was something about this woman, perhaps it was just that she was so miserable, that brought out once again after all these years her motherly instincts.

"I miss him so," said Osa.

"It hurts you."

"Yes."

"I know," the old woman said.

She had not said that it would get better with the passage of time, and Osa knew that she had come to the right person.

"I want to go to him," she said. "I want to die. Today I thought that I would kill myself, but I thought about his child in me. That's why I came to you."

"It's good that you did so," said Uyona. "It would not be good just now for you to die."

"*Ulisi*," said Osa, and she was trembling as she spoke, "I don't think that I can stand it any longer."

"Daughter," said the old woman, "Listen to me. I'm going to tell you something that you won't believe until sometime later on. Nevertheless, it's true. I know these things, because I'm very old. Nothing is put upon us that we cannot bear."

She looked at Osa, and she could see that her words of wisdom had not helped. Of course, she had known that they wouldn't. Not yet. The young woman just sat there, trembling, looking at the ground. Uyona knew that she couldn't send her away like that. She would have to do something more. She put her hands on her knees and shoved herself to her feet.

"Go inside the house," she said, "and lie down. I'll make you some tea to drink. It will help."

Young Puppy was perched atop the observation pole looking out over the wall. Everyone but he could go out there and roam, he thought. He alone was confined. He could almost feel the wind in his face as he raced along the road on the back of his *sogwili*. He pictured the deer in the woods, and he looked at the mountain there before him and thought about what was on the other side. No one, he thought, could be more miserable than he.

" *'Siyo, unali.* "

He looked over his shoulder and down to see who it was had spoken to him and called him friend. It was the Frenchman, Jacques Tournier. The Catawba, Little Black Bear, his constant shadow, stood beside him. Young Puppy smiled down at the two guests.

" *'Siyo,* " he said, and he moved back down the notched pole to stand on the ground there in front of the Frenchman and his interpreter.

"How are things with you?" Tournier asked, speaking the language of the Real People.

"Ah," said Young Puppy, "I long to be outside the wall."

Tournier gave a questioning look to Little Black Bear, who quickly translated Young Puppy's words for the Frenchman.

"*Ah, oui,*" said Tournier. "I can well understand. You see, my friend, you quickly got beyond my feeble command of your language."

Little Black Bear translated, and Young Puppy laughed politely.

"I think you're doing very well," he said. "You've only been here with us a short time."

"*Wado,*" said Tournier, beaming with pride upon hearing the translation.

The Howler had completely abandoned his post outside of Kituwah after the episode of Oliga's attempted attack on Guwisti. He was certain that the girl had seen him lying in wait there, and she would likely tell Young Puppy. There was not much point in it anymore. Besides, it was getting cold, and there would be plenty of warm weather left in the year after the winter was done.

The Howler's home was in a town some distance from Kituwah, so he decided that rather than return home, he would stay on for a while in Kituwah as a visitor. There were already several visitors in Kituwah, some staying in homes and some in the townhouse. He would go to the townhouse.

Perhaps he had been too anxious, anyway, to kill Young Puppy. Anyone could stay inside the walls for a time. Later, when the young man had been there for several moons, he would almost certainly begin to get restless. Later there would be opportunity. In the meantime, if the Howler stayed on at Kituwah, he could keep his eyes on Young Puppy. He could watch him become more and more nervous, more and more anxious to get outside. It might even be better that way.

9

The Senika People were waiting for the return of the Frenchmen, who were to bring word of whether or not their old enemies, the Cave People, far to the south, would entertain talk of peace. Should the response of the Cave People be positive, then some Senikas would return with the Frenchmen to the country of the Cave People to formally conclude the peace.

Owl was convinced that the response would be positive, and he told everyone in his town what he believed. He also made it clear to everyone that he supported the plan. Owl was known to have the ability to see into the future. No one could remember a time when he had been wrong. Therefore the Senikas all began to behave as though a peace mission to the Cave People in the near future was a certainty.

"We have to get ready for the trip," Owl said. "We have to decide who will go, and then those selected must go to the water."

At a big council meeting, the men who would make the journey were selected. It was determined that Owl would be their leader, and fourteen others were chosen to go with him. It was a great honor. The very next day, Owl led the fourteen men to a place far into the forest beside the river, a secluded place where they would not be observed by anyone else.

There, for the next ten days, the men drank medicine every morning. The medicine made them toss up the contents of their stomachs, and after they had done that, they went into the river to wash. At the end of ten days of this activity, the men would all be purified.

Once the ten days had passed, Owl sent some of the men out to kill a deer. It was time, he said, to start gathering the eagle feathers. He took the rest of the men to the top of a high hill, and he instructed them to dig a pit deep enough and long enough for Owl to lie in and be concealed.

When the digging was done, Owl got down into the pit, and some of the men covered it over with branches of trees until he was completely hidden, but there was space between some of the branches for him to be able to reach out with his hands.

Then the hunters returned with the body of a freshly killed deer. The deer was laid out on top of the branches that hid Owl. The rest of the men left the area, at Owl's instructions, and they said prayers and sang songs asking Shadageya, the Cloud Dweller, to come down.

Owl waited patiently. He had to be perfectly still. There wasn't much room inside the pit to move around anyway. He waited one whole day and one whole night, and sometime during the morning of the second day, he heard a fluttering of wings, and he could see a shadow descending. A hawk had come down to feed off the body of the deer.

"Go away," said Owl, and he shook the branches above him. The frightened hawk shrieked an indignant protest and flew away. Twice more that day, he had to frighten off unwanted birds. He waited still. Another night passed by. Another day.

It was the middle of the morning of the fourth day. Owl no longer felt his hunger, and he was not at all certain how long he had lain in the pit. He saw a large shadow darken the rack above him, and his heart pounded as he watched and listened. He heard the sounds of the big wings before he saw the bird. It landed hard on the carcass of the deer, shaking the platform of branches above him, and then he could see it clearly. Shadageya. Owl waited, his heart pounding in his chest.

Shadageya began to eat. Slowly, carefully, Owl reached out between the branches. He closed his fingers tightly on one lone tail feather. Shadageya screeched his displeasure and spread his wide wings. He rose gracefully into the air, and Owl held tight to the precious feather. The feather came loose in Owl's hand as Shadageya made his escape.

Owl felt good, but he well knew that this same ritual would have to be repeated with equal success eleven more times before he would have obtained the required number of tailfeathers, the number needed to make the journey for peace.

Ahuli, with the advice of his seven councilors, had at last made the determination. The New Moon would appear in just seven days. The leaves had all turned yellow, and many of them were already falling from the trees. Ahuli thought about the time long ago when the world had been created. It had been just like this, he thought. Just this way. He was anxious to see the Great New Moon.

The seven councilors each went to their respective clans and sent out designated hunters who would hunt for the next six days. They appointed seven men to prepare the seats and tables, and seven women to cook. Young Puppy observed all of this, and his confinement frustrated him all the more. He should have been going out with the hunters, he thought.

After some consultation with Little Black Bear and some with Young Puppy through Little Black Bear, Jacques Tournier made some notes on the events. *It is early in Octobre,* he wrote, *and it is to these people the beginning of their year. It is just about time for another of their major ceremonies.*

Oliga had spent a cold and lonely night in the mountains. It was too cold. He had not slept well. He decided that he would go to another town of the Real People, one not too close to Kituwah. He knew that his own clansmen, the Ani-Wodi or Paint People, would gladly take him in. They would feed him and give him a warm place to sleep.

Olig' had no long-range plans. He only knew that he could not face the ridicule of the people back home in Kituwah. He could not stand the look of triumph that he imagined on the face of Guwisti or the scorn on that of Young Puppy. His own parents and his other close kinsmen would feel that he had embarrassed them, and they, too, would either shun his company or tease him unmercifully.

Others would keep telling the shameful tale and keep laughing at it over and over again each time just as if they were hearing it for the first time ever. They would call him "Jisduh." He could not face them, and so he was out in the woods alone.

But it was getting cold, and he wanted a warm place to stay, especially for the nights. And he had not had a really decent meal since he had sneaked away from home under cover of darkness. Yes. He was sure that he must go on to another town, but he would have to decide which town to go to.

Ijodi and Stikoyi were both too close to Kituwah. People in those two towns would almost certainly have heard the tale already. He would have to go to some place farther off. At last he decided that he would journey north to Coyatee.

Coyatee was far enough away that people there would not likely have heard the embarrassing story. It was a hard journey over the mountains, and visits between the two towns were infrequent. Olig' thought that he would probably be able to stay in Coyatee for a good long while, perhaps long enough to allow the people back home to forget his humiliation.

It would not be an easy trip to make alone, but it would be worth the trouble and the hardship once he arrived there. No one would know him there. He would be able at last to relax, eat well and survive in comfort. His clansmen at Coyatee would treat him well. He was sure of it. Coyatee was the place to go.

IO

S triker and Woyi, the *gatayusti* players, were the first of the hunters to return to Kituwah, and they went immediately to the home of Ahuli and proudly presented him with the tip of a deer's tongue, wrapped in leaves. They also gave him the skin of the deer. The meat had been given to the cooks of the Seven Clans to prepare for the big feast to come. The next six deerskins to come in would also go to Ahuli.

In the meantime, the women from the seven clans were busy gathering together baskets full of the produce they had raised in their gardens: hard corn, beans, dried pumpkins and squash. These things were then also delivered to Ahuli who directed that they be put into the communal storehouse. Then at last the seventh deerskin was delivered into the hands of Ahuli.

"In two days," he announced, "the New Moon will appear and the ceremony will begin."

Jacques Tournier, having heard the announcement, looked up into the sky and found it dark and heavy with clouds. Then he glanced at Little Black Bear, who was standing patiently by his side.

"What will happen," he asked in French, "if the new moon does not appear in two days? What if the old conjurer is wrong?"

Little Black Bear shrugged.

"Je ne sais pas," he said. "I expect that it will appear. If not, then he'll probably make some explanation for its failure."

Tournier thought that it was amusing that the failure would be ascribed to the moon rather than to Ahuli, but he decided to keep that thought to himself. Perhaps he would put it into his notes.

For the rest of the day, the Frenchman found himself looking into the sky for any sign of the new moon, but the sky was heavy with clouds. We won't be able to tell, he thought. Ah. Perhaps that is exactly the old scoundrel's game after all.

It was well after dark when Young Puppy made his way to the house of Guwisti. He was careful that no one saw him, and the overcast sky seemed to be working in his favor. There was no moonlight, no starlight. His sneaking made him feel like a thief, but his desire drove him on. His heart was pounding, and he felt almost hot, in spite of the cool night air.

When at last he reached the house, he lay down beside it, pressing himself against the wall. He waited. No one was stirring in the street or at the neighboring houses. He had made it undetected. The plastered wall of the house was cold against his warm skin, and he thought that his heavy breathing was much too loud. He wondered if Guwist' could hear it through the wall.

He waited, hoping that she would somehow know that he was there, hoping that she would come out, or that she would at least put her head into the doorway and whisper to him to come in to her. He pressed the side of his head hard against the wall to listen for some indication, some sound of movement, her breathing even, but he heard nothing through the wall.

He wanted her so badly. He ached with desire. Did she not want him too? Did she not feel as he did? And if so, should not her thoughts connect with his? Why, he wondered, did she not know that he was out there, alone, waiting for her, longing for her, suffering? Why did she not invite him in? He thought about getting up and slipping on boldly inside the house to wake her up and to lie down beside her, but something kept him from doing so.

At last he stood up and began to skulk his way back to his mother's new house. He felt like a fool, and he was glad that no one had seen him over there. He was just walking past the entrance of the townhouse when a voice out of the darkness startled him.

" 'Siyo, Young Puppy," it said.

He stopped and looked. There in the doorway was the Howler.

" 'Siyo," said Young Puppy. "I didn't expect anyone to be awake here."

"And I, too, am surprised to see you walking around alone in the middle of the night like a grinning opossum, or an owl, or *waguli*," said the Howler. "Is something wrong? Are you restless?"

"Yes," said Young Puppy. "I— No. I just couldn't sleep. That's all."

"It must be difficult for you, a healthy young man, having to stay inside these walls while others go out to hunt and prepare for the Great New Moon Ceremony. I've heard several people say that you're a good hunter too. Is it true?"

"I was," said Young Puppy.

"Then of course you still are. One doesn't forget those things. Or you could be—if you could go out again. Where would you go to hunt, if you could go?"

Young Puppy shrugged. The conversation was making him nervous, and he was finding the company of the Howler to be more than a little annoying.

"I don't know," he said.

"Well," said the Howler, "if you were hunting deer, where would you go?"

"Oh, there's a field," said Young Puppy with a sigh, "maybe two days' walk from here to the north. It's a place that was cleared to attract the deer. That's a good place to go."

"You could get to it faster than that on the back of your *sogwil'*," said the Howler.

"The *sogwil'* is no longer mine," said Young Puppy. "I gave it to Guwisti."

"Oh, yes. She's the young woman you want to marry, isn't she?"

"Yes," said Young Puppy.

"A very pretty girl," said the Howler. "Yes. I've seen her riding on the *sogwili*. She was riding it just the other day when Olig' attacked her, wasn't she? When he tried to attack her, I mean. I saw that happen. I saw the whole thing. Did you see it?"

"No," said Young Puppy. He was becoming more irritated with the Howler. He did not like the way this conversation was going.

"If you had seen it, would you have run out to help her?" asked the Howler. "Out beyond the wall? Beyond your safety?"

"Maybe I would have," said Young Puppy, wishing that the Howler would shut up and leave him alone. "I don't know."

"It's a good thing that she was able to take care of herself," said the Howler. "You weren't there to protect her. There's no telling what Olig' had in mind for her. Anyway, she dealt with the situation well enough, and she seems as free as the wind when she rides the *sogwil'*. It's too bad you had to give it up. You must have felt free when you rode it before."

"Yes," said Young Puppy. "Free."

"Sleep well, my friend," said the Howler. "I expect that Ahuli will be waking us all up early when the Sun comes out from under the eastern Sky Vault in the morning. We should be ready."

The Howler then disappeared into the darkness of the townhouse, and Young Puppy stood for a moment staring after him. He heaved a sigh of relief. Then he turned and looked toward the path that led out of Kituwah, the town that was at once his refuge and his prison, and he wanted to cry out in his anguish.

"The New Moon will appear tonight," shouted Ahuli. "The New Moon will appear tonight."

All over town, people came out of their houses to listen. Ahuli droned on. "Tonight no one will sleep. Only the *usdis* will sleep. We stay awake with the New Moon. Tonight the New Moon will appear."

Though he had gotten little sleep the night before, Young Puppy was glad to hear the announcement. The ceremonies helped to pass the time. They gave him something to watch and something to do. They kept him from thinking constantly of what was outside the wall or of how much he wanted his Guwisti. They kept him from going crazy. Even staying awake all night was something to do. Even that would help. He glanced up into the sky and noticed that it had cleared. The Howler walked by with a wry smile on his face.

"Maybe it won't be quite so bad for you for the next few days," he said.

"Not so bad," Young Puppy agreed. The man seemed to be reading his mind. He knew that the Howler was a Wolf Person. He's trying to torment me, he said to himself. He thinks that he can goad me into leaving the town, and if I do, he or some of his clan brothers will be out there waiting to kill me.

Young Puppy wanted to get out of Kituwah in the worst way, but he knew that he could not, and he determined that he would not allow the Howler or anyone else to prod him with words into doing something rash and foolish. Let him talk all he wants, he thought. His words will not affect my actions.

In spite of his positive thoughts, the day crept by for Young Puppy, and when the sky at last began to darken, and the women began to gather around the altar in the ceremonial ground to dance, he was thankful.

Guwisti danced with them around the fire, and he watched her with burning desire. She was so lovely, he thought, and her movements so graceful. She was, of all women, the most desirable and she was his, if only he could last out the year. But why, he asked himself impatiently, why must I wait for the end of the year? We're both here in this town, and she lives alone in her own house, so why must I wait?

" '*Siyo*, Young Puppy."

Young Puppy flinched with the surprise, but he tried to cover it up as a shiver from the cold night air. He looked to his side to find Jacques Tournier standing there. He was glad that it was the Frenchman rather than the Howler. Besides, he had discovered that he enjoyed his conversations with the white man. They were pleasant and amusing. They helped to pass the time, and, he thought, he really sort of liked the man.

" 'Siyo, Tseg' Duni," he said, trying his best to pronounce the Frenchman's name. *"Tohiju?"*

"Uh, tohigwu," said Tournier. *"Nihina?"*

Young Puppy shrugged.

"I'm still here," he said.

"Yes," said Tournier, "and I'm very glad of it, my friend."

The Frenchman spoke haltingly, choosing his words with care.

"You're speaking my language better every day," said Young Puppy.

"Wado," said Tournier. "I think I'm slow, but perhaps I'm just impatient."

"Every time I talk with you," said Young Puppy, "you're doing better."

Tournier smiled, feeling a bit smug. Secretly, he was very proud of his growing mastery of the language of the Cheraques, Ani-yunwi-ya, as they called themselves. He had always fancied himself a linguist, speaking the Spanish, English and Portuguese tongues as well as his own.

"This dance of the women," he said, "it begins the ceremony?"

"The ceremony will begin in the morning," said Young Puppy.

"Then why are the women dancing?"

Young Puppy shrugged.

"They dance the night before the ceremony begins," he said. "That's all."

"Um," said Tournier. "Just as in the last ceremony?"

"Yes."

The answer was frustrating to the Frenchman, who wanted to write down in his notebook everything that happened among these people, along with an explanation for what had taken place. But he was not finding many explanations. He wondered if that was because the *Indiens* did not want him to know certain things, or because they themselves did not know.

He recalled that Little Black Bear had told him a tale about these Cheraques having killed off their own priests. Of course, he realized, there was yet another possible explanation. Perhaps reasons for things were not as important to these people as they were to him. The answers to so many of his questions, he remembered, had been preceded by a casual shrug, as if to say, it really doesn't matter, does it?

"Will they dance all night?" he asked.

"I don't know," said Young Puppy. "They might. It depends on how they feel, I guess. But we must stay awake all night no matter what they do."

"Yes," said Tournier. "I know."

It would be so much easier to stay awake the night, he thought, if they would keep up the dance. He hoped that they would. It would be a great deal easier. There would at least be something to watch. And the noise of the singing would help too.

He wondered if these people would be offended if he, a foreigner, should decide to go to bed rather than keep awake the whole night with them for the sake of their ceremony. He decided that he would not do that, however. He would stick it out, all the way, and he looked up into the clear night at a sky filled with dancing stars and a bright sliver of new moon, and the noise of the dance began for the first time to sound to his French ears something like music.

11

J
acques Tournier, his interpreter, and all of his Frenchmen spent the night,
after the dancing was done, visiting in the townhouse with each other
and with various men of the town of Kituwah. The Howler was there too.
For a while Young Puppy sat with them and talked. The talk was of nothing
important, although the Frenchman occasionally asked questions about the
ceremony which would begin as soon as the night had ended. The answers
he got were usually vague.

"Why do we sit up this night?" he asked. "We did not sit up the night before
the last ceremony."

"We always stay awake the night before Nuwadi equa," said Young Puppy.

Tournier did not bother trying to pursue his question any further. He had
gotten used to such answers, as frustrating as they were to his logical mind.
Besides, he was not really seeking information this night. He was just making
conversation to help keep himself awake.

Many of the men were smoking, and a fire burned in the center of the
townhouse floor. The atmosphere was smoke-filled, and the smoke burned the
Frenchman's eyes. He longed to lay back and close his eyes and rest them,
but he knew that if he did, he would soon fall sound asleep. And he was fully
determined to stay awake with his hosts the whole night through.

He noticed across the room one of his charges leaning back against a support post, his head fallen down on his chest. Tournier stood up and walked
over to where the man was lounging. He looked close. The man's eyes were

closed, and just then Tournier heard the man snore. He knelt beside the man and gave him a gentle shake. The man's head jerked up with surprise.

"André," said Tournier, "get up and walk around. Keep yourself awake."

"Pardonnez moi, Capitaine," said André, getting unsteadily to his feet.

"When you feel drowsy," said Tournier, "walk. Walk to stay awake."

As André started to walk, Tournier looked over the rest of his men. Then he sat down next to Dr. DuBois.

"Why are we doing this?" asked the doctor.

"We are honored guests here," said Tournier. "We are doing this to show respect for the ways of our hosts. Nothing more."

"Their ways are not our ways," said DuBois. "They are savage. We are Christian. Taking part in their heathenish rituals is blasphemous on our part, I would say. What will they think of this back in France?"

"When we get back, *Docteur,*" said Tournier, "you can find out, if you wish to complain. In the meantime, I am in charge of this expedition, and you will do as I say. You and all the rest."

Somewhere to the north, beside a clear mountain stream, Oliga cooked a spitted rabbit over a small fire. He was not sure how much longer it would take him to reach his destination of Coyatee. But he had walked a long day. He was tired and he was hungry. He turned the spit and listened for a moment as the grease dripped into the fire and hissed. Then he lay back and looked up into the night sky at the bright moon.

Back at home in Kituwah, he thought, they would all be just getting ready for the Nuwadi equa. Perhaps it had already begun. He couldn't be sure. He had a loneliness in his heart for Kituwah, for all his relatives and his friends.

He thought about the dancing that would take place around the fire. He could almost see the women circling, hear the soft rattle of the turtle shells and the voice of Ahuli leading the dance. Oh, how he would like to be there, at home.

But he would like to be there with things as they had been before he had made a fool of himself in front of Guwisti on the back of her *sogwili.* Before he had fallen down on his back in the road in front of the big beast and scooted backwards—like *jisduh.* Before the people had all started telling and retelling the tale and calling him by that new name and laughing at him. Ah, fool, he said to himself, you have ruined everything.

He could smell the cooking rabbit, and he sat up and shifted his weight around to reach over and grab the spit.

He turned it again, and the flames shot up at the dripping grease, and the fire hissed and sizzled. He thought that the rabbit was done. He lifted it off the fire and set it aside to cool a bit. It would not be cooked as well as the food his mother cooked at home, but it would ease his hunger. It would do.

He tried to get his mind off the things that he was missing at home and think about what might lie ahead. He would be treated well at Coyatee, he knew. The Real People were always good hosts, even to strangers, and even though Oliga did not know anyone in Coyatee, he knew that he would find members of his own Paint People there, and they would welcome him and take him in as a visiting relative. It would be good.

He tested his cooked rabbit and found that it had cooled enough, so he pulled off a piece of meat and took a bite. Soon he had devoured the rabbit, and he was still hungry. He wiped his hands clean of grease in the grass, then he got up and walked to the edge of the stream to get a drink. He was just about to go back to his small fire and settle down for the night when he heard a noise from the woods on the opposite side of the water.

It had not been a normal night-sound in the woods. He crouched there beside the water, keeping still and listening. Then he heard a voice, harsh and angry. He heard some crashing sounds, as if someone were running through the tangle of the forest. Then the voice again. No. Two voices. The crashing sounds and the voices were getting closer, and then he heard one of the voices clearly enough to know that whoever was shouting was not speaking the language of the Real People.

He hurried back to his small fire and picked up his war club and his knife. He did not know what was going on, but he was pretty sure that there was some kind of trouble and that it involved someone from outside, some invader into the land of the Real People.

He waded into the stream and felt the sudden shock of the cold water on the calves of his legs. Cautiously, he moved across the stream, stepped out onto the bank and pressed himself against a thick tree-trunk there. Now the sounds were more distinct. They were coming nearer. Someone or something was running through the forest, moving toward the stream. He heard a voice shout again and another respond. Suddenly a young woman came crashing out of the woods. With long athletic strides, she was in the middle of the stream before Olig' could react. By then a man had burst forth, and he caught her from behind, his fist wrapped in her long black hair.

Jerked off her feet, the girl shouted as she fell back into the cold water. The man called out something over his shoulder, as he raised his war club, preparing to strike a downward blow. Olig' had to act quickly. He shrieked out an imitation of a gobbling turkey and ran at the man, his own war club poised. The startled invader turned and blocked Oliga's blow just in time. With the two war clubs crossed, Olig' made an upward thrust with the knife in his left hand. The blade sank deep, just under the other man's right rib cage.

As Olig' stepped back and the body fell into the water, the girl, scrambling to her feet, spoke in the language of the Real People.

"Watch out behind you," she said. "There's another one coming."

Olig' turned to ready himself just as the second man appeared.

The stranger had come running out of the woods, but on seeing Olig' standing there, he tried to stop on the loose rocks there at the edge of the stream. He lost his footing and fell back. Before he could recover, Olig' was on top of him, a knee on each of the man's arms. He raised his war club and brought it down hard on the man's head with a dull and sickening thud. The man lay still, and a thick, dark pool spread slowly over the rocks beneath his head.

Olig' stood and turned to look for the young woman. She was still standing in the middle of the stream, and she was trembling, whether from the cold or from the fright, he did not know. He walked toward her.

"Are you all right?" he asked.

"Yes," she said. "Thank you. And are you unhurt?"

Olig' shrugged and ducked his head as if he were embarrassed by the whole event.

"They didn't hurt me," he said. He raised his arm and pointed toward his camp. "I have a fire just over there," he said. "Will you join me?"

"*Wado*," she said, and she walked with him back to his camp.

"You're probably cold," he said. "You fell in that cold water. I'll build the fire up. Here. You can wrap yourself in this if you like."

He picked up his bearskin robe that he had been lying on earlier and held it out toward her. She took it, and he moved away into the woods a little to gather some more sticks for his fire. While he was thus occupied, she pulled off her wet dress and wrapped herself in the robe. Olig' came back and added sticks to the fire.

"I'm Olig'," he said, "of the Paint People. I live in Kituwah."

"I'm called Tsiwon'," said the woman. "My home is in Coyatee. My people are the Long Hair People. Thank you for helping me."

"Who were those men?" asked Olig'.

"Ani-Sawahoni, I think," said Tsiwon'. "I was in the woods not far out of town when they grabbed me. No one heard me shout, I guess, and they dragged me away. I fought them, but they were too strong for me, the two of them together. I couldn't understand any of their language, but I guess they meant to take me home with them. When they stopped to camp, I broke loose from them and ran."

"I'm glad I was here," said Olig'.

"Me too. But what are you doing so far away from your home?"

Olig' laughed. "I was just going to your home to visit for a while. That's all."

"You're on your way to Coyatee?"

"Yes."

"Do you know people in my town?"

"No."

"Have you been there before?"

"Never."

"Well, you're too far east," said Tsiwon'. "It's a good thing you came across me out here. I'll lead the way from here on and take you into town."

"Good," said Olig'. "I wasn't really sure of the way. Thank you."

They were silent for a moment, and then she spoke again, a little hesitantly.

"Oliga?"

"Yes?"

"Do you have some business in Coyatee?"

"Um, no."

"Why are you traveling so far at this time of year to a place where you know no one?"

And then, before he knew what he was doing or why he was doing it, Oliga told Tsiwon' the whole tale of his foolish jealousy and the resulting actions that had led to his being an object of ridicule at home, and together they laughed at the story.

12

L ow in the eastern sky there was just a little reddish light from the emerging Sun, when criers previously appointed by Ahuli began to go through the town and call out the residents and guests of Kituwah to go to the water.

"It's time to go," they cried.

"Look straight ahead as you go."

"Do not look behind you."

"Do not look to your right or to your left."

"Go straight to the water."

As the people began arriving at the water's edge in the early-morning chill, they found Ahuli, dressed in his priestly robes, already there waiting for them. They also saw there a long table with the deerskins carefully laid out upon it.

The last to arrive were the criers. Ahuli had touched the first arrival, moving him to a certain spot there by the water, and each one thereafter, Ahuli had placed carefully, so that all the people were arranged in a straight line, facing the water. Then he had them sit down. Everyone was silent, even the children.

One of the criers then came forward with a large bundle of straight sticks, each cut to a length of the distance from Ahuli's fingertips to about halfway up to his elbow. Laying one of the sticks down for a measure, he stuck another one into the ground a stick's distance away from the water's edge.

He then proceeded to poke each stick into the ground at the same distance away from the water and about a pace apart from the next one. When he was done, the long line of sticks stretched out between the water and the line of people. With the sticks as their points of reference, the people watched the water for a time, looking for any special signs that might appear.

"All right," called Ahuli, at last breaking the intense silence. "Now. Everyone go into the water."

Everyone got up, old men and women, young people, toddlers, mothers with babes in arms, and, fully dressed, they splashed into the water. Tournier and his Frenchmen followed them. Tournier noticed that it seemed to be a particularly exuberant time. The people seemed to be going into the water with a great sense of relief. He would ask someone about that later.

He looked around, and he saw Young Puppy standing not far away from him, and he noticed that everyone was facing east. He too faced east. Then he watched as the people ducked themselves entirely under water. Mothers dipped their infants. Tournier followed their example, leaning forward and bending his knees until he was completely immersed. This was done seven times.

There seems to be something significant to these people about the number seven, he thought.

The seven dips completed, the people all turned again to face Ahuli, who was standing beside the table and praying. With his limited knowledge of the language, Tournier was only able to catch a few words of the prayer. At last Ahuli ceased praying.

He unwrapped one of the deerskins on the table to reveal a bright crystal and others to reveal a great quantity of roots. Then he called out to the people to come out of the water. Tournier started to move, but he stopped. No one around him was moving.

Then he noticed an old man step out onto the bank, followed by another old man. Slowly other old ones, all men, stepped out of the water. They walked in a straight line toward the table, and when they reached the table, they walked around it four times. Then the old man at the front of the line stopped.

He held his right hand out with its palm down over the crystal there on the table, and he seemed to gaze hard into the crystal, intent on what he saw there. Then with a seeming sigh of relief, he picked up a root, turned and started walking back toward the houses, not looking back, nor right nor left.

The next person in line stepped up to the crystal and repeated the same procedure, but Tournier noticed that one old man, having gazed into the crystal, turned and walked away in a different direction from that in which the others had gone.

Slowly the younger men began to move out of the water, until finally Tournier and his Frenchmen were allowed to emerge. They followed the example of those who had gone before them, and, as curious as he was, Tournier forced himself not to look back as he walked away with his piece of root.

He saw those ahead of him go into their houses, and so he walked straight to the townhouse, which served as the Frenchmen's quarters, and went inside. He was glad when Little Black Bear came in to join him.

"*Mon ami,*" said Tournier, "are we confined to our houses now?"

"I think," said the interpreter, "that when we have all gotten ourselves into dry clothes, we will gather again right outside this house."

"Then we must change our clothes quickly," said Tournier. "We don't want to be in the way when the ceremony resumes."

"There's time," said Little Black Bear. "From what I heard, the men go first, by age, oldest to youngest. Then the women, the same way. Then Ahuli's assistants, and last of all, Ahuli himself."

"I see. One of the old men went off by himself, *mon ami.* Did you notice that?"

"*Oui.* I saw him," said Little Black Bear.

"What was the reason for that? Do you know?"

Looking down at the ground, Little Black Bear hesitated a moment before answering. Then he seemed to frame his response carefully.

"Did you look into the crystal, *Capitaine?*" he asked.

"*Oui.* I did as the others had done."

"And what did you see there?"

"*Rien.* I saw nothing. *Le cristal,*" said Tournier, "what is its significance?"

"They say that you look for yourself in there. If you see yourself standing up, you will live until the next New Moon Ceremony. Another year. But if you see yourself lying down, you will not live so long."

"*Mon dieu,*" said Tournier. "Like a crystal ball?"

Little Black Bear shrugged.

"*Je ne sais pas,*" he said. "I do not know this crystal ball."

"Never mind that. And the staring into the water for so long? What is the purpose of that?"

"Where you look at the water between the sticks," said Little Black Bear, "if the water flows by smoothly and clearly, you will live. But if you see a fish or a leaf or something else, it could mean that something bad will happen to you."

"A bunch of foolish superstition," said Dr. DuBois, who had just come into the townhouse.

"But we are told that our Lord Jesus Christ fed the multitudes with one fish and one loaf of bread," Tournier responded. "And he walked on water too. Foolish superstition?"

"You're talking blasphemy again," said the doctor. "How dare you make comparison between the life of our Lord and Savior Jesus Christ and the antics of this Devil worship? Blasphemy is what it is."

"You may be right, of course," said Tournier, "and if so, I will surely pay for it one of these days. That will be between me and le *bon dieu*, but right here and now, in this setting and among these people, somehow I cannot think that anything is truly blasphemy, *mon ami*. I wish that you could see it as I do."

DuBois looked stern and shook his head.

"That will never be," he said.

The other Frenchmen started to arrive back in the townhouse, and DuBois snorted at Tournier and moved away from him to join the others. Tournier looked up and thought for a moment that the group the doctor had joined appeared to be conspiratorial. No, he told himself. They're grumpy because they're bored, staying in this village. That's all. And he pushed all thoughts of developing conspiracies out of his mind.

Young Puppy still stood in the water. The procession was slow, and he was among the youngest of the adult males. He wished that his turn would hurry along, because the water was cold and he was beginning to shiver. Suddenly it was his time, and, relieved, he walked out of the water. His legs felt numb from the cold.

He walked to the table and moved around it four times. Then he stopped there beside the crystal, beside *ulunsuti*, transparent, the powerful medicine crystal from the forehead of an *ukitena*. He raised his hand over the crystal to block out the light, and his eyes opened wide. He stood staring into the crystal for a long time. Then he picked up a root and turned to walk away, but he hesitated, not knowing where to go.

He did not look back, for he was afraid to look back, but he stood still, confused. The next person coming out of the water waited, also confused by Young Puppy's action, or lack thereof. Should he walk around Young Puppy? He did not know. Ahuli noticed the hold up and stepped over to Young Puppy's side.

"What's the matter?" he asked, his voice low.

"I saw myself," said Young Puppy, and Ahuli could see the confusion on the young man's face.

"Yes?" he said.

"I was neither standing nor lying down."

"Ah," said Ahuli, amazement in his voice. "Go on to your house and change your clothes. Go on as if you had seen yourself standing. You and I will talk more of this later."

The people were beginning to gather there outside the townhouse, and Young Puppy waited anxiously for Guwisti to appear. She would be one of the last out of the water, being a young woman. He knew that, and yet he was impatient to see her. Something strange had happened to him, something that he wanted to tell her about, something that he felt she needed to know. At last he saw her coming, and he hurried to meet her on the road, away from the crowd and any curious listening ears.

"Guwisti," he said, "I have to tell you. I saw myself in *ulunsuti*."

She looked into his face and held her breath, waiting for the rest of the story.

"I was neither standing nor lying down. I didn't know where to go."

"I saw you waiting there," she said. "I wondered what was wrong."

"Ahuli told me to act as if I had seen myself standing, but I was not standing."

"And you were not lying down?"

"No."

"It's a good sign, I think," said Guwist'. "It's like the other things we've been told. You will die, but you will also be reborn. That's what I think you saw in the crystal."

"Yes," said Young Puppy. "I think so too. Ahuli said that we'll talk more about it later. Perhaps then we'll know for sure."

"Yes," she said. "Ahuli knows all the signs."

The crowd around the sacred dance ground was getting large, and Young Puppy saw Ahuli approaching. He and Guwisti hurried to join the rest of the people. There at the edge of the ground a great feast was laid out. Ahuli ceremonially took up the tongue of the first deer that had been killed for the feast, and he dropped it into the fire which burned atop the altar. He told everyone to eat, and he went away from the crowd.

Ahuli left the feast and went to find the one old man who had gone off alone. He found the man standing alone at the edge of the woods near the river. The old man seemed somber, but not sad, resigned, not afraid. He was waiting there patiently for Ahuli's return.

"The image in the crystal is not final," said Ahuli. "It only tells us to look further. There's more to be done now. Come with me."

He led the way back to the water's edge, and he spread a deerskin on the same table as before. He placed *ulunsuti* in the middle of the deerskin, and he prayed aloud, a long prayer addressing spirits from the four directions. The prayer finally finished, he turned once more toward the old man, standing patiently by, waiting for further word on his fate.

"Look again," said Ahuli. "Look deeply into *ulunsuti* now."

And slowly the old one who had seen the vision in the crystal earlier of himself lying prone turned and looked. Surprise crossed his wrinkled features, and he looked toward Ahuli.

"This time," he said, "I'm standing."

He smiled, and Ahuli smiled with him and pointed toward the water.

"Go in again," he said, "and dunk yourself another seven times. You'll live yet for another year and, who knows, maybe even longer. We'll learn about that this time next year."

His duties with the old man done, Ahuli returned to the dance ground outside the townhouse. Everyone else had eaten by then, so Ahuli ate. Now he could relax. Nothing more was done that day, but when darkness fell that night, the women began to dance.

They danced joyfully throughout the night while everyone, only infants excepted, kept awake. Young Puppy spent much of the night watching the sensual movements of his Guwisti as she circled the fire. He also thought about Ahuli, wondering what the old man would say about the image Young Puppy had seen in *ulunsuti*. When the Sun crawled out from under the eastern edge of the Sky Vault early the next morning, the women finished their dancing, and the people all went to their homes. Nuwadi equa was over.

13

Young Puppy was asleep inside his mother's new house in Kituwah. Bear Meat had gone to the townhouse to visit with some of his friends and to look at the hairy-faced white men. Lolo was tending a small cooking fire just in front of the house, when she saw Ahuli approaching. She gave him a nod and a smile, and then she was aware that he was walking directly toward her.

" '*Siyo*," said Ahuli. "Is your son at home?"

"He's inside asleep," said Lolo.

"Well, I don't want to disturb his rest," said Ahuli, "but when he wakes up, I would like to speak with him. Would you tell him that for me?"

"Of course I will, but first, sit down here by the fire," said Lolo. "Let me go inside and see if he's really asleep."

Ahuli sat on a bench that was there by the fire, and Lolo ducked her head to go inside the house. Young Puppy was lying on a cot against a side wall. He was obviously sound asleep. She put a hand on his shoulder anyway. Ahuli had said to tell him after he wakes up, but she didn't want to wait. She was anxious to know what the most important man in Kituwah wanted with her son. Young Puppy was in so much trouble that anything that seemed like a good sign was something to be grasped at by Lolo. Maybe Ahuli could wait, but she could not. She shook her son gently and whispered in his ear.

"My son," she said. "Wake up. Wake up. Ahuli is here. He wants to talk to you."

Young Puppy stirred slightly and rubbed his eyes.

"Ahuli?" he said.

"Yes. He's sitting outside by the fire."

Young Puppy sat up and rubbed his eyes. He took the bear skin that had covered him on the cot and threw it over his shoulders.

"Go on now," said Lolo, gesturing toward the door. "Go on. He's waiting for you."

Young Puppy took a couple of short faltering steps, drew himself up with a deep breath, and ducked out the door. Lolo hurriedly gathered up two bowls as her son went outside.

" *'Siyo,*" said Young Puppy.

"I didn't want her to wake you," said Ahuli.

"It's all right. I was just resting."

"Are you well?" asked Ahuli.

"Yes," said Young Puppy. *"Nihina?"*

"I'm well," said Ahuli, "but I'm getting old."

Lolo stepped out just then and handed a bowl to Ahuli and another to Young Puppy.

"Wado," said Ahuli, and he took a long drink of the *kanohena.* "Ah. That's very good."

Lolo went back inside the house, leaving the two men, one old, one young, to their conversation. Ahuli took another sip.

"Yes," he said. "I'm getting old. I have important knowledge too. Knowledge important, vital even, to all of the Real People."

"Yes," said Young Puppy. "I suppose you do."

He felt a little uneasy, wondering if this old man had come to see him just to brag about his own importance. What does all this have to do with me? When will he get around to talking about the image in *ulunsuti?*

"My helpers don't even know all the things that I know," Ahuli continued. "The things you see them doing during the ceremonies—that's all they know. What if I were to die suddenly? What if I were to fall over dead right now, right here sitting by your mother's fire? Who could lead the ceremonies?"

"I—I don't know," said Young Puppy.

"There would be no one," said Ahuli. "No one. Then what would happen?"

"I—"

"There would be no ceremonies. That's what. Do you know what that would mean?"

"I—I guess it could mean the end of the world," said Young Puppy. "I've heard that. I don't know."

"That's exactly what it would mean. The end of the world."

Ahuli took another sip of the *kanohena*. Then he looked at Young Puppy so directly and so long that Young Puppy began to squirm under the gaze. Such a direct look usually was an indication of hostility or, at the least, rudeness. Young Puppy did not believe that Ahuli was being deliberately rude or hostile toward him, but he was nevertheless uneasy. He couldn't figure out what the old man wanted of him.

"What you saw in *ulunsuti*," said Ahuli, his voice suddenly low enough to make Young Puppy lean toward him to listen, "was very significant. You saw yourself neither dead nor alive. I think that you had been dead, and you were coming back to life."

"Being—reborn?" said Young Puppy, suddenly very interested in what the old man had to say.

"Yes. Just that."

"I have been told before that I must die and be reborn."

Ahuli spoke very low, and this time it was he who leaned over toward Young Puppy.

"Who told you that?"

Young Puppy looked around, as if to make sure no one else would overhear what he was about to say.

"Uyona," he whispered.

"Ah. Uyona."

"Yes."

Ahuli tipped back the bowl and drained it of its contents. He leaned forward to put the bowl on the ground beside his bench.

"I want you to study with me," he said.

"What?"

"I want you to learn to lead the ceremonies. It's very important work, perhaps the most important work there is. Someone has to learn it from me before I die. What you saw in *ulunsuti* and what Uyona told you proves that you're a very unusual young man. You've been chosen for something very special. And something happened to make you stay inside the wall of Kituwah for an entire year, just the time required for a complete cycle of our ceremonies. There was a reason for that, you know. We're not always smart enough to see it, but there's a reason for everything that happens. I think you've been chosen to lead the ceremonies after I am gone. That's what I think. Will you work with me?"

Jacques Tournier sat alone in the townhouse, squinting in the dim light, writing in his journal. The rest of the Frenchmen were clustered in two small groups on the other side of the room. Dr. DuBois seemed to be in a particularly sulky mood. Little Black Bear had gone out. Tournier wrote as follows:

I don't know if I will ever understand these strange people. We call them Cheraques because that is what all their neighbors call them, and my interpreter tells me that the word means Cave People. They certainly do not live in caves but in quite substantial houses, not by our standards in France, of course, but by a fair comparison with the other peoples of this land.

They call themselves by a name which in their language seems to mean the Real People or perhaps the Original People, and they seem to sincerely believe that their ceremonies, which they perform diligently and religiously, actually keep the world alive. Should they fail to perform even one part of just one of their many ceremonies just exactly right, the world will come to an end—for all of us. That is their belief.

Having said all that, I now note with some amazement that they seem not even to know the significance of various details of their ceremonies. When I ask for an explanation, they shrug, as if the answer to my question is of no importance, or they say, that's just the way it's done.

I have now gone through two complete ceremonies with these people. The first one they called the Bush Feast, and I have not yet learned the reason for that designation. It lasted for four days. The second one, called the New Moon Ceremony, I was led to believe was of very great significance, and it was completed in just one day. It's all very perplexing.

One final note for now. During the course of the New Moon Celebration, each individual in this town took a turn at gazing into a crystal, which they swear came from the forehead of a great and powerful creature which they call Keen-eyed. This monster is said to be like a giant rattlesnake, but with wings and antlers. The creature, they say, can fly. It breathes fire. Its very look can kill, and so can its breath. Some say if it but crosses a man's path, that man will die. Needless to say, they fear this monster very much.

But the possession of the crystal from its forehead, which they simply call "transparent," gives great power to a man, and it was into this crystal that the people stared in awe. I was told that they saw themselves in the crystal, and that if a man saw himself standing, he would still be alive for the next performance of this ceremony in just one year, but if he saw himself lying down, he would be dead before that time came around. I looked into the crystal, and I saw nothing there.

The nights are getting colder here, and I believe that winter will be hard upon us soon. We have been assured of the continued hospitality of this village throughout that difficult time of year. My only concern is that I will be able to return to the Senikas in the north before they change their minds about the promise they made to me regarding a peace between themselves and these Cheraques. I believe that an alliance between our own nation and both of these will be vital, both for purposes of trade and for future possible military reasons.

Tournier closed his journal and put away his pen and ink, just as the grumpy Dr. DuBois moved over to sit beside him.

"Still making your little notes, I see," said the doctor.

"*Oui, Docteur.*"

"And do you really believe that it will do us any good?"

"I believe that to make lasting allies, we must first make friends," said Tournier, "and to make friends with people whose ways are strange to us, we must have understanding."

"But it's all completely one-sided," said the doctor. "They are making no effort to understand us."

"We're in their land, *mon ami.*"

"We are the more advanced people," said the doctor. "We're the most civilized and the most powerful. We should not have to behave in this way toward these *sauvages*, bowing and scraping as if they are monarchs of the wilderness. From all that I have heard, the Spaniards taught them lessons with their swords."

"And, *Docteur*," said Tournier, "how many of those same Spaniards have you noticed running around in these parts lately?"

14

Young Puppy was practically living with Ahuli, and it was a very busy time for the two of them. It seemed to the young man that Nuwadi equa, the New Moon Ceremony, had only just ended, and already they were making preparations for the next ceremony, that of Ama tsunegi, the White Drink. Before he had taken on the role of Ahuli's apprentice, if someone had asked him if he knew what went on with the White Drink Ceremony, Young Puppy would almost certainly have answered, "Of course." But working under Ahuli's directions in preparation for the ceremony, he suddenly felt like he knew next to nothing about it. There was so much to do, so much to learn.

At times he wanted to tell Ahuli to forget it. He wanted to walk away from this new role, a role he had not asked for in the first place, and one that Ahuli, Young Puppy felt, had thrust upon him. Was it not enough, he asked himself, that he was a prisoner in Kituwah? Must he also be a slave to an old man who was so particular about so many and such insignificant details?

But he did not walk away, and more than once, he asked himself why he did not. Did he actually want to lead the ceremonies one day? He did not really think so. He had never wanted anything in life except to be a great hunter and a great warrior—and the husband of Guwisti. So why was he putting up with this old man, with all his tedium and all his abuse?

To pass the time more quickly and more easily, he told himself. That's why, of course. Even this is better than sitting around with nothing to do while others come and go as they please. Yes. Even this. Yet slowly he began to realize that with his new role, he had also attained a new status. Before he had started working with Ahuli, he had been regarded as almost a fugitive. Suddenly he was afforded more respect. And he did like that.

He had not been mistreated before. Far from it. He had been treated as a guest and there were rules which governed his treatment. Even so, he could tell the difference between attitudes governed by rules and attitudes of real respect. In addition, his mother was proud of him and somewhat relieved of her anxiety by his new role and his new status. Guwisti, too, was proud, and Young Puppy could not discount the feelings of Guwisti and of his mother.

He also found that, because Ahuli kept him so busy, he did not spend so much time staring at the wall or staring over it and longing to go roaming. He did not spend so much time alone moaning over the time he would have to wait to marry his beloved Guwisti. He did not, in short, spend so much time feeling sorry for himself.

Perhaps after all it was not so bad, this apprenticeship. He discovered that the worst times were not the times when Ahuli had him so busy that his head was swimming with new knowledge and with things to be done. The worst times were the times when he had to stay behind because Ahuli had to go outside the walls to gather certain plants.

Then he made the greatest and most surprising discovery of all. He woke up one morning to the realization that he was anxious to get on with his day. He was thirsting to learn more. He had found a deep and genuine interest in the ceremonial life of his people and in the things that he could learn from Ahuli. At last, it seemed, he had found his calling. He had discovered his purpose in life, his place in the complex web of the everyday comings and goings in the world of the Real People.

Oliga had been welcomed into Coyatee by its inhabitants, and once Tsiwon' had told the tale of her rescue by this visitor from Kituwah, he had been hailed as a hero. They had danced all night and fed him until he could eat no more. He wasn't at all sure that he deserved such treatment and such respect, for the events that had driven him away from home were still fresh in his mind. Still, he enjoyed his status in Coyatee.

The next morning after his arrival in town, Olig' had gone back into the forest with three men from Coyatee. One was called Black Dog. He was the leading warrior of Coyatee. The other two were Tsuwa, or Water Dog, the father of Tsiwon', and Ukusuhntsudi, or Bent Bow Shape, her brother, so called because of his lanky physique and his posture.

Olig' had led them back to the place of the fight to look at the bodies and the weapons of the men he had killed. Neither he nor Tsiwon' had been able to say with certainty just who the men were. He had little difficulty finding the place, and the bodies were lying just where he had left them.

"That means that they were alone," said Black Dog. "If there had been others, they would have taken the bodies with them."

"Perhaps there were others, but the others did not know just where these two had gone," said Water Dog.

"Um," Black Dog mused. "Perhaps."

"Who are they then?" asked Olig'.

"Ani-Sawahoni," said Black Dog. "Tsiwon' was right. I've fought them many times."

"Ani-Sawahoni," said Bent Bow Shape. "What are they doing here?"

"I think they were hunting," said Black Dog. "They're not painted for war."

"But they captured my sister," Bent Bow Shape protested.

"They were just out hunting, and they saw her," said Black Dog with a shrug. "And so they just decided to take her, I guess."

"She's a very beautiful woman," said Olig'. "Any man would want her."

"If they were just hunting," said Water Dog, "they had wandered a long way from their home. It's not normal to hunt so far away from home."

"And in someone else's hunting grounds," added Bent Bow Shape.

"Yes," said Black Dog. "This will have to be looked into further. Let's go back to town. We'll have to have a council, I think."

The meeting was held that very night, and it went as all four men had expected. It was decided that several parties of men would go out from Coyatee the next morning looking for any sign of any more Shawnee activity in their territory. It simply made no sense that only two hunters would be so far into the country of the Real People on their own.

"Will you go out with them?" Tsiwon' asked Olig'.

"Yes."

"Be careful," she said. "I've only just met you. I don't want anything to happen to you now."

Olig' was happy to hear her say what she had said, but he did not quite know what to make of it. She liked him. That much was clear. But how much did she like him? Perhaps more to the point, how did she like him? He thought that he liked her very much. He even thought that he would like to—he was almost afraid to allow the thought to finish forming in his mind—that he would like to make her his woman.

Olig' went out the next morning with the same group of men he had gone with before. Other groups went out in different directions. They stayed out all day, returning to town just before darkness, and each group had the same thing to report. They had wandered the hills and searched the woods, but to no avail. No sign of invasion had been found. No further indications of Shawnee activity had been discovered in the area. Nothing had been resolved. They would have to search further. They all agreed.

In his journal, Jacques Tournier wrote,

Ahuli, the great priest of this town, has been very busy these last few days gathering tremendous quantities of leaves from some sort of holly. I have learned that he will brew a sort of tea from these leaves that will be used in the next ceremony, coming up soon. The result of drinking this brew, a very black drink, I have been told, is a kind of ritualistic regurgitation. They do this, it seems, for reasons of purity, and for those same reasons, they metaphorically designate this black drink by its exact opposite name. They call it the white drink.

Ahuli had indeed collected large quantities of the holly leaves as well as small twigs from the same bush. With the assistance of Young Puppy, he had filled several earthen jars with the already-dried leaves and twigs. He had Young Puppy build seven small fires just outside his house and construct small rectangular racks of sticks over each of the fires. Then he showed the younger man some shallow clay dishes.

"Put one these dishes on each rack," he said, and Young Puppy did so. Then Ahuli carefully poured leaves and twigs from one of his pots out into each dish. He stayed with Young Puppy watching the process until just the right time. "See how they are roasted?" he asked. "Just that much. It's time to take them off." He left Young Puppy then to finish preparing the rest of the leaves and twigs from the pots.

The next day, when Ahuli met with his seven councillors, one from each clan. Young Puppy met with them for the first time. The councillors already knew that Ahuli had chosen Young Puppy as his apprentice, but Ahuli still made a formal introduction and explanation of Young Puppy's presence at the meeting. Young Puppy felt very important, more important even, he realized, than he had felt at the time of the victory celebrations held in his and 'Squani's honor after their successful foray into enemy territory.

Ahuli told the councillors that it was, in his opinion, time to begin preparations for Ama tsunegi, and the seven councillors agreed. The meeting was brief. They had agreed, and the seven knew what to do. They went their ways.

That night, under the watchful eye of Ahuli, Young Puppy built up the fire on the altar in the center of the sacred dance-ground, using wood from the seven sacred trees, and when the Sun had crawled under the western edge of the Sky Vault, and darkness had settled over Kituwah, the women began to dance.

From where she sat alone in her house, Osa could hear the sounds coming from the dance-ground, and she knew that she should be out there taking part in the ceremony. At least she knew that others expected as much from her. She also knew that her own Catawba people had their own set of ceremonies which they considered to be every bit as important to sustaining life as did these Real People their own. Her knowledge of two different sets of religious cycles left Osa uncertain as to which, if either, really did the trick, and her uncertainty over the matter made her a bit skeptical about it all.

There had also been the Christian teachings of the hateful Spanish priest, teachings that her late husband had taken very seriously, at least for a time. Before the time of her captivity by the Spanish, Osa had never questioned her beliefs. Having been exposed to so many different sets of beliefs now, she had to wonder if anyone really knew what it was all about.

Besides, she really didn't feel like going out at all. She was lying on the cot in her home, covered by the rug on which she had made love with Asquani. She was thinking about him, trying to remember every detail of his appearance, trying to recall the feel of his touch, his smell, the pressure of his body against her own. She tried to recall exact words he had used when he had spoken to her on different occasions, and she rehearsed in her mind for the thousandth time the many dangers they had passed together.

How she missed him. How empty was her life without him. How she longed for her own life on this earth to end so that her spirit could find his on the other side of the Sky Vault there in the Darkening Land. She hoped that she would find him waiting there. But if the Christians were right, she guessed she would find him waiting for her in the Christian hell. Well, their tales didn't frighten her. She would go even there to be with him.

But first she had an obligation to fulfill. She was carrying his child, and she could not go to join Asquani until their child was safely started in this life. She rested her hands on her growing belly and thought about the life that had started in there. What a marvel it was, she thought. What a thing to think about. Would it be a boy, and if so, she wondered, will it look like him? She hoped so. She wanted that very much.

Then she felt a movement deep inside. It startled her. She waited, and it moved again. Her child. His child. In spite of her overwhelming sadness, she felt a joy, and her eyes were suddenly filled with tears. She smiled, and she laughed, out loud but softly. Then she recalled the words of old Uyona. She sat up on the edge of the cot, and, looking down toward her belly, she said, "We have to go to her now."

15

She carried a long stick for a walking staff, because she knew that the way was rough and uneven with obstacles in the path, and it was dark. She made her way along the inside of the wall, keeping as much out of the way of other people as she could. She did not want anyone to see her and ask her any questions. She was not at the dance, and she was leaving town alone at night. Her reasons were no one's business.

She reached the passageway out of and into Kituwah undetected, and then she slipped outside. She turned to face the direction she must travel, the way into the woods that would take her by a narrow pathway to the home of old Uyona. It was dark, and she was afraid.

For a moment she thought about going back inside the wall, back to the safety of her home, even to the dance ground and the company of others, and waiting until morning light to make this visit.

She started to walk toward the woods, using her staff to poke the ground ahead of her, much the way a sightless person would. She stumbled once and slowed her pace, and then she reached the woods.

The night was even darker underneath the canopy of trees, and her own footsteps in the leaves and the tangle of the forest floor seemed especially loud in that darkness. Her heart pounded inside her chest, and down below that, she felt the *usdi* move.

She heard *waguli* sing, and farther off an owl *hoo-hoo*ed into the night. Somewhere to her right something rustled on the forest floor. She wanted to turn and run back to the safety of the town and the light of the fires of town, but she could not. She poked with her stick, and she walked ahead.

Once she tripped and fell, but she caught herself with her arms so that she did not land hard on her belly. Ignoring the scrapes and bruises, she got back to her feet and moved ahead.

At last she saw through the dark shapes of the woods a slight glow ahead, and she knew that it came from the fire in front of Uyona's house. She hurried on until she came to the small clearing. The fire was low. It had almost gone out. She stood there staring across the glowing embers toward the house.

She felt a tremendous sense of relief at having made it through the woods and arriving safely at her destination, but she also felt a new anxiety. It was late, and the fire was almost out. The old woman must be asleep, she thought. She stood in silence, shivering in the cold night air, trying to call up some courage from somewhere deep inside herself.

"Uyona," she said, and her voice was low and timid. Only the sounds of the forest at night answered her, and she had a frightening thought. Suppose the old woman had died? "Uyona," she said in a louder voice.

"Who's there?"

Osa breathed a heavy sigh of relief at the welcome sound of the crackling voice.

"It's Osa," she said. "I felt it move."

"Ah, come and sit down," said Uyona. "Let me build up the fire."

And all of a sudden Uyona was there. She bent to gather up some sticks from a pile beside her door. Then she groaned as she squatted beside the glowing embers and poked the sticks in one at a time.

"Let me help you," said Osa. She went to the wood pile and gathered more sticks which she then handed one at a time to the old woman. Soon the fire was blazing once again. Osa sat on a stool there beside it while Uyona stared silently into the flames for a space and a time.

"You felt it move inside you?" said Uyona.

"Yes."

"The first time?"

"Yes."

"When?"

"Just now," said Uyona. "I mean, I felt it, and then I came straight here to see you. Should I have waited until morning?"

"No," said the old woman. "You did right to come here now. Let me make you some tea."

She put some water in a clay pot onto the fire to boil, and then she ducked into her house for a moment. When she returned to the fireside, she dropped some roots into the water.

"It will be ready soon," she said. She went inside again and returned a moment later with a thick bear rug which she spread on the ground close to the fire. "Lie down here," she said.

Osa moved to the rug and stretched out on it, lying on her back, and the old woman knelt creakily beside her. She placed her wrinkled, leathery old hands on Osa's rising belly.

"Um," she said. "Um."

"What is it?" Osa asked.

"Hush," said Uyona. "Be still, Daughter."

The old hands moved around on the belly, feeling here and there, and the touch of them was soothing to the young woman. Then Uyona laid the side of her head to the belly as if to listen. At last she straightened up and sat back on her haunches with a heavy sigh, a sigh such as can only come from the very old and tired.

"Sit up now," she said. "Your tea is ready."

While Osa sat up on the rug, Uyona picked up the clay pot from the fire in her bare hand and poured the tea into another bowl. How can she do that? Osa wondered. Has she no feeling in her hands? The old woman frightened her. At the same time, she was more comfortable in the presence of Uyona than anywhere else. Uyona handed the bowl to Osa.

"Drink," she said.

Osa reached for the bowl, and in the light of the fire, Uyona saw the fresh cuts on her arm.

"You've hurt yourself," she said, and there was genuine concern in the crackly old voice.

"It's nothing," said Osa. "On my way here, I fell in the woods."

"Wait," said the old one, and again she went into her house. A moment later she returned with a small pot, and she took Osa by the arm. She dug into the pot and came out with some salve which she rubbed onto the scratches. She did the same to the other arm. Osa felt the soothing effects almost immediately.

"Thank you," she said. "That's much better. But I—I have nothing to give you."

"It doesn't matter," said Uyona.

"Unless you'd like to have a *sogwili*."

Uyona laughed.

"They climb on its back to ride, don't they?" she asked.

"Yes."

"I couldn't get myself up there. I don't think I want it."

"Uyona?"

"What?"

"My *usdi*."

"Um."

"Did you learn anything about it?"

"Um. Yes," said Uyona. "There will be two of them."

"Two? Twins?"

"Yes."

"Boys or girls? Do you know?"

"There will be one of each."

"Will they be all right? Both of them?"

"They will, if I help you," said Uyona. "But you must give me the little girl."

Osa fell back on the rug and stared into the flames to avoid looking at Uyona. Give away my own child, she thought. Asquani's child? How can she ask such a thing of me, the old witch? Ask a mother to give away her own child, a little girl.

But if she helps, they both will live, and I will have the boy, a little likeness of my 'Squani. Without this old woman, I might be dead already. I owe her very much. I've nothing else to give her. Besides, she might not live much longer, and when she dies, I'll have my daughter back.

"May I visit her? And you?"

"Of course, Daughter. As often as you like."

"Then I'll do as you say," said Osa, "and you will have the girl."

The dancing did not stop until the Sun began to light the eastern sky, and then Ahuli's criers called for all the people to go to the water. This time Young Puppy did not go with them. He stayed behind to take up the rear with Ahuli. At the water's edge, the assistants had already set up the sticks, and all the people were staring through them at the water, each hoping to see nothing out of the ordinary, hoping to see nothing but water flowing by. When he thought that enough time had passed, Ahuli spoke low into Young Puppy's ear.

"Tell them to go into the water," he said.

"All go into the water," Young Puppy called out. "Dip yourselves seven times."

The people did as they were told. Then they came out again and headed for their homes. When the last of them had gone on several paces toward their houses, Young Puppy and Ahuli went into the water. The coldness of the water made Young Puppy gasp.

He took a deep breath and quickly plunged his head under the icy water, once, twice, three times. He paused to take another breath. Then plunged a fourth time and a fifth. He took another breath, then went under for the sixth and then the seventh time.

He stood there quaking in the cold water, sucking air into his lungs, and he looked in the direction of Ahuli, who was already walking back out onto the shore. Young Puppy followed him, his legs jerking uncontrollably from the cold. Old Ahuli didn't seem to be bothered by it at all.

"Come along," said Ahuli. "We have to change into dry clothes now. There's still much to be done this day."

There beside the dance ground, the assistants had built up the fires. Four large pots of water had been placed on the fires to boil. Close by, smaller, empty vessels had been placed, and a strainer made like a tightly woven basket lay across the top of one of the pots. The jars of roasted leaves and twigs were also there.

The people were gathered in a circle around the dance ground waiting, when Ahuli and Young Puppy came out of Ahuli's house, dressed in dry clothing. The two men walked over to the large pots and found the water boiling. Ahuli took up one of the jars of leaves and twigs and poured its contents into the boiling water of one large pot. Young Puppy took another and did the same.

While this was going on, the assistants were busy bringing in bundles of dry river cane to arrange in a circle around the edge of the dance ground. Ahuli watched the boiling brew closely. From time to time, he added more leaves to one pot or another. He instructed Young Puppy when to add more wood to the fire. He also watched the progress of the circle of cane bundles.

No one ate that day. Mothers were allowed to feed their infants. That was all. Young Puppy felt a gnawing in his stomach for a while, but soon he forgot all about it. Tournier, seated with the others around the dance ground, saw DuBois and four other Frenchmen get up and walk away toward the townhouse. He followed them.

Stopping them a sufficient distance away from the crowd to avoid being overheard, he grabbed the doctor by a shoulder and spun him around.

"Where are you going, DuBois," he demanded, "you and these others?"

"We're hungry, *Capitaine*," said DuBois. "We're going to find something to eat."

"Did you not understand?" said Tournier. "This is a day of fasting."

"For these *sauvages*, perhaps," said the doctor. "Not for us."

"My orders are," said Tournier, "that while we are the guests of these people, we will follow their customs. Now get back over there and take your places."

DuBois stared hard into the face of Tournier, but Tournier met his gaze with a frightening sternness. It was a tense moment.

"Now," said the captain, "or I may have you taken out and shot for disobeying orders."

"*Oui, Capitaine*," said DuBois. "You win, of course. For now."

Tournier watched as the doctor and the other four moved back into the crowd. Then he went back to where he had been seated beside Little Black Bear. He spoke to his Catawba interpreter in French and in low tones.

"From now on, we must watch DuBois and the others very closely, *mon ami*," he said. "They grow impatient, and they may cause some trouble here."

16

The Sun was low in the western sky when Ahuli directed Young Puppy to take up the straining basket and hold it over the top of one of the empty vessels. Ahuli himself took a long-necked gourd dipper which he plunged into one of the large pots on a fire. He brought up a dipperful of steaming liquid and poured it into the previously empty vessel through the strainer. The liquid was a deep, dark brown, almost black.

At the same time, one of the assistants kindled a fire at the easternmost point of the circle of cane bundles in such a way as to cause the cane to start burning in a northerly direction. Thus the flames began to circle the dance ground in the same direction as did the people anytime they danced.

Among the people gathered around the dance ground watching the flames was the Howler, but his attention was not so much on the ceremony itself as it was on the new participant, Young Puppy. The young man he wanted so badly to kill was becoming a person of some importance. Howler believed in the ceremonies. He believed that they kept the world in balance.

How could he think of killing a man upon whom the whole future of the Real People might one day depend? He knew that if he should encounter Young Puppy outside the wall of the sanctuary town before the time of the next Ripe Corn Feast, he would have to kill him. But strangely, he found himself hoping that Young Puppy would somehow manage to keep himself safe inside the town for the necessary time span.

Others watched Young Puppy with special interest: Lolo, his mother, and Guwisti, his beloved. They watched with pride as he performed in public for the first time in his new role. Guwist' imagined a long life ahead as the wife of a very important man, and she knew at last that everything would work out for the best.

Ahuli spoke to Young Puppy, who then laid aside his strainer and took up a large conch shell. He held the shell out in front of him while Ahuli dipped his gourd into one of the vessels of strained liquid and then poured it into the shell. Ahuli put down the dipper and held out his hands toward Young Puppy, who handed him the shell. And Ahuli drank a long draught of the black liquid that the Real People called the White Drink.

He drank long, tilting back his head and raising the shell, swallowing in large gulps. The hot liquid ran down his chin and on down onto his chest. At last the shell was empty, and Ahuli lowered it with a loud and long sigh. He handed it back to Young Puppy, took up the gourd and refilled the shell. Then Young Puppy drank.

Four assistants came with shells which Young Puppy filled for them, and they each drank. Then Young Puppy and Ahuli refilled the shells of the assistants, and those four men began passing the shells of White Drink around to the people seated around the dance ground. Everyone drank.

And Ahuli and Young Puppy were kept busy with refilling the shells, and even they drank more. Tournier and his Frenchmen drank, but the captain noticed that the women did not drink.

Then one young man stood up and ran away from the circle. He ran toward the woods, gagging and coughing, and then the sounds of retching could be heard. A moment later another man followed, and then another.

Dr. DuBois turned to his companion on his right.

"They're puking, the fools," he said.

His companion muffled a belch, stood up and ran for the woods, and almost immediately, DuBois felt the roiling in his own guts. He ran for the woods.

The ceremony seemed to have no formal end. Eventually Ahuli and Young Puppy abandoned the pots. They had gone to the woods more than once themselves. But even after that, it seemed, if a man wanted some more of the White Drink, he went to help himself.

The circling fire had burned itself out back at the eastern point of the circle, almost where it had begun, and then the women went into the dance ground and began to move around the sacred altar fire. They danced the rest of the night away, and Ama tsunegi was done.

It was early afternoon of the next day before Dr. DuBois bestirred himself. He sat up with a groan and noticed right away that the muscles of his belly ached. Looking around the interior of the townhouse, he saw that one of his four companions from the day before was up.

"René," he said.

The other man walked over to DuBois. *"Oui, Docteur?"*

"How are you feeling?"

"Miserable," said René Gaspard. "That horrible brew they made us drink, it has my guts in turmoil."

"René," said DuBois, "that was the last straw. Do you agree?"

"I don't know what you mean," said René. "Do I agree that it was the last straw?"

"I mean that we have taken quite enough from Tournier. He is no longer fit to command this expedition. He's guilty of blasphemy. He's taking part in pagan rituals. Devil worship. And what is more, he's forcing us with his orders to take part too. He alternately starves us and forces us to ingest *merde*."

Rene shrugged.

"What can we do? He is in command."

"We can take away his command," said DuBois.

"Mutiny?" said Rene, incredulous. "We could be executed for that."

"Not if we all stick together," said DuBois. "We can kill him, and when we return to France, we can explain all of our reasons. We'll be excused."

"Ah," said René, shaking his head, "I don't know."

"I'll assume command, and I'll take all the responsibility."

"Anyone who follows you will be as guilty as you," said René. "I don't like the killing part."

"Then we will make him our prisoner, and we will make it our business to turn him over to the proper authorities, charged with blasphemy and incompetence."

"I don't know," said René, rubbing his chin. "If we go against the *capitaine*, these *sauvages* might take his side. They seem to like him."

"They cannot raise their hands against us," said DuBois. "Not in this town. They call this their sanctuary town or their peace town or something like that. They are forbidden to kill within these walls. That's why that one young man is stuck in here. Here they cannot even kill him, and he is a murderer."

"Well, maybe," said René. "Let's see what the others think about it."

"We'll talk to Marcel, Jean, and Georges," said DuBois. "I'm sure they'll be with us. We won't mention this to any of the others. Not just yet."

"All right," said René, but his voice still sounded unsure.

"Mon ami," said DuBois, "how long has it been since you've lain with a woman?"

"What?"

"You heard me right," said DuBois. "How long has it been?"

"I don't know anymore," said René. "It's been too long. Months. I don't know."

"Have you noticed all the lovely young *femmes sauvages* in this village? What has Tournier said to us about them?"

"He's ordered us to keep away from them."

"Or be shot, by him personally. *Non?*"

"*Oui*," said René. "That's what he said."

"And do you think that's right? Why should we not— Why should you not enjoy the pleasures of their young bodies before they are given over to some *sauvage* for a wife?"

"I don't see anything wrong with it," said Rene.

"*Non, mon ami*," said DuBois, "and neither do I. And neither would I, were I, and not Tournier, in command of this force."

Tournier wrote,

Novembre, and I have been through three of the ceremonies of these people, the Cheraques. I begin to see some pattern to the things they do and make at least some little sense of their beliefs.

Their language is extremely difficult, but I continue to make slow progress in learning it.

I believe that we will have to spend at least two months more and maybe three here in this town because of the winter, but at the first real sign of spring, we will once again head north to the land of the Iroquois to meet with the Senikas and bring their peace delegation here to treat with the Cheraques. If I can be successful at that, I will have obtained for *le roi* two of the most powerful allies in this land.

I am worried about DuBois and a few others of my men. They are disgruntled and display signs of rebellion. I am watching them very closely these days for any indications of improper behavior. I don't know if we'll manage to make it through the winter without some unpleasantness from them.

In Coyatee, Olig' and his new friends prepared to make a longer search of the area around the town. Their first time out, they had gone only as far as they could go out and back in one day. Four different groups had gone out from town a half-day's travel and then returned. This time they would be gone for four days if need be. There would still be four groups, and they would still go out in the four directions, but they would search farther away and longer. If there were any more Shawnees in the area, they meant to find them.

They carried food with them, so they would not have to take time away from their search for hunting, and they carried weapons in case they should encounter the enemy. The morning of the first day, they were relaxed. They were covering ground they had already searched. But after the Sun had reached her daughter's house just overhead in the center of the Sky Vault, without any directions or orders, without even a suggestion from anyone in the group, they became more vigilant.

Oliga's group—the same group he had gone out with before, Black Dog, Water Dog and Bent Bow Shape—had gone east. They were out of the mountains and into low foothills. They were still walking trails through thick woods.

Now and then they took side paths and checked out the banks of nearby rivers or streams. At the end of the first day out, they had seen no evidence of foreigners in their land. They found a clear spot just up a hillside from a clean running creek, and there they made their camp for the night.

They built a small fire and prepared a meal, which they washed down with water from the creek below. Bent Bow Shape moved away from the fire to watch while the others slept. Water Dog, his father, was preparing himself a spot on the ground near the fire.

"Water Dog," said Oliga, "I'm far away from home, and so I can't do things the way they should be done. I like your daughter."

Water Dog sat down on the ground.

"Well," he said, "I think she likes you too."

"I want to marry her," said Olig'.

"That's a matter for the women to decide," said Water Dog.

"I know," said Olig'. "The women of her clan should talk to the women of my clan. Her mother should speak to my mother. But my mother is in Kitu-wah. It's a long way back there."

"Then there's nothing to be done about it that I know of," said Water Dog.

"Unless you two just run away together," said Bent Bow Shape, from his place in the darkness.

"Yes," said Water Dog. "There is that way."

Oliga had not considered that. Of course, that was a way to marry without going through the tedium of the clan negotiations. He was surprised that the suggestion had been made by the brother of Tsiwon', and even seconded, it seemed, by her father. For a moment he was silent.

"If Tsiwon' and I should run away," he said, "and then if we came back, would we be welcome in Coyatee?"

"I can't speak for her mother," said Water Dog, "but I would welcome you. I see nothing wrong with elopement. It's an honorable way to marry. As long as the girl agrees."

"Oh," said Olig', "I would never take Tsiwon' away against her will."

"Then maybe you should talk to her when we get back," said Water Dog. "Now I'm going to sleep."

Oliga could not sleep, though. He thought about Tsiwon', and he considered the prospect of elopement, something he had never really thought about before. He had always assumed that when the time came for him to marry, he would go through the standard procedures.

He tried, but he could not even recall having ever known anyone who had eloped. He knew that such things happened, for he had heard tales, and, of course, he knew that men sometimes came home with wives from other peoples. But elopement. It sounded like an adventure. He liked the idea, and he decided as he lay there that he would take his future father-in-law's advice and speak about it to Tsiwon' as soon as they got back to Coyatee.

Still he couldn't sleep for thinking of Tsiwon' and imagining what would happen in his near future. He also thought about his inglorious flight from Kituwah. He smiled to himself there in the darkness. How things had changed. He smoothed a spot across the fire from where Water Dog was already sleeping, stretched himself out and pulled his robe up to his chin.

It was cold already. The day had been cool, but with the Sun on the other side of the Sky Vault, it was cold. At last, in spite of the cold and the jumble of his thoughts, he drifted off to sleep.

17

Oliga found himself standing alone upon a narrow ledge of rock. He looked down. Far below, a dizzying distance, was a winding, clear-running mountain stream, its banks nothing but jagged rocks. Between the rocky stream below and the ledge on which he stood was a wall of sheer, slick rock, almost straight up and down. There was no way to climb down. There was nothing below but a fall to certain death. Off in the distance an eagle cried.

Olig' looked to his right, and he saw that the ledge on which he stood narrowed until it simply vanished into the wall of the cliff. He could have taken two, maybe three steps in that direction, but that was all. He looked to his left. There was no place there to go, for the ledge simply appeared to have been chopped off abruptly.

Beginning to feel giddy from the height, Olig' pressed his back firmly against the rock wall and looked up. The ledge on which he was so precariously perched must have been only about half the way up the face of the cliff, for it looked to him to be as far on up to the top as it was down to the bottom.

But again he saw no way to move. The wall did not go straight up above him. It jutted out, so that if someone had lowered a long rope from up above and let it hang down straight, by the time it had reached his level, it would have been much too far away for Oliga to reach it, even by a jump.

He was trapped, and he was getting dizzy. The cliff behind him and the valley below seemed to swirl around him. The wind blew harder and colder, and he was afraid that he would fall, or be picked up bodily by the strong wind and hurled out into space. Slowly, carefully, he slid his back downward on the smooth rock behind him, bending his knees, until he was sitting on the ledge. He felt a little safer in that posture, not quite so much as if he would pitch forward from his dizziness at any moment.

Sitting there on the narrow ledge, his back pressed against the cliff face, shivering from the cold and howling wind, he hugged his knees into his chest. He felt like a frightened child.

Then even over the roar of the wind, he heard the eagle scream again, and this time it seemed very close indeed. He looked around, but he did not see it. He couldn't find it, but he knew that it was near. He pressed himself hard against the rock wall, wishing he could scoot back even more, wishing he could shoot backwards like a crawdad in a rocky stream.

"Jisduh," he heard them say. "Jisduh."

He was afraid. His flesh was slick with salty sweat, even though he shivered in the cold. Then he saw it. Coming from straight ahead. Swooping toward him. Getting closer and closer. Its frightful beak was opened wide. Its deadly talons reaching forward, ready to clutch and tear. Its hideous shriek long and loud. He screamed and ducked his head and felt it strike him a glancing blow as it swept on by.

He looked up just in time to see it turn. A graceful turn. Beautiful and frightening. It came back toward him then riding on the wind with a deadly speed, and it shrieked again as it came. He tried to prepare himself for the force of the strike, and as the great bird came closer, he shifted his weight to the side, and when it would have struck, he leaned quickly to his left, managing to dodge the blow. A wing slapped him hard as it swooped on by.

Again it turned. It would not give up. He looked desperately around himself on the ledge for his weapons, but he saw none. He wondered just how he had gotten himself onto this ledge, and he wondered where his weapons might be. He thought about trying to defend himself with his bare hands. He had to do something. He couldn't just sit there like a frightened mouse and wait for the deadly blow that would rip him open.

The screaming eagle came close again and closer, and he reached out with both hands, grabbing for its throat. At the last instant, it veered and flew straight up, and Olig' lost his balance and pitched forward, falling headlong toward the rocky shore below.

Gracefully, he turned and looked at clouds above, and then he turned again and saw the rocks below. They seemed larger, seemed to be rushing toward him. He wondered if he would feel the impact when he hit, or if he would be killed too quickly to feel anything.

And then he sat up straight and quick and made a noise as if someone had slipped up on him in the dark and frightened him. He looked around himself. He was sitting beside the campfire across from Water Dog. He looked back over his shoulder and there was Black Dog. Both men were sound asleep. He hoped that he had not made a noise loud enough for Bent Bow Shape to hear, but before he had thought about it long, he had his answer.

"Oliga, is something wrong over there?" Bent Bow Shape said.

"No," said Olig', trying to make himself heard by the sentry without waking the others. "I just woke up. That's all."

His body was wet with perspiration in the cold night air. He put aside his robe, stood up and, taking up his weapons, walked toward the place from which he thought Bent Bow Shape watched.

"Where are you?" he asked.

"Over here."

Olig' turned toward the voice and kept walking.

"I'm awake now," he said. "I'll watch and let you sleep."

"Good," said Bent Bow Shape. "I'm getting sleepy. *Wado.*"

Standing alone away from the fire, Olig' thought about the frightening dream. He wondered if he should tell the others. If he should tell them, he wondered, what would they say? Would they abandon the search for Shawnees and go immediately back to Coyatee? They might. The dream could be a bad sign. To dream of eagles, he had heard, was a sign of death.

Ahuli and Young Puppy were busy preparing for the coming ceremony of Ado huna. There was not much time, and Ahuli spent much of it in teaching the younger man the words to one special song. Once Ado huna was done, there would be no more ceremonies until the arrival of spring. Ahuli could have been content with performing this pressing ceremony himself, but he very much wanted Young Puppy to begin taking a more active and more important role, and so he pressed very hard with his instructions.

When Ado huna was behind them, and the long cold period, the hardest part of the winter, would be upon them, he would have plenty of time to prepare Young Puppy for the remaining ceremonies of the year, the ones that would begin again in the spring.

It was good, Ahuli thought, to have a young man studying the forms, good to know that one's knowledge would not go with him to the Darkening Land. And Young Puppy was intelligent, a fast learner, but even more important than that, he had been chosen. Ahuli was certain of that; and lately, it seemed, Young Puppy himself had even come to that realization.

There had been only one day between the finish of the Ceremony of the White Drink and the meeting Ahuli had called with his seven councillors to determine the exact time of Ado huna. Again Young Puppy had attended the meeting, sitting quietly and respectfully, watching and listening to the proceedings, learning all he could.

Ahuli and the councillors had determined that Ado huna would begin in seven days. The next morning, a runner was again sent out to notify all the nearby towns and to invite everyone to attend.

A woman from each clan was selected to lead the dance, and musicians were appointed. Seven men were selected to clean the sacred dance ground, and seven hunters were sent out in seven different directions to hunt for game for the feast. Another seven were sent out to gather seven plants for purification: cedar, white pine, hemlock, mistletoe, evergreen briar, heartleaf, and ginseng. The sacred fire on the altar was once again renewed with wood from the seven sacred trees.

The next morning, Ahuli, Young Puppy, the seven councillors, the seven women selected to lead the dance, all began to fast. They were allowed to take a small amount of cornmeal mush at night, just before retiring. At the same time, the seven hunters and the seven gatherers went out to begin their hunts.

Olig' and his companions began their search the second day, and although Oliga was strangely silent and somber, no one spoke to him about it. Olig' tried to keep his mind on the search. He knew that if he blundered carelessly upon some enemy, he could get himself killed, maybe even cause another's death, but he could not stop thinking about the eagle dream.

He was like a man haunted, and he found himself looking up into the sky at every third or fourth step he took. He saw no eagles though. They stopped close by a stream to rest when the Sun was overhead, and Olig', restless, paced away from the others. He wandered close to a muddy shore, and he almost overlooked the footprint there. He saw it, though, and he hurried back to where his companions were resting.

"I saw a footprint down there in the mud," he said. "Come with me. I'll show you."

The others followed him, and Black Dog moved in close to study the imprint in the mud. He squatted on his haunches and stared at it for a long time, until the others grew impatient with him.

"Well," Water Dog finally said, "what do you make of it?"

Black Dog stood up and turned to face his anxious companions.

"Shawnee, I think," he said. "Let's look around for more."

It wasn't long before they found more prints, enough to determine a probable direction of travel. It was more northerly than the direction they had been moving, so they shifted to a slightly northeastern line of march. The sighting of the footprints shocked Olig'—though he did not forget his dream—back into caution and attention to the problems of the present.

Everyone was alert from there on. They moved slowly and silently through the forest, not knowing what to expect, trying to be ready for anything. Before nightfall, they were out of the trees and onto a grassy plain. There, still in the land of the Real People, they found the Shawnees. Not lone hunters. Not a war party. They found a Shawnee town, well populated, fortified and completely walled-in.

René Gaspar stood leaning against the outside of Kituwah's wall. He was watching Guwisti as she tended her horse. Ah, how he wished that she would climb on its back and ride, ride somewhere beyond shouting distance back to town. He would leap on the back of any one of the French horses and follow her and have his way. But she showed no sign of mounting up. She seemed only to be moving the animal to another grazing spot, not far away, still near the wall.

"Hey," he called out to her.

She looked at him and smiled, then went on about her business.

"Hey, pretty lady," said René.

Guwisti looked again and shrugged, as if to say, I do not understand you.

"Mon dieu," said Rene. He started walking toward Guwist'. "Hey. You want to go for a ride with me? I'll get another horse."

"René," a voice called sharply, and René stopped and looked back over his shoulder to see Dr. DuBois standing there at the opening in the fence. He grinned, shrugged and turned to walk over to stand beside DuBois.

"You told me you saw nothing wrong with it," he said.

"I do not," said the doctor, "but I'm not in command here, either. Not yet anyway. I wouldn't want to lose my right-hand man over such a small thing as this before it's time for us to make our move."

"Ah, well," said René. "She is such a pretty little thing. Don't you agree, *Docteur*?"

"Yes, yes," said DuBois. "Have you talked to the others?"

"I talked to just about everyone, and I found out what I already knew."

"And what is that?" asked the doctor.

"That Marcel and Georges and Jean might go along with us," said René. "They have no love for *le capitaine*, but they are afraid of him."

"I'll talk to them myself, then," said DuBois. "I'll bring them around to our way of thinking. What about the others?"

"They're loyal, to a man. Don't even hint of mutiny in front of one of them. He'd run to *le capitaine* immediately."

"And we'd be shot for our troubles. Yes," said DuBois. "Well, that makes the problem a little bigger, but not yet impossible to solve. When the time comes, we'll simply have to disarm them all just before we make our move."

René looked toward Guwisti with a leer.

"And when will that be?" he asked.

"When the time is right," said DuBois. "When I say and not a moment before. You understand me?"

"*Oui*," said René.

"In the meantime, do nothing to make Tournier suspect us. If he says jump, you click your heels and ask him, Over what?"

Guwisti, finished with her chore, walked back to the entryway. She almost had to brush into René to get past him on her way back into town. René turned and watched as she moved on through the passageway. When she was gone from his sight, he turned to face the wall, pressed himself against it and pounded it with his fist. He growled, then turned back to face DuBois.

"*Docteur*," he said, "don't wait too long. I beg of you. I beg you, and I warn you."

18

Osa did not go home again. She remained there with Uyona and became in fact like a daughter to the old woman. Uyona watched her almost constantly, telling her what to do and what not to do for the safety of the two children growing inside her. And Osa did not resent the attention. Far from it. She thrived and doted on it.

She had felt so alone since the death of her Asquani, that she eagerly, if not joyfully, embraced the new relationship. She depended on it for survival, her own and that of her coming children, and for her sanity. She had worried about the new life growing in her womb. With Uyona she felt secure.

The clever old woman had taken Osa to the water one night under the light of a full moon, and there she had prayed and divined with the black and red beads. As she studied the beads, the red one balanced between the thumb and index finger of her boney right hand, the black on her left, the red bead had begun to tremble and move of its own power and will, and old Uyona had smiled.

"We'll have success," she had said.

She had brewed a strong tea of the bark of *dawoja*, the red or slippery elm, and she had given this tea to Osa to drink.

"This will make you slippery inside," she'd said, "so that when the times comes, the little ones will slide out easy."

And she had brewed another drink from the stems of *wālelu uhnaja luhgisgi*. This, she had said, when the right time came, would frighten the infants, and make them jump out in a hurry.

She had made more tea to ensure long life for the infants to come, and this she had brewed from roots of *ganuhgwadliski nigalo itsei* and cones from the *notsi*, both of which are evergreen.

"Good health and long life will come from these," she had said.

Every morning Osa, accompanied by Uyona, went to the nearby creek, and there they washed their faces, hands and feet in the cold, clear, running water. Osa thought that it was a brisk and happy way to start the day.

And Osa helped Uyona as much as she could with the chores around the house, but the old woman insisted on preparing all the meals by herself.

"Uyona," said Osa, one morning after coming back to the house from the creek, "tell me again about my babies."

"I've already told you everything there is to tell," said the old woman.

"I know," said Osa. "I just like to hear it."

"A boy and a girl," the old woman said with a smile.

"Both will live?"

"Both will be healthy and live long lives, the boy with you and the girl with me."

"Can we all live here together?" Osa asked.

"When they've jumped out," the old woman said, "you must go back to your house in Kituwah with your boy. The girl and I will stay here. But you may come and visit every seventh day."

And Osa was content with her arrangement with old Horn. The company of the old woman, the chores around the house, all helped to pass the time and kept her from being lonely and depressed. The old woman's vast knowledge, her advice and guidance, her careful preparations and precise directions, all helped keep Osa's mind at ease regarding the coming births and the future well-being of her children.

"They've moved a whole town into our country," Bent Bow Shape said, amazed.

"What will we do?" asked Water Dog.

"There's nothing we can do just now," said Black Dog. "There are only four of us. We'll return to Coyatee and report what we have found out here. But first, let's study this town well, study all approaches to the town, and then on our way back home, study the trail, so that we'll be able to make a full report and plan carefully our return."

They did so for four days, and then they started home, and all the way, Olig' worried about his eagle dream. He wondered what it meant. Did it indeed mean death? If so, for whom? For him? He had only just begun looking forward to his future, only since meeting with Tsiwon'.

He also worried because he had kept his dream to himself, for he and his companions had been in potentially dangerous situations together, and his dream had been an omen of possible death in the near future. He felt guilty, wondering if he should have warned them of that danger by telling them about the dream.

Olig' was therefore greatly relieved when he and his companions all reached Coyatee together and safely. They were the last of the four groups to return. The others were all back, having nothing to report, and all were safe and unharmed.

A council meeting was called, and the entire population of Coyatee crowded into their townhouse, for the night was cold. Black Dog reported the findings, and much discussion followed. Everyone agreed that something must be done, but just what it would be was not defined. At last it was decided that they would meet again in four days' time, and everyone went home.

It was early morning when seven men, one from each clan, rekindled the sacred fire in the altar. They used wood broken from the dry, lower limbs on the east side of black jack, locust, post oak, sycamore, redbud, plum and red oak trees.

As soon as this was done, women began to appear from all the houses in Kituwah. Having been required to extinguish all flames at their homes that morning and to clean up and throw out all the ashes, they came to the newly kindled sacred fire to replenish their own at home.

The grounds had been swept clean, all old ashes removed, and the altar had been repaired and restored to its proper height. Just in front of the altar were placed a table and bench, each having been formed by the placing of a wide plank across the tops of sections of log stood on end. Seven poles had been planted firmly in the ground. All of this had been freshly painted white.

The table and bench were covered with white deerskins, and deerskins were draped on the tops of the poles to form a canopy. Pots and dipping gourds were on the table. Two of the firekeepers took up a large pot and carried it to the altar where they placed it carefully on the fire. Then all seven walked in single file four full times around the altar.

"*Yuuuu*," they sang together. "*Yuuuu. Yuuuu. Yuuuu*," and they finished with a whoop. Then each of the seven took a dipping gourd from the table, and they all walked to the water.

Returning to the dance ground, each man in turn walked one more time around the fire, poured the water from his gourd into the pot, and then replaced the gourd on the table. That done, they walked together to the home of Ahuli.

"Everything is ready," said one man.

Ahuli and Young Puppy came out of the house at once. Ignoring the seven men, they walked straight to the town storehouse. Ahuli stood by watching while Young Puppy opened the door to the storehouse and reached in for a large basket which was filled with the seven plants for purification. He took out the basket and walked with it toward the dance ground. Just as he was about to walk onto the ground, Ahuli stopped him.

"*Hesdi,*" Ahuli said.

Young Puppy stopped. He stood there holding the basket, waiting, while Ahuli said a prayer for purification. When the prayer was done, Young Puppy walked on in toward the altar. Ahuli stopped him again, just by the table, and there he prayed again. He asked for all impurities from the year just passed to be wiped away.

Ahuli nodded curtly to Young Puppy then, and Young Puppy, still carrying the basket of plants, moved on. Followed by Ahuli, he walked to the altar and circled it, stopping on the north. Ahuli reached into a pouch at his waist and drew out a handful of *tsola gayunli* which he tossed into the flames. Then he produced the wing of a white heron from under his feathered matchcoat, and he wafted the smoke from the burning tobacco in each of the four directions.

They circled again, and again Ahuli put ancient tobacco into the flames. Again he waved the heron's wing through the smoke. They circled a third and then a fourth time, and after the fourth, Ahuli looked at Young Puppy and gave a nod.

Young Puppy stepped up close to the altar. He lifted the basket in both his hands, holding it over the pot of boiling water, and he moved it back and forth over the pot four times. Then he lowered the basket and its contents into the pot and stepped back out of the way. Ahuli then moved up and waved the heron wing through the steam that was rising now through the contents of the basket. He waved the wing four times, then led Young Puppy to the bench by the table, and they both sat down.

The seven firekeepers then reappeared in a wide circle around the periphery of the dance ground. Together they sang loud and long.

"*Yuuuu.*"

They sang it seven times, and then they shouted a quick "*Wah,*" and faded back away. By this time, the crowd was large around the ground. Probably all the residents and all the guests of Kituwah were there, and each person in the crowd was holding a fresh suit of clothing.

Ahuli stood up, and with great pomp and flourish, produced a white robe, which he carried a short distance toward the altar. Then he called Young Puppy's name. Young Puppy followed him and stood, facing east, while Ahuli placed the beautiful white robe on his shoulders. That done, Ahuli handed Young Puppy a white gourd, filled with pebbles. He went back to his seat, leaving Young Puppy there alone.

All eyes were on the young man in his newly acquired splendor as he assumed an important role in a ceremony vital to all life. He stood for a moment, silent. Then he lifted the gourd rattle and shook it.

"Yuuuu," he sang as he walked around the altar. He finished with a whoop and left the dance ground. With that for their signal, the seven men who had earlier swept the ground started walking toward the storehouse, singing all the way, each carrying in his right hand a long sycamore rod.

When they reached the storehouse, they circled it and began lashing at the eaves with their rods. Then they sang again while walking to the nearest house. The song finished each time just as they reached a house, and then they lashed its eaves. They kept going in this way until they had lashed every house in Kituwah. When they finished back at the dance ground, placing their rods on the table, the Sun was high overhead.

The seven firekeepers went to the storehouse and gathered up the meat which the seven hunters had placed there, and they delivered it into the hands of the seven women who had been chosen as cooks.

While they were thus employed, Young Puppy, in his new white robe, went to the rear of the townhouse. A notched pole was waiting for him there, leaning up against the eave of the roof. He climbed the pole, his heart pounding in his chest with anxiety. He stepped onto the roof and walked to its highest point, and he began to sing.

> *Hiyo wa yakani.*
> *Hiyo wa yakani.*
> *Hiyo wa yakani.*
> *Hiyo wa yakani.*
>
> *Hide huyu yakani.*
> *Hide huyu yakani.*
> *Hide huyu yakani.*
> *Hide huyu yakani.*
>
> *Hiwa taki yakani.*
> *Hiwa taki yakani.*

Hiwa taki yakani.
Hiwa taki yakani.

Hihi wasasi yakani.
Hihi wasasi yakani.
Hihi wasasi yakani.
Hihi wasasi yakani.

Hiani tsusi yakani.
Hiani tsusi yakani.
Hiani tsusi yakani.
Hiani tsusi yakani.

Hiyowa hiyeyo yakani.
Hiyowa hiyeyo yakani.
Hiyowa hiyeyo yakani.
Hiyowa hiyeyo yakani.

Hiani heho yakani.
Hiani heho yakani.
Hiani heho yakani.
Hiani heho yakani.

Following each of the seven stanzas, Young Puppy rattled his gourd and sounded a long high note. When he had finished, he went back down the notched pole and back to the dance ground, where he walked around the fire. He stopped, facing east, back at the spot where Ahuli had placed the white robe on his shoulders.

"I am heard," he shouted, and the crowd answered him with a long and loud *"Waaah."* Ahuli stood and walked over to a spot just behind Young Puppy. He removed the robe from Young Puppy's shoulders and took it back to the table where he carefully folded it and laid it down. Both men sat back down at the table.

Then the seven keepers of the sacred fire took up seven dipping gourds. One at a time they filled their gourds from the pot on the altar fire. Then each firekeeper handed his gourd to a different clan leader in the crowd, who in turn, passed it around among his own clanspeople. Thus, before they were done, each person in town had drunk from the gourd and had rubbed some of its contents over his body. After this, mothers were allowed to feed their infants. No one else ate food.

Then, from his place at the table, Young Puppy sang his song again. When that was done, Ahuli called out for everyone to go to the water. Carrying their extra clothing, the people hurried to the water's edge. There seemed to be no order to their going. They rushed ahead, some nearly running over others.

But when Ahuli and Young Puppy arrived behind them, they were standing quietly in an orderly line facing the water. Each person's extra clothing was neatly folded and lying at his feet.

"Go in," Ahuli called, and the people plunged into the water. Men moved a little upstream and women downstream, but once in the water, all faced east. Then almost together, almost as if by command, though no command was given, they ducked their heads entirely under the water. Coming back up, they turned to face the north, and dipped again, then again to the west and then to the south. Turning back east, they dipped themselves three times more to make it seven.

Only then did they wipe their faces, and then they began removing their clothes, which they allowed the drifting current to carry away downstream. Then they walked naked, clean and pure out of the running water and dressed themselves in their new clothes.

In silence, everyone walked back to the dance ground, followed by Ahuli and Young Puppy. When all of the people had taken their places, and the seven firekeepers had formed a semicircle in front of the altar, Ahuli stepped into the circle. He walked to the altar, and Young Puppy followed.

One of the firekeepers handed Ahuli the tongue of a deer, and Ahuli held it up high and prayed. Then he carefully placed the tongue in the fire on the altar and sprinkled it with sacred tobacco. They stood quietly and watched it burn.

Then a firekeeper handed Ahuli a stack of seven neatly folded deerskins. Ahuli took them to the table and placed them there. He reached into a pouch underneath his matchcoat and drew out *ulunsuti*, which he placed on top of the stack of skins. He prayed again, and then he gazed into the crystal for a long, silent time.

The Sun was now low in the western sky. Soon she would crawl under the western edge of the Sky Vault and disappear for the night, leaving the world in darkness while she moved along the top side of the Vault heading back toward the east, where she would once again crawl under to start another day. Standing by the altar, Young Puppy sang his song again. When he was done, Ahuli called for food.

And food was brought. Great quantities and great varieties of food. Meat, squirrel and rabbit, bear and deer, pounded and boiled, cornbread, mush, hominy, potatoes, beans and squash. All kinds of foods were there. Ahuli prayed again, and then, at last, the people ate.

The people ate, but not Ahuli, nor Young Puppy, nor the seven cooks, nor Ahuli's seven councillors. None of these had eaten since the meeting seven days before the ceremony had begun.

When the people had finished their meal, they began to dance around the fire. A dance leader sang the songs and led the dance, and the others, men and women and children too, followed him as he moved in the sacred direction around the altar.

They had been dancing for some time, and it was well into the night, when Ahuli at last spoke into Young Puppy's ear. Young Puppy then went alone to the water. He waded into the cold stream, and he dipped himself seven times. Then he returned to the dance ground, and only then was he allowed to eat. By that time, the others who had fasted with him were eating too. A crier made an announcement that those who did not wish to stay awake all night could now go home, and some few did. Many danced all night. The first day of Ado huna was done.

19

Tournier wrote:

The language of these people is most difficult. I know that I have said that before, but I must emphasize it here again. We have just completed the first day of another ceremony, my fourth among the Cheraques, the name of which I cannot with any degree of confidence put down. It may be Friendship. It may be Propitiation or even something else.

Whatever its proper name, it seems to me to have to do with cleansing or purification, physical, mental and spiritual, and it is by far the most complex of the ceremonies I have witnessed yet.

I continue to watch most carefully Monsieur Le Docteur DuBois and his close associates, René Gaspar, Jean Claude Larousse, Georges LeGrue and Marcel Debonnet. Lately they have given me no trouble, but they seem somewhat surly in their manner. Perhaps nothing will come of it after all.

Young Puppy should have been exhausted. He had gone seven days without eating, had taken an important and tiring role in the first busy day of the Friendship Celebration, and then had stayed up all night for the dancing. But he was not exhausted. He was not even tired. He felt exhilarated and ready to go again.

It was this new life of his, he thought. Strange, how he had never considered it before Ahuli had come to him and almost forced it on him. But Ahuli had been right. It must be right, for it felt good and right and proper to Young Puppy, and he was sure that it was for this role in life that he had been born.

He had never felt so much alive as when he had been singing his song, singing in front of all the people, singing the most important song of Ado huna, singing from the top of the townhouse with the white robe draped over his shoulders, singing for continued life for all the people and even for the life of the world itself.

He knew that when this ceremony was done, he would have some leisure time before the next, for three long months, the hard, coldest months of Gola, would be upon them soon, and nothing more would be done until the spring. And a part of him was anxious for the leisure time so that he could spend some of it in talking with his mother and with Guwisti. He knew that they were both proud of him in his new role, and he'd had but little time for either of them lately.

But another part of him did not want to see the end of the ceremony. It told him there could be nothing better in his life than what he was now so thoroughly engaged in, that life from this time on would be waiting from one ceremony to the next.

The second day of Ado huna was much the same as the first had been, except that the people in general were free to eat whenever they pleased. But Ahuli and Young Puppy and the others who had fasted for so long were not. They would not eat again until after dark, as they had done the day before.

And the second day was a little disappointing for Young Puppy, for the day's events did not include the singing of the song. The third day was like the second.

But the fourth day was like the first, almost exactly, and again Young Puppy sang his song three times. This night everyone stayed awake while only the women engaged in dancing all night long.

When the Sun appeared the next morning, the morning of the fifth day, the dancing ceased. Ahuli made another sacrifice to the fire, and then he took the basket from the pot. He held it out for all to see until its contents had quit dripping water onto the ground, and then he took it to the table and emptied the contents onto a deerskin. He set aside the basket and folded the deerskin.

"Now I'm going home," he said.

He took up the folded deerskin under his arm and walked away, and as he walked, the crowd called out behind him, "Wah." Young Puppy followed him. Then the seven councillors arose and walked away, going toward their homes.

Finally the people, a few at a time, got up to leave. It was all very orderly. All was quiet. Everyone went home. The ceremony was done.

Oliga could keep his dreadful secret no longer. He was not alone in danger because of his dream. Death could come to someone, anyone, who was near to him. He sought out Water Dog to confide in.

"I had a dream," he said. "Awohali was in it."

Water Dog's face took on a grim expression.

"You know what it means when an eagle comes into your dreams?"

"Yes," said Olig'. "I know."

"You, or someone close to you, will die."

"Unless I have an Eagle Dance," said Olig'.

"In order to have an Eagle Dance," said Water Dog, "you need eagle feathers."

"Of course."

"But you can't get them for yourself. It's forbidden for just anyone to kill an eagle. You must go to an Awohali-dihi."

"Yes. I know."

All of the Real People knew of the specialist, the man known as the Eagle Killer, who alone knew the proper forms and the proper words which allowed him, and only him, to kill the sacred bird.

"Olig'," said Water Dog, "we have no Eagle Killer here, and we have no one here who knows how to lead the Eagle Dance."

Oliga smacked himself hard on the forehead and paced away from Water Dog. What was he to do? No Eagle Killer and no Eagle Dance leader. Did that mean that he was to just sit around and wait to die? Or wait for someone else, someone near him, to die? Such a thing was unthinkable to him, especially when he knew what needed to be done.

"Is there no one near?" he said. "No one in another town?"

"We're a remote town here," said Water Dog. "Our nearest neighbor is the Shawnee town we found the other day."

Oliga thought about the irony of his situation. He had sought out Coyatee because of its remoteness, and now that very quality was working against him. Had he stayed at home in Kituwah, he could have gone to Ahuli. Ahuli, he was sure, was an Eagle Killer. But then, if he'd stayed home, would the eagle have come into his dream? Of course, he could not know.

"I'll just have to go home then," he said, "to Kituwah. There's a man there who can help me, an Eagle Killer. I'll go to him."

Water Dog put a hand on Oliga's shoulder and thought a moment before he spoke.

"Let's talk to Black Dog first," he said.

Olig' waited a moment for more, but Water Dog gave no further indication of his intentions. Instead, he stood up abruptly and motioned for Olig' to follow him. They walked straight to Black Dog's home and called for him to come outside and talk. Water Dog told Black Dog about Oliga's dream and about his plans to return to Kituwah to enlist the aid of Ahuli.

"I'm sorry to lose a good fighting man," said Black Dog, "with what we're facing here, but there's nothing else to be done. He must go."

"But what if I go with him?" Water Dog asked. "I could tell the people there at Kituwah about the Shawnee town here in our country. Maybe they would send some men back with us to help us out."

Black Dog rubbed his chin and thought for a moment.

"When do you plan to leave here?" he asked Olig'.

"As soon as I can," said Olig'. "With the morning light. I don't know how much time I have to get the Eagle Dance performed. And the days are getting colder. I should go now."

"You're right, of course," said Black Dog. "We don't have time to call a council meeting over this matter. It's important to act quickly. If you want to go with him, Water Dog, then I suggest you go. I'll tell the council that you've gone to seek some aid from Kituwah. Maybe they'll decide to wait for word from you before we take any action against these Shawnees."

Back at his wife's house, Water Dog announced his intentions of traveling to Kituwah with Oliga. As he was gathering his things for the trip, Tsiwon' spoke up.

"I'm going too," she said.

"No," said Water Dog. "It's dangerous."

"To travel in our own country to visit another town of Real People?" Tsiwon' said.

"There could be winter storms."

"I can take the cold as well as you," she said. "Maybe even better. You're getting old."

Water Dog looked toward his wife for assistance, but she only shrugged.

"Take her with you," she said. "Otherwise I'll have to listen to her complain the whole time you're gone."

Water Dog sighed and dropped the bundle he was working on.

"There's more," he said. "I wasn't going to tell it, but Oliga had a dream. He had an eagle dream. That means that he could die, or someone near to him could die. He's going to Kituwah for an Eagle Dance. And so, Daughter, I don't want you along on this trip, and I don't think that Oliga would want you along, either. We know you want to marry Olig'. You're too close to him. You might be the one to die."

For a moment no one spoke. Then Tsiwon' turned and began gathering up her things for travel.

"What are you doing?" Water Dog said.

"I'm going with you," she said. "If I'm the one to die because of the eagle dream, I'll die here as well as on the way to Kituwah. Besides, I think the Eagle Dance will be done in time."

In Kituwah, the ceremonies were over for a time. The people were all tired from the festivities they had just gone through, and the days and nights were getting colder. For those reasons, everyone seemed to sleep longer and more soundly.

Dr. DuBois sat up slowly in the night. The flickering light from the central fire in the townhouse showed that everyone else was asleep. Carefully and quietly he crawled to the side of René Gaspar. He put a hand over the mouth of Gaspar and clamped down hard. René stirred and then struggled. He snorted and then came awake to look wide-eyed at the doctor there.

"Hush," whispered DuBois. "It's only me."

He released René slowly and he sat up, looking nervously around the large room.

"Don't worry," said DuBois. "They're all sleeping like babies."

"What is it?" asked Gaspar.

"Tonight's the night," said DuBois.

"Tonight? So soon?"

"Aren't you the one who warned me not to wait too long?"

"Yes, but—"

"Never again may we find everyone so sound asleep and so much off their guard as now," said the doctor. "We must take advantage of the times. Besides, when I saw you slobbering over that young woman, you did not say, 'So soon?' "

"All right," said Gaspar. "Tonight it is."

"You know what to do," said DuBois. "So do it."

Gaspar got up slowly and quietly and, taking his shoes in his hands, he headed toward the door. DuBois watched him until he went outside. Then the mutinous doctor moved over to where Jean-Claude Larousse was sleeping.

"Jean," he said. "Jean. Wake up."

Larousse lifted his head, rubbing his eyes.

"It is I," said DuBois. "René has gone for the weapons. Wake up Marcel and Georges. Be quiet, but hurry. We must be ready."

René shivered as he stepped out into the cold night. He pulled on his shoes, and then he reached under his jacket to feel the haft of the knife that he had secreted there. Then stealthily he made his way to the wall and the passageway that would lead outside the town.

In the darkness, the landscape outside Kituwah looked to him like a wilderness, full of danger and evil. He gripped the knife hard, and he was aware that his palm was sweating. He looked to his left beyond the herd of horses tethered there, and he could see the glimmer of the small fire where the sentry stood guard over the cache of French weapons which Tournier had stacked there at the insistence of Trotting Wolf and others.

"They will have us as their guests," Tournier had said, "but they will not have our weapons inside the walls of their peace town."

Well, as it turned out, that was working to the advantage of DuBois and his rebellious companions. There were but five of them, and they were outnumbered by the rest of Tournier's company, not to mention the Indians. But the guns would make all the difference. Gaspar stayed close to the wall and walked toward the fire. He was trembling, and he could feel his heart pounding in his chest.

"Who goes there?" came the voice of the sentry.

"René Gaspar. Is that you, LeBlanc?"

"*Oui.* What are you doing out here, René?"

Discovered, Gaspar strode boldly on toward LeBlanc, who stood holding a blunderbuss across his chest.

"Ah, you know, I couldn't sleep. The smoke in that blasted townhouse was burning my eyes. Everyone else is asleep. I don't know how they manage it in there. *Sacre bleu.* I'm going crazy in this Indien town."

"It's better than being out in the wilderness with winter coming on," said LeBlanc, "and all kinds of wild animals. Maybe even devils. Who knows?"

"I suppose you're right about that," said Gaspar. "Say, *mon ami,* do you have a pipe and some of that Indien tobacco on you?"

"*Oui,*" said LeBlanc. "I have some here, I think."

He lowered the blunderbuss into the crook of his right arm and reached into a deep coat pocket, and as he did, Gaspar drew out the knife, lunging forward with an underhand thrust. The blade bit deep. LeBlanc gasped, blood gurgled in his throat, and he sank forward, lifeless, into the arms of Gaspar. Gaspar looked over his shoulders. No one was around. He lowered the body onto the ground and turned his attention to the cache of arms.

20

Tournier woke up to the touch of cold steel against his temple. He rolled his eyes to see a primed and cocked pistol in the right hand of René Gaspar. I've been a fool, he thought. I should have watched them all more closely.

"Sit up slowly, *Capitaine*," said Gaspar.

Tournier sat up, and then he saw that Larousse, LeGrue, and Debonnet were holding guns on all the rest of his company, including Little Black Bear, the Catawba interpreter. DuBois was standing in the middle of the townhouse, hands on his hips, two pistols in his belt, and a wide grin on his face.

"*Capitaine* Tournier," said DuBois, "I wish to inform you that I have assumed command of this expedition because of your general incompetence. I also wish to inform you that I am placing you under arrest, and that formal charges will be made against you."

"You fool," said Tournier. "What charges?"

"Endangering the lives of everyone in this company by placing us inside a village of *sauvages*, outnumbered and unarmed, and taking part in and forcing us all to take part in heathen worship services. Gaspar, bring him down here and bind him fast."

Gaspar pulled Tournier roughly to his feet and shoved him out into the center of the townhouse. He pulled Tournier's arms behind his back and tied them tight with a rope which he had been carrying over his shoulder.

"You won't get away with this," said Tournier.

"I think that I already have," said DuBois. "It's true that we're outnumbered for right now by your—loyal followers, but we have all the guns. Besides, in time I think they'll come around to my way of thinking, especially when they see René and Jean and Marcel and Georges enjoying all the favors of the *jeunes femmes sauvages* while they have only their five fingers to relieve their pain."

"DuBois," said Tournier, "I beg you not to harm these people. They've been gracious hosts to us, and they are important potential allies."

"They're *sauvages*," said DuBois, "hardly people at all. Besides, I'm not talking of harming them, as long as they obey."

"Listen to me, DuBois," said Tournier, "before it's too late. All of us together would be no match for the people of this town. They could kill us all in a matter of minutes."

"You do think that I'm a fool, don't you, *Capitaine?*" said DuBois. "I've listened while you prattled on about these *sauvages*. So you see, I know that they are forbidden to kill inside these walls."

"DuBois, listen—"

"*La ferme.* René, put him over there with his minions, and keep him quiet. Then go find the devil priest and bring him here to me."

Ahuli was startled awake by the sudden intrusion of René Gaspar into his home. Gaspar held a torch in his left hand and a pistol in his right. Ahuli, though he had not seen many pistols fired, knew what it was and what it could do.

"Come along with me," said Gaspar, but, of course, he was speaking in French, and so Ahuli did not understand. "Come on, I say."

This time Gaspar gestured wildly with the pistol, and Ahuli understood the gesture. He stood up slowly, gathering a bear skin around himself. Gaspar shoved him roughly out the door and followed close behind. From a dark corner of the interior of Ahuli's house, unnoticed by Gaspar, Young Puppy watched.

He waited for a moment, then crawled to the doorway to look out, and he could see that the Frenchman was marching Ahuli toward the townhouse. He waited another moment, then slipped out the door and ran.

He ran to his mother's house and stopped just outside the door. He hesitated a moment, and when he spoke, it was in a low voice, a rough whisper.

"*Etsi,*" he said. "*Yona Hawiya.*"

No one answered. He raised his voice a little.

"Bear Meat. Father. Are you in there? Wake up. It's Young Puppy calling you."

"Young Puppy? Is that you?"

It was his mother's voice. He answered quickly.

"Yes, Mother. Is Father awake?"

"Come in," said Lolo. "What's the matter?"

Young Puppy crawled inside. By then Bear Meat was awake, sitting up and rubbing his eyes.

"Is something wrong?" he asked.

"One of the *yonegs* came to Ahuli's house and woke him up," said Young Puppy. "He had a fire stick, one of the short ones, and he pointed it at Ahuli and made him go with him to the townhouse."

Bear Meat got up quickly and reached for his war club.

"Your war club won't be any good against the fire sticks," said Young Puppy.

Bear Meat thought for a moment, put down the war club and picked up his bow and a quiver of arrows.

"Come on," he said.

"Where are you going?" said Lolo.

"First," said Bear Meat, "to find Trotting Wolf."

"Why do you want to remain loyal to this man?" DuBois was saying to the Frenchmen. "He has gone mad. He has been dancing every night with *les sauvages*. He makes us sit up all night through their heathenish ceremonies. He makes us fast. He denies us the pleasures of their women. What kind of a leader is that?"

There was some low mumbling among the captured Frenchmen, and DuBois allowed it to go on for a moment before he resumed speaking.

"When we return to France, I mean to have *le capitaine* Tournier formally charged with blasphemy, with heresy and with incompetence. In the meantime, I do not intend to continue to behave as if these Indiens are our lords and masters. I will show them that we are the masters. And so I'm giving each of you another chance to join me. Are you with me?"

No one spoke up.

"Anyone?"

"I'm with you," said one man. He stepped forward. "If you promise me a woman."

"Then step over here with us, Raoul," said DuBois. "You shall have one tonight. Anyone else?"

Raoul looked over his shoulder.

"Charles?" he said.

The man he addressed gave a shrug and stepped out to stand beside him.

"Oh, yeah," he said. "Why not. It's been pretty boring around here lately."

DuBois waited a moment, looking over the rest of the crew. None of them stepped forward. None spoke.

"Then bind the rest of them," said DuBois.

In a few moments the hands of all the Frenchmen who remained loyal to their deposed commander had been bound tightly behind their backs. DuBois and his crew of mutineers shoved them all to the ground, all except Little Black Bear.

"Bring him along with us," said DuBois, "and the devil priest as well."

He led his followers and their two native captives outside and into the dance ground where he stoked up the fire on the altar for light. Then he turned to Little Black Bear.

"Wake up the town," he said. "Call them all out. I want everyone in town gathered here to listen to what I have to say."

Little Black Bear hesitated, and DuBois slapped him across the face.

"Do as I say," he demanded, "or I will have you killed right here and now."

"Wake up," shouted Little Black Bear, speaking the trade language. "Wake up and come to the dance ground. Wake up."

"René," said DuBois, "stand just over here close by the devil priest and hold your pistol to his head."

A few people looked out of their houses to see what was going on, and some who did not know the trade language asked others who could understand it to tell them what was being shouted. Soon they began to gather nervously around the dance ground.

"Ask them if everyone is here," DuBois said to Little Black Bear.

"Is everyone here?" the Catawba asked in the trade language.

A man standing in front of the crowd looked around himself for a moment before answering.

"I think so," he said. "What is this all about?"

"They're all here," Little Black Bear said in French.

"*Bon,*" said DuBois. "Tell them that Tournier is no longer in charge. Tell them that he and his followers are my prisoners."

Little Black Bear rendered DuBois's startling words into the trade language, and the man in the crowd who had answered him before, translated into the language of the Real People.

"What is he saying?" asked DuBois.

"He's telling them what I just said," answered Little Black Bear. "I do not speak their language. I speak only the trade language. Some of them know it, and some do not, so—"

"All right. All right. Tell them now that their devil priest is also my prisoner, as they can easily see, and tell them that if they do not obey me in every way, he will die right here and now in front of their eyes. Tell them that I am not afraid of their law. I am not afraid to kill inside this town."

Little Black Bear translated again, and again the other man translated a second time. Everyone in the crowd looked at Ahuli, standing there with his arms tied behind his back, the big Frenchman holding him by one arm and pointing a pistol at him with the other.

"Now," said DuBois, "ask them if they understand what I have said."

As the question was being translated and then retranslated, the crowd parted a little, and Trotting Wolf stepped boldly to the front. He held a war club in his right hand.

"Tell the *yoneg* we understood his words," he said.

Across the dance ground from Trotting Wolf, Young Puppy's father, Bear Meat, stood at the front of the crowd. He held a bow with an arrow nocked and ready. Not far to his right was the Howler. The young men Striker and Woyi also had come forward, also armed. There were a few others as well.

René Gaspar's eyes shifted nervously from one armed Indian to another. With a sweaty thumb, he cocked the pistol he held to Ahuli's head. DuBois and the other Frenchmen cocked and raised their pistols.

"DuBois?" said René. "What shall I do? If I kill him, we have no hostage."

"They can't kill here," said the doctor. "They're bluffing. This is their peace town. They're not allowed to kill in here."

"Well, what are we going to do? They're all around us."

DuBois raised his pistol and aimed at the chest of Trotting Wolf.

"I can kill this one, and we'll still have our hostage," he said. Then to Little Black Bear, he added, "Tell him to drop his club on the ground, or I will drop him. Now."

"He says that he will kill you, if you don't drop your club to the ground right now," said Little Black Bear. "And I think he will do it."

Trotting Wolf looked past DuBois to Bear Meat on the other side. He held his arms out to his sides in a seeming gesture of surrender, and he loosened his grip on the handle of his war club, allowing it to slip from his fingers. Just as the war club hit the ground, Bear Meat loosed his arrow. It sank deep into the right shoulder of DuBois.

The doctor shrieked in pain and dropped his pistol, which discharged harmlessly as it hit the ground, barking and spitting sparks. People in the crowd yelled and ducked and ran for cover.

The Howler let fly an arrow only an instant after Bear Meat, and his shaft struck René Gaspar in the neck. Gaspar's pistol fired into the air. He dropped it, and reached for the deadly missile which protruded from both sides of his neck. Gripping it with both hands, one on each side, he staggered a few steps on rubbery legs, and then he fell.

Trotting Wolf picked up his war club and rushed upon Larousse, but before he reached his target, Larousse and the other five remaining Frenchmen had all dropped their weapons and fallen to their knees. Trembling and folding their hands in an attitude of prayer, they babbled what to Trotting Wolf and the other Real People was a jumble of meaningless noise.

Trotting Wolf bashed in the skull of Larousse as he was begging for his life. Striker was about to do the same to Debonnet, when a shout from Ahuli stopped him.

"*Elikwa.*"

Just then Young Puppy came into the dance ground with Tournier. He had cut the ropes that bound the captain's hands. Tournier looked around in horror.

"Are any Real People hurt?" he asked.

"No," said Little Black Bear.

"Thank God for that," said Tournier.

Trotting Wolf and the others were binding the arms of the Frenchmen they had been prevented from killing, including DuBois, whose shoulder was smashed. The doctor screamed with pain as they bound him. Tournier stepped over to face Trotting Wolf.

"My friend," he said, speaking haltingly in the language of the Real People, "what can I say? These men are bad men. They did not act according to my wishes. They made me their prisoner. They have dishonored me and their country. I hope that you will not hold their actions against me, or allow what they have done to keep us from fulfilling our pledges to one another."

Trotting Wolf looked Tournier directly in the eyes.

"We'll talk of this in the morning," he said. He turned and walked away.

Tournier stepped over to DuBois, who half lay in the dirt, bleeding and groaning.

"You fool," he said. "Do you see that you may have ruined everything we've been working for? And for what? For what?"

"I don't understand," said DuBois. "It was supposed to be their sanctuary town. They're not allowed to kill inside these walls."

"Idiot," said Tournier. "You scoffed at me for studying the ways and the beliefs of these people. Do you know what they call themselves?"

"Real People?"

"*Oui*, and if they are the Real People, what does that make us? Something less than real perhaps? We don't count in here, DuBois. Of course they can kill us—anywhere they like. You fool."

21

The following morning, while Ahuli, Young Puppy and some other men were busy cleaning and purifying the sacred dance ground, Tournier had DuBois, LeGrue, Debonnet, Raoul and Charles lined up against the outside wall of Kituwah and shot. Most of Kituwah's residents stood by and watched in fascination. When the grim task was done, Trotting Wolf walked over to Tournier.

"It's a bad time of year," he said. "I don't like to do this to you, but I must. I have no choice. We'll help you all we can with robes and food for the journey, but you can no longer stay here in Kituwah, or in any other town of the Real People. Many of my people are saying now that we made a mistake when we let you come in, and it was I who talked for you."

"I understand, my dear friend," said Tournier, "and I would not even beg you to reconsider your decision. I thank you for your hospitality for the time that we were here and for the supplies you offer for our trip. And I deeply regret the unfortunate incident caused by these bad Frenchmen."

"You made them pay for what they did," said Trotting Wolf. "That much is good. When you come back with the Ani-Senika, camp there in the pass where we first met. We'll talk out there."

"*Wado*, my friend," said Tournier. "I will come back. You can count on that."

With the supplies provided by the people of Kituwah, Tournier ordered his men to pack up and prepare to move out immediately. Riding horses were saddled and packhorses were loaded. As a final gesture of his goodwill, the captain, knowing, of course, that he had eight fewer men to have to consider, the seven conspirators and the murdered sentry, gave eight riding horses to Trotting Wolf. Then the Frenchmen left Kituwah, their captain with a heavy heart. From the top of a notched pole leaning against the inside of the wall, Young Puppy watched them go. He, too, was saddened by this parting.

Traveling north, Tournier watched the sky nervously. He knew that if he wasn't careful and failed to plan ahead wisely, one good winter storm could wipe out his entire command. He therefore stopped early the first night, making sure that he had a good, sheltered campsite. They hadn't traveled very far that day, in fact had not yet even gotten out of the country of the Real People, but safety was far more important than haste, he thought.

Tournier was more than disappointed. He was angry, but the people he was angry at were now all dead, and so the anger was useless, even burdensome. But what an educated fool, that damnable DuBois, he thought, and how much work he has come near to destroying. The captain tried hard to put the anger away and concentrate on ways in which he could salvage something worthwhile out of the mess that DuBois and his rebellious crew had created. Perhaps, after all, it was not all as bad as it seemed.

The Senecas, he thought, would probably still be willing to go along with the peace proposal; nothing had happened to offend them, and Trotting Wolf had given every indication that he and the Cheraques would, too, in spite of what had happened.

So the important thing, Tournier told himself, was to live through the winter and manage to make the trip to the Senecas in safety. Perhaps they could even find a village of some other tribe of Indians along the way who would be willing to put them up until spring. Perhaps. Somehow, he insisted to himself, he would make sure that all his work had not been done in vain. He would not allow the bastard DuBois a victory in death.

Young Puppy was sorry to see the Frenchmen go. He had made a friend of Tournier, and the Frenchmen with their different ways had helped to pass the time. He tried to figure out DuBois and the others who had caused the trouble, but he could not. He could not understand how a few men could turn against the authority of their own group. It could never happen among the Real People, he told himself.

Then he recalled the story of the revolt against the ancient priesthood, the Ani-Kutani. The priests had been the rulers over the Real People. They had governed every aspect of the people's lives. And then they had taken the wife of a man while he was out hunting, a man named—what was it?—Edohi.

They had killed the woman in a ceremony, used her as a human sacrifice, and when Edohi had come home and found out what had happened to his wife, he had organized a revolt, and the people had killed off all the priests. Or almost all—two, at least, had survived.

Having thought the old tale through, Young Puppy told himself that it was not the same at all as with DuBois and his followers. Tournier had not been a tyrant. He was a good man, and he had treated all his people well. And it had not been all the Frenchmen rising up against a tyrannical authority. It had been a few against the many, a few who were jealous, it seemed, of the power of Tournier. No. It had not been the same. Or had it?

Young Puppy decided that he would probably never understand the Frenchmen, but he knew that he would miss them, at least for the remainder of his time of confinement in Kituwah.

It was a good thing, he told himself, that he had his new duties to keep him busy, to keep his mind occupied, to keep the time from seeming to stand still. He was anxious, though, for the next three months or so to pass so that he could get back to the ceremonies, so that he could make himself busy again. Idle, he could think only of Guwisti and how much he wanted her embrace.

Oliga knew that he would be laughed at when he got back to Kituwah, and he was not looking forward to that. The Real People could be vicious in their ridicule of one another. It was a way of keeping people on the right path. One always did one's best, partly because one wanted at all costs to avoid the verbal barbs and jabs that followed meanness, foolishness or incompetence.

He had left Kituwah for exactly that reason. He had thought that he could not stand the teasing and the laughter. Now he was going back, and it had been his own decision to do so. He was going back to save his life or the life of someone close to him, perhaps even that of Tsiwon'. Perhaps his parents. He had no way of knowing, and so he had to go back.

For he had dreamed about an eagle, and such a dream meant that a death would follow, unless the dreamer sponsored an Eagle Dance. To have an Eagle Dance, one first had to have eagle feathers, and only the specialist, the Eagle Killer was allowed to get them. There was no such specialist at Coyatee, and so Oliga could think of nothing else to do except return to Kituwah and enlist the aid of Ahuli.

In addition, he was going back to save his country from invasion. The population of Coyatee was small. The men there would be no match for the large Shawnee town that had somehow established itself in the land of the Real People. Olig' knew that when Trotting Wolf and the other Wolves found out about it, they would be more than willing to join forces with the men of Coyatee to drive the Shawnees out. After all, the Wolves had given themselves the assignment of keeping all foreigners out of the land of the Real People, and they had done so, too, until they had let the Frenchmen come in to stay the winter at Kituwah.

"How much farther is it now to your town?" asked Water Dog, as the three travelers huddled close together one night around a small fire.

"I'm not sure," said Olig'. "Two more days perhaps. Maybe not quite so long as that."

"This is a bad time for traveling," said Water Dog. "It's getting colder every day."

"Yes," said Olig'. "Every night, I'd say."

Water Dog nodded in agreement.

"You feel it especially at night, when the Sun has gone to the other side of the Sky Vault."

"There was nothing else to be done," said Tsiwon'. "We all know that we had to make this trip, so there's no point in complaining about it. Besides, we're not doing so badly. We can do two more days of travel easily, even in this cold."

Olig' looked at her and smiled. He was tired, and he was cold, but he was proud of this woman. If she was tired, she denied it, and she certainly did not show it. She took the cold in stride just like a furry animal. She was a strong woman, and a brave and determined one. And she wanted Oliga for her man. He was proud of her and he was anxious for her to be his wife. Two more days of travel, he thought, or less. One day and a half, maybe. Then the Eagle Dance, and then the Shawnee town. How long, he wondered, would it all take?

It was early afternoon, and many of the people of Kituwah were gathered outside the wall around the horses. Guwist' was there with her own. Osa's horse was there, but no one had seen Osa for some time. Then there were the six horses that Tournier had given to Trotting Wolf.

Guwist' had put the saddle on the back of her *sogwili*, and others who had watched her, and thought that they could do as well, put saddles on the other animals. Guwist' mounted up and rode out a ways from the rest. She stopped and turned her horse to look back at them. Woyi jumped on the back of a *sogwili*, and the saddle slipped. The would-be rider fell hard on the ground, sending up a cloud of dust, and all the others there laughed uproariously.

"I thought the *gayahulo*"—one called, between bursts of laughter—"was supposed to be on its back, not under its belly."

Others mounted up while someone tried to right the slipped saddle. Some of them could ride with some skill, having had lessons from the Frenchmen. Others were trying for the first time. It seemed as if all the young men and young women of the town wanted to try to ride. Everyone was having fun.

Guwist' turned again to ride away, and that was when she saw them coming, Olig' and two strangers. She started to turn her horse and ride back into the crowd. Her last dealings with Olig' had been unpleasant. But there were two others with him, and to turn her back on them would have been rude. She rode to meet them instead.

" '*Siyo*, Olig'," she said, looking down at him from the back of her *sogwili*. She was conscious of the fact that the whole trouble between her and Young Puppy on the one hand and Olig' on the other had been because of this animal she rode. "We didn't think we'd see you back in Kituwah so soon."

" '*Siyo*, Guwist'," said Oliga. "The last time we met, I was wrong. I behaved badly toward you, and I deserved the ridicule that I received as a result of my bad and foolish behavior.

"These are new friends of mine from Coyatee. This is Tsiwon'. She's going to be my wife, I hope. And this is Water Dog, her father. My friends, this is Guwisti of Kituwah. She's the young woman in the tale I told you, the one in which I made such a fool of myself and earned the name of Jisduh."

Tsiwon' smiled and stepped forward, reaching a hand up toward Guwisti.

"That was a good story," she said. "You taught him a lesson he won't soon forget, and I think you made him a better man for it. I owe you my thanks for that. I'm glad to know you."

"Come on," said Guwist'. "We'll go into town. You must all be hungry and tired after your journey."

The travelers ate and got cleaned up. They changed their clothes. And though Olig' did have to put up with some laughter and some ridicule, Water Dog soon told all the people of how Olig' had saved his daughter from two enemy Shawnees, killing them both. And Tsiwon' told them that he had told on himself the tale of scooting backwards like a crawdad. Everyone decided that Olig' had indeed learned his lesson, and that he had redeemed himself with an act of bravery. After that, all was well again between Olig' and his townspeople.

But Olig' had to see Ahuli, and Water Dog needed to talk with Trotting Wolf, and so the arrangements were made. Olig' introduced Water Dog to Trotting Wolf and left the two to talk, while he went on to seek out Ahuli. He found him in the company of Young Puppy, and he knew that once again he would have to humble himself.

"'*Siyo*, Ahuli," he said. "I came to see you on a matter of great importance, but I did not know that Young Puppy would be here. If you will allow me to do so, I should say something first to him."

Ahuli nodded his assent.

"Young Puppy," Olig' said, "I treated you badly before. It was wrong of me. Now I'm a changed man."

"So are we all," said Young Puppy. "We change with time. Welcome home, my friend."

"*Wado*," said Olig'. "But now I must speak with Ahuli."

"Speak," said Ahuli. "This man is my student and my assistant. You can speak to both of us."

Olig' showed surprise at that news, but he recovered from it quickly.

"That's good," he said, and he paused a little before going on. "I had a dream of an eagle," he said. "I was at Coyatee, and there is no Eagle Killer there, and no one there knows how to lead the Eagle Dance. I hurried back here to see you."

"It's good you did," said Ahuli. "There may still be time. I'll have to get some feathers, but before I go, I'll give instructions to Young Puppy here, so that he can be preparing for the dance."

Alone, Young Puppy thought about the time that Olig' wanted to ride his *sogwili*, and when Young Puppy had tried to put him off, he'd insisted. Then Young Puppy had tricked him and caused him to be thrown from the animal's back.

He thought about the time Olig' had tripped him in front of the townhouse while he had just been standing there talking with his father, and, of course, he remembered the attempted assault on Guwisti. Young Puppy had no reason to like Olig', but Olig' seemed truly repentant of his old ways. And in his new role, Young Puppy was required to be forgiving. He would do his best. Anyway, somehow it all seemed to have happened a long time ago.

Walking away from his meeting with Ahuli and Young Puppy, Olig' felt ashamed. He thought that Young Puppy had every right to turn him down, to refuse to help in any way, because of the way in which Olig' had treated him in the past. But Young Puppy had forgiven him, at least it seemed so, and it made Olig' want to hang his head in shame. Well, there was nothing he could do about the past, but for the present, he could use the other young man as his example. He would try to do as well with his own life.

When Water Dog told Trotting Wolf about the Shawnee town, Trotting Wolf sat and stared for a long while before he spoke.

"It's well inside our boundaries?" he said. "There's no mistake?"

"I've seen the town," said Water Dog. "I've been there. There's no mistake. They must know that they're on our land, and two of them tried to carry off my daughter. She was saved only by Olig' of your town. He killed them both."

Trotting Wolf stroked his chin and mumbled to himself, seemingly in deep thought.

"It's not good," he said. "This Shawnee town. Yes. You're right, of course. They must know where they are. They must be daring us to attack them. They must want to have a war with us. Well, all right then. I think that we'll play ball with them. We'll see how well they play. I think that we'll go with you back up there to drive the Shawnees out, but, of course, we'll have to have a council first, and then there will be certain preparations. It will take some time."

Of course, everything takes time.

22

Young Puppy had thought that he would have some leisure time to spend with Guwisti during the cold months when there would be no more ceremonies to take up all his time, but then Olig' had returned, and Ahuli had given Young Puppy a great many things to do in preparation for the coming Eagle Dance. Ahuli himself had gone out in search of an eagle, so he was not hanging around town to keep a watchful eye on his young apprentice, but somehow knowing that only made the young man want to do a better job. Ahuli trusted Young Puppy and depended on him, and he was determined that he would not let Ahuli down.

Ahuli had done some certain things alone in preparation for his eagle hunt, things that even Young Puppy had not been allowed to see, for Young Puppy was only being prepared for the role of a dance-ground leader of ceremonies, and not for that of an Eagle Killer, a specialty unto itself. Perhaps that would come later, Ahuli had thought, but for now, he has enough to learn.

Then Ahuli had left Kituwah alone, carrying his bow and a few arrows, nothing else. Those who watched as he left town saw him walk toward the distant mountains, but no one knew exactly where he would go or what he would do when he got there. That knowledge was his alone. He alone was Uwohali-dihi, the Eagle Killer.

Young Puppy, in the meantime, was busy building a small, round hut at the edge of the dance ground. Ahuli had given him the specifications, and he was being careful to follow them exactly. It would be called "the place where the feathers are kept," or simply "the featherhouse," and it would have to be ready for the time when Ahuli would have the feathers brought back to Kituwah.

Since Young Puppy could not leave town, and because the planned Eagle Dance was for Olig', Olig' had been sent out by Young Puppy to hunt. He had been told to kill a deer and a scarlet tanager and bring the bodies back to town. Then Ahuli had told Young Puppy to have some woman of his own choice cook some corn.

Young Puppy went to see Guwist'.

"I haven't had much time to visit you," he said.

"I know," she said, "but I know too that you've been busy with important work."

"Yes," he said, "I have been very busy. I don't know if I'm worthy of all this. There's a great deal for me to learn."

"You'll learn it all in time," she said. "I know you will. I've been watching you. You're doing very well, and I am proud."

"Ahuli's a good teacher," said Young Puppy. "He's patient."

"Yes," said Guwist', "and I think he has a good student, too."

"Guwisti," said Young Puppy, looking at the ground, "do you think— Will you mind very much if I don't become a warrior? Will you still want to be my wife?"

"Don't be silly," she said. "Of course I will."

"You mean it?"

"It's you I love, Young Puppy," said Guwist'. "And I'm proud of you for what you're doing. When you were in the townhouse singing, everyone in town could see you and hear you, and they all know that you're going to be my husband. It made me feel good."

Young Puppy felt puffed-up and proud, but he tried not to let it show. In his new role, he knew, he had to show humility. He looked at the ground between the two of them and tried to swallow his pride. It was not an easy thing to do.

"Guwist'," he said, "I have to have a woman cook some corn for the Eagle Dance that will be held. Will you cook the corn for me?"

"Yes. Of course I will," she said. "And it's a good thing for you that you didn't ask anyone else to do it for you."

Olig' had taken his bow and some arrows. He had also taken with him a blowgun and some darts. The arrows were for the deer; the darts were for the small bird. He left Kituwah and headed for the browsing area, a place where they had killed the trees and burned them off to create a pasture to attract the deer.

He had left Kituwah as soon as the Sun had begun to crawl under the eastern edge of the Sky Vault, and she was overhead on her way to her daughter's house by the time he reached the place. He settled down to wait and watch. No deer were present.

While he waited there alone, he thought about the irony of his present situation, how he was receiving both aid and instruction from a young man he had only recently wanted very badly to harm. He had even wished success to the Wolf People who wanted to kill Young Puppy, and he had gone so far as to plot with the Howler, trying to come up with some scheme with which to draw Young Puppy out of town so that he could be killed.

Looking back on all of that, Olig' felt foolish, and he felt ashamed, but then he thought, If I had not behaved so foolishly, then I would not have been teased by everyone so unmercifully. I would not have left Kituwah to escape the teasing. If I had not left Kituwah, I would not have met Tsiwon'. Everything happens for a reason, he concluded. Everything works out for the best.

And just then he saw the deer, a healthy young buck, and then he drew his bow.

Right now, he said quietly, let the red *gatlida* strike into the very center of your soul.

As he released the arrow, he concluded the words with *"Yu."* And the shot was true. Olig' ran through the tall grass to the side of the fallen deer. He pulled a knife from a scabbard which was hanging at his waist and quickly cut its throat.

"I'm sorry, Brother Awi," he said, "to have to do this to you, but it's necessary in order for me to protect my loved ones."

On his way home, Olig' looked constantly for the small red tanager, but he saw none. Back in Kituwah, he asked his mother and Tsiwon' if they would prepare the skin of the deer and cook the meat. Of course, they agreed. Olig' himself would have to go out hunting once again, this time looking only for the small red bird.

Ahuli fasted and prayed alone in the mountains for four entire days. On the morning of his fifth day out, he killed a deer. He slung the carcass over his shoulders and climbed to a place of high cliffs, a place he knew the eagles would come, and there he placed the body of the deer upon a rocky ledge.

Then he moved to a crevice in the rocks not far away where he could conceal himself, but from where he could still keep his eyes on the deer he had placed on the ledge for bait. He waited, and while he waited, he quietly sang the songs to call the eagle down, songs known only to the Eagle Killers. Then it came, the Pretty Feathered Eagle, Uwohali. Ahuli had little time to admire its beauty. He would have to shoot fast, and he had to make sure that his shot would not cause the Pretty Feathered Eagle to fall off the ledge beyond retrieving.

He waited as Uwohali tore at the carcass, ripping off bits of flesh. He waited until the great bird was in just the right position, and then with a prayer, he let fly his arrow.

It was a good and true shot. Uwohali died almost at once, and as fast as he could go on the dangerous ledge, Ahuli moved over to its side.

"Uwohali," he said, "it was not I who shot you. It was Asquani, a Spaniard."

There was a reason for the lie. Now the spirit of the dead bird, if it should decide to seek vengeance for the killing, would look for one of the hated Spaniards, and not for one of the Real People. Then, leaving the dead eagle where it lay, Ahuli turned and began his journey back to Kituwah.

Olig' wandered through the woods with his blowgun and darts. Every few steps he stopped to look up into the trees. Small birds flitted here and there, the ones that had not gone away for the cold part of the year. He saw *dojuhwa*, the red bird, and *dlayhga*, the blue jay, and he heard the songs of many others as he walked. He heard the harsh *"ga ga"* of *kog'*, the crow, and somewhere not far off *dalala* was driving a hole in a tree with the rapid hammering of his hard beak.

The Real Bird, Tsisquaya, the sparrow, seemed to be everywhere, on the ground and in the trees. Olig' saw birds of every kind, of every color. Their songs were all around him, and he wondered if one of the songs he heard was the song of the bird he sought. And then he saw one, but it was female, yellow below and greenish above. The red male, he told himself, should be somewhere near.

He stood still watching, breathing easy. He put a dart into one end of his blowgun to be ready. The birdsongs were all around him, filling his ears with their music, and now and then he could hear *saloli* chatter and run and jump from tree to tree.

He saw another tanager, a male, and he put the blowgun to his lips, but did not blow. It was young and not yet fully turned to red. Its head and back were red, and red was halfway down its breast, but the rest of the underside was yellow still, and the tail and half the wings were green. He let it go.

He waited longer still, and he was growing hungry, but he refused to allow himself to grow impatient. At last he was rewarded with the sight of an all-red male. Landing on a branch in front of him, it seemed to flash bright red in the light from the Sun. His heart thrilled as he pointed the long cane pole and prepared to blow the dart. The red bird flew, but it didn't go far.

It lit again on a low branch just ahead. He aimed the gun, and he sucked air into his lungs and his cheeks until they could hold no more, and then he blew, a quick, hard puff of breath. The sharp dart flew. The small red bird dropped, and it hit the ground with a pat. Olig' ran to get it. He made a small apology, pulled out the dart and tied the bird to the sash around his waist. Thrilled with his success, he headed home.

Young Puppy, acting under Ahuli's instructions, had selected Woyi, Striker and two other hunters to wait for the Eagle Killer's return. Striker was just outside the entrance to the town when he saw Ahuli walking toward him. He waited there, and when Ahuli was just about to pass him by on his way back into town, the hunter heard the announcement he was expecting.

"A snowbird has just been killed," Ahuli said, and he kept walking. He went inside the town and straight to his house, where he went inside. He spoke to no one else that day but stayed to himself and fasted and prayed.

Striker knew that Ahuli had killed an eagle, and he also knew that the Eagle Killer had refused to say its name in case the spirit of any eagle should happen to be nearby to overhear. He turned to go back inside the town to tell the other hunters and Young Puppy what he had heard. In four more days, he knew, he and the other three would be sent out to bring the feathers in.

Far to the north Owl, the Senika, lay once again in the shallow pit covered with a grid of branches. Once again on top of the grid was laid out the body of a freshly killed deer. Owl prayed again for Shadageya, the Cloud Dweller, to come down from on high.

Between his prayers, the old man was alert for any shadow or any sound that might indicate the descent of the Cloud Dweller. Still his mind could wander. He thought about the purpose of his long ordeal. He thought about the number of lives that would be saved by the making of peace between his people and their longtime enemy, the Cave People, who lived to the south.

He considered the number of women who would not be made widows, the number of children who would not lose their fathers, the mothers who would not mourn over lost sons, the numbers of people, men, women and children, who would not become captives in a strange land.

Owl had no love for the Cave People. He himself had lost an uncle and a son as well as a number of friends to them. He had fought them in his youth, and he had killed his share. But the white men had come as mediators with an offer of peace, and such an opportunity was not to be taken lightly. He had to put aside his personal hatreds and consider what was best for all the people.

Besides, he was wise enough to know that hatred was a habit passed on from one generation to the next. It could be nothing more, for if he were to ask another of his people, Why do you hate the Cave People? that person would likely answer by telling of some recent raid they had made on his town or of some friend or relative who had been killed by one of the Cave People.

But then Owl thought, one could ask the same question of the Cave People, and they would give the same kinds of answers. But could anyone say with any certainty when it had been that they had first become enemies? And what it had been that had started the first fight? He did not think that anyone could answer those questions. He knew that he could not.

He did know, though, that his people and the Cave People were relatives who had split apart long years ago. Had they become angry at one another and then divided, or had the anger come along after the split had already occurred? Of course, he could not know, but lying there alone in the cold pit waiting for the Cloud Dweller to come down again it seemed to Owl that it was right that old relatives stop fighting with one another. It was good, this peace that the Frenchman had proposed.

He was hungry, and his back was hurting from pressing into the hard, cold ground. He was tired. It had been a long vigil, this gathering of eleven feathers from the tail of the Cloud Dweller, and he needed but one more. He was cold, lying there in the pit. His breath came out in visible puffs like clouds.

Then at last it came. And when it came, the coming was so hard and fast that it almost frightened him, even though he well knew what to expect. It hit the carcass with such force that Owl thought for an instant that it would crash right through the branches above and land inside the pit with him. But it did not. The grid held. He saw it and heard it shaking just above him, as the great bird pulled at the meat, gripped it with his sharp talons and ripped at it with its powerful beak.

He waited, his heart pounding fast in his chest, for the Cloud Dweller to become totally involved in the business of scavenging food for its young, for it to turn at just the right angle, and when at last it did, he reached out through the latticework of branches and grasped a large and beautiful tailfeather. He held it hard and pulled downward slow and steady.

The Cloud Dweller shrieked and turned in search of an unseen enemy. It spread its great wings and raised itself into the air, and as it did, the feather came out of its tail. Owl had it. It was number twelve. Now he would be ready when the Frenchmen came back.

Up on the narrow ledge, Striker, Woyi and the two other hunters who had been selected by Young Puppy found the body of the eagle just where Ahuli had said it would be. It had lain there four full days, and it was time for the gathering of the feathers. While three watched and waited, Woyi moved forward on the ledge until he came to the spot where the carcass of the deer and the carcass of the eagle lay. He looked down from the ledge, the dizzying distance to the ground below, but only for an instant.

He stripped the eagle's body of the large tail and wingfeathers, and as he did, he handed them back to a second hunter who wrapped them carefully in the deerhide that had been secured by Olig' and prepared by Tsiwon'. When the gathering of the feathers had been completed, the four men left the ledge and started on their way home. They left the bodies on the ledge where they had found them.

Back in Kituwah, the hunters gave the feathers, still wrapped in the deerskin, to Young Puppy. He took the precious bundle to the featherhouse, where he hung it up inside. On the ground beneath the bundle of feathers, he placed a bowl of cooked venison and corn. The meat was from the same deer as was the hide above. Tsiwon' had cooked it. The corn had been cooked by Guwist'.

"Eat," he said, speaking to the unseen feathers. "Eat."

Then he tied the body of the small red bird to the roof, allowing it to dangle there in front of the bundle of feathers from Uwohali. Ducking low, he went back outside. Olig' watched from a distance, as Young Puppy walked straight to the home of Ahuli. Standing outside the door of the house, Young Puppy spoke out loud.

"All is ready now," he said.

23

Ahuli wore only his breechcloth and moccasins, but he was painted red all over, except for the left side of his face, which was painted black. He stood beside a table at the edge of the dance ground as six men, similarly attired but painted white, walked by him on their way into the dance ground. Each man carried a gourd rattle in his left hand. As they passed him by, he handed each an eagle-feather wand from off the table.

Then came seven women. They followed the men, and each woman also received from Ahuli a feather wand as she passed him by. The last of the wands, the fourteenth, Ahuli kept for himself.

Each wand was made of a stick of sourwood about as long as Ahuli's arm. The sticks were straight and smooth and as big around as a thumb. A shorter and more slender piece of sourwood had been bent in the shape of an arc and tied to the center of each wand, and to each of the arcs, ten or more eagle feathers had been attached.

Young Puppy had once again built up the fire on the altar in the center of the circular dance ground in preparation for the Eagle Dance. At the southern point of the large dance circle a man sat with a drum. The six male dancers lined up from east to west, almost in the center of the circle.

The seven women came into the circle and lined up on the other side of the fire, facing the men. The lead woman, alone at the head of her line, was wearing shackles of turtleshell rattles strapped to the calves of her legs. Ahuli moved into the circle to stand directly across from her, at the head of the line of men.

He shouted a signal, and the man with the drum began to sing and to beat the drum. Ahuli lifted his gourd rattle and joined in the rhythm of the drum, and the lead woman began to stomp her feet in time. The dancers all turned toward the west, took a step forward, turned around again, and began to dance toward the east.

Being first in line, Ahuli had only taken a few steps before he had reached the edge of the circle. He turned to his right and started to move around the edge, headed toward the north. The lead woman stepped in line behind him, the next man behind her. When the line had been completely formed in single file, it alternated man and woman.

Sometimes Ahuli shuffled. Other times he stomped. He stood upright for a while, and then he stooped low. All the other dancers followed his example, and they sang with the drummer as they danced, and they raised and lowered the feather wands in unison. After some time, Ahuli raised a whoop. The music stopped abruptly and with it the dancing. The dancers then all walked out of the circle to take a rest.

Olig' watched every detail of the dance. He was fascinated. He was like a man who had been climbing a high mountain and could see the top just ahead. He was alive, and no one in his family had died. Tsiwon' was safe too. He had dreamed an eagle, a dreaded sign, but now the Eagle Dance was in progress, and everyone was still all right. It had all been done in time.

He hoped it had all been done in time. Of course, the dance was still in progress, and Oliga did not know if death could still strike before the dance had been completed. He did not think so, if for no other reason than that he felt so good about what was happening. Even so, he was still more than a little anxious.

After a brief rest, Ahuli announced the second round of dancing, but he did not go into the circle himself. Neither did any of the men and women who had danced the previous dance with him. Instead, Young Puppy and six new male dancers took their places, facing seven new female dancers. Young Puppy, like all the other men, was painted white. Guwisti had the place directly across from him, and he was proud of that.

In a crouch, the men danced a circle around the fire, going from east to south to west to north and back again to east, just opposite the normal movement, while the women, in a separate line, between the men and the fire, danced in the usual direction.

All sang along with the man at the drum. Sometimes he sang a line alone, and the rest made a singing response. Sometimes they sang all together. The dance was livelier than the previous one had been. Now and then the men came out of their crouch to leap around the fire. Young Puppy danced with an arrogant strut, the dance being the one time and place that allowed him to indulge his puffed-up sense of self-importance, allowed him to show off, allowed him to openly display his pride.

He dipped low, almost touching one knee to the ground, and he waved the feather wand, moving the rattle in the other hand along with it and all in perfect time with the music. When he came alongside Guwisti as they passed by each other moving in opposite directions, still holding his head up high, he looked at her and smiled, and he could see that she was proud, and she smiled back at him.

He was disappointed when the dance ended and the next break came, much too soon, it seemed. He felt as if he could have danced on and on. He could have danced away his time of confinement in Kituwah. He saw himself dancing his way out of town and up into the mountains. He even saw himself dancing on a cloud.

When Ahuli next called out the dancers, most of the night had gone. It would be morning, with the Sun crawling out from under the eastern edge of the Sky Vault by the time the dance was done.

Again the women formed a circle around the fire, and again the men formed theirs around the women. This time they faced each other. This time all the dancers were out at once, and there were even pairs who had not yet danced at all that night.

Ahuli faced the lead woman dancer once again. Young Puppy faced Guwist', and Olig' now was opposite Tsiwon'. He felt like he had reached the mountain crest at last. The ordeal was over. This was the time for celebration. He was dancing on the mountaintop.

To the rhythm of the song, the men and women took one step toward each other, then one step back. With the first step forward, the men waved their feather wands over the heads of the women. With their next step forward, the women waved theirs over the men.

Young Puppy and Guwisti smiled at one another as they danced. Oliga and Tsiwon' did the same. Everybody's mood was festive. They were in the final movement of the Eagle Dance, and they all knew that a life had been saved. And they all knew that they had taken a part in the ceremony that had saved it.

They changed positions at a certain point in the song, and for a time the men formed the inner circle, surrounded by the women. They danced as before, a step toward each other, a wave of the wand, a step back. During the long song, four such shifts were made, and when the singing stopped, the men once again formed the outer circle surrounding the women.

This time, though, Ahuli did not call for a break. All of the dancers kept their positions, and right away, following a very short pause, time enough only for him to take a good deep breath, the singer began a new song. For a time, the dance was as before, a movement forward, a wave of the wand, a movement back.

Then all the dancers turned to their left, and the two circles began to move in opposite directions. When they stopped circling and faced each other once again, it was with different partners than before. They circled again and faced each other again several times, until at last the original partners faced each other once more, and the dance was done.

The pause was brief again. The singer started to sing a new song. All the dancers, men and women, faced outside the circle, waving their wands toward the skies. Then the men turned to face the women, and then they danced toward them. When they had come up close to the women, the men turned again. The women also turned, and the partners danced then back to back.

Then there was another pause, and then another song. Everyone knew that this would be the final round, and though they were tired, they were also joyful, and they danced with renewed energy. For this last dance, Ahuli led them all in a single line in the standard direction around the fire. The men followed Ahuli. The women followed the men.

It was a long song and a long dance, and even Ahuli seemed not to want to let it end. Each time the dancers thought that it was done, Ahuli shouted out the beginning of another round. At last he stopped it with a whoop, and laughing and joking, the dancers immediately broke up their formation, each walking out of the circle in his own direction.

The feather wands were all returned to Ahuli. Near by, Oliga's mother, with the help of some of her clan sisters, had laid out a pile of skins, mats, baskets and pots, and those were then presented to Ahuli as his payment for having gathered the feathers and having performed the Eagle Dance. Ahuli gave the payment and the eagle-feather wands into the charge of Young Puppy to put away, and then everyone's attention was turned to a lavish feast, laid out also by Oliga's clan.

The major ceremonies done for a time and the special Eagle Dance having been taken care of, the people's minds would ordinarily have turned to the coming winter hunt, but Olig' had brought Tsiwon' and her father down from

Coyatee. The news they brought was bad, and it called for immediate attention.

It was the wrong time of year for war, and yet they could not simply ignore the arrogance of the Shawnees in building their town in the country of the Real People. Trotting Wolf called a council, but not before he had thought these matters through. He would go before the people with recommendations. He knew the decision he wanted them to reach.

"We cannot go to war this time of year," he said to the gathering of men and women in the smoke-filled townhouse. "It would not be good. And we have the winter hunt to consider. But we cannot let these Shawnees get away with what they've done. We can't ignore them until the time for war gets here.

"This is what I think. I think that we should prepare ourselves for the hunt, just as we always do, and while we're doing that, we should send a message to this Shawnee town, telling them to get out. If they don't listen to our warning, then when the proper time arrives, we'll attack and drive them out or kill them off. That's what I think we should do."

The people argued into the night, some in favor of Trotting Wolf's proposal, some against, and the meeting ended without any decision having been reached, other than to meet again in four more days. When the four days had passed, the men having consulted with their clan matrons in private, the meeting was reconvened. They argued for a while again, but in the end they all agreed to Trotting Wolf's plan of action.

Water Dog knew that Olig' and Tsiwon' had thought to run away together in order to become man and wife, but things had gone so well that he began to think that a proper wedding might be arranged after all. He sought out, among the residents of Kituwah, some women of the clan of his wife and daughter.

"Olig' and my daughter want to get married," he told them, "but my daughter's mother is in Coyatee. I wonder if something can be done."

"We'll take care of it," said one of the women. "We'll talk to Oliga's mother and her sisters. Don't worry. We can get it done."

"*Wado,*" he said, and he went to find his daughter. "Tsiwon'," he said. "I have some news. You'll have a wedding right here in Kituwah. I spoke to your clan sisters here."

Tsiwon' was ecstatic with the news. She wanted to run immediately to find Olig' and tell him about it, but her father held her back.

"Let the women take care of things," he said. "They'll tell him. They'll arrange it all."

At just about that same time, Trotting Wolf was approaching Olig' near the townhouse.

" 'Siyo," he said.

" 'Siyo."

"I've come to talk with you about a thing of some importance," Trotting Wolf said.

Olig' nodded, and his face took on a serious and somber expression. No one had ever approached him in that manner before, especially an important man like Trotting Wolf. He wondered what the man could possibly want with him.

Olig' had left Kituwah not so long ago in disgrace, but since then much had happened. He had killed two Shawnee enemies, rescuing a woman of the Real People at the same time, and now that woman was to be his wife. He had dreamed of an eagle, and then he had sponsored an Eagle Dance. And he had come home to Kituwah with new friends from Coyatee to warn of a Shawnee encroachment onto land of the Real People. His status in Kituwah was much improved, he thought, from when he had first slipped out of town.

"You were at the meeting?" asked Trotting Wolf.

"Yes," said Olig'. "I was there."

"You know the plans, then?"

"Yes."

"Do you speak the language of the Ani-Sawahoni?"

"No," said Olig'. "I do not."

"The trade language, then?"

"Yes," said Olig'. "A little."

"A little?"

"Enough to get along."

"Good. You've been to Coyatee," said Trotting Wolf, "and you've seen the Shawnee town. Someone has to take a message to those Shawnees. The message we decided on. Will you go?"

Olig' took a deep breath and let it out in a long sigh. When the decision had been made in the meeting to send a message to the Shawnee town, it had never occurred to Olig' that he might be the messenger. It was a dangerous assignment and an important one. But it came at a time when he was thinking of marriage—that was important too. He thought about Tsiwon', and he thought about his earlier behavior and his recently acquired and still-fragile status.

"Yes," he said. "I'll go."

"It may be they will kill you," said Trotting Wolf. "They should honor the status of a messenger, but we can't count on the Ani-Sawahoni to always do what's right. After all, they put that town there. So you should know that they might kill you."

Oliga shrugged.

"And maybe they will not kill me," he said.

The wedding was rushed, and the people of Kituwah provided provisions for the return trip to Coyatee and Oliga's trip on over to the Shawnee town. Ahuli taught Olig' to sing songs of peace, songs which the Shawnee, too, would recognize. He also gave him strings of beads, white feathers, a pipe and a pouch of tobacco. Olig' would be recognized as an emissary of peace and not an enemy. Still, there was no guarantee that the Shawnees would honor those signs and not decide to kill him.

They left early one morning: Oliga, his new wife and his father-in-law. It was cold as they began retracing their steps. First they would return to Coyatee and inform the people there of the events that had taken place and the decisions that had been made in Kituwah. Then, from Coyatee, Olig' would take the warning on over to the Shawnee town.

24

Olig' walked toward the entry to the Shawnee town. He walked straight and tall, and he walked at a steady pace, not too fast, not too slow. He had to maintain the dignity of his role. He could show no fear, but at the same time, he could not appear to be too haughty.

He carried a heavy, white clay pipe, fitted with a long stem of river cane, across his right arm. In his left hand, he carried a fan of white heron feathers, and across his left forearm, strands of beads dangled. As he walked he sang the songs of peace in a strong and clear voice that would carry inside the walls of the town.

Back behind him at the forest's edge, hiding just inside the trees and brush, watching to see what would happen, were Water Dog, Black Dog and Bent Bow Shape. There would be nothing they could do if the Shawnees should decide to capture or kill Oliga, but they would know, and they would be able to tell the others at Coyatee, at Kituwah, and at other towns of the Real People.

Olig' was close enough to the town for the Shawnees inside to hear the song he was singing, when four men stepped out of the passageway to stand abreast, watching him approach. He walked closer, close enough to toss a war club and hit a man's head, and then he stopped, and when he stopped, he ended his song. He looked at the four men standing there with angry faces, and he felt some fear, but he knew that he could keep the Shawnees from seeing it.

"Do you speak the trade language?" he asked.

The man standing to the far right of the group smiled and surprised Olig' by answering his question in the language of the Real People.

"Better than you," he said, "but as you can tell, I also speak your language."

"That's good. I'm Oliga," Olig' said in his own language, "of the Real People, and I've come here with a message from my people to you. I come in peace, as you can see."

"My name is Stone Heart," said the Shawnee, "and I've killed many of your—Real People. You come in peace clothes, singing the peace song. Did you come to sue for peace?"

"I came here in this manner," said Olig', "hoping that you will not kill me before you've heard what I have to say to you."

"Come inside," said Stone Heart. "We'll hear what you have to say—before we kill you."

Young Puppy perched at the top of the notched pole to look over the wall. He watched the various groups of hunters as they left Kituwah for the winter hunt. A few able-bodied men, mostly Wolves, remained behind to watch the mountain pass and to defend the town if necessary, but most of them had gone to hunt. They left in groups, some to hunt *yansa*, the buffalo, some to hunt *awi*, the deer, some *awi-ekwa*, the elk. Each group had danced a special dance, and each would hunt only the animal whose dance it had done.

Except for the few defenders of the town, left behind were mostly old people and children—and Young Puppy. For the first time since he had begun taking part in the ceremonies, Young Puppy keenly felt the pangs of his confinement. He felt useless once again. He thought that he should be out on the hunt making a contribution to the living of the town. Left behind, he was doing nothing. He was worth nothing.

Even young women had gone on the hunt. Guwisti had gone, and so had Lolo. The hunters would be away so long, that the women would set up camp and cook their meals. After the hunt, they would also skin and butcher the game. Young Puppy's face burned with humiliation as he watched them go.

Ahuli himself led the group of buffalo hunters. He had determined when and where they would go by the singing of his songs and other esoteric ways and means known only to himself. He had led the hunters in a buffalo dance in Kituwah, and he took with him the buffalo mask and hide that he had worn in the dance.

Yansa would be moving south along the ancient trails that wound sometimes through the hills, sometimes over mountain crests and sometimes across the open prairies. But old Ahuli knew a special place where the hunters could intercept them on a high mountain crest, and if his powers were working, they would get there just at the right time to meet the herd.

They had left Kituwah in four large dugout canoes, seven people to a boat. The canoes, with flat bottoms and straight sides, had each been fashioned of one large cypress log from a tree that had been felled by a storm. They had been fashioned by a combination of burning, hacking and scraping.

There was room in each *tsiyu*, as the boats were called, for several more people, but that space would be taken up by meat and hides on the return trip, if the hunt was successful.

Ahuli led them north for four days on the waterways, and then he had them pull the boats ashore and secure them. They took up their weapons and their packs and walked toward the mountains. One day's walk, and Ahuli stopped. The light from the Sun was not quite gone.

"Here is where we'll camp," he said.

Olig' sat inside the Shawnee townhouse, facing a group of Shawnee men. Stone Heart and the other three who had met him outside the town were there. Because he could speak the language of the Real People, Stone Heart had been designated interpreter for this talk.

"Now, Oliga," he said, "what is this message that you bring?"

"I was instructed to talk to you like this," said Olig'. "Your people and mine have been enemies for a long time now. Many people have been killed on both sides. Many captured. Among the Real People, we had a great warrior once who was known as the Shawnee. Perhaps some of ours live still among you. We don't know. We have a long and bloody history between us of things that neither side will soon forget.

"But we have not built towns in your country. We have not insulted you in that way. We wonder if maybe you got lost and don't know where you are. This town of yours is in the land of the Real People, and I was sent here to ask you to leave this town and go back to your own country."

The sense of Oliga's statement was rendered into Senika by Stone Heart, and then the Senika men had some discussion among themselves. At last Stone Heart turned again to Olig'.

"When we came here," he said, "we found no Real People living here. And we are not lost. What is your claim to this land?"

"This land has always belonged to the Real People," Olig' said. "No one has ever disputed that fact."

"We are here to dispute it now," said Stone Heart. "This town you're standing in disputes it. I think you're the one who is lost."

"This is not the time of year for war," said Olig', "but when that time comes around, our warriors will be here to see if you have left. If you're still here, they'll drive you out."

"We will not be frightened off like rabbits," said Stone Heart. "If your warriors come here to fight, they'll find us ready for them, and they will not find it such an easy task to drive us out."

Olig' stood up facing the Senikas.

"Is that the answer that I should take back to my people?" he asked.

Again the Senikas conversed in their own language, and Olig' stood patiently waiting for a response. He hoped that the Shawnees could not detect the trembling he felt inside his breast. At last there was silence, and Stone Heart turned to him again.

"No," he said. "Our answer to your people will be this—that you will not return to them at all. You are our prisoner now. You just might die here in this town—where you got lost."

Ahuli situated the hunting camp on a flat plain below a high bluff. They were not too close to the bluff, and to their back was a clear-running stream. Along the banks of the stream on both sides trees grew thick. There was water and there was wood.

While the rest of the men and women were busy setting up the camp, Ahuli climbed alone to the top of the bluff. There he found the familiar buffalo trail. He knew that the great shaggy beasts traveled the same route year after year, and he had used this same spot many times before. He knew it well.

The only trick was to arrive at the place at just the right time, just before the herd would make its appearance on the bluff on its way over to the other side. A quick glance at the trail was all Ahuli needed to assure himself that the buffalo had not already passed. The question then was, How soon would they arrive?

He walked north along the trail for a distance, and then he climbed to the highest spot around. Reaching the crest, he stared off toward the north. He threw the buffalo robe around his shoulders and donned the buffalo mask, and then he sang some songs.

By the time he'd made his way back down to the plain, the camp was all prepared. Cooking fires had been built, and the sweet smell of corn soup was in the air. He walked straight to the small thatched shelter someone had prepared for him during his absence. Standing at the small doorway, he turned. The hunters all had gathered up around him and were anxiously awaiting his words.

"Be ready in two days," he said.

"Something's gone wrong in there," said Water Dog. "Olig' should have come back out by now."

"They could be talking still," said Black Dog, "but I don't think so. I'm afraid you're right."

Water Dog looked around for the tallest tree that he could find close by. He gestured toward it with his chin.

"Do you think that you can climb that one?" he asked his son.

Bent Bow Shape took a quick look.

"Yes," he said. "I can."

He walked to the tree and stood close and tipped his head back to look at it and study for a while. Then he embraced it with his arms, and his right leg bent out at a sharp angle allowing him to press the sole of his foot against the bark.

He looked like a spider walking up the tree until he reached the lower branches. Then, with something to get hold of and something to step on, he climbed even faster until he was almost out of sight to those below.

Water Dog and Black Dog looked after him until their necks began to hurt. Then they looked at one another briefly.

"Can he see anything from up there, do you think?" asked Black Dog.

"I don't know," said Water Dog. "Maybe he can. It's a tall tree."

"Olig' might be in a house."

"Yes," said Water Dog. He looked up again. He wanted badly to call out to Bent Bow Shape and ask what he could see, but he knew better than to do that. The sound might carry to the town below.

Black Dog stared at the town, but the only movement he could see was rising smoke. Then Bent Bow Shape came back down. He stopped at the low branches for a moment, then he dropped to the ground.

"Could you see anything down there?" asked Water Dog.

"I saw them," said Bent Bow Shape. "They dragged him out of their townhouse and tied him to a pole. They've made him their prisoner. He went to them with the white feathers and the pipe, singing the peace songs, and they've taken him captive."

"What will we do?" asked Water Dog.

"We can't attack them," said Black Dog. "There are only three of us. Besides, we went to Kituwah for help because there aren't enough of us at Coyatee. This is a large town."

"Kituwah isn't planning any action until Gogi comes," said Water Dog, "and even if they would come up here now, it would take too long for us to go and get them."

"We should do something," said Bent Bow Shape. "I don't want to have to tell my sister that I left her husband here."

"What can we do?" said Water Dog.

"We can go in at night," said Black Dog. "While the Shawnees are all asleep. We can go in quietly and try to bring him out."

"We might be able to do that," said Water Dog. "Or, if we try, they might have all four of us for captives instead of only one."

"That would be the chance we take," Black Dog agreed.

"Well, I say we try it," said Bent Bow Shape. "The Shawnees have insulted us already by building their town here. Now they've taken my brother-in-law captive while he was dressed for peace. That's too much for us to take from them. I'm angry with them now. I want to show them what it means to insult the Real People. I want to go in and bring Olig' out of there."

"And I," said Black Dog.

"Then I agree," said Water Dog. "But we had better go tonight, while he's still alive."

25

Olig' knew his predicament. It was an obvious one. Tied to a pole and tormented for a while, he would then be left alone at least overnight while his captors decided just what they would do with him. And he knew, too, what their options would be.

They might decide to turn him loose after all, rather than risk a war, but he doubted that. He might become a slave, likely to someone who had lost a husband or a son to the Real People. That was a fairly common practice. But much more likely, he thought, they would simply kill him, and if they decided to do that, they would probably do it slowly.

The practice of slowly torturing a captive to death had grown rapidly since the arrival of the Spaniards, so much that it was beginning to be commonplace. Even the Real People were engaging in it. Well, he told himself, if that was to be his fate, he would face it bravely. He would not give these Shawnees the satisfaction of watching him flinch or cringe nor of hearing him whine or cry out in pain.

Instead he would brag to them out loud about the two Shawnees he had killed, and he would sing a song in the face of pain and death. Olig' was not afraid of dying, but he did hate to think that he had only just recently met Tsiwon', and even more recently she had become his wife. He thought about her, wishing that he'd had more time with her. He wondered if the Eagle Dance had not been done in time, after all.

But he had known full well, when he had accepted the mission from Trotting Wolf, that the outcome could easily mean his death, and he had accepted willingly and with pride. He had been entrusted with an important job, and, he told himself, if he had it to do over, he would still do the same thing.

The night was dark, but there was some light from the moon and stars. Between the forest and the town the ground was flat and clear. From somewhere in the trees, whippoorwills sang their *waguli* song into the night sky, and occasionally owls *hoo-hoo*ed their chilling call into the already-cold night air.

Widely separated, Black Dog, Water Dog and Bent Bow Shape inched along the ground. They knew that the only chance they had of success was for at least one of them to reach the Shawnee town and enter it unseen. They pressed their bodies tight and flat against the ground and crept so slowly that no one who might be looking would detect any movement.

The night was more than halfway through by the time the two older warriors reached the wall, one on each side of the passageway that would lead them into the town. They stood and pressed their backs to the wall and still moved slowly toward each other, toward the entryway. No one had seen them yet.

Bent Bow Shape had stopped some distance from the wall, just as they had planned. Directly in front of him, a single Shawnee sentry looked out over the top of the wall. The Shawnees in the town, he thought, must feel fairly secure. He was glad of that for the sake of the present mission, but he also thought that such an attitude from them in their present location was yet another insult to the Real People. Well, he told himself, they'll learn soon enough.

Not knowing that Olig' had been accompanied on his journey by three who stayed back in the woods, the complacent Shawnees probably thought that he would not yet be missed. And, of course, it was not yet the time of year for war, so only one sentry watched.

Bent Bow Shape saw his father when he stood up at the wall. He saw him slowly move along toward the entryway. He waited until he was sure that Water Dog was almost ready to go inside the town, and then he got up slowly to one knee, fitted an arrow to his bow, took careful aim and said a little prayer.

It was a crucial shot. It had to hit the mark, and it had to be deadly at once. They could not afford to have the sentry cry out and give the alarm to the town. A quick and silent death was called for. Bent Bow Shape let go the string, and the arrow flew, and the twang of the string and the zip of the arrow in its flight sounded loud to his ears there in the stillness of the night. Then there was the sound of the arrow striking into the sentry's chest just below the throat, the soft sound of the sentry's quickly-exhaled puff of breath, and then the body slumped forward, silently, to hang there on the wall.

Bent Bow Shape breathed a sigh of relief. Had the sentry fallen back, the thud of his body as it landed on the ground would have made the loudest noise of all and might have attracted some attention.

With the sentry dead, Bent Bow Shape stood and ran toward the entry in the wall. He quickly stepped inside and moved through the passageway. Black Dog was already there, waiting just inside. Holding his bow ready with an arrow nocked, he stepped to his left and watched in that direction. Bent Bow Shape nocked another arrow and watched to the right.

Water Dog had moved in a low crouch until he reached the pole where Oliga was tied.

"Son-in-law," he said in a whisper, "it is I."

Olig' made no sound, but he was instantly watchful for any signs of danger. He could feel the tugging at the ropes as Water Dog worked to free him. This was an option he had not considered when he had contemplated his fate. His new in-laws and their friend were making a bold move, and he hoped that nothing would happen to them because of him.

At last he felt his hands free, but still he did not move. Water Dog stood up behind him, put a hand on his shoulder and gave him a shove in the direction of the passageway. With a quick glance at Water Dog, Olig' crouched and ran.

He stopped between Black Dog and Bent Bow Shape, and he was about to turn and look back for his father-in-law, when Bent Bow Shape put a hand on his back and shoved him toward the outside.

"Go," Bent Bow Shape said in a harsh whisper, and Olig' ran. At the same time Black Dog was gesturing wildly for Water Dog, who had stayed behind to cover Oliga's escape, to hurry along on his way. Water Dog put his war club on the ground at the base of the pole, then ran. The two others let him run on through. They looked around quickly one last time. No Shawnees were up. No one had suspected anything. Black Dog nodded for Bent Bow Shape to go first, and then he followed.

They met at the edge of the forest, the four of them, and they looked back at the Shawnee town. There was no pursuit.

"I thought that I would never see any of you again," said Olig'. "I thought that I would never see my wife. *Wado*, my friends."

"We did it," said Bent Bow Shape. "I wasn't sure we could."

"Neither was I," said Water Dog, "but we did. We made fools of the Shawnees. I left my war club there for them to find, so they'll know who came to see them."

"And I killed one of them," said Bent Bow Shape.

"It was a good shot," said his father, pride in his voice.

Black Dog looked again toward the town.

"Right now," he said, "let's get ourselves as far away from this place as we can before the Sun comes out to light the sky."

On the edge of the high bluff, bending low, he danced there, a slow dance, with an undulating movement from side to side. On his back he wore the shaggy robe, and on his face was the buffalo mask, carved of buckeye wood and stained dark red, the eye-holes lined with black. Buffalo hair was glued between the horns.

In the cold air, his breath came out in short puffs that looked like smoke. He snorted, and he bellowed, and he danced a *yansa* dance.

And while he danced, he sang. He sang the songs to call the buffalo, the *yansa* songs. He sang them low as he danced along the edge of the bluff, high above the hard rocks down below. He was a bull, and he sang a song to call the cows.

"They are coming to me," he sang.

And the people down below who watched were amazed at Ahuli's skill.

"He looks like *yansa* up there," one said.

"He has become *yansa*," said another. "He is *yansa* now."

"That's just what *yansa* thinks, too. That's why he'll come," said yet another.

Ahuli danced near the edge of the bluff, not far from where a large protective boulder jutted up out of the ground. The ancient buffalo trail ran along the top of the bluff, parallel with the edge. On the other side of the wide trail, more rocks rose out of the ground and just beyond them, the forest resumed. Seven hunters waited there, hidden behind the rocks.

Down on the flat ground below the bluff, about halfway between the rocks at its base and the hunting camp, the rest of the hunting party, men and women, waited. A few had bows and arrows. Most held clubs. All wore knives at their waists.

Then, as Ahuli sang and danced, the buffalo herd came up the trail. They snorted and bellowed as they came, and their breath came out like puffs of smoke. The sounds made by the hundreds of beasts filled the air, and Ahuli could no longer hear the words to the songs he sang. Still he sang and still he danced. And then the buffalo were there on the trail on top of the bluff.

He bellowed and stamped, and he rolled in the dirt. He sang the *yansa* songs and called out to them to join him there in his frolic. The big bull in the lead paused and cocked his head, looking at Ahuli with curiosity. He shook himself and bellowed, and then he started to move again, but he veered to his left, moving toward where Ahuli danced and sang and rolled in the dirt. The rest of the giant beasts followed his lead.

His back toward the edge of the bluff, Ahuli continued to dance and sing as the herd drew closer and closer. He danced himself nearer to the protective boulder, as the animals drew near to the edge. He could hear their heavy breathing, their snorts and bellows. They were upon him now. He could almost feel their breath. Then he heard a shout from the rear, and he dropped quickly to safety behind the rock.

The seven hunters behind the herd had begun to scream and shout and wave their arms. Some waved buffalo robes and bear robes in the air. They raced toward the animals to the rear of the herd, making as much stir as possible.

Calves bawled and ran for their mothers. Cows ran from the commotion, plunging into the herd ahead of them for imagined protection from the unknown disturbance behind. As the next wave was hit, it moved ahead, and then the next. Suddenly all was confusion, bawling and bellowing, snorting and stamping. The pounding of hundreds of hoofs began to shake the ground, as huge, hairy bodies crashed into one another and pressed together.

Ahuli watched from his place behind the boulder, as the lead bull and the others around him were pressed to the edge of the bluff by the mass behind them trying to run. He could see the terror in their eyes as they looked out over the edge into the vastness of space, and he heard the first one scream as it fell.

One by one they plunged off the edge of the bluff. One by one they crashed into the rocks below. Then all at once the scene was transformed into a brown cascade. The air was filled with their frightful roars and screams and the sounds of the heavy bodies smashing first against the rocks and then onto the growing heap of flesh and bones and fur.

Clouds of dust rose from the massive pile of dead and dying that was forming at the base of the bluff. And when finally the last beast had fallen, it was a writhing, moaning, bellowing mass. Many of the animals were hurt only with broken bones. The hunters rushed in then with their clubs. The ones with bows and arrows shot some of the livelier beasts, the ones who had fallen last and had more cushion for their landings.

There was a frenzy of killing then, with the cracking of skulls and the shooting of arrows into the bodies of wounded beasts. It was a massive killing that wore out the arms and the legs of the killers and left them exhausted, gasping for breath and covered with blood. The air was filled with the stench of death.

But even when the killing was done, the killers could not rest. Immediately they went to work on the fresh carcasses, skinning and butchering. They would be a long time at this job, and when it was done, the meat and the hides would have to be wrapped and packed and hauled back to the waiting canoes to be loaded for the trip back to Kituwah.

26

A huli and the buffalo hunters had not been the only group of hunters to go out from Kituwah. Other groups had gone out to hunt deer, or elk, or bear, or turkeys. Before setting out, each group had first danced the appropriate dance. Each group had also returned successfully, and danced one more time upon its return to town. Kituwah was well supplied with meat. Of course, other towns of the Real People had sent out other groups of hunters as well. It was the way that things were done.

Young Puppy sulked for a time after the hunters had returned. It was the hardest time of year for him. His time of confinement in Kituwah weighed heavy on him. He was inactive, and he felt useless. Worse than that. He felt he was a burden on his parents and the town.

But soon Ahuli had him busy once again. When the cold part of the year was over, there would be more ceremonies to perform, more songs to sing. Young Puppy still had much to learn.

Sometimes late at night, with the snow on the ground outside, the people would gather in the townhouse, a fire burning in the center of the floor. The air would be filled with the smoke from pipes, and old men would tell their tales.

"This is how we got the dances and the songs," Ahuli said. "I heard this tale from old men when I was but a boy.

"A long time ago, near the beginning of time, all of the people were out on a hunt. They were high up in the mountains, and one man had gone ahead to scout, to watch for enemies or look for game or something. I don't know, but he was high up on a ridge, and down below him on the other side, he saw a river there. On the other side of the river was another ridge, and the scout could see an old man walking there, carrying a walking cane.

"But the cane was not made of wood—it seemed to be made of some shiny stone. While the scout still watched, the old man stopped and pointed with his cane, and then he sniffed its end. He walked a few more paces, stopped and did the same thing again. He kept that up until he happened to point it in the direction of the hunters' camp. That time he sniffed it long, and the scout could see a smile form on the old man's face.

"The old man started walking once again, and this time he was walking straight toward the hunters' camp. He walked slowly with his cane, the way an old man will. But when he came to the water's edge, he stopped and threw his cane out into the air, and it became a bridge of rock and stretched all the way across the river.

"The old man walked across the bridge, turned to pick it up, and it was once again his cane. He started up the mountain, walking toward the camp.

"The scout was afraid, and he ran back to the hunters' camp as fast as he could run. He ran the shortest way he knew, and when he got there he was out of breath, but he had beat the old man there.

" 'What's wrong with you?' the hunters asked.

"He told them what he'd seen, and then the wisest man among them stepped out in front.

" 'I've heard of this old man,' he said. 'His name is Nuh yunuwi, Dressed in Stone. The stick he carries guides him like a dog, and his skin is stone. His meat is human flesh. He wanders these mountains looking for hunters to catch and eat.'

" 'Let's kill him, then,' a hunter said.

" 'That's very hard to do,' the wise man said. 'His skin is solid rock.'

" 'Let's run away before he gets here,' said another.

" 'His stick will guide him to us, no matter where we go.'

" 'Then what will we do?' they cried.

" 'There's only one thing to be done,' the wise man said. 'Old Stone Coat cannot stand to see a woman in her bleeding time of month. It makes him sick. Hurry up. Find seven women in that state and bring them here.'

"So the hunters ran to find the women, and they did find seven of them in that condition. They hurried back to the wise man with the women they had found. The scout had been watching the approach of Stone Coat, and so they knew the path that he would walk into their camp.

"The wise man led the seven women out onto the path. He left one near the camp and then went on a distance before he left the next, and so on until he had them all spaced out along the path. Then he had them all undress. They did. And then they waited.

"By and by old Stone Coat came along, and when he saw the first woman, he paused and made a face. He put his hand in front of his eyes. 'You're in a bad way,' he said. He walked on, moving closer to the camp, and then he saw the second woman standing there. He shuddered. 'Ah,' he said, 'you're in an awful state,' and he hurried past her, but he was vomiting blood as he went.

"He met the third one, and he staggered by her, blood running all down his chest, and then he met the fourth. He choked and gagged as he walked on by. He tried to cover up his eyes, but still he saw the fifth, and he stumbled to his knees.

"Using his cane, he got himself back up to his feet and staggered on. The blood was spewing from his mouth. Then he saw the sixth. He howled in pain, spat blood and dropped down to both knees. He crawled slowly and painfully ahead.

"And then he came to the seventh woman standing naked in the path, and he collapsed. The blood ran freely from his mouth to form a widening pool.

"Then the wise man ran out into the path with seven sourwood stakes he had prepared. He drove the stakes through Stone Coat's body and on down into the ground. He pinned him there.

"The hunters came with firewood, and they piled it over the body of Stone Coat, who was moaning and barely moving. They started a fire on him then, and everyone gathered around to watch.

"Then Stone Coat began to talk, and he told them the plants to use for medicine for different ailments. It grew dark and the fire continued to burn, and Stone Coat talked long into the night.

"Then he began to sing, and he sang the hunting songs for deer and bear and buffalo and all the rest. The flames began to burn lower, and Stone Coat's voice grew weak, and by the time the Sun came out from under the eastern edge of the Sky Vault, the old man was dead. There was nothing left but a heap of white ashes.

"The wise man had the hunters sweep the ashes away, and there he found an *ulunsuti* stone, which he picked up and kept. There was also a lump of red stone there, and the wise man had the people all line up while he pounded and ground up the stone and made some paint. Then he painted them red, one at a time, and whatever they wished for while he was painting, was theirs. The hunters had all wished for success on the hunt, and of course, they were successful after that. And we still sing all of those songs today."

Sounds of pleasure and of awe and even some of disgust came from the crowd gathered there in the townhouse, but everyone had enjoyed listening to the tale, and no one wanted the evening to come to an end just yet. They quieted down a bit, and someone said, "But they already had the arrowpoints, the flint."

"Yes, of course they did," said Ahuli. "And I'll tell you how they got it.

"It was way back toward the beginning of time, the time when all the animals could talk to one another, the time when the world was young.

"Tawiskala lived up in the mountains. He lived alone, because all the animals hated him. They hated him, because he had helped to kill many of their brothers, for he was made of flint, and his name was Flint.

"Sometimes the animals got together to have a council, and they would talk about ways to get rid of Flint, but nothing ever came of the talk. They were all afraid to go near his house.

"Then one day Jisdu got tired of all the talk.

" 'I'm not afraid,' he said. 'I'll go alone, and I'll find him and kill him.'

"Some of the animals laughed at him. 'He's just bragging,' they said, but others believed that he would really try to find Flint and kill him, and they thought that they'd never see the rabbit alive again.

"The next morning, Jisdu set out alone, and sure enough, he found Flint's house. Flint was standing out front when Jisdu arrived.

" 'Siyo,' said Jisdu. 'Are you the one called Flint?'

"Flint looked at the arrogant rabbit standing there.

" 'I'm Flint,' he said.

"Jisdu wanted to get inside Flint's house, but Flint didn't invite him in. Jisdu looked around.

" 'Is this your house?' he asked.

" 'This is where I live.'

"Still Flint did not invite him in. Jisdu thought a moment.

" 'Well,' he said, 'I'm Jisdu. I've heard so much talk about you that I decided to come and see you for myself. I came to invite you to visit me at my house.'

" 'Where is your house?' asked Flint.

" 'Just down there near the river, in the broom grass field.'

" 'Well, maybe I'll drop in to see you one of these days,' said Flint.

" 'Why not come along with me right now?' said Jisdu. 'We'll have supper at my house.'

"Flint grumbled and made excuses, but Jisdu argued with him, and finally Flint gave in.

" 'All right,' he said. 'All right. Let's go.'

"They walked together down the mountain, and Jisdu led the way to his hole near the edge of the river.

" 'Here's where I live,' he said, pointing to the hole, 'but in the summer I usually eat outside.'

"Jisdu built a fire and cooked a big meal, and each time Flint emptied his bowl, Jisdu gave him some more. At last they'd eaten everything up, and Flint was stuffed. He stretched out on the ground to take a nap. Soon he was sound asleep.

" 'Flint,' said Jisdu. 'Did you have enough to eat?'

"Flint didn't answer.

" 'Are you sleeping now?' said Jisdu.

"Flint just snored, so Jisdu knew that he was sleeping soundly. That was all he wanted to know. He jumped down in his hole and right away came back out with his knife and a heavy mallet. He used his knife to cut a branch and sharpen it on one end. He spoke again to Flint to make sure he was still asleep. Flint gave no answer.

"Jisdu crept up close to Flint, carrying the sharp stick and the mallet. Carefully, he placed the sharp end of the stick on Flint's chest, and then he struck it hard with all his strength. As soon as he swung the mallet, he dropped it and turned and ran as hard as he could go for his hole.

"He heard a loud explosion behind him, and as he made a desperate dive for his hole, pieces of flint were flying all around. One piece flew past him and struck another rock. It ricocheted and split the rabbit's nose. That's how he got that way, and that's the reason we find flint so many places now."

Young Puppy did his best to pass the time with his studies, but he found that the songs were easy for him to learn, and he memorized the movements for the dances of each coming ceremony without any trouble. He spent time at his mother's house, visiting with Lolo and with Bear Meat, and occasionally he found a way to sit and talk with Guwisti.

Those were perhaps the hardest times. They couldn't think of things to talk about beyond their mutual desire for the year to pass and how anxious they were to be married and live together in Guwisti's house.

He looked forward to the nights and the storytelling times, and he wished that he had more to do to keep him busy. Other men went out to hunt deer when the days were not too cold. Other men were free.

Then, just when he thought that he could take no more, Gola was gone, and with it, almost half his time was gone. He rejoiced with the warm air and the thawing. He quietly congratulated himself on his staying power. He gave thanks that he had endured.

The cycle of ceremonies would soon begin again, and he knew for the first time since his ordeal had begun that he would make it through to the end of the year. He would last until the Ripe Corn Ceremony was done, and he would be reborn.

27

I t was Gogi. It was the time of leisure. The hard cold time of year was over, and they had survived it well. They had more than survived. They had lasted through until the coming of Gogi, the warm time of year, with a surplus of food. The people were healthy and well, and everyone rejoiced over the arrival of the comfortable days, and the signs of new life.

It was early in Gogi, and after a time of rest and recreation, it would be time to forage in the woods again hunting game and gathering wild foods. Soon it would be time for the women to plant their crops. It was the female time of year.

Men gathered around the playing fields and played the *gatayusti* game, the game that had been invented by the monster Untsaiyi, the game where they rolled the disc of stone and tossed the spear after it. Those who did not play made bets on who would win.

The ball players began to train and practice, running long races and avoiding all kinds of food that might make them slow, confused, weak or sluggish, or food that might make their bones break easily. Before much longer there would be games to play.

And it was the time of the snake, the time when snakes came out from their homes in the World Below, a time to watch out for snakes, especially *ujonati*, the one with rattles on its tail. If a person were to come across a rattlesnake by chance out in the woods, that person was supposed to say, "Let's you and I not meet one another again this year," and then go on about his business. To kill one was forbidden.

Once long ago, they said, a woman went outside her house and met a rattlesnake. It startled her, and, without thinking, she killed it.

Her husband was out walking in the woods, looking for some game to kill, when, all at once, he found himself surrounded by rattlesnakes. Their heads were up, and their rattles were sounding. The largest of the snakes stood up tall, as tall as the man, and it spoke.

"Just now," it said, "your wife has killed my brother. Go home, and send her back outside for water, so that I may kill her."

The man went back to his house and did as the rattlesnake had told him to do. The woman went outside to go for water, and the rattlesnake bit her, and she died. The man had no other choice.

Young Puppy was glad to see this time of year arrive, but in a way, it made him all the more restless. All the young men were active. They were gaming or hunting or fishing. Several of them were riding the horses the Frenchmen had left behind. Young Puppy did what he could inside the wall, but it wasn't the same. There was nothing that he could do to satisfy the natural spirit for adventure that the time of year excited in the breast of the young and restless.

He studied, but that did not take up too much of his time. He worked in the garden with Guwisti and the other women, and he didn't even worry too much that some of the men might laugh at him for that. It helped a little to pass the time away.

But it was also the time for war, and one day Oliga returned from Coyatee. Tsiwon' came with him, and Water Dog and Bent Bow Shape. And this time Black Dog came. After they had been greeted by everyone and well fed, they met with Trotting Wolf.

"What happened there at the Shawnee town?" he asked them.

"I told them just what you said," said Olig'. "They laughed when I said that they were on our land, and then when I told them to move off before the time for war, they captured me and tied me to a post. They would have killed me, I'm sure, had not these three come in at night and released me."

Trotting Wolf sent seven young men out to all the nearby towns to tell the people there that he would hold a council in Kituwah in seven days' time. The talk would be about the Shawnees who had dared to build a town in the Real People's land. It would be a council of war, and all were invited to attend.

———

When the seven days had passed, and it was exactly the night for the council of war in Kituwah, out in the woods at the home of Uyona, Osa felt a pain. She cried out to the old woman.

"I think it's time," she said.

"Good," said Uyona. "Everything is ready. Everything will be all right."

Osa's pains continued, while Uyona brewed a tea of the bark of wild cherry. She put some in a cup and handed it to Osa.

"Drink this," she said, and she went outside. She walked to the eastern corner of her house and stood there facing east.

"Hey, Little Man," she said, "jump up quick. An ugly old woman is coming. She's almost here. Jump up and run away."

She walked to the north corner of the house and stood there facing north.

"Little Woman," she said, "jump up quick. Your grandfather's coming to get you. Just there. Jump up and run away."

She walked over to the west corner and repeated what she had done at the east. She moved finally to the south corner and repeated what she had done at the north. Moving back to the east, she began again, but she changed the words.

"Little Boy," she sang, "Little Boy, hurry and come out. I see a bow out here. Let's see who gets it. Hurry now."

And on the alternate corners she sang these words:

> Little Girl, Little Girl,
> hurry and come out. I see a sifter here,
> Come out. Let's see who gets it.

She went back inside the house to check on Osa. Everything seemed all right, but Uyona meant to take no chances. She knew that the Raven Mockers watched for times like this. A woman giving birth was particularly vulnerable to their attack, as were newborn infants. Raven Mockers, knowing their weak condition, would try to steal their remaining years away from them to add to their own evil lives. Uyona knew that many of the people feared her and believed her to be a Raven Mocker, just because she was so old. The fools, she snorted.

She looked over her shoulder to make sure that she was not being watched, but Osa, of course, was too much concerned with her own predicament to worry about what the old woman was doing. Uyona reached under her cot and pulled out a basket. She took a small bundle or pouch out of the basket and unwrapped it to reveal some sacred tobacco. From that, she filled the bowl of her pipe. Then she took up six sharpened sticks which had been standing in the corner of the room.

She went outside again, and then she lit her pipe. Once more she went around the house. This time, though, she wasn't calling out the babies. She was calling to the spirits of the four directions for protection against all kinds of witches. She was working to keep them out of her house during this critical time.

As before, she went from one corner of the house to the next, moving from east to north to west to south. But this time she smoked as she went, and she stopped at each corner to push one of the sticks into the ground there. She pushed them into the ground with their sharp ends at the top and pointed out at an angle. And each time, she sang these words.

> *Red Man in the cold land up above,*
> *Just now we, too, made your arrows ready*
> *in the path of the Night-goer.*
> *If he comes we'll take his Soul.*
> *We'll cut his Soul in two.*

The children had been called out, and the house had been protected. Back inside, Uyona found Osa lying on her back on the bear rug on the floor, breathing hard, perspiration broken out on her forehead. She was on the verge of giving birth.

"Come on," said Uyona, and she moved behind Osa, reaching under her arms to help her up into a sitting position, and she leaned her back against a house post there. Then the old woman moved around to face Osa, to be ready for the two *usdis*, as soon as they decided to jump down.

People were gathering in Kituwah from Stikoyi, from Ijodi and from other neighboring towns. Trotting Wolf and Black Dog were pleased to see so many young men there. All would be anxious to make names for themselves by earning honors in a war against the enemies of the Real People. All of them would be ready and anxious to move against the Shawnee invaders.

"We have an army here," said Trotting Wolf.

"That's good," said Black Dog.

Young Puppy felt his warrior's blood stir, and for a while he felt a deep resentment toward Ahuli, who had taken the warrior's life away from him. He was still a young man, still had lots of fight left in him. A priest's life was more suited to an old man, he thought, one who could fight no more.

Why couldn't he have left me alone? he asked himself. But then, of course, he knew that even if he had not taken on this new role in life, he would not have been able to go to the Shawnee town with the others. He could not leave Kituwah.

The night was warm. Even so, they crowded into the townhouse. A fire was burning there in the center of the floor, and many smoked their pipes. The air inside was soon smoke-filled. Trotting Wolf stood to speak, and everyone was quiet.

"We've been called together this night because of a situation which our brothers and sisters of the town of Coyatee have told us about," he said. "Up there, to the north, near Coyatee, on our lands, some Ani-Sawahoni have built themselves a town."

He paused to allow the crowd to murmur their astonishment, resentment and anger to one another before he went on.

"We thought that maybe these Shawnees had done this thing in ignorance," he said, "and so we sent a message to them, to tell them that they were on our land and ask them to move off. Oliga, from our town here, took the message to them, and now I will let him tell you what happened to him there."

Trotting Wolf stood aside to allow Olig' to take the speaker's spot and tell his tale. Olig' had never before addressed a council, and he was nervous, but he tried not to let it show. He stood in front of the large crowd and looked them over. Many of them he knew. Some he did not. He felt his knees shake, and he took a deep breath, hoping that his voice would not quake as he spoke.

"I went to the Shawnee town," he said. "My father-in-law, Water Dog, my brother-in-law, Bent Bow Shape, and Black Dog, all of Coyatee, went with me. But when we reached the Shawnee town, they hid in the woods and waited to see what would happen to me.

"I went to the Shawnee town carrying the beads of peace and the pipe and the white feathers, and I sang the songs of peace as I walked. They saw me, and they heard me, and they brought me in. I told them they were on our land. I told them to move off before the weather changed.

"They laughed at me and said that it was not our land, and then they took hold of me and tied me to a post. I think they meant to kill me, but they didn't say. That night, when the Shawnees were asleep—all but one sentry who watched over the wall—Water Dog, Black Dog and Bent Bow Shape came down to the town. Bent Bow Shape killed the sentry, and Water Dog came inside the town, all the way to the pole where I was tied, and cut me loose. The four of us escaped unharmed."

As Oliga moved back to his seat, and Trotting Wolf stepped back up to the speaker's place, the crowd murmured again to each other, speaking in unbelieving tones about the arrogance of the Shawnees and their shameful behavior in laying hands on a messenger who had been singing the peace songs. When Trotting Wolf was ready once again to speak, they quieted down.

"Our friends from Coyatee have come to us for help," he said. "This Shawnee town is near to them, but its presence there is not just their problem. The Shawnees built their town on land that belongs to the Real People. It belongs to all of us.

"You see how they've insulted us. They settled on our land, and when we sent a man to talk to them under the signs of peace, they made him a captive. There is only one thing left for us to do. We must drive them out or kill them off. We must make war on those Shawnees."

Trotting Wolf turned abruptly and walked out of the townhouse. His mind was made up. He would listen to no debate. Anyone wanting to argue the issue further could stay inside and talk all night, but Trotting Wolf had nothing more to say. It was a dramatic gesture, one carefully calculated to impress his audience with his determination and with the firmness of his belief in the position he had taken.

The crowd was quiet as if stunned following Trotting Wolf's departure. Oliga stood up and followed him outside. Then Black Dog and Water Dog followed. And though he could not go himself, Young Puppy left the townhouse to show his support for Trotting Wolf.

Inside the townhouse, no one spoke at all. More and more walked out, and soon the townhouse was empty. No voice of opposition to Trotting Wolf's proposal had been raised. There was no debate. The decision had been made. It was for war.

The little girl had jumped down first, and then the little boy. Uyona had bound and cut the cords after she had caught them. Then she had taken a tiny bit of puffball and put it on the navels. She washed both the babies in warm water, which she had prepared beforehand, and finally she dried them off.

She brewed another tea and gave it to Osa to drink in a cup. After Osa had finished the tea, Uyona helped her lie down again.

"Rest," she said. She picked up the boy and handed it to Osa to hold. "Here is your 'Squani-usdi," she said, "your Little Spaniard."

Taking up the girl for herself, the old woman went to sit on the edge of her cot. She put the infant's head on her shoulder, and she started to rock and hum the tune of a lullaby.

"My child," she said. "You little girl. You're mine. You came into my old age like a little whirlwind, and that will be your name. Gano luh'sguh."

28

An old man with a face and body covered with tattoos and scars climbed up onto a large tree stump there outside the townhouse in Kituwah and waved his arms to get the attention of the young men gathered there. Gradually, enough of them noticed him to quiet down and pay attention to what he had to say.

"Young warriors," he said, "I wish I could go with you still, but I am past my fighting time of life. I'm no longer good for anything but dandling grandchildren on my knee. This is a good cause you go to fight for, for these Shawnees, longtime enemies of ours, have flung insults in our faces.

"I've killed Shawnees before, and other enemies of the Real People. More than my share. More than I can count. And on my old withered body are the scars from their arrows and clubs and knives. Now it's your time, young men. Shoot all your arrows, and when your arrows are all gone, use your war clubs until they're drenched with the blood of our enemies.

"Fight bravely and fight well, and when you return victorious, we'll have a dance for you. Earn honors in the fight, and you'll be honored here at home."

The old man's martial speech was followed by whoops and yells, and another man, not quite so old, climbed up on the stump.

"Kill as many as you can," he said. "Show them what it means to challenge the warriors of the Real People. Drive them back to their own lands. Drive them out or kill them all. It doesn't matter which.

"If you cannot overcome, if you are overwhelmed by large numbers of enemy, then die bravely, fighting, with bloody war clubs in your hands. Don't let them capture you to make a sport of you for their women back in their town. If you can't escape, die fighting, like warriors of the Real People."

Several more older warriors, men past their fighting time, got up to make inflammatory speeches, and all were well received. The young men who planned to go to war became more and more agitated. They screamed, whooped, yelped and jumped into the air. They were more than ready for a fight.

Suddenly a woman broke into song, and at once other female voices joined hers, and the song was a song to the men who were about to fight, a song to stir the blood. The words encouraged the young men to be brave and ferocious in battle and not to fear the enemy. "Carry your red war clubs high," the women sang.

"If you show yourselves to be cowards," one woman shrieked, as the song came to an end, "don't bother coming back home to us. We won't lie on our backs for cowards. We won't put up with you. We'd knock you on your heads ourselves."

"Kill the Shawnees," shouted another woman.

"Drive them out of here," another yelled.

"Come home covered with their blood."

Everyone, young and old, male and female, was caught up in the frenzy. While all of this was going on, Trotting Wolf went alone to the dance ground and kindled a new fire there. That done, he went into his own house. When he returned shortly thereafter, he had painted himself black and red, and he was wearing on his face a wooden mask carved like the face of a man.

On top of the head of the mask was carved a coiled rattlesnake. The face of the mask was painted red, and the eyes were lined with black. Trotting Wolf carried in his right hand a gourd rattle, also painted red. As he made his way back to the dance ground, he called out for the young men to join him there, and they came.

He whooped and started to move around the fire, starting at the east and moving to the north. Striker fell in right behind him and began to sing the war-dance song with him. Woyi was not far behind. Then a woman stepped into the circle, wearing the turtleshell rattles strapped to the calves of her legs, and then the others fell in line.

The Howler danced, and Oliga, and Dangerous Man and High Back. Black Dog, Water Dog and Bent Bow Shape from Coyatee danced with them. And there were many more.

They danced and sang all night, and when the Sun showed herself in the morning, Trotting Wolf and all the men who would accompany him in his attack on the Shawnee town went into the townhouse. No one else followed them there. No one else was allowed.

There in the townhouse, Trotting Wolf prepared a large pot of the black drink which was called the White Drink, the Ama tsunegi, and all the young men drank excessively and vomited to purify themselves. They ate no food and would not, until they would all emerge from the townhouse after four days of isolation, fasting and purification. When they slept, they would sleep on ashes gathered from the sacred fire.

It was during the fourth day in the townhouse, when from somewhere Trotting Wolf produced the *kanesa-i galuhq'diyu*, the sacred box which contained the ancient war medicine. Wrapped in buckskin, the wooden box was nearly square.

It was a solemn moment when Trotting Wolf unwrapped the box to reveal the beautiful stylized rattlesnake designs painted around its sides and the fierce redheaded woodpecker on its lid. The young men almost held their breath in awe and in anticipation.

Trotting Wolf removed the lid, and then, one item at a time, he took out a scale from the body of an *uk'ten'*, a wing bone from Tlanuwa, the ancient giant hawk, the rattle from the tail of a monstrous rattlesnake, tailfeathers from an eagle, and other holy objects. Some of these things were older than anyone could remember. Many of the younger men had never seen them before. The last item Trotting Wolf took out to show was *ulunsuti*, a crystal from *ukitena*'s head.

As Trotting Wolf was replacing the ancient objects in the box, Ahuli came into the townhouse. He carried a small clay pot with a lid. Holes had been cut into the sides of the pot, and smoke was coming out of the holes, leaving a trail behind Ahuli where he walked. Inside the pot was a burning coal from the sacred fire which burned outside in the dance ground.

Ahuli handed the pot to Trotting Wolf, who then placed it inside the box with the holy relics. He closed the lid and rewrapped the box. Ahuli left. Then Trotting Wolf called for Olig' to come forward.

"I choose you," he said, "to carry *kanesa-i galuhq'diyu* into battle."

Oliga's mouth fell open in surprise. It was a great honor and a tremendous responsibility to be in charge of the sacred box. The success of the mission, the safety of the warriors, the welfare of all of the Real People depended on its care.

"Do you accept this duty?" Trotting Wolf asked. "Will you carry the box?"

"Yes," said Olig'. "I'll carry it with pride."

Trotting Wolf strapped the box to Oliga's back.

"Never let it touch the ground," he said. "Of course, if the enemy should get it from us, everything would fall apart."

"Yes," said Oliga. "I know. The Shawnees will not get the box from me, not while I am alive."

The final day of the warriors' ordeal in the townhouse, some of the women brought dishes to the door and left them just outside. The women would not go inside during this special time. Trotting Wolf went to the door and brought the dishes in, and all the men in there enjoyed a feast of deer meat.

When the four days were done, Trotting Wolf and all the fighting men emerged from the townhouse whooping and yelling and leaping around, waving war clubs menacingly in the air. Then almost mysteriously, the noises they were making seemed to come together clearly into the words of a war song which they sang as they left Kituwah, marching single file.

There were forty of them altogether. Trotting Wolf led the way, and Olig' marched close behind him, the sacred box strapped firmly on his back. All were painted red and black, and they carried bows and arrows, spears, war clubs and knives.

Outside the wall, Trotting Wolf stopped at a post set in the ground and painted red. He took the bundle off of Oliga's back, unwrapped it and removed the precious crystal. Carefully he placed the crystal on top of the red post, and then each man walked by and looked to see if *ulunsuti* would sparkle for him in the sunlight. The crystal did not turn back a single man.

That done, Trotting Wolf replaced the sacred crystal, rewrapped the box and strapped the bundle once again onto the back of Olig'. The march and the song were resumed, but according to the war plan of Trotting Wolf, the last ten men in line, selected earlier for this purpose, put saddles on the backs of the ten horses owned by the Real People of Kituwah, mounted them, and rode them slowly behind the men on foot.

Trotting Wolf had selected these young men because they were the ones who had been riding the most. They had become skillful in their handling of the mounts. They weren't quite sure why Trotting Wolf had them bring along the horses. The Real People had always fought on foot. It was their way. But Trotting Wolf had some plan of war that would involve these ten animals and ten riders, and so they rode.

Osa went back to her own house in Kituwah after only a couple of days. She was feeling strong enough. She took the Little Spaniard with her, and she nursed him at her breast. His eyes were green, and his wavy hair had a reddish tint. He was the image of his father, and she loved him with all her soul.

She had not seen the little girl, the one that old Uyona was calling Whirlwind, since the day of the birth of the twins, for the old woman had taken the girl child almost immediately out to her *osi*, her winter house or hothouse, the small domelike structure which stood to one side of the main house. There she fed Whirlwind on the liquid of *kanohena*. The child would eat nothing else and would see no one else, not even its mother, for a period of twenty-four days.

That was all it would take. Uyona sang more songs and smoked tobacco around her house to make sure that no one would get near to spoil the raising of the child in the way that she intended. She fed the child only at night and only the liquid from the *kanohena*. When the twenty-four days was done, if no one had come around, if everything had gone as it should, the process would be complete.

Then Whirlwind would always get what she wanted. When she grew a little and began to crawl, she would play with the Little People out in the woods. No one would have to watch her or worry about her. She would take care of herself.

When she was grown, or nearly grown, she would fly through the air at will. She would be able to dive under the ground and swim through the earth just as if it were water. She would walk on the beams of the Sun.

She'd be able to do all of the work of a woman, simply by wishing it done. If she tossed the meat into the pot, it would be cooked just right, right then. If she threw her seeds out onto the ground, her crops would grow and thrive. If she took her basket out to the field, it would be filled at once with corn.

Ah, what a life, Uyona thought. What a way to be.

Whirlwind would be able to take on any shape that she wanted at any time. She could take the form of a man, if she liked, or that of another woman. She might decide to look like an owl or a raven, a fox or a deer.

A man might be talking to his wife, thinking that they were alone, while all along, Whirlwind, in the shape of a bird or a bug, might be listening to every word.

She might take a fancy to some woman's husband and want to try him out for herself. She could do that, and no one would ever know, for the man might think that he was lying down beside his wife one night, and it would really be Whirlwind there. Uyona chuckled to herself just thinking about it.

And there was even more. There was no end to the powers the girl would have. She might wonder, for instance, what it was like to be a man and lie with a woman. Whirlwind would be able to satisfy even such a wild curiosity as that, for some unsuspecting woman might be lying underneath her man one night, on her own bear rug, in her own house, and it might not be her man on her at all. It might be Whirlwind there.

But even that was not the most or the best of it. If someone ever dared to do her wrong, if anyone did anything to displease her, Whirlwind could merely think them sick, and they would languish, waste away and die.

Or she could send an invisible arrowhead into a body to make a person sick or to kill him. All these powers and more would belong to Whirlwind. There would be nothing that she could not do, no power she would not have, no desire she would not be able to fulfill.

Uyona chuckled at all these thoughts. She thought about the way the people in Kituwah had shunned her all these years, shunned her, of course, until they needed her help. Just because of her age, they thought that she was a witch, a Raven Mocker even. They wanted to kill her. She knew that. But they were afraid to come near. Just wait, she thought, until my Whirlwind's older. She'll take care of you for me. If you thought that I was one to fear, just wait.

"Well," she said out loud to the babe, "they just think that I have power. They only think they have me to fear. You'll have powers they've never seen the like of before in all their lives combined. You'll have your way with them all."

And so, through the life of Whirlwind, Uyona would have her way.

29

As they moved closer to Coyatee and thus to the town of the invading Shawnees, the Real People from Kituwah moved more slowly, carefully and quietly, for there could easily be Shawnee hunters out in the woods so near to their town. Once they came across two such hunters, and Trotting Wolf and the Howler killed them quickly, left them there and went on their silent way.

At Coyatee, they picked up another twenty men. Anticipating the arrival of the men from Kituwah, these had already fasted and danced and were properly prepared to go to war. That brought their total strength to sixty.

On the march from Coyatee, they would have to be especially cautious. It would not be easy to keep secret the approach of sixty men. Trotting Wolf planned carefully, consulting the Howler and High Back and others. Usually the Real People raided in small parties into the enemy's own land. The goal was different here.

The enemy town was in the Real People's country. The object was not to steal from them, or kill a few or get a captive or two. It was to drive them out and destroy the town, and it required a different tactic from their normal warfare.

The Shawnee town was down the river from Coyatee and built on the same side of the river, the south side, in a low river valley overlooked by tree-covered mountains to its south and west. The town itself was in a wide, flat clearing, but behind it, along the riverbanks, were more thick woods.

Black Dog told Trotting Wolf about the point in the woods on the side of the mountain from which he and Water Dog and Bent Bow Shape had watched as Oliga went down into the town singing the peace songs. Trotting Wolf then decided that would be his place for this battle. From there, he and nine more men would watch and wait. Twenty men would cross the river and approach the Shawnees from the other side. Twenty more would approach from the south side.

Once near the town, those two groups would divide themselves again, ten men attacking from each of the four directions. The ten men on horseback would be held in reserve at the edge of the woods. The plan was laid. The trick was to get everyone in position without alerting the Shawnees.

They left Coyatee, all except the horseback men, in war canoes and rode the river halfway to the Shawnee town. From there they walked, keeping close to the woods. Lone scouts went out ahead to help ensure the secrecy of their approach.

On the morning of the second day of the walk, Trotting Wolf separated the men into the different groups and sent them each out in their own directions.

When at last he reached his own designated spot, Trotting Wolf assumed that all his men were in place and ready and waiting for his signal. He stood at the edge of the woods, up on the hillside, overlooking the Shawnee town. Behind him were Olig', the sacred box on his back, and eight more men.

To his left, at the bottom of the hill but still hidden in the edge of the woods, were the ten horsemen, led by the young man called Striker. The Howler and nine others waited east of the town, concealed by the trees along the river. Black Dog led the group that would come from the north. High Back and others waited to the west, Dangerous Man in a group to the south.

Because of the angle of the river and the placement of the town, farthest from the town was the attacking group of Dangerous Man to the south. Their approach was across the open prairie.

Trotting Wolf looked out over the terrain below one last time. Then he put his hands to his mouth, took a deep breath, and gave out a long and loud imitation of a wild turkey's call. From his right an answer came, and almost immediately, Dangerous Man burst forth from his hiding place, followed by nine more men.

Whooping and shrieking, they ran toward the town. They waved war clubs over their heads. The heads of Shawnee sentries appeared, looking out over the wall. Some Shawnee men, armed with bows and arrows, came running out of the passageway. They lined up there, prepared to meet the attack, but Dangerous Man and the others stopped, just beyond range of a bow shot.

They stood there, shouting insults, waving their war clubs, taunting the Shawnee men, daring them to come out farther away from town to fight. A few more men came out of the town.

Trotting Wolf watched as Dangerous Man ran dangerously close to the waiting Shawnees. Several of them sent arrows in his direction, and he turned and ran back to his group. Facing them again, he shook his war club in the air and shouted at them that they couldn't hit the wall around their town.

The Shawnees still kept close to town. Well, they're not stupid, Trotting Wolf told himself. The peculiar behavior of Dangerous Man and his group made them suspect that the Real People were trying to draw them out into an ambush. They held back, waiting.

Dangerous Man built a small fire and sat down beside it. He took out his pipe to smoke. Others sat down with him. Some two or three continued to shake their clubs and shout insults and dares.

The Shawnees bunched up together to have a talk, trying to figure out what was going on, trying to decide what to do about it. A few more men came out to join them. Trotting Wolf wanted as many of the Shawnee men outside the town as possible. He waited. Then came some more. Still, there were not more than twenty. There should be more fighting men than that, he thought.

Then a few of the Shawnee men nocked arrows, ran some steps toward Dangerous Man and his group and let the arrows fly. They missed the mark, and the Real People there around the fire stood up and laughed and waved their arms and shouted insults.

The Shawnees conferred among themselves again. They seemed to be arguing. Then half of them walked out away from the rest. They moved toward the ten warriors around the fire.

"Now is the time," said Trotting Wolf, and a man standing to his right shot an arrow almost straight up into the air. Dangerous Man saw the signal. "Now," he said, and one with him also sent an arrow flying high.

High Back, Black Dog, Howler and the rest saw the signal arrows and rushed toward the town from the west, the north and the east. They ran forward, shouting, whooping and imitating the wild turkey's fierce gobbling sound. Close enough for bow shots, they stopped and sent volleys of arrows over the walls into the town.

The Shawnees who had moved toward Dangerous Man and his group to the south were about halfway across the open space when the ten mounted Real People came rushing out of the woods. Confused, some of them turned to run back toward the town, but the riders quickly and easily cut them off.

The men at the entrance fired arrows, but none of them hit the mark. They turned and ran inside. The others, cut off now from retreat, decided to fight. They rushed toward the group at the fire. The horsemen had ridden past them by that time, and they turned their mounts to charge again.

Dangerous Man and the lead Shawnee met each other in the open field and closed in combat with their war clubs. Then others rushed together. The two groups were about evenly matched, until the horsemen returned, charging through the mass of fighting men, scattering them in all directions.

Woyi was knocked to the ground by a larger, stronger Shawnee. The Shawnee raised his club and was about to fall on Woyi, when the Striker saw them there, turned his horse and raced forward, knocking the Shawnee aside. Woyi quickly got to his feet.

The fight was over quickly after that. Two of the followers of Dangerous Man were hurt, but none were killed. The Real People killed all but three of the Shawnees. They let them run back to the town.

"Let them tell the rest in there how well we fight," said Dangerous Man. "Come on."

He led his men closer to the wall, and there they joined the other three attacking groups in sending arrows into the town. Then four of the horsemen took flaming sticks out of the fire. Leaning low over their horses' necks, they raced for the wall, each placing a torch against it at different points.

The Shawnees inside were huddled against the arrows raining down, and so no one took a shot at the riders, and they got back safely away from the town. Then the arrows stopped. The Real People all retreated back to a distance outside the range of a bow. They waited.

Trotting Wolf knew that most of the arrows had already been used. The supply was low. If the Shawnees wanted to fight some more, his next tactic would have to be an all-out assault on the town. He watched as the flames licked higher on the wall.

He would not have his men run into the town single-file through the narrow passageway. Such an attack would be foolish. He would wait until the wall had burned away in several places. Then they would be able to rush in from different directions all at once.

While he was contemplating all these different possibilities, a lone Shawnee man came out of the town, walking out the passageway, holding his arms out in front of himself, draped with white beads and feathers, singing a song. He moved toward Dangerous Man and the others, still there around the small fire.

Trotting Wolf walked down the hillside, moving toward the same goal. The horsemen were still milling around over there too. Closer, Trotting Wolf could make out the sounds of the peace song. He held himself erect, and his chest swelled. Carrying nothing with him but his war club, he walked to the fire.

Trotting Wolf and Dangerous Man stood side by side, the others stood behind them.

"Striker," said Trotting Wolf.

Striker rode forward to see what was wanted.

"Take four other mounted men with you," said Trotting Wolf. "Ride wide around that man. Come up behind him in a line, and follow him the rest of the way over here."

The Shawnee did not flinch when he saw the riders circling him. When they disappeared behind him, he did not look back. He kept walking straight ahead. Within a few paces of Trotting Wolf and Dangerous Man, he stopped.

"You're too many for us," he said, speaking the trade language, "and you have the white man's big dogs. We did not know you had the big dogs, and you caught us by surprise. We've had enough of this fight."

"You were told that we would come," said Trotting Wolf. "You should not have been surprised."

"We didn't know that you would come so soon."

"We sent a man to you," said Trotting Wolf, "carrying white beads and white feathers and singing the peace song, and you tied him to a post."

"But he escaped," said the Shawnee, "so no harm was done."

"Our people brought him out," said Trotting Wolf. "You would have killed him, I suspect."

"That decision had not yet been made," said the Shawnee, "but you could take me now and kill me, if that's what you want. I knew that when I came out here. I'm not afraid to die."

"And why should we not kill you?"

"If you do not kill me, and if you agree to what I ask, my people will leave this town and not come back."

"And what is it you want us to agree to?" asked Trotting Wolf.

"Say that the fight is over. Let us depart in peace. Nothing more. If you refuse, we'll fight you to the end, and you will win, but many of you will die."

"Go back to your town," said Trotting Wolf, "and when the Sun comes out in the morning, come out here again. Then we'll talk some more. In the meantime, there will be no more fighting."

As the Shawnee walked back toward the town, Trotting Wolf sent one of the horsemen with a message to all of the different groups.

"Tell them to build two big fires well apart," he said, "and keep them burning all through the night. Have the Howler, Black Dog and High Back come and meet with me back there."

He indicated the spot from which he had watched before, the place where Olig' and the others waited for his return, and the rider left. Then Trotting Wolf turned to Dangerous Man.

"As soon as the Sun goes down," he said, "send a few men over there and build another fire. He nodded toward his right. "And Striker," he said, "you take your *sogwili* back over there and build two fires. Don't place them too close together."

When darkness fell the Shawnees would look out and see that they were surrounded by twelve campfires. Already having admitted defeat, they would feel completely overwhelmed by the Real People, and they would surely not change their minds about giving up.

Trotting Wolf met with the other leaders that night and told them what the Shawnee had said. Dangerous Man had not yet had enough.

"Kill them all," he said.

"We could," Trotting Wolf replied with a shrug.

"If we kill them all," said the Howler, "some of ours will be killed too. Right now we have only two hurt. That's all."

"And if we kill them all," said Black Dog, "other Shawnees are sure to come seeking revenge. These have said that if we let them go, they won't come back."

"That's true," said Trotting Wolf. "What do you want to do?"

"Let them go in peace," said High Back.

Black Dog said, "Let them go."

"I agree," the Howler said.

Dangerous Man looked at the ground and said nothing. He was outvoted. It made no sense to argue further. Trotting Wolf stood up.

"Then it's decided," he said. "We'll let them leave in peace, but we'll watch them until they're out of our country. Go back now to your men and tell them what's happened here. Tell them also that I'm meeting the Shawnee when the Sun comes out to tell them that we agree, and they can go in peace."

30

Back at Kituwah, Trotting Wolf and the others who had gone to war had to undergo purification. They also celebrated their victory with a dance and feast. Then they had a meeting of all the people there, the residents of Kituwah and all their guests.

"In Coyatee," Trotting Wolf told the people gathered there, "they told me that they are but a small town with only a few warriors. They're on our border too. Enemies can come into our country that way. The Shawnees showed us that.

"The people at Coyatee think that we should have another town up there, near where we burned the Shawnee town. I think so too. But they're small, and they can send only one or two families out to make another town. Maybe some of us should go up there."

He let it go at that. Let them think about it awhile, he told himself. Some might decide that they would like to go and take part in building a new town, a town to protect the northern border of the country of the Real People. They would meet on the matter again one day and make some decisions.

When Whirlwind's twenty-four days were done, Osa took the Little Spaniard in her arms and walked out to Uyona's house again. She could hear the child screaming before she got to the house.

"What's wrong with her?" she said, rushing toward where old Uyona sat rocking the baby back and forth under her lopsided arbor. She put the Little

Spaniard down on a mat that was lying there, and reached for the girl, as if she were rescuing her from the arms of an old witch.

Whirlwind reached out her little arms, clutching for her mother, and when Osa took her, the baby nuzzled for her breast. Soon she was happily feeding. "You see?" said Uyona. "She gets what she wants. She hasn't cried until today, when her time in the *osi* was done, and then she started screaming for her mother's milk, and then you came along." She laughed out loud. "She gets what she wants. She always will. You had no choice. You had to come to her," she said.

"I only came to see my baby," said Osa. "You told me that I could come today. I don't know what you're talking about."

Uyona laughed and laughed. She laughed so hard that she fell down on the ground beside the little boy. The process had worked, and no one knew about it but she alone. It was her secret, hers and Whirlwind's.

Guwist' was glad to have the horses back, especially the one that Young Puppy had given her. She had gotten used to her almost daily rides, when the weather permitted, and she had grown fond of the animal by giving it constant care and attention. She was also proud that it had taken an important role in driving out the enemies of the Real People.

She visited with Young Puppy when she could, but the visits were awkward. They made small talk and avoided telling each other how they ached to embrace. So Guwisti spent her time with her *sogwili*, tending her crops, and helping her mother around the house.

Osa gave almost all of her time to her baby boy, but every seventh day, with the permission of old Uyona, she visited her daughter there at the old woman's house. She had been afraid at first that the little girl would sicken without regular feedings of her mother's milk, but instead Whirlwind seemed to be thriving. She was at least as healthy as Little Spaniard.

The days grew warmer, the forest greener, and all kinds of new life sprang up around Kituwah. It was the creation of the world and all of life all over again. Men went out alone or in small groups to hunt or to fish, and life went on as it always had and, everyone assumed, as it always would.

At last the time was near for the next ceremony in the great yearly cycle, and Young Puppy was much relieved. He had taken as much of forced idleness as he thought he could bear, and so he was grateful and glad when Ahuli at last called him in to rehearse his part in the coming event.

Then Ahuli sent for his seven councillors once again for a meeting. They counted the nights since the last new moon and looked deep into Ahuli's *ulunsuti*. They determined as close as they could when the first new moon of spring would appear.

As soon as they had made that determination, they sent messengers out as usual to all the nearby towns, and once again they sent the hunters out to kill deer, turkeys and other wild game. The hunters were given specific instructions regarding the manner in which the slain deer should be prepared. Men and women were selected to be responsible for the preparation of the feast. Everyone was involved in getting things in order for Ani-Sinuhdo, the Ceremony of the First New Moon of Spring.

Soon the storehouse was full of food, for everyone contributed, including those who came in from neighboring towns.

Then at long last came the day when Ahuli had said that the full moon would appear. Everyone gathered there in Kituwah to watch and wait. Young Puppy, under the guidance of Ahuli, had once again repaired the altar in the dance ground. The firekeeper had gathered the inner bark from the east side of one of each of the seven sacred trees and placed it there on the altar, and the sacred fire was once again rekindled there. And the full moon did appear in the sky, just as Ahuli had said that it would, and the women danced a friendship dance long into the night.

Early the next morning, Young Puppy brought a full-dressed deer to the altar. A massive crowd was gathered there already around the dance ground to watch his every move. Young Puppy laid out the body of the deer with its head near the altar.

He took up a bowl of turkey's blood and dipped into it with some blades of grass. He sprinkled the blood in a line from the nose to the tail of the deer. Then he reached into a pouch and withdrew the powerful *ulunsuti*. It was the first time Ahuli had allowed him to handle this sacred object, and Young Puppy thought that he could feel it almost burn his hand.

He placed it carefully on the line of blood on the body of the deer. Then he dropped some wildflowers and some old tobacco leaves on the carcass. The Sun appeared just about then, and Ahuli came out to the dance ground.

"Let's all go to the water," he said.

Then, just as they had done before for Nuwadi equa, the Great Moon Ceremony, almost six months before, the people lined up there at the water's edge, a row of sticks between them and the water, and in silence they watched a space for any bad signs that might float by. Then, at a word from Ahuli, they all plunged into the water and ducked themselves under seven times.

When they came out again, each passed by *ulunsuti* and looked, and then they went their ways back home for the rest of the day.

The day was a day of fasting. After the Sun had paused at her daughter's house almost directly overhead, only infants were fed. When the Sun was low in the west, all of the people gathered together again around the dance ground. The firekeeper had kept the sacred fire burning throughout the day.

Ahuli and Young Puppy stood west of the altar, facing the east. The seven councillors stood in a crescent-shaped line behind them. Ahuli produced a handful of tobacco flowers and flung them into the fire.

He then cut off the tip of the tongue of the whole deer, still lying there by the altar. He held it up over his head in his right hand for a moment, then put it into the fire. He and Young Puppy and the seven councillors watched it intently.

Then, at Ahuli's call, some men and women came out to prepare the whole deer to be eaten. They brought a great pot of corn mush to go with it. Nothing else could be eaten at this time. Nothing else could be eaten until this was all consumed.

The women danced again all through the night, and everyone stayed awake. Only infants were allowed to sleep. When the Sun appeared again, the ceremony had officially come to an end.

Ahuli took the deerskins and a goodly portion of what was left of all the food as his pay. He gave some of it to Young Puppy, who was thrilled at last to have something he had earned. He almost ran with it to the home of Osa, and he was disappointed when he did not find her there. He left most of the food and deerskins at the house and carried the rest away to divide between his mother and Guwisti.

The ceremony was done, but the people did not go home. Various activities continued. A sacred Night Dance would be performed in seven days, and on that seventh day, new fire would be made. The seven councillors named people to take care of those tasks. Every fire in town was put out. The altar and all hearths were cleaned.

During this time, young men were scratched and bled. Older men, skilled in the practice, drew lines on the young men's backs. Using a piece of flint or a rattlesnake's tooth or the bone of a fish, the older man would scratch the younger with a continuous line from the shoulder, down the back, the buttocks, the back of the thigh and the calf, once on the right and once on the left. A young man thus scratched would run fast.

On the morning of the seventh day, a new altar was prepared, and a new fire was kindled from dry goldenrod by a man who twirled a stick between his palms. Once he had started the fire in the goldenrod on a block of wood, he kindled it anew on the altar. Then every woman in town came by to get some fire to take to her own house.

That night the women danced throughout the night. Everyone stayed awake. Young Puppy had no trouble keeping up that night, even though he was tired from the ceremony and the activities that had followed it. He was glad to be busy again. He was thankful that his period of idleness was at an end. He knew that soon it would be time for the Green Corn Ceremony, and soon after that the Ripe Corn Ceremony, and when that was done, he would be free to leave Kituwah whenever he should choose, and he would be free to marry Guwist'.

31

It was a busy time of year for Ahuli. One ceremony followed on the heels of the last. The new fires having been kindled, it was time already for him to call in the seven councillors again. It was time to be watching the corn. As soon as the new corn was fit to taste, it would be time to begin Selu tsunegi sdi sdi, the Ceremony of the New Green Corn, the early or preliminary corn festival.

Early one morning, Ahuli examined the corn in the field, and he found that it was time. He called the seven councillors together, and they concluded that the messenger should be sent out. Along his way, he would take an ear of corn from each of the seven clan fields, and he would carry the message to surrounding towns. Upon his return, he would give the seven ears of corn to Ahuli.

The messenger went out on his way, and the hunters were sent out from Kituwah to hunt for six days. While they were gone, Ahuli, Young Puppy and the seven councillors would fast in the townhouse.

On this occasion, High Back was appointed chief hunter, which meant that he had to bring down the first buck. He waited at a well-known watering spot early in the morning, and he let several deer go on their way in peace. Then he saw the one he wanted: a large, healthy buck with a heavy rack.

His arrow struck the mark, but the buck was strong. It ran. High Back ran after it, sometimes following a trail of blood. He ran until the Sun was high up overhead, just about at her daughter's house, and then he found it dead. He pulled out his sharp flint knife as he approached the body.

He pulled out the tongue and snipped a bit off of the right side of the end. Then he took out some old leaves from a pouch he wore and wrapped the piece of tongue. He put it carefully back in the pouch.

Late in the evening of the sixth day, people flocked into Kituwah from all directions. Everyone brought something to eat, already prepared, and all the food went into the general storehouse to be distributed later at the proper time. No one ate. Everyone but infants stayed up all night. A silent, solemn dance was held. The altar had been repaired.

Early in the morning, the beginning of the seventh day, the first day of the ceremony, the people gathered around the dance ground to watch the messenger turn over to Ahuli the seven ears of corn. Seven firemakers, with inner bark from the east side of the seven sacred trees, lit new fire. Ahuli counseled all the people there to fast, to stay awake, to do no work nor play.

The solemn day dragged by. Then, just before dark, Ahuli appeared in the dance ground. He walked to the altar, followed by Young Puppy and the seven councillors, and he took in his left hand, holding it between his thumb and forefinger, the tip of the tongue of the first buck killed. In his right hand he held seven kernels of corn, one from each of the seven ears taken from the fields of the seven clans. He raised both hands above his head.

Then he said an ancient prayer, so ancient that some of the people could not even understand some of the words, but everyone knew it to be a prayer of thanks for a bountiful harvest and a plea for plenty for the rest of the year.

Finished with the prayer, Ahuli placed the tongue and the corn in the fire. Then he drew out of his pouch a handful of ancient tobacco. He sprinkled that over the corn and the bit of tongue. He and Young Puppy and the seven councillors watched the fire closely until the meat was consumed by the flames.

"Bring out the food," Ahuli said, and seven men and seven women brought it out and spread it before all the people. No one ate until all had been served. When the time came, Young Puppy said simply, "Eat." Yet he, Ahuli and the seven councillors did not eat. They waited for the Sun to crawl out from under the Sky Vault to darken the sky; by that time, most of the rest were done. And only then did they eat.

For the rest of the night the women did the Friendship Dance, and for the next five days, nothing more was done. People ate when they were hungry, and most of them slept during the day, for each night they stayed awake. Each night the women danced.

With no special duties to occupy his time, Young Puppy sat and watched Guwisti move around the fire. He never tired of watching her. He thought that there was no such dancer in all the world as she. She moved with grace, with an eloquence of motion, and it seemed to him that the meaning of all of life could be seen in her supple young body.

And he found a surprising maturity settling into his own body, for he watched her without lust. He watched with pleasure and pride. And he watched with a new and amazing patience. He felt as if he could sit and watch her dance for the rest of his life.

On the evening of the seventh day a general feast was laid again. This time Ahuli, Young Puppy and the seven councillors ate with all the rest, and this time they ate the fruits of the new year, not just those of the old. The ceremony was done. The women danced again that night, and most of the people stayed awake.

Osa suddenly felt compelled to go to Uyona's house to see her daughter. It wasn't the seventh day. It wasn't time for her to go, according to the schedule the old woman had set. She was afraid that maybe Uyona would drive her away, but she was no longer afraid of the old woman, and besides, she felt compelled to go.

She bundled Little Spaniard onto her back and picked up the long staff which she carried with her on her treks into the woods, and she started out. A few people spoke to her as she moved through the streets of Kituwah, but not many people were out.

Most of them, she knew, had been up all night with the dance. She was glad for that. She didn't really want to see anyone. She didn't want anyone asking her where she was going. Or why. It was none of their business, and besides, even she did not know why she was going. Something was making her do it. Something was calling her to go.

She walked through the long, narrow passageway that would take her out of town, and she thought about the parents of her dead husband. Of course, they were interested in their grandchildren, but they asked her so many questions. They were easiest for Osa to deal with when they were playing with Little Spaniard.

"He's just like his father," Potmaker would say, and Carrier would agree with her, of course.

But then they would ask about the little girl.

"You call her Whirlwind?" Potmaker had said. "What kind of name is that for a little girl?"

"You can't mean to leave her with that old woman," Carrier had said. "What will become of her out there?"

"They say the old woman is a witch," Potmaker said.

So Osa was glad to be alone, and she was glad that most everyone had stayed awake all night the night before. She managed to get out of town without being seen by more than two or three people who bothered to speak to her, and none of those had tried to engage her in conversation. None had asked her where she was going.

She felt anxious as she moved into the woods onto the trail which had become so familiar to her, the path she had now traced back and forth so many times. She was anxious, and she did not know why. It was a feeling. That was all.

She heard the crying before she could see the house, and she knew that it was Whirlwind. She hurried on. When she reached the little clearing, she could see the smoke still rising from a fire that had almost gone out there in front of the wretched, crumbling house. Whirlwind was crying loud.

"Uyona," Osa called. "Where are you?"

Receiving no answer from the old woman, uninvited, she rushed on into the house. Whirlwind was lying there on the floor on top of a bear rug, screaming as loudly as she could. Osa dropped to her knees beside the baby and reached for her.

"*Usdi,*" she said. "I'm here. It's all right. Your mother has come to see you." She picked Whirlwind up and held her close, talking all the while.

"And see? Your brother came to see you too. Stop crying now. We're all together. The three of us. There, there."

Whirlwind stopped crying all at once. Osa unslung Little Spaniard from off her back and sat down on the edge of Uyona's cot with a child on each knee. She bounced her knees.

"Here we are," she sang. "All of us together. Etsi, Asquani-usdi-no, Gano-luh'sguh-no. We three. Everything will be all right. Everything is good."

After a while, Osa began to wonder where old Uyona might be. It was unusual for the old woman to leave the baby alone. At least, Osa thought that it was. And it was almost unheard of for Uyona to allow anyone to come into her house unchallenged.

Perhaps she had gone out to find some herbs or something. Even so, she shouldn't be far away from home. Osa had never before come to the house and not found Uyona right there waiting for her. The old woman seemed always to know if anyone was coming, and always she was waiting there.

"Where has the old woman gone?" she asked little Whirlwind, as if she thought that she would get an answer. Of course, she did not. "What has she done? She went off and left you all by yourself, didn't she? Bad old woman. Old Uyona. Where can she be?"

She looked around the interior of the small house, as if something there might provide her with some answers, and she sat quietly for a moment, listening for the sound of approaching footsteps. All was silent, except for the songs of birds and the chattering of squirrels outside.

"Let's see what we can find," Osa said at last, and hefting the two infants up onto her shoulders, she stood up. "Let's go outside," she said, "and see what we can see."

Out in front of the house, she stood and looked around.

"Uyona?" she called, but there was no answer. She walked over to the arbor and looked under the sagging roof. No clues were there. She walked back past the glowing embers from the dying fire and over to the *osi*. Bending down, she tried to look inside, but she couldn't manage it.

She put the babies down, got down on her hands and knees and peered into the dark, round house.

"Uyona?" she said.

There was no answer. She stuck her head practically inside the *osi* and squinted against the darkness there. No one was inside. She scooted back and got back up on her feet. Perplexed, she looked around. She glanced at her babies on the ground. They were sitting up and smiling, reaching out toward each other.

"Don't worry," she said. "I'm not going far, and I'll be right back."

She walked around the house, and she almost missed it. The tiny, crumpled body was almost hidden underneath the clothes, looking like a carelessly discarded pile of rags. Osa had not ever noticed before just how small the old woman had been. She had fallen there against the back wall of her house, and she was dead.

Osa knelt beside her and looked at her wrinkled old face. She seemed peaceful and calm. Her face wore an expression more pleasant than any Osa had ever seen on it alive. Suddenly, she wondered just how old old Uyona had been.

She stood up, walked back around the house and picked up her babies. She had not touched the body. Something should be done for old Uyona, she told herself, but she would not do it. She could not. She had her babies to care for. Back in Kituwah, she would tell them. Someone there could take care of the body.

———

"Have you heard about Uyona?" Diguhsgi asked her daughter.

"No," said Guwisti. "What about her?"

"Osa went to see her and found her dead."

"Oh."

"It's too bad," said Diguhsgi.

"She was very old. How old was she, do you think?"

"As long as I can remember," said Diguhsgi, "she was very old. She outlived six husbands, you know. That's what they say."

"Well," said Guwist', "it was time for her to go."

"I guess, but I had wanted to visit her one more time. In thirty days or so, it will time for the Ripe Corn. When that's done, the time will be up, you know. The time she told you and Young Puppy to wait. I wanted to go see her again after the ceremony and see if everything would be all right."

"You mean for us to marry?"

"Yes."

"She told us already that it would be all right," said Guwist'. "There was no need to ask again."

Jacques Tournier knew that he was back in the country of the Cheraques, but he also knew that he was still a few days away from Kituwah. It was August, and the weather was warm. He recalled how cold it had been when he had left back in the early part of the winter.

That DuBois, he thought. The son of a bitch. The trouble he caused. Because of the doctor's actions, Tournier had been forced to leave the Cheraque town much sooner than he had planned. He had lost eight men to the doctor's ill-fated revolt and another six to the harsh winter trip.

His journal, in which he had been detailing the ceremonial cycle of the Cheraques, had been abandoned and would have to remain incomplete, at least for the time being, and perhaps forever. Tournier was not at all sure that he would ever again be allowed back inside a Cheraque town.

He had known at the time that they had made a special exception to an otherwise hard-and-fast rule when they had allowed him and his men to come in. Then DuBois and the others had violated their hospitality in the worst of all possible ways. It is a tribute to the very liberal hearts of those people, Tournier said to himself, that they did not kill us all.

But he was back in their land, and in his company were fourteen Senika men, headed by one called Owl, ready to conclude a peace. In spite of DuBois, Tournier's efforts were meeting with success. He was confident, and he was anxious to get it done.

They were camped for the night beside a small stream, and Tournier was sitting on a log beside the fire. Owl walked over and sat beside him.

"We're almost there," said Tournier, speaking the Senika tongue. He had been pleasantly surprised at finding similarities between that language and the language of the Cheraques, and because of the progress he had made in the one, he found it easier to pick up the other. Then he had stayed long enough with the Senikas to be able to carry on a basic conversation in their language.

"Three more days," said Owl. "Maybe four."

"You've made this trip before?" asked Tournier.

"Several times," said Owl. "But always before to kill."

"I see," said the Frenchman. "Well, this time it will be to make peace."

"You really think the Cave People will honor the promise they made to you?" asked Owl.

"Why yes. Of course they will."

"Some of my people think that you have brought us down here to let the Cave People kill us. They think that they will never see us at home again."

"Surely you don't believe that of me?" said Tournier. "Surely you trust my word?"

"I trust you," said Owl. "Otherwise I wouldn't be here with you in this country."

"You'll see," said Tournier. "You'll see soon. And so will those others back at your home. They'll see, when you come back with beads of peace from the Cave People."

Owl stared for a moment into the fire.

"I wonder what it will be like," he said.

"What?" asked Tournier.

"I wonder what it will be like to shake the hand of a Cave Person, rather than to crack his skull."

32

J ust twenty days had gone by since the conclusion of Selu tsunegi sdi sdi,
the Green Corn Feast, when Ahuli once again called in the seven councillors. Young Puppy met with them again, and this time he felt as if he
would not be able to contain his excitement and anticipation, for they were
meeting at last to determine the time of Donah Gohuni, the Ceremony of the
Ripe Corn, the end of which would also finally mark the end of Young Puppy's
long confinement in Kituwah.

With a mighty effort of the will, he managed to keep the turmoil inside
himself and remain seemingly dignified and restrained. All nine men had
looked at the corn in the fields, and so the discussion was brief. They all
readily agreed with everything Ahuli said. They announced a dance to be held
in Kituwah in just four days.

The sequence was always the same, year after year, so everyone knew just
what to expect once they had heard the announcement. The time of the Ripe
Corn would be given out at the dance. It always was. They also knew that the
Ripe Corn would be held in just about another twenty days after the dance
was done.

Ahuli, Young Puppy, the seven councillors and all the other people they
would pick for various jobs connected with the ceremony would need all
twenty days. There was much to be done. And much excitement followed the
announcement of the dance.

It was one of the biggest and by far the most joyous of all the cycle of
ceremonies. It was a time of renewal and thanksgiving and forgiveness. It was

a time of feasting and laughing and joking and happy dancing and singing. It was always the best time of the year.

The four days went by quickly for Young Puppy, for he was busy with the preparations, and then they held the dance. They danced all night, and in the morning they announced the time of the Ripe Corn Ceremony and appointed various people to various tasks. It was time for the work to really begin. Hunters were sent out again to bring back plenty of game, for Kituwah would be the host to all who would show up for the feast. Women harvested their crops and gathered wild foods from the woods and prepared them all to eat.

And there was even more than that to be done, for this was the biggest and most important ceremony of them all, and therefore more elaborate preparations were called for. An arbor had to be constructed there beside the dance ground and covered with green boughs. Just opposite the arbor, a booth containing benches had to be built, and, most difficult of all, and most impressive of all once it was all done, a beautiful, bushy-topped shade tree had to be cut down, near the roots, moved in one piece to the dance ground, and there stood up again to look as if it grew there.

To accomplish that amazing feat, a hole would have to be dug in the center of the dance ground, and the whole, felled tree placed upright there and set, just the way a pole would be set. People were assigned to all these tasks.

The morning after the dance, the messenger went out, and all the others set to work on their assignments.

But the Wolf Clan still had its old job to do, and the Howler was high on the ridge overlooking the pass below, the pass that led into Kituwah, when he saw the approach of the Frenchmen and the Senikas. They had been expected, of course, but just exactly when they would arrive had not been known. There had been no way to know.

It had been a long time since Tournier had left Kituwah headed for the land of the Senikas, and so their actual arrival was a surprise, as well as a major event. Leaving his comrade Wolves in charge on the ridge, the Howler rushed back down and into Kituwah to search out Trotting Wolf as fast as he could. He found the War Chief lounging in front of the townhouse.

"Trotting Wolf," he called, running. "Trotting Wolf!"

"What is it?" asked Trotting Wolf. "Why are you in such a hurry?"

"The Frenchmen have come back," said the Howler, "and they have some Senika men with them."

"Ah," said Trotting Wolf. "So soon. Are they coming to Kituwah?"

"No," said the Howler. "I think they stopped to camp."

"Where are they, then?" asked Trotting Wolf.

"They've just come into the pass."

Trotting Wolf decided that he and the Howler should ride out to meet the Frenchmen on the backs of *sogwilis*. He had two of the animals saddled and asked the Howler to accompany him. Holding themselves up straight, they rode slowly toward the campsite.

They found Tournier and his men there busy setting up tents and shelters in the pass. The two Wolf Men rode up close to the camp and remained sitting on the horses' backs. Tournier saw them and rushed forward anxiously to greet them.

" '*Siyo*, my friends," he said, happy to be speaking their language again. "You said that I should camp out here when I returned. Is this all right?"

He gestured with an arm toward the activity behind him.

"It's good," said Trotting Wolf, and he climbed down off the back of the *sogwili*. The Howler followed his example.

"Welcome back," said Trotting Wolf, and he reached for the hand of the Frenchman. "You haven't forgotten how to speak our language."

"*Wado*," said Tournier with a broad smile. "It's good to be back among the Real People. It's good to see you, my friends. I've brought someone for you to meet."

They knew who it was he meant. Trotting Wolf and the Howler exchanged glances. Then they followed the Frenchman. He took them to meet Owl and the other Senikas. The introductions were formal and stiff. Owl and Trotting Wolf, especially, eyed each other as wary old enemies.

"I never thought to meet with you like this," said Owl. "But this is good, I guess."

"Yes," said Trotting Wolf. "I suppose it must be for the best, otherwise this Frenchman would not have been sent to bring us together."

"Well," said Tournier, sensing the tension in the air between the two men, "we have some food being prepared over here. Will you eat with us?"

"Yes. Thank you," said Trotting Wolf. "But then we'll have to leave you for a few days to yourselves. You arrived just as our Ripe Corn Ceremony is about to begin. It can't be delayed, but as soon as it's done, I'll come back to see you again, and we'll talk about the peace."

Nothing more of business was discussed that day. They ate, and Trotting Wolf and the Howler excused themselves, mounted up, and went back to Kituwah. Watching them ride off, Owl walked over to stand close beside Tournier. He spoke softly in the Frenchman's ear.

"I don't like this," he said. "We came down here to make peace. We traveled a long distance away from our homes. Why are we being left out here to make our own camp, when festivities are taking place in town? Don't these Cave People know how to treat guests?"

"It's all right, my friend," said Tournier. "I assure you. Let me try to explain. These people had shut out all foreigners from their land because of the hated Spaniards. When I came along, they made a special exception and let me come in with my men. They made us welcome, and kept us as their guests for several weeks. They were most excellent hosts, I assure you.

"Then some of my men did a bad thing. They brought their weapons into town, and they turned on me. They captured me and my loyal followers, and then they threatened the lives of the Cave People. They tried to take over the town, and they caused the spilling of blood on the sacred dance ground inside the wall of this peace town.

"I was afraid that they would not ever allow me to come back at all, but they said that they would keep their word and make the peace with you, but that when I returned, we would have to stay out here, outside the town."

Owl paced away from Tournier, thought it all over for a moment, then turned back toward the Frenchman and nodded.

"All right," he said. "We'll wait."

Later that day, seven men came out of Kituwah bringing great quantities of food to the camp of the Frenchmen and Senikas.

"You see, my friend," Tournier said to Owl, "they are very busy with the big ceremony, but even so, they do not ignore us. It's just as I told you. They are excellent hosts."

Young Puppy and Ahuli were at the dance ground overseeing the final stages of the setting of the tree and the covering of the arbor. It was a spectacular sight. The dance ground did not even appear to be the same place as before. It looked as if a full-grown tree had sprung up overnight, and the still-green boughs on the arbor glistened in the sunlight, changing the hue and tone of everything around.

Striker and Woyi, or Pigeon, stood to one side watching. They huddled close together and spoke to one another now and then in low tones. Then they would look at Young Puppy or at Ahuli. Young Puppy noticed the behavior of the two young men, and he thought that perhaps they were wanting to talk to Ahuli. He waited for his chance and then walked over casually to join them.

" 'Siyo," he said.

" *'Siyo,*" said Striker.

Woyi nodded, looking at the ground.

"Well," said Young Puppy, making conversation, "things are just about ready here."

"Yes," said Striker. "It's beautiful. This is my favorite time of year."

"Yes," said Young Puppy. "It will be a good ceremony, and it will mark the beginning of a good year, I think. We're even going to have peace now with the Senikas, it seems."

"We went out to the camp to see them," said Woyi. "There with the white men. I've never talked to a Senika before. Have you been out there?"

"No," said Young Puppy.

Striker nudged Woyi with an elbow.

"Oh," said Woyi, remembering Young Puppy's status in Kituwah. "No. Of course not. Well, you'll see them later, I guess."

"Yes," said Young Puppy. "And I have seen Frenchmen and Senikas before. Well, I suppose that I should get back to my work."

He turned to walk back to the dance ground, but Woyi stopped him, calling out perhaps a little too loudly and quickly. "Young Puppy," he said.

"Yes?" Young Puppy paused and turned back to face the other two young men again.

"Striker and I—" said Woyi. "Well, we have something important to ask."

"What is it?" Young Puppy asked.

"We went to fight the Shawnees," said Woyi, "up near Coyatee."

"Yes," said Young Puppy. "I know. You two rode *sogwilis,* I heard, and you did well in the fight."

"Striker did better than I," said Woyi. "I had been knocked down, and a Shawnee warrior was just about to bring his war club down on my head. He would have killed me, but just then Striker rode hard into him with his *sogwili* and shoved him aside. Striker saved my life."

"We want to make friendship," said Striker.

"I see," said Young Puppy. "That is usually done at the time of Ado huna, I think."

"Yes, we know, but can it not be done at other times?" asked Woyi.

"I don't know," said Young Puppy. "I never thought about it before now. I'll talk to Ahuli as soon as I can. I'll find out for you and let you know."

"*Wado,*" said Woyi.

"Thank you, Young Puppy," said Striker, and the two young men watched as Young Puppy made his way back to the dance ground.

———

It was evening of the day before the ceremony was to begin, and the people came into Kituwah from all around, bringing baskets of food as their contribution to the feast. Every man who showed up for the ceremony carried a green bough in his right hand. And the mood was not solemn, but festive.

That night the women danced the Friendship Dance, and many of the people stayed up all night to watch them dance, to visit with their friends and clan relatives, or just because they were too enthusiastic about the coming ceremony to go to sleep.

In the morning, the ceremony was begun. It started with the men, away from the dance ground, singing loud. Then, carrying their green boughs over their heads, they were led single-file by Ahuli, dressed all in white with otter skins on his arms. On his head, he wore a cap of red feathers.

He led the song and led the dance, and the song was punctuated with much whooping and joyful shouting and a loud pop or bang now and then, and the dance was a dance of leaping and running and jumping for joy.

The occasional pops or bangs, almost like the noises made when one of the Frenchmen fired a pistol, were being made by a man who sat beside a large rock. He had a pile of charcoal chunks, and he would put one on the rock and at the proper time, he would smack it hard with a wooden club.

The men danced in a circle in the typical direction, and Ahuli led them around seven times before the song was ended, and even then they didn't stand still.

They walked around a bit, catching their breath and repositioning themselves behind Ahuli, two abreast. In front of them, standing alone, Ahuli started another song, and they danced behind him in a straight line until they came into the dance ground. Then Ahuli shouted a command, and they all turned and ran yelling back to the place they had started from. And charcoal popped again.

They sang joyfully about the rain and the fruits of the harvest, and the popping charcoal was Thunder, the bringer of rain, the Real People's friend. He had been their friend ever since the long-ago days when the little boy, one of the Real People, had saved his life in his fight with the monstrous uk'ten'. There were some who said he was also Kanati, the husband of Selu or Corn.

Ahuli began the song again, and the men danced the whole dance again. They repeated it several times more, and when they finally stopped, it was time to eat. Everyone relaxed for a while. Like everything else that day, the mealtime was festive. People ate and talked and laughed. They joked with one another, they bragged about the food, and they remarked about how beautiful the dance ground was.

Then the women dancers gathered in the center of the dance ground, and they lined up side by side. Their leader was wearing the turtleshell rattles strapped to the calves of her legs, and a singer with a drum, a man, sat alone off to one side of the dance ground.

With the commencement of the singing and the drumming, the women started to dance slowly toward the singer, but when they got close to him, they danced back again to where they had started from. This movement was repeated several times, and about the middle of the song the tempo increased. The song and the dance continued as before, but faster. At last, it stopped abruptly.

Then the women started to sing a new song, with responses sung by the men. The women danced in a circle around the dance ground in the typical direction, but this time they danced, not around the fire, but around the tree and under its shade.

When the second song was finished, the women lined up yet again. They sang a third song, and again they danced in a straight line, the way they had danced the first one. They danced back and forth as before.

The song came to an end, and there was only a brief pause before a loud shout came from the men at their place away from the dance ground. A lump of charcoal popped. Immediately after the shout and the pop, the men started to sing and dance again. With their shuffling step, they moved toward the dance ground. When they reached the edge, they danced on in, and Ahuli led them around in a circle, but he led them in the opposite direction from usual.

The women were still in the center of the dance ground, and the men danced around them, and as they danced, their circle got smaller and tighter around the women, until there was almost no more room. The women squealed as if they were afraid of the men, and Ahuli shouted, and the men all ran back to their starting places. They did this again and again.

The song changed then, and the men danced into the dance ground and joined the women, side by side, to circle around and under the tree. When they finished the song, they paused only for a brief moment, then immediately started to sing another song. With this one, the men sang a line, and the women responded, and so on, back and forth. And as they sang this song, they circled the tree, just as they had before.

It was early evening by the time this song was over, and it was time for another break for yet another meal. This time a great feast was laid out before them, and everybody ate again. They ate until they could eat no more. They overindulged. They ate because the food was good and because it was fun to eat.

It was an informal time, and Young Puppy sought out Guwisti to sit with for his mealtime. They looked at each other and smiled.

"It will be time for our wedding soon," Guwisti said.

"Yes," said Young Puppy. "I think of almost nothing else. One year ago, I didn't think this time would ever come. I didn't think that I could last the year."

"I never worried about it," she said. "I always knew you would make it."

33

But the day was not yet done, and after the big meal, when everyone's belly was full, even though they felt they could hardly move, still they danced some more. In a little while, the Sun would crawl out under the western edge of the great Sky Vault and leave the Earth in darkness for a space again. It would be the last round of dancing for the ceremony that day.

Once again, the women circled the tree in the dance ground, and once again the men came from outside. When the men had entered the dance ground, again they surrounded the women and moved in close. The song changed then, and the men and women danced together again around the tree, and then the Sun was gone, and the sky was dark, and the ceremony was done for the day.

Some people went on home to bed, some sat and visited with friends, while some of the women went back once again onto the dance ground to do the Friendship Dance. It wasn't a part of the ceremony at all. It was strictly a voluntary dance for the ones who just couldn't seem to stop. Their Friendship Dance would be followed by a long sequence of animal dances—beaver, buffalo, ground hog, spring frog, pigeon, partridge and raccoon—that would last all through the night, for those with desire and endurance enough to keep going.

Jacques Tournier and the others at his camp could clearly hear the singing and shouting and laughing coming from the town. They heard the loud pops of the charcoal pieces, too, and Tournier wondered if they had some pistols in Kituwah.

He had, of course, witnessed some of the ceremonials of the Real People before, during his stay in Kituwah, but nothing that he had heard had sounded anything like this. He was jealous that he could not be inside the town to see what was going on in there and maybe even to take part in it. He was curious about the raucous jollity he heard. In his frustration, he took out his journal and wrote.

Ah, how I long to be inside the town of Kituwah right at this moment with the Cheraques, for they are surely having a joyous time in there. I can hear singing, shouting and laughing. In all the time I spent with them, I never heard anything quite like this before. Never.

This must be the most joyful time of year for them. It's the time of their festival of the mature corn, and it brings to mind the ancient harvest festivals of Europe which we have read about. A feast of thanksgiving, I believe, for a good year past, a bountiful harvest of crops and of the fruits of the forest, and a prayer for a good year to follow.

He closed his journal and set it aside. Then he stood up and walked a few steps toward Kituwah, and he stood there alone and stared through the darkness and listened to the songs and the laughter. Suddenly he felt very lonely, and he did not know if he was lonely for Kituwah or for Paris. He decided that he would stay awake and listen throughout the night.

The Ceremony of the Ripe Corn in Kituwah lasted for four full days, with each day being the same as the first, the same sequence of dances danced to the same cycle of songs, the same feasting and overeating, the same laughter and visiting and jokes. No one seemed to want it to end, but it did end, of course, as everything must, and when it was over and done at last, and before the still-jubilant people had yet begun the series of animal dances that would last throughout the final night, as they had done the three previous nights, Ahuli stepped forward to make an announcement.

Donah gohuni was over, he said, and everyone was free to go his own way. Those who were so inclined could dance throughout the night as before. However, he told them, there would be two special ceremonies performed in the morning. They would take place right there in the dance ground, and everyone was encouraged to attend.

"They won't last very long," he said.

It was a sly move on Ahuli's part, for he knew that curiosity would get to almost everyone. He knew that he would have almost all of the crowd still there in the morning, just wondering what it was he was going to do. He thanked them for their time, for their participation and their contributions of food, and then, he said, Trotting Wolf had something he wanted to say before the assembly broke up.

"This has been a good time for us all," said Trotting Wolf, "and we of Kituwah are glad that all of you are here. We've had a good year. The crops have been good, the hunting's been good, and the forest has given us plenty. Now we're looking forward to another one just as good as the last. We pray that it will be so.

"Ahuli has invited all of you to gather here again in the morning to witness two brief but special ceremonies. I mean to be here early myself, for I'm like the rest of you, and I'm wondering just what it is that he's going to surprise us with.

"But whatever it is, when he's done with us, I want everyone to gather up again over by the townhouse. It will be time then to talk about some serious things that we have put off long enough.

"The Frenchmen have come back, and they've brought some Senika People with them to make the peace that we promised them we would make. We've kept them waiting patiently for us, camped out there in the pass, while we celebrated our Ripe Corn here in town. But the ceremony's done now, and now we have to play the hosts again.

"We need to talk again about the new town we propose to build, up where we ran the Shawnees out, up there near Coyatee. Those of you who came here from other towns, I hope you'll stay with us tomorrow to talk about these things and help us make decisions. That's all I have to say for now."

Some of the women immediately prepared to dance the Friendship Dance, but most of the people, gathered in small groups here and there, sat and talked for a while longer. It was a busy time. Just finished with their major ceremony of the year, they had the peace with the Senikas to conclude. Representatives from the old enemy were actually there, just outside of town. The Frenchmen were back, and they had brought the Senikas along with them.

Ahuli was promising two surprise ceremonies the following morning—"special" ceremonies, he had called them, and no one seemed to know what they would be.

"What do you think it will be?" they asked each other, and the answer they got was, "I don't know. Do you?"

Then there was talk of building a new town. Sometimes towns were moved, usually when the fields were tired and needed a rest—that happened for each town, maybe once in ten years. Sometimes when the population of a town grew too large, some of the people would leave to build a new one. But this was different. This move would not be to break up a large population, nor to find a fresh and healthy planting field. This move would be to create a new town for the sake of defense.

"Would you take your family and move up there?"

"I don't know. I haven't seen that country."

"It's not as good as this. The time for growing crops is shorter."

"My wife's mother lives up there. I've been there. It's not much different from here. Maybe we will move. Someone has to go."

"It's right there on our northern frontier, isn't it? Any enemy who tries to come in from the north will come through there. The people who settle there might have to be fighting all the time."

"If there's going to be fighting, I think I'll go. I'm always ready for a fight."

The dancing started, and the talking continued, and only a few of the people went home to bed. Some few fell asleep right there beside the dance ground. There was too much to do, too much to think about, too much to talk about and too many people to see. It was an exciting time for the Real People.

Young Puppy and Guwisti stayed awake and danced the whole night through, for like most of the others, neither one of them could sleep. Between the dances, they talked.

"This has been a good time," said Guwist'. "I don't like to see it end."

"I'll be glad to see it end," said Young Puppy. "I've been waiting for it for a year."

"Well, yes," she said. "In that way, I'll be glad. I just meant that it's been fun. I've had a good time with you here."

"I know what you mean," he said.

"Young Puppy," said Guwisti, "will we talk to our mothers tomorrow about the wedding day?"

"I don't know," he said. "I want us to marry as soon as we can, but Ahuli is doing two more ceremonies in the morning. I don't know how long they'll last."

"What are they?" she asked. "Do you know?"

Young Puppy shrugged.

"He didn't tell me any more than he told the rest," he said. "I heard about it the same time you did. We'll see in the morning, I guess. After that, it seems, we'll have a council to talk about the Senikas and then about the new town to be built in the north. If I get a chance, I'll ask my mother about our wedding."

"I'll ask mine for sure," she said. Someone started a new song, and she took him by the hand. "Shall we dance this one?" she asked.

"Yes," he said. "Let's go."

34

Young Puppy was tired and drowsy by the time the Sun came out, but
then, so was everybody else. The four frenzied days of ceremony had
been energy-draining, although it had not seemed so while it had been
going on. It seemed, though, all of a sudden, that all the activity of the past
four days had ended abruptly and that, as abruptly, an overwhelming weariness
of body and of soul had followed. Young Puppy had his arm around the shoulders of Guwist', and they were leaning on each other, practically holding each
other up.

People were gathering again, or were still gathered, there around the sacred
dance ground. Some were rising up from where they had slept on the ground.
Others, rubbing their eyes, were staggering out of their houses. They all looked
to Young Puppy as if they felt the same as he. Yet they were there. They, as
he, wondered what Ahuli was going to do. They, as he, would stay awake to
find out. Then Young Puppy noticed that Striker and Woyi had appeared at
the edge of the dance ground.

They were fully dressed, each in what must have been his best suit of
clothes: moccasins, leggings and breechcloth, buckskin shirt and sash, and
each of the buckskin items was finely decorated with dyed porcupine quills
formed into beautiful designs.

Then Young Puppy knew what was about to happen. He was suddenly eager
to see it, and he felt almost alert again. It was a ceremony he had heard about
before, but he had never seen performed. Ahuli came out of his house and
walked straight into the dance ground, not looking right nor left, not pausing

to speak to anyone. He raised his arms for attention. It wasn't necessary. All eyes were on him, and everyone was quiet. Ahuli thanked the people there for having stayed.

Then: "There are two young men with us here today," he said, "two warriors. Recently they fought against the Shawnees who had made a town in our country. They rode *sogwilis* into battle. Now they are about to make friendship."

"Ah."

The sound came up from the crowd, as if they said at once, So now we know.

"Striker of the Deer Clan of Stikoyi and Woyi of the Bird Clan of Kituwah," he called out, "come on out here into the circle."

The two young men walked into the circle of the dance ground and stood near Ahuli. They stood facing each other, self-conscious, to be sure, yet assured.

"There is nothing more pure than the friendship of two warriors," said Ahuli, "and there is nothing more lasting than friendship. This Earth will even die one day, but friendship lasts forever, for the souls of friends will find one another in the Darkening Land on the other side of the Sky Vault.

"A man will die for his friend, and a man will live for his friend. The making of friends renews the heart and renews the body. It renews the two men making friends. It renews us all."

He stopped addressing the crowd and turned his attention back to the two young men.

"Go ahead," he said to them, and they both, together, pulled their shirts off over their heads. Each then held his shirt out to the other, and the other took it and put it on. Then they took off their moccasins and their leggings and exchanged those things. When they were done, they had changed clothes with each other completely, there in front of the crowd. Woyi was dressed in the clothes of Striker, and Striker in those of Woyi, and they embraced.

Everyone who had witnessed the ceremony of the making of friends between these two young men knew that the two would be inseparable from that day on. If Woyi went to hunt, Striker would go along. If Striker went to war, Woyi would be beside him. The changing of clothes had signified to all that each young man had given himself to the other. Anyone who tried to fight one, would have to fight two. And when they married, they would marry women whose houses were close together.

Ahuli held up his arms once more and said a prayer, many of the words to which were ancient, and the people gathered there could not understand. When he had finished with the prayer, he said, "They have just made friendship. We are done."

As the two young men walked out of the area of the dance ground, they were warmly congratulated by all those who could easily reach them. Ahuli allowed that to go on for some time before he called once more for attention. When the crowd had quieted again, he caught the eye of Young Puppy and gestured for him to come forward.

Caught by surprise and wondering what was about to transpire, Young Puppy moved into the dance ground to stand before Ahuli, but Ahuli took him by the shoulders and turned him to face out toward the crowd.

"Most of you remember," he said, "when this young man came into Kituwah. It has been a year ago now since that day, and most of you know why he stayed in here all that time—why he couldn't go out to hunt with the other young men, and why he couldn't go north to fight the Shawnees. All that is over now. It's done.

"We've just finished with Selu tsunegi. Now no one among us is guilty of any crime from the past. No one among us should harbor any resentments or any ill feeling toward anyone else. No one must think of revenge or retaliation against anyone else for anything that might have happened in the year just past. All from the past is wiped out. All is forgotten. Everything now is new and pure. Our hearts are pure.

"The young man who came here to live among us one year ago, the man we once knew as Young Puppy, is no longer here. He is dead."

Ahuli pointed a long arm in Young Puppy's direction, and Young Puppy felt a chill run over his body. He recalled the words of Uyona. "He will have to die." Ahuli continued.

"You see standing before you now a new man with a new name. You see a man who has died and then come back again. You see here Tsule-hisanuh-hi, Comes Back to Life. From now on, when you speak to him or when you speak of him, call him by that name."

As Comes Back to Life stepped out of the circle of the dance ground, Guwisti was there to throw her arms around his neck and hug him tight. Then his mother was there, and she held him too. Bear Meat clapped him on the shoulder, and others crowded around to congratulate him on his success, on his new name and his new status. From a distance away, over the heads of the crowd, Trotting Wolf, the head of the Wolf Clan, caught his eye, and he smiled.

As the people were slowly making their way to the townhouse for the meeting Trotting Wolf had called, Trotting Wolf went first to Ahuli.

"Do you think," he asked slyly, "that since all of the past year is now forgiven, as you said, do you think we might let the Frenchmen come back in and bring the Senikas with them?"

Ahuli looked thoughtful for a moment, then slowly nodded his head.

"I think so," he said, "but we should ask the people first. Don't you agree?"

"Yes. Of course," said Trotting Wolf, "but I wanted to hear your opinion before I even mentioned the idea in front of the others."

"That's good," said Ahuli. "Good. Go ahead and ask them, then."

In addition to his generally persuasive manner, Trotting Wolf had two advantages over the people gathered there before the townhouse on that day. They were feeling generous because of the recently concluded joyous ceremony, and they were tired. They agreed almost at once to his request. That accomplished, he looked around the crowd for the Howler.

"Would you go out and invite them in?" he asked.

"Yes," said the Howler. "I will."

"And," said Trotting Wolf, "will you take Comes Back to Life along with you?"

The Howler paused. He recalled the time he'd wanted more than anything to get Young Puppy outside of Kituwah's wall, in order to be able to kill him, but all that was in the past, and Young Puppy was no more.

"Yes," he said. "Of course."

"Ride *sogwilis*," said Trotting Wolf. "The white men are impressed by that."

Comes Back to Life took his first step in over a year outside Kituwah's wall, and then he stopped. He had waited a lifetime, it seemed, for this moment, longed for it and dreamed about it. There had been times when he had despaired of ever seeing it arrive. There had been times when he had thought that he would run out early and probably be killed.

He had imagined the actual moment many times in many different ways. He had seen himself running toward the mountains. He had imagined jumping on the back of his *sogwili* and riding as fast and as far as it could go. He had dreamed of flying over the tops of the mountains and on up into the clouds.

He did none of those things, of course, as he stepped out of Kituwah. He stood a moment, breathing in the air and thinking that it really did taste differently from that on the other side of the wall, and then he walked alongside the Howler to where the horses were kept. They saddled two of them, mounted and rode side by side to the camp of Tournier.

"You're invited into town," said the Howler. "All of you."

"*Wado,*" said Tournier, and then he called to his men and to the Senikas to prepare themselves to go into Kituwah. Then he took Comes Back to Life warmly by the hand. "Young Puppy, it's good to see you again, my friend," he said. "And you're outside the town. Your time has expired, and you are free?"

"Yes," said Comes Back to Life, "and that name you just called me has been thrown away. I'm now called Tsule-hisanuh-hi."

Tournier smiled.

"I'm glad for you," he said. "I'm very glad. I knew that you would last the required time."

Most of the rest of the day was taken up with discussing the terms of the peace and with feeding the newly arrived guests. Trotting Wolf saw that he would not get all his discussion into one day. The meeting broke up in the early evening, and everyone went to get some sleep. The Frenchmen and the Senikas slept in the townhouse.

The next four days were spent in seeming idleness, but Trotting Wolf and men from each of the other six clans were busy at home, talking to their mothers and aunts. When the meeting reconvened, everyone was rested.

Trotting Wolf and other Real People made speeches, and so did Owl and each of the other Senikas who had come with him. Nothing of substance was said. No promises were made. They spoke of the end of the longtime war, and said that they were now friends. Then gifts were given on both sides. The peace was made. They had a feast that night in honor of their new friends, the Senikas, and their old friends, the Frenchmen.

The next day, in front of everyone in Kituwah, residents and guests alike, Guwisti handed a basket full of corn to Comes Back to Life, and he in turn gave her a bowl of venison. Wrapped together in one blanket, they went into Guwisti's house.

It was yet another four days before they met again, and again Trotting Wolf easily had his way. Everyone present readily agreed with him that a new town should be built there where the Shawnees had been. Anyone who wanted to go could make the move, they said.

Comes Back to Life, having discussed the matter first with his new wife, went to see Ahuli.

"I'd like to go with my wife to help build the new town," he said.

Ahuli turned away and stared long into the sky. Then at last he turned back.

"It's been good to have you working with me for a while," he said, "but they'll need someone there in the new town, and I'm too old. I don't want to move. Go with them, then. Go on, but when you go, take some of the old fire from here with you."

And so it was decided. Lolo and Bear Meat chose to go along with their son and his new wife. Osa did not want to remain in Kituwah. She would take her two *usdis* to live in the new town. Oliga said that it was proper that he live near the parents of his new wife, and so they decided that they would go too. And Diguhsgi wanted to go, to be near her daughter Guwist', and Striker and Woyi thought that it would be a great adventure for them. Besides, as it was, they lived in two different towns. The move to the new town would solve that problem. The Howler and High Back and others would go.

Tournier asked if he and his Frenchmen, and the Senikas on their way home, could travel along with the people who would build the new town. That was when Comes Back to Life became fully aware of his new role. In the new town, he would be like Ahuli. He would be the Peace Chief, and as such, he was the only one so far identified in the new group with any kind of authority. They turned to him to answer the Frenchman's request.

"Of course," he said. "We'll be glad for your company along the way."

But then, he thought, a War Chief really should have made that decision. It had to do with outsiders and not with the life of the people in town. So he asked the people to vote for one among them to fulfill that role, so he would not have to make that kind of decision again, and someone called out the name of Olig', and someone else, that of the Howler. Olig' stood up to speak.

"I'm honored," he said, "that some of you would name me to be your War Chief, but this man, the Howler, is older than me. He has more experience than I've had. He's a Wolf Person, and I am not. My voice is for the Howler for War Chief."

There was more discussion and at last a lull. The Howler stood up in the silence. His powerful figure dominated the scene, and all eyes turned toward him.

"Oliga recently made a fool of himself and ran away," he said. "Since then he has distinguished himself so much that some of you have spoken for him to be War Chief of our new town. I say that he has further distinguished himself by facing his past foolishness, and finally, he has shown maturity and a good heart by speaking for me, his rival, for this office. I say we make Olig' our War Chief."

So the two major roles for the new town government were filled even before there was a town. Later, advisors would have to be selected, but there would be plenty of time for that. There was a journey to be made. There was a town to be built.

Guwisti stood close beside Comes Back to Life, and he put his arm around her. She smiled and looked up into his eyes.

"Are you happy to be going?" he asked her.

"Yes," she said. "It's just as it should be, I think."

"What do you mean by that?" he asked.

"You've been reborn," she said, "just like old Uyona said. Now you'll start your new life, and we'll start our new life together, in this new town."

"Yes," said Comes Back to Life. "We'll start again in New Town."

Back in his house alone, Ahuli calculated how many days of rest he would have before he should call in the seven councillors once again. It wouldn't be long. There was never much time between the Ripe Corn Ceremony and that of Ela talegi, the Bush. He decided that he'd better get his rest while he could. Soon there would be no rest. The cycle had begun again.

PART TWO

New Town

35

The decision had been made. A new town was to be established on the northern frontier of the country of the Real People. The land of the Real People was vast, and it called for continual vigilance to keep out unwanted invaders. The Real People were used to watching out for invasions from their traditional enemies the Senika, the Delaware, the Shawnee, the Creek and others they had known and warred with intermittently for generations.

But there were new threats in this new and perilous age. New people, completely unknown until recent years, were threatening the peace and the territory of the Real People and all of their neighbors as well.

At first they had simply called these strange invaders "white people," or "people with hairy faces," but then they had made the remarkable and frightening discovery that there were several different tribes of these men from across the great water. And they had eventually learned to differentiate them one from another.

The first they had encountered had been the Spaniards. They had heard tales about them for some time before they actually saw any. The Spaniards had come to the land of the Timucuas and Calusas far to the south of the lands of the Real People, and tales about these strange and cruel beasts had reached the Real People through traders and other travelers, both their own and those of other peoples.

Eventually the Spaniards had reached as far north as their own country, and some of the Real People had even actually fought against them. The Real People had not suffered nearly as much at the hands of these "Christianos" as had other people, but they had certainly seen enough of them to know that they wanted as little to do with them in the future as possible.

Then had come the Frenchmen, and the Real People had learned that they were not like the Spaniards. They learned that they could get along with the Frenchmen, and slowly, they had even come to call some of the Frenchmen their friends and had promised a trade alliance with them.

The Frenchman Tournier had gone so far as to act as the go-between to establish a peace between the Real People and their longtime enemies the Senikas. However, the Real People had made a strange discovery about the Frenchmen. Some of them had turned against their own leader while they had been guests of the Real People in the town of Kituwah, so even with those white men that they called friends, the Real People had to still remain alert, for among those "friends" were some bad men.

More recently, they had heard rumors of still another group of white men, not Spanish, not French, and both the Spanish and the French, who seemed to hate each other, hated this new group.

So the Real People, who had always been wary of their neighbors, had become even more watchful and more suspicious than ever before. There was more reason to be so. Their existence had become more dangerous and more precarious than ever before.

So when a breach in their northern border had been discovered, they had made the decision to patch it with a new town. People mostly from Kituwah and from Stikoyi would make up the population of the town, which was already being called Gaduhuh Itsei, or simply, New Town.

Any town needed a government, and the basis of the government of New Town had been formed right in Kituwah while the preparations for the journey were still being made. The town would have to have two main leaders, one to deal with internal matters of the town, the ceremonial life which governed the routine matters of daily existence—hunting and planting and harvesting, marriages, births and deaths.

That responsibility had fallen on the shoulders of Comes Back to Life. He was a young man for such a tremendous responsibility, but he had been apprenticed to Ahuli, the ceremonial leader of Kituwah. So when the time had come to select people for leadership roles at New Town, Comes Back to Life had been selected as the ceremonial leader, or Peace Chief.

But New Town was planned as a frontier town, one which would almost certainly have to deal with people from outside, and that was the job of a War Chief. Oliga, from Kituwah, had been the first of the Real People to spot the invading Shawnees.

He had killed two of them and rescued a woman of the Real People whom they had captured. Then he had helped to locate the Shawnee town and later joined the force that had successfully driven the Shawnees out of the territory of the Real People. Olig' would be War Chief of New Town.

There were other roles to be filled, but they would be dealt with later, after the town had been fully established. In the meantime, enough people had volunteered to be part of the population of New Town for them to make the move.

The expedition would be led by Olig', who would be accompanied by his new wife, Tsiwon', the woman from the northern town of Coyatee, the same woman he had rescued from the two Shawnees. Once they reached the site of New Town, the leadership would be taken over by Comes Back to Life, who would oversee the building of the town and its ceremonial life. He, too, would be accompanied by a new wife, Guwisti of Kituwah, who had waited patiently for him during his year as a refugee in Kituwah.

Bear Meat and Lolo, the parents of Comes Back to Life, had decided that they, too, would go along, as did Diguhsgi, the widowed mother of Guwisti. Another widow, Osa, was going with them.

Osa's husband had been Asquani—Spaniard—the half-breed, the man who had been killed by Comes Back to Life. His death had occurred before the birth of Osa's twin infants, Little Spaniard and his sister Whirlwind, but Osa had been assured of a good living, for Comes Back to Life had sworn to take care of her and her children. She would also have with her the parents of her late husband, Carrier and Potmaker, who, having lost their son, could not bear the thought of being separated from his children.

There was much enthusiasm over this expedition to build a new town. It was a major move on the part of everyone involved. There was much work to be done in preparation for the move, food to be prepared, clothing to be made, weapons for defense and for hunting, tools for use in building and in planting. Then there would be packing for the trip and at last the journey itself.

There would be the actual building of the town once they had reached their destination, and then the getting used to their new situation, a new location, new neighbors, a new town government.

But in the midst of all this enthusiasm, none were more excited than the two young men, Woyi, or Pigeon, and Striker. Woyi had barely reached the age of a warrior. He had, in fact, taken part in his first action as a warrior in the attack on the intrusive Shawnee town. During that fight, his life had been saved by Striker, only a couple of years his senior.

After that, the two young men had become fast friends. They had gone so far as to pledge their eternal friendship to each other in the public ceremony known as the Making of Friends. They had exchanged clothing with each other, one item at a time, in front of a huge gathering of Real People in Kituwah, until each had been fully dressed in the other's clothes.

They were friends for life, inseparable. Each would gladly die for the other and everyone knew it. They were also very young and full of the spirit of adventure. They longed to do battle, side by side, with the enemies of the Real People, whoever those enemies might be. They had talked late into the night with each other on numerous occasions about the adventures they imagined to be ahead of them.

"Who do you think we'll have to fight?" asked Woyi.

"I don't know," said Striker. "It could be almost anyone. The Shawnees might decide to come back."

"They promised to stay out of our country," said Woyi.

"Yes, I know, but you can't trust them. We humiliated them. They'll be wanting to get even with us for that. If not the same ones, then maybe it will be some of their friends or relatives."

"Yes," said Woyi. "Of course. Some other Shawnees who made no promises to us. They might come into our country."

"They might try," said Striker.

The young men laughed, the cocky, confident laugh of youth who believe themselves to be invincible and capable of accomplishing any daring feat. But with these two young men, there was an added ingredient to their boldness, and it was the belief that together, they could do anything, together, nothing could stop them.

"Yes," said Woyi. "They might try, but we'll be there at New Town to stop them. You and I."

"You and I. Together," said Striker.

"It could be Delawares or Powhatans," said Woyi. "Or any of the people of the League, except the Senikas. We just made a peace with the Senikas."

"Even they might change their minds," said Striker. "It doesn't matter. We'll fight anyone who dares to come into our country."

"What if it's white men?" said Woyi.

Striker shrugged as if to say, It doesn't matter.

"Spaniards, bad Frenchmen, or those others we've just heard about," he said. "It could be any of them. Our job at New Town will be to keep invaders out. Any invaders who dare to try to come across our borders."

They were both packed and ready to go, and it was all they could do to wait for the rest of the people to get ready for the journey. They talked with each other about what could be taking the others so long.

Then one morning, while they were hanging impatiently around the townhouse in Kituwah, Trotting Wolf, War Chief of Kituwah, came walking up to them. "It will be time for you to be moving to your new home soon," he said. "We're ready now," said Woyi. "We're just waiting for the others." Trotting Wolf smiled, recalling the exuberance and impatience of his own youth.

"Another day or two, I think," he said, "and you'll be on your way. Will you walk with me outside of town?"

Woyi and Striker looked at each other and shrugged, almost together. "Of course," said Striker.

They walked to the wall and through the narrow passageway that led outside, and just outside the wall, they found two horses waiting, *gayahulos* on their backs. They recognized the *sogwilis* and knew them to be part of the bunch that the Frenchman Tournier had given to Trotting Wolf.

"You're starting a new town," Trotting Wolf said. "Osa has a *sogwili* that belonged to her husband and Guwisti has one that her husband gave to her. I have more than I need, and you can both ride. You rode well when we attacked the Shawnee town. I give these two to you, so New Town will have four of them. The rest of them will stay here at Kituwah."

The two young men were amazed, and they thanked Trotting Wolf over and over again, until the older man became embarrassed and excused himself. He turned to go back inside the town, leaving Woyi and Striker alone with their horses. The young men looked at each other, their faces beaming with joy and pride.

"Shall we ride?" asked Woyi.

"Yes," said Striker. "Let's do."

They practically vaulted onto the backs of the animals, and kicking and yelling, they raced toward the mountain where the road turned to run east and west alongside its base. Reaching the fork in the road, they wheeled the horses around, laughing out loud with joy and youthful abandon, and raced back to the wall, where they had started. Side by side the whole way, they reined in the animals close to the wall, stirring up a great cloud of dust.

"It's wonderful," Woyi shouted.

"Now," said Striker, "nothing can stop us."

"You and me together with our two *sogwilis*," said Woyi. "The enemies of the Real People had better watch out for us."

36

The mood of the two young men was somewhat dampened when the expedition finally started to move north, and they found their two beautiful, recently acquired steeds, along with those of Osa and Guwisti, being used as beasts of burden. Even the horses of the Frenchman were carrying packs on their backs instead of saddles and men.

They didn't grumble about it, though, at least not within hearing of any of the others, for there was a great deal to pack along. Anything the horses couldn't carry had been tied onto the backs of dogs, onto little travois dragged by dogs, or was on the backs of people. It was hard work keeping the dogs in line, and it was hard on the backs of the people who were carrying the heavy loads.

Because Osa had two babies to tend, and because her husband had bound himself to look after Osa, Guwisti offered to carry one of the little ones for her. She had started to take Whirlwind on her back, but the little girl had set up a tremendous howl. There were no tears. There was only a loud, protesting and insistent howl. So Osa had carried Whirlwind on her back, and Guwisti had taken the Little Spaniard. He made no complaints. He never did. Everyone commented that he was a well-behaved child.

Walking along with the smug and contented Whirlwind on her back, Osa thought about the first few weeks of the baby girl's life, how the old woman Uyona, the Horn, had insisted on keeping her, and how she had kept her from everyone's view, even from Osa's, for a specified period of time starting right after her birth. The old woman had fed the infant only on the liquid of *kanohena*, and had not allowed her even to suckle at her own mother's breast until the time was up.

"She'll always get her way," Uyona had said, and so far, Osa had to admit, the old woman had been proved right at least about that. She had said other things, too, about Whirlwind and what she would turn out to be, and the things that she would be able to do, but Osa didn't think about those things. She would worry about them later, or perhaps not at all. For now, she had two babies to raise, and that was all that mattered to her.

Recognizing the symptoms of rash youth in Woyi and Striker, the explosive, energetic and impatient exuberance, Oliga sent the two young men ahead of the column as scouts. There was not likely to be any danger as long as they were deep in their own country, but Oliga reasoned that it was best to be always alert. Besides, one never knew what one might encounter along the way. It was also best to give the young men something to do to keep their minds occupied and their pride fed, something to keep them out of mischief and out of trouble.

Their excitement thus tempered a little by their new and sobering sense of heavy responsibility, Striker and Woyi raced ahead of the column together, leaving the rest to plod along behind. The first day's march was uneventful, and the people camped that night alongside a clear, cool stream. Jacques Tournier took advantage of the time and sought out Comes Back to Life.

"My friend," he said, speaking in the language of the Real People, "I've not had a chance to speak with you since you took on a new name."

Comes Back to Life took Tournier's hand in friendship and smiled. He had really come to like the Frenchman over the past several months.

"We have been busy since that time," he said. "Much has happened."

"Yes," said Tournier. "And things have changed much in your life too. I remember not so long ago when you thought that you would not last the year out. You were miserable. Now you're a free man again. You have a new name, a new wife, and a new and very important role to fill with your people."

"Yes," said Comes Back to Life. "I have been very fortunate. Everything is good."

"And I am very glad for you, my friend," said the Frenchman.

"*Wado,*" said Comes Back to Life.

Potmaker and Carrier sat beside their small fire, with Usdi, their little daughter. They had just finished their meal, and the little one was toddling around, picking up rocks and sticks and leaves for examination. Now and then she would run on her short legs to show one of her discoveries to one or the other of her parents.

Carrier smiled to himself, but Potmaker saw the smile.

"What is it?" she asked.

"What?"

"What is it that amuses you?"

"Oh," said Carrier, "I was just thinking that we are like the bear people, you and I. Following our children when they leave home."

Of course, they were not, strictly speaking, following their children. Not exactly. Potmaker's son, whom Carrier had adopted as his own, had been Asquani, he who was dead. Their own child, Usdi, was with them, but they were the ones taking her along. She was much too small to leave home on her own, although sometimes she seemed more than willing to try it.

They were following their daughter-in-law, Osa, and her twin babies, their grandchildren, the son and daughter of 'Squani. But Potmaker understood her husband's meaning.

"Yes," she said. "I guess we are like that."

Even though Potmaker had not been born a Real Person, she had lived with the Real People, her husband's people, for a good many years. She had become a Real Person, both by assimilation and by adoption, and she knew most of the old stories of the Real People. Therefore she readily recognized the reference her husband had made to the bears.

They said that a long time ago, there was a boy who liked to play outside all the time. That was all right for a while, but there came a time when the little fellow started showing up late for his meals. As more time went by, he began to not show up at all at mealtime. His mother became concerned about his behavior.

"You're staying out too long," she said.

"I like it out in the woods," he said.

"You don't come home to eat," she said.

"I find plenty to eat out in the woods."

Then came a day when the boy failed to come home even at night. He had been gone for a long time. When at last he came back home, his mother sat him down to talk.

"I don't want you to stay away from home for so long," she said. "You were out a long time. I was worried about you."

"The next time I go out," the boy said, "I think I won't come back home at all."

"Never?" said his mother.

"No," he said. "I think I'll just stay out in the woods to live."

"But you'll get hungry," his mother said.

"No, I won't," he answered. "There's always plenty of food out there in the woods."

He was talking about the berries that grow on the bushes and the nuts that fall from the trees and the honey that the bees make. His mother grew very sad.

"We'll miss you," she said. "Your father and I, and your brothers and sisters. We'll all miss you if you don't ever come back to your home."

"Well," the boy said, "you can come with me. All of you. There's plenty for all of us to eat out there in the woods. If you think that you'll miss me so much, come with me, then. I'll be leaving in the morning, as soon as the Sun has come out."

The boy went to sleep, and his mother woke up her husband and talked to him. She told him what their son had said, and they decided that they would go with him, for they knew that if they let him go off by himself, they would miss him so much that they would always be sad.

The next morning the boy, his mother and father, his brothers and sisters, all left the town and headed across the open field toward the woods. The people of the town saw them going, and they ran out to talk to them.

"Where are you going?" they asked.

"We're going to live in the woods."

"Will you be coming back?"

"No."

"We'll miss you."

"Then come with us," the boy said. "There's plenty for all of us to eat out there in the woods. But if any of you don't want to come along, that's all right too. There may come a time when you'll get hungry and you have trouble finding something to eat. When that happens, you can kill one of us to eat."

Some of the people followed the boy and his family, but others stayed behind. The ones who stayed behind watched as the group led by the boy walked across the field toward the woods, and they saw an amazing thing. As those people walked across the field, as they got closer to the woods, their manner of walking began to change. Their steps grew heavier. They began to lumber and waddle. Then, just before they disappeared into the woods, the people watching from town saw their bodies begin to grow fat and hairy. They had become the bears.

Not far from where Carrier and Potmaker sat with their Usdi, Osa sat holding both her little ones. Comes Back to Life walked over to squat down beside her small fire.

" *'Siyo,*" he said. "Are you all right?"

"Yes. Thank you," she said.

"Are your babies well?"

She smiled down at the two infants in her lap and nodded.

"They're fine."

"Yes," said Comes Back to Life. "They certainly look healthy and happy."

"I think they are," said their mother.

"Is there anything that you need?" Comes Back to Life asked.

"No," said Osa. "Thank you. I'm doing well enough for now. Your wife has been much help with the Little Spaniard."

"Well, if you should need anything," said Comes Back to Life, "let me know. Anytime. I don't want you to go without, you and your little ones. Be sure to tell me."

"*Wado,*" she said. "I will, but just now, really, we're doing fine."

Comes Back to Life straightened up just as Guwisti was returning from the stream. She stood a moment and watched her husband leaving the campfire of Osa. Then she walked over to take his place there. She sat down on the ground.

"Osa," she said, "do you need any help with these two?"

"They are getting heavy," said Osa, "both of them at once."

"Here," said Guwisti, reaching toward them. "Let me have the Little Spaniard for a while."

The little fellow reached out toward Guwisti eagerly, and she took him in her arms and held him close.

" *'Siyo,* little man," she said, "Little Spaniard. Did you miss me? I'm getting to be just like your other mother. Yes, yes, yes."

The next morning, the people broke camp early and started on the second day of their journey. Woyi and Striker again went out in front as scouts. Oliga walked at the head of the column with Comes Back to Life at his side. Not far behind them, Guwisti still walked along with Osa and carried the Little

Spaniard on her back. Osa carried Whirlwind. Toward the rear of the group came the Frenchmen and the Senikas. They walked, too, for Tournier would not have his people ride while the main body of the group of Real People with whom they traveled was on foot. He had even allowed his riding horses to be used as beasts of burden. At first, a few of the Frenchmen had moaned over that, but Tournier had shut them up quickly.

"I'll have no grumbling from any of you," he had said. "No complaints. Be thankful that I haven't put packs on your own lazy backs. A little walking will be good for you anyhow."

Some distance ahead of the others, Striker and Woyi walked along the road. They were a little more relaxed than they had been the day before. They had actually begun to think that they were really unnecessary as scouts. The first day on the road had been almost boring. They had seen nothing out of the ordinary.

What's more, they had each decided, independent of the other, they were not likely to see anything of any real concern. The chances of any outsiders having gotten past Kituwah were very slim, and the direction of their march was only taking them deeper into their own country.

Once they reached and passed by the halfway mark in their journey, they would begin moving ever closer to the far northern boundary of their land. Then, perhaps, there would be more reason for constant vigilance, but even then, they thought, there would not be much real likelihood of anything to worry about. Coyatee was there, and to its east was the place where the Shawnee town had been. They had already driven the Shawnees out. No. They did not expect trouble, and therefore, they had begun to feel useless. And bored.

The road they traveled wound its easy way through thick, lush woods, and even in the middle of the day, they moved in deep shadow because of the thick canopy of dark green leaves above. All kinds of birds sang a rich variety of songs all around them, and squirrels, too, chattered up above as they scampered from branch to branch and tree to tree. Leaves rustled on the ground to their left and to their right as some small creature or other skittered on the forest floor, an opposum perhaps, or a raccoon. The brush was too thick to tell.

Suddenly both young men were startled by the sudden appearance in the road just in front of them of a large buck deer. It sprang into the road from their right, then bounded off into the bramble on the left. The scouts looked at one another.

"Let's get it," said Striker.

"Do you think we should?" asked Woyi.

"Of course," said Striker. "Let's go."

And he ran headlong into the woods just there where the deer had disappeared, and Woyi followed him close behind.

37

Striker could hear the sounds ahead of him of the big buck crashing through the tangle of growth in the woods. He ran after the sounds. Woyi ran hard trying to keep Striker in sight. Low-hanging branches lashed at his face, and tangles of brush reached for his legs, trying to wrap themselves around him to trip him up, or at least to slow his progress. He tore them loose with the forward motion of his legs as he ran, and they in turn ripped at his skin.

Then he felt the ground rising ahead of him, and as he looked down, struggling through the brush, he lost sight of Striker momentarily. They were climbing the hillside, and it was getting steeper with each step. He moved to his left around a boulder and then to his right around a thick tangle of brush. Looking up, startled, he found himself just a couple of steps behind Striker, who was standing still. Carefully, quietly, Woyi stepped up to stand just beside him.

"Up there, I think," said Striker, his voice low. "On top of the hill."

Woyi nodded.

"Let's go," said Striker, and again they started to climb, seeking out the path with the fewest obstacles. It wasn't a difficult climb, and soon they found themselves on the crest. It was a long, low hill, with a wide, flat ridge running its length, more or less parallel to the road below. On the far side, the hill dropped off into a low valley, just before the mountains rose sharply again beyond.

Almost all was tree-covered, but here and there the view was dotted with small clearings, and rivers and streams snaked their ways easily through the otherwise seemingly impregnable mass of lush greenery.

For a moment it seemed still and quiet from their prominence as the young friends looked around. Were they searching for the elusive buck or taking in the grandeur of the breathtaking view around them?

Woyi's eyes swept the valley to his right. They almost passed it by, something that didn't belong there in that scene. He looked back and found it, a barely perceptible wisp of smoke at the base of the western side of the hill.

"Striker," he said, his voice low. "Look."

Striker turned to look in the direction Woyi pointed, and he, too, saw it. He stared at it, his brow knit.

"What is it?" asked Woyi.

"It's a campfire, I think," said Striker. "It looks to me like smoke from the fire of someone who doesn't want to be seen."

"Why do you say that?"

"It's a small fire. Very small. Almost without smoke. And it's on the wrong side of the hill. Any of our own people traveling along this way would be camped over there along the road."

"Yes. Of course," said Woyi. "What shall we do? Run back and tell the others?"

"No," said Striker. "Not yet. We can't just tell them that we saw a little smoke. Let's get closer and see if we can tell who it is and how many there are. Then we'll decide what to do."

Woyi's heart pounded with the excitement. At last there was something to investigate. If Striker was right, it would lead to more than that. If Striker was right, it would be some invader down there, someone with no business in the country of the Real People, and it could easily lead to a fight.

They walked north along the ridge for a distance, and then, to avoid being seen by the others, whoever they might be, they dropped down the side of the hill a little and continued in the same direction. In doing so, however, they lost sight of the smoke. At last Striker stopped.

"We should be just over them now, I think," he said. "Let's go back up now where we can see."

They went back to the top of the hill. The trees grew all the way to the top there, and so they were not exposed to the view of whoever might be down below. But they could not find the smoke. Woyi looked up into a tall tree with lofty branches and thick foliage.

"I bet I could find it from up there," he said.

The trunk was thick and straight, but there were no branches until well above the reach of either of the two young men. Striker studied the tree for a moment.

"Can you climb it?" he asked.

Woyi handed his weapons to his friend.

"Watch me," he said.

He took off his moccasins to better grip the trunk with the soles of his feet, and he reached around the trunk with his arms. Then he began to inch his way up. The rough bark scraped the insides of his arms and his chest and belly, as he moved steadily upward. At last he reached the lowest branch, and he grasped it with his hands and pulled himself up. He stopped there to look, but he could not find the smoke. He climbed higher.

Striker watched from below until he lost sight of Woyi in the thick leaves overhead. Then he turned his own attention back to the valley below. Anything could be down there, he thought, for in addition to all the animals, with whom all the Real People were familiar, the woods, he knew, were full of Little People, Immortals and all manner of spirit folk. He had never seen any of them personally, but he had heard tales.

He heard the rustling of leaves, and he looked back up into the tree just in time to see Woyi reappear. Lowering himself by the bottom branch, Woyi once more hugged the trunk. He scooted down enough to make the fall an easy one, then he pushed himself slightly away from the trunk and dropped to the ground. He landed on his feet, but then fell over on his backside. He got up quickly and brushed himself off.

"I found it," he said. "Just there."

He indicated a spot just to their left and down on the valley floor.

"Come on," said Striker, handing back to Woyi his weapons.

Picking their way carefully, they started down the back side of the hill. About halfway down, they could see the smoke again. They moved more slowly, more carefully, trying to make no noise, trying not to rustle leaves or loosen small rocks with their steps. They stopped behind an outcropping of boulders about three-quarters of the way down.

From this vantage point, they could see below them the small fire, and seated around it, they counted eight people. A closer examination revealed that one of the figures was a woman, and she seemed to have her arms bound behind her back. The others moved about freely. All, except the female captive, of course, appeared to be well armed. Woyi's eyes were wide.

"*Gago?*" he whispered. "Who are they?"

Striker shrugged and shook his head.

"The woman is one of us," he said. "The others—I don't know."

"Are they Shawnees?"

"I don't think so," said Striker.

"What shall we do?"

"There are too many for just the two of us to fight," said Striker. "I'll stay here and watch them while you run back to the others to get help. Tell Olig' what we've found here."

"We should both go," Woyi protested.

"No," said Striker. "What if they leave this spot while we're gone? Go on. I'll be all right. I'll just watch them. When you come back with the others, if I'm not right here in this same spot, look around carefully. If I have to go, I'll leave you a trail to follow."

Reluctantly, Woyi left his friend there alone watching over the camp of seven enemy men. What if they spotted Striker there on the hillside? He would be no match for all seven. But Woyi knew that Striker had been right. One of them had to go back to tell Oliga what they had found. And, in case the enemy decided to move along, one of them had to stay behind to watch.

He moved back up the hillside as quickly as he could without being so careless as to take a chance on exposing himself. When he reached the top of the hill, he took one quick look over his shoulder, then headed down the other side.

Back down on the main trail, he forgot about caution and ran toward the column of Real People. He ran as fast as he could, and still he felt as if it were taking him an extra long time to get back. He knew that it wasn't, really—it was only his anxiety. He was worried about Striker. He didn't like leaving his friend alone in a dangerous situation. At last he saw the head of the column moving toward him, and he raced on up to meet Oliga.

"Woyi," said Oliga. "What's the matter?"

Scarcely breathing hard, even after his long run, Woyi answered.

"We found a party of strangers camped on the other side of the mountain," he said. "We saw their smoke, and we went over to take a look. There are seven of them, and they have a captive. One of our people. A woman."

"Who are these strangers?" asked Olig'. "Do you know?"

"No," said Woyi. "Neither Striker nor I could tell."

"Were they white men?"

"No."

"Where is Striker?"

"He stayed behind to watch in case they should move."

Oliga had a strategic decision to make. He could not just go charging ahead after these invaders, whoever they might be. He had a whole column of people to consider, and there were women and children among them. Yet something had to be done about the seven strangers, the woman of the Real People who was their captive, and Striker who had stayed behind alone to watch them. Something would have to be done soon, for there was no way of knowing what the strangers might do next or when they might decide to do it.

Olig' called a halt to the march and had the people all gather around for a quick council. Then he had young Woyi address the entire crowd, telling them what he had seen, repeating what he had just told Oliga.

When Woyi was done, the crowd murmured, their voices both astonished and angry. Olig' allowed them a short while, then stood up and raised his arms for quiet.

"We cannot abandon this group to rescue the woman and drive out the invaders," he said. "We'll have to take a small force away from here to do that. Woyi said there are seven men. Let's send a party of fourteen to run them down."

"I want to go," said Woyi. "Striker is my friend."

"Of course," said Oliga. "You have to go to show us where you left them. And I, and then twelve more."

Just then, the Howler, who had been remarkably quiet on this trip, stepped forward.

"I'd like to say something," he said. "I think that Oliga should stay with this group. He is charged with the safety of everyone here. So, unless anyone objects, I volunteer to lead this party against the unknown enemy, and perhaps some of our new friends would like to join me in this pursuit."

Everyone grew very quiet. The Howler had not mentioned any names, but everyone knew that he had just issued a challenge to the Senikas and perhaps to the Frenchmen as well. Oliga considered the Howler's comments for a brief moment before speaking again into the tense silence.

"I give over the leadership of this party to the capable, brave and wise Howler," he said, and he stepped back out of the way.

The Howler moved over to stand beside Woyi.

"Who goes with us?" he called.

Jacques Tournier stepped forward to answer the challenge laid before him by the Howler.

"I and my Frenchmen," he said, speaking in the language of the Real People, "we will go along gladly, if you will have us."

"You're welcome," said the Howler.

Then Owl moved up beside Tournier.

"I and my Senikas will go," he said, "and that should be enough."

It was enough, for the party was thus already larger than the fourteen Oliga had called for in the first place, and yet it included only two Real People— Woyi and the Howler. Oliga called for the rest of the people to set up camp. They would spend what was left of the day and the night in that spot, allowing the party of warriors to get ahead of them and make sure the enemy was taken care of before moving on. Tournier approached the Howler.

"Do you think that we should use the *sogwilis?*" he asked.

The Howler glanced at Woyi.

"Are our enemies on foot?" he asked.

"We saw no *sogwilis* with them," answered Woyi.

"Yes," said the Howler, looking back toward Tournier. "That would be good."

Tournier ordered some of the Frenchmen to unload the horses and saddle them, and that seemed to please everyone. The Frenchmen had not liked walking; the Senikas and the two Real People were excited about being mounted; and even the horses seemed pleased to have their packs replaced by saddles once again. They stamped and snorted, anxious to run.

In a short time, nearly thirty mounted men rode away from the camp of Real People. Oliga watched them go. He had felt the pomp of his new office for a while. For the first time, he was feeling its burden. He decided that he should post guards around the camp. One never knew what to expect these days.

38

The Howler was particularly anxious to catch up with the seven invaders, whoever they might be. As a prominent member of the Wolf Clan, he felt personally responsible for any breach in the security of the lands of the Real People. He wanted to know just who these invaders were and where and how they had gotten past the sentries posted by his clansmen. Then he wanted to teach them a severe lesson regarding the consequences of daring such an invasion.

However, when they reached the place where Woyi had last seen Striker, there was no one around. Striker was gone, and so were the invaders with their prisoner. Angrily, Howler led the way down the hillside to the abandoned campsite.

It was clear that there had been a camp, and that seven or so people had been there, but not much else was clear. Whoever these people were, they had covered their tracks pretty well.

"Striker told me," said Woyi, "that if they moved before we got here, he would follow them, and he would leave a trail for us to follow."

"I don't see any trail," said the Howler.

"He wasn't down here," said Woyi. "He was watching from up there."

Woyi pointed to the rocks up on the side of the hill where he and Striker had hidden to watch the campsite below.

"We'll go up there and look around," said the Howler, "but there's something else we have to consider."

"What is that?" Woyi asked.

"Maybe Striker didn't follow them. Maybe they captured him, too."

That thought had not entered Woyi's mind. He had thought only that Striker would do exactly as he had said he would do. He would follow the strangers and leave a trail. Now that the Howler had mentioned the other possibility, Woyi was worried. He could hardly stand to think about Striker in serious danger, alone without him. They were friends until the end of life and even beyond. They were supposed to be inseparable. Woyi began to feel extremely anxious and even a little guilty.

It was true that Striker had told him to go back for the others. Even so, Woyi couldn't help feeling that he had abandoned his friend. Something inside kept telling him that he should have stayed with Striker. He tried to push those thoughts aside.

"I believe that he followed them," he said, almost angrily, "and he left us a trail to follow. Come on."

He ran up the hillside toward the rocks where he had last seen his friend. Down by the campsite, the Howler issued some instructions, and his followers, including the Senikas and the Frenchmen, began to fan out, searching the area around the campsite and on the hillside.

Woyi looked frantically around the rocks. He could not even find any indication of the direction Striker might have gone when he left his hiding place. That could mean, he thought with horror, that the strangers had indeed captured him, and when they left with him they had carefully covered their tracks.

Just then one of the Senikas called out in his own tongue. Woyi looked up to see the man on the slope to his north. He also saw Owl running to join the man. Woyi, too, ran. When he drew near, Owl was pointing at the ground.

"Look at this," he said.

Woyi looked and saw three fist-sized rocks placed carefully in a line. He felt a thrill and a relief, and he almost shouted out loud in his sudden exuberance.

"It's Striker," he said. "He's pointing us north. I told you."

Everyone else had gathered around by then, and the Howler got down on one knee to look at the rocks. Then he picked one up. He examined the rock closely and then the ground beneath it. He picked up the other two rocks one at a time and did the same. Then he stood.

"This is the sign that Striker left for us," he said. He then divided his force into three parts, each division consisting of both Senikas and Frenchmen. He placed himself at the head of one group, Woyi at the head of the second and Owl the third, which included the Frenchman Tournier.

"Woyi," he said, "continue to follow the signs on this side of the mountain.

Owl, with your group, go back to the road on the other side where we left the sogwilis. Mount up and follow the road. I and the third group will walk along the ridge in between. If either of you come across any sign of the enemy, send someone to tell me. We'll all get together again before we make any plans to attack."

Tournier rode beside Owl, the others following. They walked the horses. There was no point in getting too far ahead of the other two groups.

"My friend," said Tournier, "what will we do if we should come upon these people suddenly?"

"Kill them," said Owl. "What else?"

"But the Howler said that we should send word to him before we attack."

"We will," said Owl, "if we can."

"But there are only seven of them, according to Woyi. We should be able to capture them easily."

"Perhaps we'll leave one or two alive for the Howler to question," said Owl. "But if, as you said, we come on them by surprise, and they try to fight us, the Howler cannot expect us to refrain from killing them."

Tournier rode along for a little in silence. Of course Owl was right.

"My friend," he said, "something puzzles me. This party is made up almost entirely of your people and mine."

Owl smiled.

"We're being tested by the Howler," he said.

"Tested?"

"Of course. We are old enemies, his people and mine," said Owl, "and very new friends. He's testing that new friendship. He wants to see if we will kill his enemies."

"And will you?"

"Of course," said Owl, with a shrug. "Why not? Will you? You're new friends, too."

On top of the ridge the group led by the Howler moved along. From their position, they could usually see both groups down below. The Howler moved from one side of the mountaintop to the other to check on the two groups. They were all keeping up pretty much the same pace. So far, things were going much as he had planned. What frustrated him was that, even from high on the ridge, he had not yet seen anything of either Striker or of the invaders, whoever they might be.

On the far side of the mountain, Woyi, at the head of his group, watched the ground carefully as he moved along. He had instructed other members of the group to look ahead, to keep them from walking into some kind of a trap or of blundering into the enemy.

But he watched the ground for any signs that Striker might have left along the way. He still felt certain that his friend was not a captive of the strangers. Rather, he was following them, and that meant that he would be leaving some kind of trail for them to follow. They had already found the three stones back close to the campsite. Woyi was sure they'd find more. It had been some time and distance, however, since the three stones, and he was beginning to worry.

Then he saw a large, flat stone that had been turned over, and a smaller stone had been placed on top. It must have been done by Striker, Woyi thought. It was certainly deliberate. He stopped and turned to face the men who were following him.

"Look," he said. "They've gone this way. Striker must have done this. We're still on the right trail. Someone run up to the top and tell the Howler."

One of the young men raced toward the hillside as Woyi moved forward, followed by the others. It wasn't long before Woyi came across another sign. This time it was three stones again, but they were lined up not north and south, but east and west. He stopped and stood for a moment puzzled. The others caught up with him and saw the rocks.

"They've turned," said Woyi, "but which way?"

A few men walked toward the left and a few more to the right, east, toward the hillside. "Up here," one of them shouted. Woyi ran. The others were close behind him. Again a large, flat rock had been turned over, a smaller rock placed on top of its exposed belly.

"They headed up the mountainside here," said Woyi. "Let's all hurry up to the top to join the Howler and tell him what we've found."

They made the ridge in good time and found themselves, in fact, a little ahead of the Howler and his group. But they could see them coming.

"We'll wait here," said Woyi, "and look around for another sign. We need to know which way they went from here."

Soon they found another line of three rocks, and it was lined up north and south. The enemy was going north again, this time along the mountaintop. The Howler's group came up, and Woyi stepped up to face the Wolf Person.

"We found a sign below," he said, "that indicates that they came up to the top just here. Then this." He pointed to the line of stones. "They headed north again, walking along the ridge just as you've been doing. We're standing in their tracks."

"Let's go," the Howler said.

"Maybe it would be good," said Woyi, "if I scouted ahead—alone."

The Howler studied that suggestion for a moment, then nodded. "Yes," he said. "Go on, and be careful."

Woyi ran ahead. He wasn't really worried about running up on the enemy, for he was still certain that Striker was following them and that he would run up on Striker first. When he found Striker, he figured, the enemy would not be far ahead.

He ran, thinking with almost every step that he would soon see Striker. He did see another line of stones, and so he knew that he was still on the right track. He kept running. Then suddenly he stopped. There was another line of stones, this time formed from east to west. They had turned again. Which way?

He moved to the eastern slope, and there he found another line running off the ridge and down the eastern side of the mountain. They had headed back down toward the road, along which the group led by the Senika Owl rode on the backs of *sogwilis*. He debated with himself for just a moment what to do. Then he ran back to the Howler.

"What have you found?" the Howler asked.

"Just up ahead," said Woyi, "they went down again. Down toward the road."

He led them to the place where the signs had been left, and they all turned to descend the slope. Below on the road, Owl saw them coming, and he halted his column to wait. The Howler explained to Owl, Tournier and the others what they had found.

"They came down here," he said.

"The question, then," said Tournier, "is which way did they go from here?"

Owl pointed straight ahead on the road.

"How do you know?" asked the Frenchman.

"They just came down from the west," said Owl. "They did not go south on the road. They would have met us. To the east the woods are thick. No one has crashed through there recently. If they had, we could tell."

"I see," said Tournier. "You're right, of course."

"Shall I scout ahead?" asked Woyi.

"No," said the Howler. "Let someone else go this time. Don't wear yourself out."

"I'm all right," Woyi insisted.

"You're anxious for your friend," said the Howler, "and that's the way it should be. But for now, stay with us."

The Howler sent another scout ahead, and, together again, the entire group moved north along the road. Woyi mounted a *sogwili* and rode alongside the

Howler. Who were these people, he wondered, who had dared to enter the country of the Real People and capture a woman? He was anxious to find his friend Striker and to be sure that Striker was safe, and once that had been taken care of, he would be just as anxious to punish these rude intruders, whoever they might be.

But he didn't worry, not really, until he saw that the Sun was low in the western sky, and still there was no sign of Striker or of the enemy. There had been two more markers left by Striker, they all presumed, but that was all. He told himself that it was good. As long as they kept finding signs, it was good.

Still he worried. He had expected that they would catch up with Striker easily before the day was done. It was almost over, and still Striker and the enemy were somewhere up ahead. How far ahead, they couldn't tell.

It was almost dark, and the Howler called a halt.

"We'll camp here for the night," he said.

Woyi didn't want to stop, but he knew that the Howler was right, and so he kept quiet. But he wouldn't sleep that night, he knew. He would roll around, thinking of his friend, wondering where he might be, worrying about his safety, wishing for the Sun to hurry and appear again so they could once more take up their pursuit.

39

Striker crept as close to the camp of the enemy as he dared. Again, they were camped around a small fire. They knew that they were still in the country of the Real People, and they were still being cautious. He wanted to get a better look at these invaders to see if he could determine just who they were. And if he could get close enough, he thought, he might even be able to hear them speak. He knew the languages of a few of the neighbors of the Real People well enough to get along, and there were others he could identify by the sound.

He moved forward on his belly, slowly, gliding almost like a snake, careful to keep himself pressed tight to the ground and out of sight, careful to make no noise which might alert the enemy to his presence. At last, as close as he dared to go, he could see them clearly in the light of their small fire, and he could hear their voices. But it did him no good. No good at all.

If anything, he was more frustrated than before, for he could hear them speaking, but he did not understand the language, and he could see the features of the men, but he did not recognize them from their hair styles, their clothing or their markings.

He wondered then how far behind him Woyi might yet be and how many men would be coming along with him. It would be foolish for Striker to try anything by himself against seven men. He lay still, wondering just what he should do next, and then he heard the woman speak, and he understood her words, even though she was not speaking in the language of the Real People.

She was using the trade language, the jargon tongue which was widely used and understood.

"I'm hungry," she said. "Do you mean to starve me to death?"

"You'll get something soon enough," one of the men answered. Then he spoke to the other men in their own language. Striker listened carefully then, hoping that the man would speak to his captive again, or she to him, hoping to hear something more that he could understand, anything that would help him figure out what to do. It was a while before it happened, but eventually the man walked over to the woman and stepped around behind her.

"I'm going to untie your hands now just long enough so you can eat," he said. "Don't try to run away. You won't get far, and if you try, I won't untie your hands again. Not for any reason."

He loosed her hands and another man handed her a bowl. She took it without saying anything and ate. While they ate, the men conversed among themselves in their native tongue, unintelligible to Striker and ugly to his ear. They watched her closely all the while. As soon as she had finished her food, the man who had untied her hands, tied them once again.

"My people will come after you," she said. "You'll all be killed for this."

The man who spoke the trade language laughed and said something to his companions. They all laughed. Striker figured that he had translated her words for the others. He must be the only one who knows the trade language, Striker thought. Then he thought, if they found her threat humorous, they'll learn soon enough to take it seriously. Woyi and I and the others will teach them.

"If any of your men dare to follow us too far," the man said, "they'll find you with the Spaniards, and the Spaniards will kill them for us."

"You're taking me to the Spaniards?" she asked.

"Of course," said the man. "Do you think we would have any use for you? You Chalakee? No, but the Spaniards pay us well for slaves."

So that was it. Striker knew that the Spaniards had not been anywhere near the land of the Real People for several years. They were far to the south, in the land of the Calusas and the Timucuas and other places, but apparently they now had allies among the native people of this land. Allies who would actually hunt for slaves for them.

Striker felt a sudden intense hatred and disgust for these men. He himself would not sell a captive Creek or Delaware—or even Mohawk—to the hated Spaniards. He would not traffic in slaves or anything else with those monsters. Even these repulsive men—these . . . Slavecatchers—he would kill, but he would not capture one and sell him as a slave to the Spaniards.

He had started out determined to help this woman and to kill at least some of these invaders, to teach them the consequences of invading the country of the Real People, but this new knowledge made him the more resolute. A hard scowl came over his face. He kept quiet, and he lay still. He waited.

Eventually the Slavecatchers began to lie down around their fire to sleep. One stayed up to watch the captive. She sat up scowling at her guard for a while, but soon she, too, lay down. Then, to Striker's surprise, so did the final Slavecatcher. Striker waited a little longer to give them all time to fall asleep. Then he crept closer. No one stirred in the camp.

It was a dangerous idea, but, he thought, with all of the Slavecatchers asleep, he might be able to rescue the woman without waiting for Woyi and the others. He moved slowly, sometimes barely moving at all, but at last he had reached her side.

He noticed that the rope which bound her hands behind her back had one long, trailing end, and that the Slavecatcher who had gone to sleep last was lying on that end of the rope. Striker crept up very close to the woman. His heart was pounding, noisily he thought, in his chest. Slowly he reached out and put a hand gently over her mouth. She woke up with a start, but she made no noise.

Her eyes opened wide, and she looked right into those of Striker. She recognized him at once by his hair and by the markings on his face as one of the Real People. He took his hand away from her mouth and reached for his knife. Carefully he began slicing at the rope just below where it was wrapped around her wrists.

Then one of the Slavecatchers, the one farthest away from Striker and the woman, sat up. Striker stopped moving. He lay as still as he could. The Slavecatcher rubbed his eyes for a moment, and then he saw Striker. His face first registered surprise, but it very quickly changed to anger. He reached for his war club and shouted something out as he rose rapidly to his feet. He rushed toward Striker, a heavy, ballheaded war club brandished over his head, as his companions, startled from their sleep, groped for their own weapons.

Before any of them had a chance to get up, the first one was almost on Striker, and he was beginning the downward swing of his club. Striker ducked low and made a quick jab with his knife, plunging it deep into the belly of his attacker. He felt the warm gush of blood over his hand and forearm as he twisted the sharp, flint knife and pulled it free.

With an agonized groan, the Slavecatcher fell forward. Striker moved aside to avoid the falling body. He looked frantically toward the woman, but the remaining six Slavecatchers were coming at him fast. He couldn't fight them all. He didn't have time to worry about the woman. He would have to leave her. He turned and ran into the darkness of the night.

Behind him, the woman scrambled desperately to her feet as fast as she could, but the man who had been sleeping on the rope end grabbed it with both hands and gave it a hard jerk. She fell back to the ground with a thud. Two of the men ran after Striker, but they didn't run far. It was too dark. They turned and went back to their fire where the six men had a frantic discussion in their own language.

Safely away, Striker chastised himself severely. He had failed in his attempt to rescue the woman. Had he made too much noise? Had he moved in too quickly, not allowing the Slavecatchers enough time to fall soundly asleep? He should have gotten her away from them, he told himself. He would not get another chance like that one. Surely, after what had happened, they would not be so foolish as to all go to sleep at the same time again, at least not until they were well out of the territory of the Real People. Ah well, he told himself, there had been seven. Now there were only six. When, he wondered, would Woyi and the others catch up with him?

Oliga was worried about the Howler and the others who had gone out in search of Striker and the unknown invaders. He had thought that they'd be back before dark on their first day out. There were only seven men, Woyi had said, and Woyi had known just where to find them. The Howler had taken a large force after them. There should not have been any problems.

Even if the enemy had moved out of their camp before the force arrived, Striker had been there to follow and to mark the trail. The Howler and the others should have caught up with them, killed them, and been home by now, Olig' told himself. He asked himself if he had, after all, been wise to trust the mission to the leadership of someone else. It was not that he did not have faith in the ability of the Howler. Of course he did. It was only that he, Olig', was the one who was ultimately responsible for all their lives and safety. It was as if he had put a burden on the shoulders of someone else, when by right, it should have been his own.

The travelers were camped for the night, and in the light of their small fire, Tsiwon' could see the worry in her husband's face. She moved over to sit close by his side and put an arm around his shoulders.

"Don't worry about them," she said.

Olig' looked at his wife with some surprise.

"Have you been listening to my thoughts?" he asked her.

She smiled.

"I can tell what you're thinking," she said. "They'll be all right. It's just taking them a little longer than we expected. That's all."

"You're right," he said, "of course."

Comes Back to Life came walking over to their fire to join them just then.

"Sit with us," Olig' said, and Comes Back to Life sat down. "Will you have some food?"

"Just a little," said Comes Back to Life. "Guwisti fed me well tonight."

Tsiwon' dipped into the pot beside the fire and handed him a bowl of soup made from dried corn. He drank from the bowl.

"It's good," he said, and he finished it off, then set the bowl aside.

"Things are going well," he said. "Everyone in our camp is well fed. We're traveling well. I think our journey will be a successful one."

"My husband is worried about the ones who went after the invaders," said Tsiwon'.

Olig' looked briefly into the face of Comes Back to Life.

"Was I wrong," he said, "to let the Howler lead them in my place?"

"My friend," said Comes Back to Life, "Woyi saw only seven men. The Howler is leading men enough to take care of twice that number easily. If they're not back yet, that means the others are running from them. That's all. Unless—"

"What?" said Oliga.

"Unless there are more than the seven Woyi saw. If that's the case, then we could be in danger here, and that's all the more reason you should be with us. You were right to let the Howler go."

"There are only two Real People," said Olig'. "Woyi and the Howler. The rest are Senikas and white men. Can we trust them?"

"I think we can," said Comes Back to Life. "These Frenchmen have fought with us against our enemies before. Their friendship has been tried."

"And the Senikas?"

"They're friends of the Frenchmen, too, and I think that our new peace with them is good. Even if they planned to turn on us, they'd have the French to deal with."

Olig' nodded and muttered a feeble agreement. The assuring arguments of Comes Back to Life and his wife were good ones. Still he worried. Perhaps that was part of what it meant to be War Chief, he decided: to worry.

Comes Back to Life looked across the way toward his own small fire. No one was there. He looked toward the fire of Osa, and there he saw his wife, the little boy in her arms. Across the fire from her, Osa sat, holding the girl. It had become a familiar sight. Comes Back to Life, newly wed, had found himself with two women to support and two babies. But then, he thought, he, like Oliga, was really responsible for all.

The Slavecatchers, with their captive, were up and moving early the next morning. The Sun had only just begun to light up the far eastern horizon. Striker placed some rocks to mark the trail to their campsite. Then he placed some more on the other side of the camp to mark the direction of their travel. Staying a safe distance behind, he followed.

He noticed that they were moving east then, moving into and through the woods. And a little later, they had turned southeast. Of course, he thought, they're headed toward the Spaniards. Or at least, they're headed toward their own home, which must be somewhere near the Spaniards. They're allies; they must live somewhere close to them.

· The Slavecatchers were moving fast. They had lost a man to one of the Real People, a man alone who had managed to sneak into their camp. They had been careless, cocky. It would not happen again. They would hurry out of the territory of the Real People as fast as they could go. If they should have to sleep another night before reaching the border, they would almost certainly post a guard.

They had no way of knowing if there were other men with the one who had killed their companion, if they might suddenly be overwhelmed by a larger force. They hurried on their way.

The woman knew all this. She could tell by the looks on their faces and by the tension in their voices as they talked with each other. She could tell by the way they rushed their pace. She also knew that the man who had tried to rescue her would try again.

He was one of her own people, a Real Person, and he knew of her trouble. He had failed in his first attempt, but he would not give up. He would be back. The next time she would be watching and ready to help.

40

ere," said the Howler. "Here they left the road. Look."

There were three stones left by Striker, but even without them, it was obvious that someone had moved into the woods. The brush was freshly trampled down, ground cover was disturbed. The signs were unmistakable, even though a wide path had been there before.

"I'm going on ahead," said Woyi, and this time the Howler did not even bother to answer the rash young man.

The Howler watched as Woyi ran down the path into the cool, dark forest. He'll be all right, he told himself. He'll come upon his friend before he encounters the enemy, unless the enemy have already killed or captured the Striker. The Howler turned around toward the Frenchmen and the Senikas behind him. "Let's go," he said.

The going was slower through the woods, even with the path there. The Howler noticed right away that winding their way through thick trees and brush, there wasn't really much, if any, advantage in having the *sogwilis*. The big animals would be useful in traveling fast or in fighting only in open spaces. In this kind of terrain, their major use would be as pack animals. He wondered if he should have had his party abandon the beasts back at the road, but they were already moving along the forest path. He kept his thought to himself.

The Sun was high in the sky, just about ready to stop for her daily visit at her daughter's house directly overhead, when Woyi came across the site of the last camp of the invaders. He looked around carefully for any sign. The ashes from the fire were cold. They probably abandoned this place early in the morning, he thought. Then he saw the dark spot on the ground. He squatted beside it and felt it with his fingers. It was blood. Was it animal or human blood? He couldn't be sure. And if it was human blood, then whose blood was it?

He felt a panic rise up within him. Striker could not have fought all seven by himself and survived. But if they had killed Striker, where was the body? He tried to settle his thoughts. He needed to be calm and search the area. He looked around. If the strangers had killed a deer or something else to eat, there should be some indication other than a spot of blood. A carcass or some bones at least. There were none.

He looked further. There were footprints around the campsite, but none he could identify. They told him nothing more than what he already knew. He stood and turned around slowly, examining the area around the campsite. The woods were thick on either side of the path.

He was facing back the direction from which he had come, back toward the road, and off to his right he noticed two marks on the ground. He went for a closer look. Something had been dragged along here, he decided, and on into the woods.

Following the marks on the ground, he noticed that the brush had been disturbed. The marks on the ground disappeared as they went on into the tangle of the forest floor, but he moved on into the woods in the direction they had indicated. The ground rose sharply just ahead. Large sharp rocks formed a wall. He moved closer.

There were cracks and niches in the rock formation, and Woyi traced a line from the drag marks he had seen to the rocks. There was a dark recess, wide enough for a man to get inside. He moved cautiously toward it. To his left, on the ground, a blacksnake slithered quickly away, rustling the grass and fallen leaves. Woyi flinched at the sudden sound, saw the disappearing snake, took a deep breath and moved ahead.

Standing at the edge of the dark recess, he put a hand on the cold rock wall and leaned forward, peering into the darkness, squinting his eyes.

It took a moment for his eyes to make the adjustment, but then he saw the body. In the dark crevasse, it was little more to Woyi than a shape stretched out there on the ground. Whoever it had been, the burial had been hasty and perfunctory.

Woyi's heart pounded in his chest. He wanted to know who the body had belonged to. He tried not to let his mind tell him that it could be that of Striker. He fought to keep that thought away. Something told him to go inside and get a closer look, but the closeness and the dankness of the cell repelled him. He felt completely useless, alone and frightened.

Then he heard the sound of horses' hoofs approaching, and he turned and ran back to the clearing where the camp had been. The Howler rode up close and reined in his mount. The others were close behind him.

"They were here," said Woyi, "and someone was killed. There's blood, and through there I found a body. I don't know who it is. It's in a cave."

Tournier had ridden up beside the Howler to hear what Woyi had to say. He looked toward the woods in the direction Woyi had indicated.

"Well," he said, "let's drag it out and see."

He glanced at the Howler whose only response was a quick nod. Tournier swung a leg over the back of his horse and dropped to the ground.

"Étienne," he said, speaking in his own language, "come with me."

Another Frenchman dismounted and followed Tournier. Woyi moved along behind them, and when they could see the rock wall, he pointed.

"Right in there," he said.

Étienne moved on ahead and squeezed himself into the crevasse. In another instant, he was backing out, bent over, dragging something. He backed out a few more steps, and Woyi could see that he was pulling the body by its ankles. Woyi moved closer to get a better look. Then he turned, a wide smile on his face, and he ran back out to the clearing.

"It's one of the strangers," he shouted. "Striker has killed one of them."

Étienne came dragging the body out for all to see.

"Who is he?" asked Tournier, looking at the Howler and then at Owl. "From what tribe? I mean."

Owl only shrugged. The Howler looked more closely.

"I don't know for sure," he said, "but I would guess that he comes from south and east of here, from the coast near the big water."

Tournier knelt beside the body and hooked a finger under the leather belt which was around the dead man's waist. He pulled it away from the body, lifting up the silver buckle.

"I think you're right, my friend," he said. "See this? It's Espagnol—Asquani. He's either killed a Spaniard or he's been trading with them."

Suddenly Woyi dropped to his knees beside the body. He pulled out his knife and plunged it into first one eye socket and then the other. The Frenchmen watched in amazement, but neither the Howler nor the Senikas seemed to think there was anything unusual in the action. Tournier was about to say something, about to ask a question, when Woyi spoke, seemingly to the corpse on the ground.

"If you should come across my friend someday in the Darkening Land," he said, "you won't see him. You won't know who is there."

The Slavecatchers kept up their fast pace all through that day, not even stopping to eat. When it got too dark to travel anymore, they stopped to rest, but they did not build a fire. They ate cold food, and two of them stayed awake all through the night. They started out early again the next morning.

The woman watched almost constantly for any sign of the return of the man who had tried to rescue her, but she knew, of course, that her captors were doing the same. She also knew that if anything was to be done, it would be best to have it done that day. By nightfall, they would be outside the lands of the Real People.

Striker continued to follow the party of Slavecatchers. He kept back far enough so that they did not see him, but not so far as to lose sight of them. It was a tricky business, but he managed it. He had to move as fast as they were moving, but he also had to be careful to avoid rushing up on them without meaning to. When he could, he kept to higher ground than they, to give him a longer view.

He did not know what he would do. He knew that he could not simply attack them. He was not afraid of them, not even all six at once, for he was not afraid to die. But his death at the hands of the vile Slavecatchers would accomplish nothing. It would certainly not save the woman, and that was his main purpose.

He watched behind his back, hoping to see some sign of Woyi with help coming up from the rear. So far he had seen no such sign. But he continued to mark his trail to help them along the way. He knew that Woyi was back there somewhere. Woyi would not abandon him.

But he did wish that Woyi and whoever might be with him would hurry along, for he knew that they were fast approaching the frontier. If they did not manage to dispatch these Slavecatchers soon, they would be in the lands of the Saras and Catawbas. It would not be impossible to save the woman after that, but it would be much more difficult. He wasn't even at all sure just what the current relationship was between his own people and the Saras or the Catawbas. The Real People in the eastern border towns would know.

That last thought suddenly lifted his spirits just a bit. Approaching the frontier had its disadvantage for the Slavecatchers, too, especially if the Wolf People there were as diligent about guarding the frontiers of the Real People as they were around Kituwah. The Slavecatchers had managed somehow to slip past the Wolves coming. Would they be so lucky trying to get out again?

The Slavecatchers were also well aware of the contradictory nature of reaching the frontier. They were anxious to get out of the Real People's land, but they knew that the frontiers were well watched. In fact, their earlier cockiness had resulted, at least partly, from the knowledge that they had managed to elude the border guards.

They had hoped to make the crossing in daylight, but the timing did not work to their advantage. When they had at last reached the area known as the frontier, the vague area between the lands of the Real People and the lands of the Saras, the Sun was low in the western sky. They would have to stop for the night.

Though she could not understand their strange language, the woman could tell that they were arguing among themselves. She guessed that they were arguing over the best way to approach their difficult situation. Would they be wise to attempt to elude the Wolves at night under the cover of darkness? The darkness would cover the Wolves as well as they. Or should they wait for the morning light? They would then be able to see any Wolves, but again the reverse would be true.

At last it became apparent that the ones who argued for waiting until morning had won the debate. They settled in for the night. Again they did not build a fire, not even a small one. Again they ate cold trail food. Again they did not all sleep at once. Someone stayed awake to watch.

The woman did not sleep that night. She stayed awake to watch, thinking that the man might show up again and wanting to be ready to help him in any way she could. She tried to remember his face from the one time she had seen it. She had seen it close, but it had been dark. Even the small fire had burned down low, and, of course, the situation had been tense and things had happened fast.

Still, she thought, she had seen enough to know that it had been a young and handsome face. And she knew that it belonged to a brave and good man, a young man who had risked his own life for her sake. She was anxious to see that face again.

She tried to analyze her feelings. Of course, she was anxious to be rescued from these vile men, and he seemed to be the best chance that she had of that. She knew that explained her feeling for the man to some degree. But there was more, she thought. There was that face. She knew that he would be warm and kind. She knew that he— Well, she knew that she wanted to know him better.

Thinking such thoughts in her present situation made her feel a bit foolish, and she forced herself to concentrate on her surroundings. She would have to be ready for him if he came. She would have to do what she could to help. If nothing else, she could jump up and run when the other men stood up to face him.

Of course, she wasn't at all sure that he would confront the men as directly as all that. It wouldn't make sense for him to do so. Still, she needed to remain alert. Anything could happen.

They were, after all, in the frontier. There should be Wolves nearby, even a border town of Real People. Help could come from either one of those. She waited, and she watched, and the Sun peeked out from under the eastern edge of the Sky Vault, and it was another day.

41

They were up early, and they rushed her on. One of the men went out ahead of the others. He was moving fast, but he was also stealthy. They knew that the border was well guarded, and they would have to sneak out carefully, or they would have to fight. They also suspected that they were being pursued.

She lost sight of the man who had gone ahead to scout, but she kept looking back over her shoulder for some sign of the Real Person who had tried to rescue her. The man behind kept pushing her. She stumbled and fell, and he grabbed her and pulled her to her feet. He pushed her and said something she could not understand, probably telling her to hurry along. She did, but she realized that she could slow them down by stumbling, by falling occasionally.

A little later she fell again, this time deliberately. The man again pulled her to her feet. He struck her across the back with his arm and spoke to her angrily and threateningly. Then he shoved her again. She moved forward.

Just about then the scout reappeared. He was grinning broadly, and he was holding something bloody in his left hand. He spoke to the others, and they rushed ahead to join him. As they moved closer, she could see that he was displaying a freshly taken scalp. She could tell what it was, though she had never seen one before.

Her captors engaged in a hurried conversation, and then they started moving again. In a little while they came across a body. She recognized it as a man of the Real People, and she saw where the grisly trophy had come from. She imagined that the man had been one of the Wolves who guarded the borders. They rushed past the body.

She was sorry for the death of the man, even though she did not recognize him. He was one of her own people, and his death meant that her captors might be able to slip past the Wolves. She was glad, though, to find out that it had not been the other man, the one who had tried to save her, that the scout had killed. They hurried on.

Striker knew that he was not far behind the hateful Slavecatchers, even though he did not have them in sight. They were moving fast, not taking time to cover their tracks. He figured that they were probably in a hurry to get out of the country of the Real People. He was hoping that the Wolves would slow them down, even capture or kill them. Thus far, he had seen no sign of Woyi coming along behind him.

He was certain that he left marks clear enough for Woyi and the others to follow, but the Slavecatchers had moved away from their first camp soon after Woyi had left to go for help, and they had been moving at a brisk pace. He knew that Woyi was coming. He wished that his friend would hurry.

He decided that it was time to rush forward and get his prey in sight again, but just as he topped a rise, he saw his path blocked by four angry-looking men. His heart skipped a beat before he recognized them as Real People. Wolf People, he thought.

" *'Siyo,* " he said. "I'm known as the Striker. I'm a Deer Person originally from Stikoyi, but I and some others, from Stikoyi and Kituwah, are going north to build a new town near Coyatee. There where some Shawnees had built a town in our country."

The faces remained stern, but one of the men spoke to Striker.

"Yes," he said. "We heard about that Shawnee town, but if you're going to that place, what are you doing here?"

"My friend Woyi and I were scouting ahead of the others. We came across some strangers at a camp. They had captured one of our women. He went back for help, and I stayed to watch. The strangers left, and I've been following them, marking my trail for my friend to follow."

"And you followed these strangers here?" asked the Wolf.

"Yes. I think they're not far ahead."

The four men seemed to relax a little then, and the one who had spoken to Striker stepped forward, extending his hand in friendship. Striker took it.

"I'm called the Wild Man," he said. "These are Traveler, Go-Ahead and

Tobacco Stem. We're all Wolf People from Itowah, a town near here. We came up here to relieve one of our guards, and we found him killed."

"Ah," Striker groaned at the news. "It must have been the ones I'm following."

"It would seem so," said Wild Man. "How many are they?"

"There were seven," said Striker, "but I killed one of them, so there are six."

"Do you know who these invaders are?"

"I heard one of them speaking to the captive woman in the trade language," said Striker. "They're Slavecatchers, trading with the Ani-'Squan'. When they spoke among themselves, I couldn't understand their language. Well, I'll be going. I don't want to lose their trail."

"Wait," said Wild Man. "Go back to Itowah with us. We'll give you something to eat, and then some men from Itowah will join you in hunting down these Slavecatchers."

"I think that I should keep going," said Striker.

"You can't fight six," Wild Man protested.

"But I can do what I've been doing. I can keep them in sight and mark the trail. My friend Woyi should be coming along soon with others. Tell him what's happened here and where I've gone."

"We'll watch for him, and we'll tell him," said Wild Man. "We would join you now, but we can't leave this place unguarded, and we have the body of our friend to take back home. Some of us will join your friends, though, and we'll come after you."

Striker hurried ahead. He knew that he was still on their trail, but he wanted to get them in sight again. He would have to be careful, though, for he was coming down out of the mountains and moving onto plains. It would be more difficult to get close to them without being seen.

A wide stream ran down from the mountains and out onto the broad plain, and much of the stream seemed to be lined with trees. Striker decided to follow the stream. That was most likely what the others were doing anyhow, he thought. The trail he was following led right down onto the open plain at first, but then it veered toward the trees and vanished.

They had finally taken the time to cover their tracks, but, he said to himself, it was too late. He knew where they were headed. He ran toward the trees. He felt vulnerable on the flat land out in the open. All his life had been spent in mountains and forests.

It was better in the trees beside the stream. He relaxed a little. He stood quietly for a long moment listening, and he heard nothing but the sounds of the stream and of the small, narrow patch of woods which ran along its banks, of birds and squirrels.

He moved ahead cautiously, watching for any sign of the Slavecatchers. He noticed a broken branch on a clump of brush, and he wondered if the woman had managed to do that to mark the trail for him. It seemed likely, but he couldn't be sure. He kept going.

When at last the Sun crawled out from under the western edge of the Sky Vault, and the world was lit only by the Moon and the Stars, Striker had to admit that another day was gone, and he had not caught up with the Slavecatchers, nor had Woyi caught up with him. He was still alone.

He was alone, pursuing six Slavecatchers, and they had left the land of the Real People. Striker wasn't sure, but he thought that they were in the country of the Sara People. He wondered what would happen should he encounter any Saras. Then he wondered if the Slavecatchers themselves were Sara or friends of the Sara. If so, his task would get much more difficult if he failed to conclude it soon.

He moved on in spite of the darkness, hoping that the Slavecatchers had stopped for the night. But he moved very slowly in order to stay quiet. The light from the Sun's brother, Moon, helped him watch where he was stepping, and the lazy lapping of the water of the stream helped cover sounds at least a little.

Then he thought he saw a faint glow up ahead, a light in the woods or on the water. He couldn't tell. He continued forward, watching the light. The stream wound around, and after he had negotiated the curve, he saw that the light was coming from a small campfire not too far ahead. He had found them.

At the campsite, one of the men was leering at her. They were much more relaxed than they had been at any time since the attempt at her rescue. She knew that they had left her country, and she was pretty sure, from their actions and their attitudes, that they knew it too.

They had built their first fire also since that time, and they had cooked their food. They were all well fed. They had even fed her well. She had thought that they would sleep, but she had been wrong. The six men were all still sitting up around the fire. They were talking among themselves in the strange language that she could not understand.

Now the one man was leering at her, and he was rubbing himself in an unmistakable way. She knew what he was thinking about. So far they had not bothered her in that way, and she had begun to think that they would not.

Now she could tell that at least one of the men was giving it serious consideration.

She tried to decide what she would do. Her first impulse was to fight with him if he tried to touch her, but then, she knew, the others would come to his aid. Besides, she wouldn't be able to fight effectively with her hands tied behind her back. She could kick until they managed to overcome her. But the end would be the same. Still, she couldn't stomach the thought of giving in willingly to any of these men.

Then the one who had been leering at her spoke to the others. They all looked at her then. Some of them smiled. They all leered. One chuckled, and then they all laughed. She saw one shrug as if to say, "Why not?" Then the man started walking toward her. Two other men got to their feet. She saw them walk around behind her, and she fought off an impulse to turn to face them, for the other, the original leering man, was still in front, still walking toward her.

She decided to get to her feet so that she could at least give him a few swift kicks, but just as she tried to rise, she felt hands grab her from behind and pull her onto her back. Struggling on her back, she looked up into two grinning, laughing faces.

The other man moved closer, and she kicked at him. He jumped aside, avoiding the blow, laughed, and said something to the two men still sitting by the fire. They got up and walked over to join in the action.

One of them knelt beside her. Grabbing her skirt, he pulled it up over her waist. She kicked and twisted, and they all laughed. Then they grabbed hold of her legs, one man on each side of her, and they pulled her legs apart, holding tight. Still she struggled.

The man in front of her now stopped still and looked down at her. He was no longer smiling. He unfastened the thong that held his breechcloth in place and let it fall to the ground, revealing himself in all his lust.

She made a noise of disgust and wrenched herself violently in one last futile attempt to escape. The men holding her down and holding her legs apart laughed. The other man did not laugh. He stepped in close standing between her legs. He dropped down to one knee.

Then the night air was shattered by a loud and shrill cry like the sound of the turkey, and out of the darkness came a rush. Before the Slavecatchers had time to react, Striker swung his war club with all his strength, and his aim was true. The stone head of the club buried itself in the brains of the would-be rapist and he fell back dead. The other five Slavecatchers ran for their weapons.

"Get up and run," Striker shouted. "Run back the way we came. My friends are coming!"

As she struggled to her feet, he placed himself between her and the five Slavecatchers. They had their weapons, and they spread out in a line to face him. Seeing the position he was in, the woman hesitated.

"Run," he said. She ran into the night. Striker's war club was still stuck in the head of its latest victim. He pulled out his flint knife and braced himself for the attack. He told himself that he would soon be dead.

Three men came straight toward him, while the two on the opposite ends of the line moved farther out and began to circle around him. If he turned to face either of them, the other four would be at his back. Then the three in front ran toward him. He struck out with his knife, but they jumped back. He could no longer see the two who had circled around him. Then he felt a hard blow to the back of his head, and he felt himself falling, and then he knew no more.

42

Woyi was the first of his contingent to reach the guarded mountain pass, and therefore the first to encounter Wild Man and the other Wolves. When he saw them, he jumped down off the back of his *sogwili* and walked forward to meet them. They were expecting him, but the horse was a surprise to Wild Man.

"I didn't know that any of the Real People had those animals," he said.

"We got them from the white men called 'French,'" said Woyi, dismounting. "We have several *sogwilis*, and we have even used them in battle once."

"Where are the others in your party?" Wild Man asked, still looking at the horse in amazement. "We were told that there would be more."

"They're coming along behind me," said Woyi, slightly puzzled. This man seemed to know all about what Woyi and the others were doing. "Not far. Our leader is the Howler."

"Ah, yes, I know of him," said Wild Man. "He's a Wolf, and a good man. I met him once. It's been a long time, though."

"But—have you seen my friend Striker, then?" asked Woyi. "Is that how you know all about this?"

"Yes. We talked with him when he came through here."

"Is he all right?"

"Yes. He seemed well and strong. He was in a hurry to get on his way."

"How far ahead is he?"

"You should be able to catch up with him in a day, maybe less, riding on that beast."

"Did you see the strangers that he's following?"

Wild Man frowned, shook his head and looked at the ground.

"We talked with Striker yesterday," he said. "He went on alone to continue marking the trail. He told us that the men he's following are Slavecatchers for the Ani-'Squan'. He couldn't understand their language, though. These Slavecatchers killed one of our guards right here at this spot and then got out of our country. We never saw them. When the rest of your party arrives, I'll take all of you into Itowah. Then maybe some of our men will join you in chasing down these Slavecatchers. We need to even things for the one they killed here."

But when the Howler arrived with the rest of the men shortly thereafter, the situation suddenly grew tense. No one had prepared Wild Man and his companion guardians of the pass for the presence of a large number of mounted Senikas and white men. He was unaware of the recent events at Kituwah and knew only that the charge to his clan was to keep out all foreigners, and the sting of their recent failure with the Slavecatchers was still fresh and rankling.

Woyi and the Howler had to talk long and hard to explain to these Wolves from Itowah how the two groups of foreigners came to be with them inside the country of the Real People.

"We had a council there at Kituwah," said the Howler. "It was called by Trotting Wolf, and at his urging, everyone agreed to make an exception to our rule for these people. The Frenchmen are not like the Spaniards, and they have become our friends. They went from us to the Ani-Senika and back again to make this new peace. When we heard from Woyi about these invaders, they agreed to help us run them down."

Wild Man frowned and rubbed his chin. He had never heard much good about Senikas before, and he had never heard anything good about white men. He had heard rumors that there were different tribes of white men, but this talk of Frenchmen was the first confirmation he had of those rumors.

"Well," he said at last, "I know Trotting Wolf. He is loved and respected throughout our country. Still, I'll have to go into Itowah first and ask in council if these men may come into our town."

"Of course," said the Howler.

"That will take too much time," said Woyi. "I don't want to go into Itowah anyway. The Slavecatchers are getting farther ahead of us while we stand here talking, and my friend is out there following them alone."

"These men we're leading need some food and rest," said the Howler. "So do the *sogwilis*. I say we should wait for Wild Man to seek permission for us to take the Senikas and the Frenchmen into Itowah."

"Then you wait with them," Woyi said. "I'm going on."

He did not wait for any response from the Howler or from Wild Man. He jumped onto the back of his *sogwili* and headed down the mountainside toward the plains below. Wild Man watched him for a moment, then turned back toward the Howler.

"This Woyi is a rash young man," he said.

"He and Striker exchanged clothing in the Making of Friends Ceremony," said the Howler.

"Ah," said Wild Man. "I see."

The Sun had just reached her daughter's house high overhead, and Woyi had gotten well out on the flat grassland when he saw the woman coming toward him from the trees that lined the stream off to his left, to the north. She hesitated, as if she were uncertain of his identity or his trustworthiness. Of course, he thought. My *sogwili*. Quickly he dismounted and took a few steps toward her.

" 'Siyo," he called to her. "You're the woman who was captured by the Slavecatchers."

She walked toward him on tired, unsteady legs, still a little uncertain, and he could see that her arms were tied behind her back. He started to speak, but she called out to him first.

"Are you one of those who's been following us?" she asked.

"Yes."

Again she started walking toward him. This time he walked, too, to meet her halfway.

"My friend and I saw you at the camp of those Slavecatchers. We were alone, just two of us, so he stayed to watch while I went for help. We've been trying to catch up with him and with you ever since."

While he talked, Woyi untied the woman's arms. Free at last, she rubbed her wrists and hands.

"He said that you were coming," she said.

"Striker?"

"I don't know his name. He came into the camp one night and tried to cut me loose, but they woke up. He killed one of them before he had to run. Then he came again. Last night. He rushed into the camp and killed another one and yelled at me to run. He said, 'My friends are coming!' I ran."

"What happened to Striker?" Woyi asked, desperation in his voice.

"I don't know. I ran. He told me to run, and I did. He was there in the camp with five of them."

Woyi turned as if to follow Striker. He turned back to the woman. He didn't know what to do. Striker had put himself in danger to save this woman, and Woyi couldn't abandon her now. But Striker might be in serious trouble. The woman had left him facing five Slavecatchers alone. They might have captured him, or even killed him by this time.

"I—I—" he stammered. "Are you all right?"

"I'm tired and hungry," she said, "but I'm all right."

"I'm Woyi," he said, "of the Bird People of Stikoyi."

"I'm called Awiakta. I'm a Deer Person from Nikutsegi. What will we do now about your friend? Striker?"

"Yes. Striker," said Woyi. "I don't know. If he was here to tell me what to do, I think that he'd tell me first to see that you're safe, and only then to come after him."

"I'm safe now," said Awiakta. "And I can help you fight those men. Three against five is not so bad. Let's go after them and help him if we can."

Woyi thought for a moment. She was young, and she looked strong. He didn't want to waste time by going back to the others or to Itowah.

"All right," he said. "My *sogwili* can carry two. But first, let's get something to eat and let you rest a little."

When Striker came to his senses, his head was throbbing from the blow he had suffered. He groaned and started to sit up, and then he realized that his hands were bound behind his back. Then he looked up and around. He was still at the campsite where he had attacked the Slavecatchers to save the woman. The five remaining Slavecatchers still sat around their small fire.

They were talking among themselves, and again he heard the strange language. It was unlike any he had ever heard before. And there was something else strange about these men, something about their appearance. They did not seem to be all of the same people. Each had his own distinctive style of dress, hair and markings on his body. Who, he wondered, are these Slavecatchers?

And why did they not kill me? And the answer came to him almost as quickly as his mind had formed the question. Of course—they meant to sell him as a slave to the Spaniards. They had lost the woman, but they had captured him.

Casually he wondered whether a man or a woman was worth more to the Spaniards. Had these Slavecatchers come out ahead by taking him in place of the woman they lost? He put the question out of his mind. But what would life be like as a slave to the Spaniards? He decided that he would not suffer it in any case. Woyi would come along soon with help.

Even without the appearance of Woyi and the others, he would look for his chance to escape from these wretched men. Even if he were to get himself killed in the attempt, he thought, that would be preferable to life as a slave to the hated Spaniards. He groaned again, and one of the Slavecatchers turned to look at him. It was the man he had overheard before talking to the woman in the trade language. The man stood up and walked over close to Striker.

"Was it worth it?" he asked, speaking the jargon. "To rescue the woman?"

Striker didn't answer, but he thought that, yes, it was worth it to get a woman of the Real People out of the hands of such as these.

"Do you speak the trade language?" the man asked.

"Yes," said Striker. "I speak it."

"You rescued the woman," the Slavecatcher said, "but now we have you, and soon you'll be sold to the Spaniards as a slave. That's your reward for your boldness. You're a fool. You and all you Chalakees. We got in and out of your country easily enough. Right under the noses of your guards. We killed one of them."

"And I killed two of you," said Striker.

"Yes," said the Slavecatcher, "and look where you are now."

He put a foot on Striker's chest and shoved him back to the ground, laughed and turned to walk back over to the fire to rejoin his companions. They talked with each other briefly. Then they all stood up. The jargon speaker looked back toward Striker.

"Get up on your feet," he said. "We're leaving."

Striker struggled to his feet with a groan.

"Where are we going?" he asked.

"You'll find out soon enough," said the Slavecatcher. "And you won't like it, either."

Tsiwon' was walking beside her husband and Comes Back to Life at the head of the column of migrating Real People when Coyatee first came into their sight.

"We're here," she said. "There's my town."

"Yes," said Olig'. He glanced toward Comes Back to Life. "And not far from here is the site of New Town. We'll stop here first, and let the people here know that we've arrived."

"They'll feed us, too," said Tsiwon', "and we can all rest here before we go on to the site of New Town. Probably some of the people will even go with us and help to build the town."

"Look," said Comes Back to Life, "someone's coming out of Coyatee."

"It's my father," said Tsiwon', and she ran ahead to meet him. Olig' looked at Comes Back to Life and smiled.

"Let's go meet my father-in-law," he said.

The people of Coyatee put on a great feast to welcome their migrating kinsmen from Kituwah and Stikoyi. They had, of course, known of the plans to build New Town, and so they had been anticipating the arrival of the people who would be the inhabitants of that town.

Just as Tsiwon' had predicted, several of the residents of Coyatee right away announced their intentions to help build New Town. They boasted to the travelers of the bravery and prowess of their new War Chief Oliga, for, they said, they had seen him in action against the Shawnees. They knew that Olig' and his followers would be valuable neighbors, and they were certainly welcome.

The travelers were happy and relieved to be so near the end of their journey, and the people of Coyatee seemed just as happy to have them there. The only thing to keep the situation from being completely joyous was the knowledge that Woyi and the Howler, accompanied by the Senikas and the Frenchmen, were out on a mission to catch up with the Striker, chase down some intruders and rescue a woman of the Real People.

Of course, Oliga told the tale to the people in Coyatee. He told them how Woyi and Striker had been scouting ahead and how Woyi had returned with the news, leaving Striker to follow the invaders. He told them how the Howler had been selected to lead a party in pursuit and explained how the party came to be made up of almost all Senikas and Frenchmen.

The thing that was worrying Oliga and others was the fact that the Howler and the others had been gone for so long. They had expected a quick and easy operation. Woyi had reported seven strangers with a captive. The woman should have been rescued and the strangers killed or captured easily, and it should not have taken so long.

"Who were these strangers?" someone asked.

"Striker and Woyi did not recognize them," said Oliga. "We don't know who they are."

The discussion continued far into the night. Some of the people of both groups wanted to go after Woyi and the others and help to teach the strangers, whoever they might be, a strong lesson. But Oliga overruled that suggestion with reason.

"We don't know where they are," he said. "We don't even know which direction to take. We'll just have to wait to find out what has happened out there."

At last, everyone settled down for the night, either as guests in the homes of clan relatives or in the Coyatee townhouse. Whirlwind screamed in the townhouse while poor Osa tried to manage both her and her brother, until Guwisti, having heard the clamor, came to the rescue.

Comes Back to Life followed his wife and watched as she took the Little Spaniard into her arms. Whirlwind stopped screaming at once and snuggled her little face into her mother's shoulder. But before she hid her face, Comes Back to Life noticed that her big, dark eyes were dry.

She wants her mother to herself, he thought, and she gets her way. She is a strange one. It will be interesting to watch her grow. He slept that night in the townhouse with Guwisti and the Little Spaniard and, very near, Osa and Whirlwind. There seemed to be no other way to sleep near his wife and to keep the little girl quiet at the same time. If Whirlwind was not kept quiet, it seemed, no one in all of Coyatee would sleep.

43

The hated Slavecatchers seemed to be in a hurry once again. One had gone ahead as scout, far enough ahead to be out of sight. Two of the remaining four led their small column along at a fast pace. Striker followed. Then the last two came along behind him. If he failed to move fast enough to suit them, the man directly behind him pushed, shoved or hit him, and barked out some unintelligible words. He moved on.

They had moved out of the trees in order to walk faster and were traveling along the edge of the woods just out on the prairie, so that it would be easy enough for them to duck back into the trees at any sign of trouble. The only trouble Striker could imagine for them was the arrival of Woyi and the others, and he was wondering what was taking them so long.

Of course, it would have taken Woyi some time to get back to the main group after he had left Striker there on the hillside watching the Slavecatchers' camp. Then Oliga would have had to decide what to do, who to send. There would probably have been a quick council with some discussion. That would have taken some time. By then the Slavecatchers had abandoned their camp-site, and Striker had been following them.

And, of course, Woyi and the others, even if they were riding *sogwilis*, would not be moving very fast. They would be looking for signs along the trail. Striker had done his best to make that task easier for them. Even so, it took time to watch for sign. Perhaps they had even stopped to talk with Wild Man and his Wolves back at the mountain pass. If they had gotten that far. He wondered if they were riding or walking.

Now that the Slavecatchers had moved out of the territory of the Real People, what would Oliga, or whoever might be leading the rescue party, decide to do? Would they keep going farther into the land of the Saras? He thought that they would. These Slavecatchers, after all, had killed a Wolf back at the pass. Some of the Wolves from Itowah would almost certainly join Woyi in his pursuit. But the land of the Saras?

That gave Striker a whole new line of thought. He didn't know if these Slavecatchers were themselves Sara, or if they were friendly with the Sara. Somehow he didn't think that they were all of the same people, but still they could be Sara allies, or one or more of them could be Sara. If that were the case, his situation was the more dangerous, and so was that of Woyi and anyone else who might be coming to the rescue.

If not, though, if these men were not Sara or Sara allies, then the Saras might attack them. Such a development could work either to the advantage or the disadvantage of Striker, and there could be danger to Woyi and the others with him once they entered the Sara country.

He had no idea what to expect. He should have questioned Wild Man about the Saras before charging into their country. He had been in too much of a hurry. He had been rash and foolish. Ah well, it was too late to worry about that. Still, he wished that he knew what the current relations between the Sara and the Real People of Itowah were like. They could be such as would turn the Real People back at the border.

The others might decide to turn back, Striker thought, but not Woyi. Woyi would never abandon him. He knew that. He glanced back over his shoulder to see if he could spot Woyi somewhere out on that vast and open prairie, but he saw nothing there. He did notice that the two men behind him were walking very close together.

He turned suddenly and rammed his shoulder hard into the chest of the man just behind him. That one in turn stumbled, crashing into his own companion, and both Slavecatchers fell back hard, the one landing on top of the other and knocking all the wind out of his lungs. The one on the bottom made only a *whuffing* sound, but the other screamed and shouted words unintelligible to Striker's ears.

The two up ahead turned to see what was the matter, but by that time Striker was running out across the open plain as hard as he could go. With his hands tied behind him, he was hampered in his running. Still he ran fast. The two men on the ground struggled to untangle themselves from each other and get to their feet, but the other two ran after Striker, shouting at him as they ran.

He had no idea how close behind him they were. Looking back over his shoulder would slow him down. He looked straight ahead, and he ran. He could hear the shouts behind him. He ran. His chest heaved as he sucked in great gulps of air, and his legs seemed to move with a will of their own. His feet seemed not to touch the ground. He ran, not on the ground, but over it. He ran for his freedom. He ran for his life.

Then he was conscious of at least one Slavecatcher close behind him. He could hear the feet slapping against the ground. He could hear the heavy breathing. He strained to run faster. He felt fingers touch the back of his neck, and he surged forward. The nails scratched his neck as the man tried in vain to get a grip on him. He ran on, but the other was still close behind.

Then he felt the hand again, and this time it moved around his throat. His pursuer managed to get an arm around his neck and jerk him violently to one side. Then he felt himself flying through the air. He landed hard on a shoulder and rolled, and as he tried to scramble back to his feet, he looked up, and he saw the other coming at him.

He was up on one knee when the Slavecatcher kicked him on the side of the head, and Striker was knocked back to the ground. The man kicked him again, this time in the side. Then another man was there, and he was kicking too. Striker rolled over, his face toward the ground, and drew his knees up under his chest. The kicks kept coming. He was certain that by this time all four men were there, all four were kicking and beating him. He could tell from the voices and from the number of kicks and blows that were raining over his body. Were they angry enough to kill him, in spite of his value to them as a commodity? Apparently they were not, for at last they stopped.

They pulled him roughly to his feet and shoved him back in the direction of the trees. He looked ahead, and he was amazed at the ground he had covered in so short a time. It had been a good run, but not good enough. If only his arms had been free, he thought—but they were not. They had caught him, and that was that.

He walked back toward the trees, his body aching from the run and from the beating, but the men pushing him along had run hard, too. They were not walking very fast. When he felt one of them give him a shove, he walked faster. He didn't think that they would try to slow him down, and so he walked faster.

It was a small bit of arrogance on his part, a little revenge, a tiny way to torment his captors. Would they admit, even to each other, that they could not keep up with him after having chased him down and beaten him? Would they want to appear to be more worn-out than he? He walked toward the trees at a lively pace, and they were forced to keep up with him.

In spite of his pain, in spite of the cuts and bruises to his body, he noticed with some joy that the four Slavecatchers were breathing harder than was he. By the time they reached the point where he had first broken out of their line, his own breathing was even again. Theirs was not. They still gasped for air. Their chests still alternately heaved and sank.

Between pants and gasps, they snarled ugly words at him, and now and then one of them reached out to strike him across the back. He held his head up and continued to walk at a steady pace. They were back beside the trees, walking as they had been before he made his attempt. Nothing had changed, except that he had slowed them down a little. He had tired them a little, and he had angered them. He told himself that it had been worth the beating.

Soon he saw the fifth man up ahead, the one who had gone forward alone as scout. He was standing in their path not far ahead, waiting for them to catch up. He was the one who spoke the jargon. When they were close enough together, the man said something to his companions. Even in the strange language, it sounded to Striker like a question.

The one walking just behind Striker, after a couple of pants and wheezes, shouted some angry words, apparently in response to the question, and gave Striker a blow on top of the head with his open hand. Then they came to a halt. The jargon-talker stepped up to Striker and looked him rudely in the face. His mouth twisted into an ugly grin.

"So you tried to get away," he said.

"Any man would try," said Striker, with a shrug.

"Perhaps," said the other, "until he's learned that it's no use."

He turned and walked into the trees again, and the others followed him, shoving Striker in that direction. They walked the short distance through the woods to the banks of the stream, and there they pulled aside some brush to reveal a dugout canoe, obviously hidden there by them before.

Striker's spirits fell at the sight. They would be able to move much faster by water than they had been doing by land. Since he had seen no sign of Woyi following them, he had decided that Woyi and the others were still some distance behind. This canoe would only increase that distance and make Striker's chances that much more grim. He wondered if his rescuers were coming on *sogwilis* or on foot. He hoped that they were coming. They might have lost his trail and turned back in despair.

And even if Woyi continued to follow alone, what would he be able to do, one man in this land of the Saras, against five men? What if these Slavecatchers should meet up with others of their kind before Woyi could track them down?

Was Woyi still coming, or was he back there somewhere wondering where the trail had gone? Since his capture, Striker had not been able to mark the trail as he had done before. It would not be so easy to follow, or to find again if it was once lost.

Then he remembered the woman. She was free, and if she had done as he had told her, she would be walking back toward the land of the Real People, back toward where Wild Man and his Wolves guarded the mountain pass. She would be able to tell them—Wild Man, Woyi, or whoever she might encounter back there—that the Slavecatchers were following the stream. She would be able to get them back on the right trail.

Two of the men shoved the heavy boat into the water, and two of them shoved Striker into the boat. Soon all five Slavecatchers were in, and the dugout was gliding swiftly through the water, headed east and a little south. The speed at which it moved depressed Striker. For the first time since Woyi left him at the boulders overlooking the Slavecatchers' camp, he felt really alone.

He no longer believed that even Woyi would find him. He decided that he would have to find his own way to escape from these men. He had tried it once and failed, but the attempt had been impulsive. The next time would be planned, carefully planned. He would not give up. He would not willingly or easily submit to being the slave of any man, and if the time ever came when he saw his captivity as an absolutely hopeless situation, one that there was no escaping, then he would die.

44

They began by sweeping the site of New Town absolutely clean of any remains of the intrusive Shawnee town that had been there before. That task alone took several days to accomplish. Next they marked the outlines of the townhouse, or council house, and the dance ground nearby. The council house would be the first building to go up, for it would provide shelter for everyone while their individual homes were under construction.

But even before work was begun on the council house, the dance ground was laid out and a new altar built. Using wood from the seven sacred trees, Comes Back to Life kindled a sacred fire there on the new altar from the fire he had brought from Kituwah and prayed for the success of New Town. Everyone, the residents of New Town and the helpers from Coyatee, stood around the dance ground and watched and listened.

That small ceremony done, Comes Back to Life announced that work on the townhouse could begin. Large trees had to be felled and trimmed for the logs that would form the seven-sided structure.

But not everyone would be involved in felling the trees and setting them in place and building the townhouse. Others would be gathering the poles necessary for the construction of the fence which would surround New Town, for, after all, it was a town which would exist primarily for defense of the border. The Shawnees who had been there had promised not to come back, but the Real People knew that the Shawnees of one town could not speak for those of another town, just as the Real People of Stikoyi could not speak for those of Kituwah or Coyatee—or New Town.

Defense was a primary concern, and so the wall would have to go up soon. One crew went into the woods to select and secure the necessary logs, long and straight and perhaps twice as big around as a man's arm, lots of logs, enough to form a solid stockade wall around the entire town. Because of the fairly recent presence of the Shawnees at this same site, the crew had to go farther into the woods in search of what they wanted.

Oliga, being War Chief and therefore being directly responsible for the safety of the town and everybody in it, was especially concerned with the building of the fence. He wanted it done quickly, and he wanted it done right.

Some of the women began to build homes, starting with two rows of saplings. They bent the saplings at the top, pulling them together to form the framework of the walls and the roof. Other women began to work on the gardens. Food crops would have to be planted as soon as possible, for the population of New Town would have to be fed. The people from Coyatee would help, but the New Town residents did not want to place too heavy a burden on their new neighbors. They didn't want to wear out their welcome before they had even settled in, and, of course, they wanted to become self-sufficient as soon as possible.

Others constructed *weirs*, fish traps, from river cane and placed the weirs in the river in strategic locations. They would soon have fish to eat and fish to use as garden fertilizer. And men were out hunting.

Everyone had something to do, and work was progressing fast and well. A person who refused to help with the work would not share in the benefits later. Everyone knew that. It was part of life, and no one had to be coerced into doing his part.

Even so, one evening after the Sun had crawled under the western edge of the Sky Vault and the darkness was settling in for the night, the people, tired from their long day's work, gathered around the fire in the ceremonial ground to relax by listening to tales told by some of the older ones, and one old man told them the following tale, as being particularly appropriate for their present situation.

A long time ago there was a drought. It went on for a long time. The animals kept watching the sky, but no clouds came. No rain. The waterholes got low, and the rivers ran low, and it looked like they were in for hard times. Finally they had a council, and they decided they would have to dig a well.

All the animals started to work digging the well, and they all worked hard. All except the rabbit. Jisdu just sat back and relaxed and watched the other animals working. The other animals, the ones who were working hard the way they should, got mad.

Finally one of them went over to Jisdu there where he was lounging in the shade.

"Jisdu," he said, "if you don't help us dig this well, you can't have any of the water."

"I haven't seen any water yet," said Jisdu.

"Well, the ground down there is getting damp," said the other. "We've gone down pretty deep now, and it won't be long. You come on and help dig the rest of the way down, or you don't get to share in the water."

"I don't care," said Jisdu. "I don't need your water. I get all the water I need from the dew on the grass in the early morning. I'm not going to wear myself out digging your stupid well."

So the animals kept digging, and Jisdu just kept watching and laughing at them. They had dug down a long ways and the well was deep. It was so deep that, in order to get down to work and then get back up again, they had to carve a pathway in the wall of the well. It went around and around all the way down.

One morning when the animals started down the path to go to work in the bottom of the well, they noticed some footprints along the path.

"Those look like Jisdu's tracks," said one of the animals.

"You're right," said another. "That lazy rabbit is sneaking down here at night to steal water."

"Water which he refuses to work for," said yet another.

So they went back up and confronted Jisdu.

"Those aren't my tracks," he said. "I get my water from the dew on the grass. I don't need your well-water."

The animals didn't know what to do. They went away from Jisdu, where he couldn't hear what they were saying, and they had a little council.

"I know they're Jisdu's tracks," said one.

"Of course they are," said another.

"But he denies it, and we haven't actually seen him go down in the well and steal water."

"So what will we do?"

"I have an idea," said one, and he explained his plan to the rest. They all liked the plan. It was a good one, and they went to work on it right away. They cut some sticks, and they tied them together to look like a man. One stick for a torso, two for arms and two for legs.

Then they tied some grass to the sticks to give them some shape, and finally they got some sticky sap from a tree, and they covered that shape they had made with sticky sap. They covered it all over, and then they stood it upright in the path leading down to the bottom of the well.

At the end of the day, they all went to bed, and Jisdu waited until he was sure that they were all sound asleep. Then he sneaked over to the well. He looked around one more time to be sure that no one was watching, and started down the path into the well.

It had been a long, hot, dry day, and Jisdu was real thirsty for some cool water. He chuckled as he started down the path. He was thinking how easy it was for a smart fellow like him to fool those stupid animals.

Why should he work when he could always get someone else to do the work for him? He was feeling real proud of himself when, just then, he saw the thing standing in the path.

It startled him. It made him jump, and his heart even skipped a beat or two. He hadn't been expecting to find anyone on the path in the middle of the night.

It was dark, because it was night, and because he was down inside the well, so all he could see was the shape. But he could see enough to tell that it was someone standing there in the path, guarding the water supply.

"Hey," he said. "Who are you?"

He got no answer.

"You won't talk, huh?" he said. "Well, then, get out of my way."

Still he got no answer, and the thing didn't move out of his way. Of course, it couldn't move, but Jisdu didn't know that.

"Get out of my way, I said. You're blocking my path."

The thing just stood there. Jisdu started to get pretty angry. You know, he likes to have things his own way all the time.

"Maybe you don't know who I am," he said. "If you knew who you're dealing with, you'd pay more attention to what I say."

He paused for a little while to see if that got any response, but it didn't. He stood up real straight and crossed his arms over his chest.

"Well," he said, "I'm Jisdu. Have you heard of me?"

He stood there trying to look real fierce, but he still got no response from the thing that was guarding the path.

"I'm a great warrior," he said, "and if you don't get out of my way right now, I'm going to knock you out of the way."

The thing just stood there, and Jisdu drew back his right arm to deliver a mighty blow.

"I warned you," he said, and he swung his fist with all his strength, and he hit the thing right on the side of its head, and his fist stuck there in the sticky sap. He pulled and tried to get loose, but he couldn't. He was stuck.

"Let go," he shouted. "Let me go, or I'll hit you again."

When he got no response, and the thing didn't turn him loose, he swung his left fist, and it stuck on the other side of the head. Now he was really mad, and he was a little bit scared too. He kicked the thing in its belly, and his right foot stuck, and he kicked again, and his left foot stuck.

He screamed and shouted, and he butted the thing with his head, and his head stuck, and then there was nothing he could do. Oh, he struggled for a while, twisting, turning, pulling, jerking, but it didn't do him any good. It just wore him out. He was stuck.

At the first sign of morning light, the hardworking animals started down the path to the bottom of their well, and they found him there, still stuck.

"Ha," they said, "we knew it was you."

"Let me go," he cried. "Get me out of here."

They carried him up out of the well, and danced around him, laughing and making jokes. He called them names and threatened them. He begged, and he cried, but they kept on teasing him and making fun of him for a long time, before they finally pulled him loose.

Then someone suggested that they cut off his head to teach him a lesson, and Jisdu said for them to go ahead and cut it off.

"It's been tried before," he said, "and no one's been able to do it."

Finally one of the animals, disgusted with Jisdu's behavior, picked him up and tossed him out into a thicket. He thought that he'd just let the lazy rabbit lay out in that tangle and die. But, of course, he didn't die in there. That was where he lived. So Jisdu outsmarted the other animals in the end anyway, at least a little bit.

The people gathered there all enjoyed the tale. Small children listened wide-eyed. The adults had all heard it before, of course, but they always liked to hear a story told again. They smiled and nodded their heads in agreement with the lesson of the tale. One who refuses to do his share of the labor cannot share in the benefits.

Osa listened carefully to the tale so she could add it to those she would tell her own children. She knew her own tribal tales, and she knew some of the tales that her late husband had learned from the Spanish priest, the tales from the big book. But she had become a Real Person, and her children were being raised as Real People. She wanted to raise them right, and she was still learning.

When the tale-telling was done, she stood up, Whirlwind in her arms, and started to walk toward the house which she and Guwisti had been working on together. Guwisti followed her close behind carrying the Little Spaniard. Then Comes Back to Life came along, and soon the three adults were walking side by side.

As they passed by a small group of people, Comes Back to Life heard someone say, "I think that he has two wives now."

45

They traveled the river for the rest of that day, the captive Striker and the five Slavecatchers. More than once Striker thought about throwing himself out of the boat and into the water, but he wasn't at all sure that he would be able to swim with his hands tied behind his back, and he was not yet ready to kill himself. As long as there was any hope for escaping from these horrible men, he would stay alive.

They stopped late in the day to make a camp for the night, and one of the men had started to untie Striker's hands. His heart thrilled. He would have a chance. With his arms loose, he knew he could outrun them. He recalled with glee how winded they had been the last time he had made them chase him, and he told himself that if his hands had been free that time, he would be a free man now.

But before the man could manage to get the knots loose, the jargon-talking one noticed what was happening. He jumped over close to other man, pushed him rudely away from Striker and spoke sharply to him at the same time. Then the jargon-talker started to check the ropes to make sure they were still tight.

Striker glanced to his right, and he could see there the man who had been pushed. The face of the insulted one wore an expression that was a combination of sulk and deep anger, and while the jargon-talker's attention was still on the ropes, the other drew a Spanish steel knife out of a scabbard which hung at his side. He snarled something and rushed at the jargon-talker, raising the knife up over his head to deal a deadly blow.

Just as the blade was descending, the jargon-talker saw it, and he screamed his surprise and jerked Striker around between himself and his angry opponent. Striker tried to duck, but it was too late, and he felt the sharp, cold steel slice his skin and scrape his bone just above his ear on the left side of his head.

The force of the blow carried the attacker on past the other two, and at the same time, the jargon-talker shoved Striker aside and to the ground. Striker landed on his side, but he quickly scrambled to his feet and stepped back out of the way of the fight. He could feel warm, sticky blood running down the side of his head.

There in front of him, the two Slavecatchers were faced off for a fight. Striker figured that the insulted one had been about to free his hands in order to make him help with setting up the camp, but the jargon-talker, who seemed to fancy himself the leader of the group, took exception with that choice.

He might have prevented the fight had he simply told the other man what he thought, but he had shoved him roughly and shouted at him. The man had taken offense and rightly so, Striker thought. That was no way for a leader to make his wishes known.

The two men circled, each looking for an opening, for a way to attack, and the jargon-talker now also held a knife in his hand. This looked to be a fight to the death. They said things to each other, but in a language Striker did not understand. The tone was clear enough though, as they spoke through snarls: boasts, insults, threats.

Suddenly the jargon-talker lunged with a deep, underhand cutting motion, but the other jumped back, barely evading the move. They continued circling cautiously. Then the other one stepped forward with another overhand swing, but the jargon-talker caught the knife hand by the wrist and held it tight, at the same time thrusting again with an underhand, and the other managed to catch his wrist. Thus they struggled, each holding away the other's knife.

Striker found it difficult to decide which man he was siding with in this fight. He did not like any of them. They were hateful Slavecatchers all, but the jargon-talker had been especially rude to him, and he would enjoy seeing the man killed. On the other hand, none of the others seemed to be able to speak the jargon, and with that man dead, Striker would not be able to communicate at all with his captors.

He watched them struggle, straining against each other, knife blades coming sometimes dangerously close, yet being held back. The other three Slavecatchers were shouting encouragement at one or the other of the antagonists. They seemed to be enjoying the fight tremendously.

These were very strange men indeed. Striker thought that if two Real People were locked in mortal combat with one another, he would certainly not be reacting in such a manner. He would be horrified. The worst possible thing a Real Person could do was to kill another Real Person.

Just then the jargon-talker reached out with a leg to trip his opponent, and both men fell heavily to the ground, the jargon-talker on top of the other. Each still held tight to the other's wrist. The jargon-talker pressed hard, and his blade moved close to the other's face.

Desperately the man on the bottom strained with all his might to hold the blade away, but to no avail. It moved closer, and he turned his head away just as it plunged downward, slicing through his ear and burying itself in the ground. He screamed as the blood flowed freely from the cut ear, and he rolled and shoved with all the weight of his body.

The jargon-talker, off balance with his knife stuck in the earth, was tossed to one side, and the other moved quickly, planting a knee firmly on the wrist of the jargon-talker, just above where he held the haft of the knife. His other knee came down hard on the jargon-talker's chest.

The jargon-talker reached up with his free hand, clutching at the other's face, his fingers digging for eyeballs. Almost calmly, the other reached around behind his own back and slowly sank the steel blade of his knife into the stomach of the jargon-talker.

"Ahhh."

It was more a moan than a scream, a moan and a death sigh, and the clutching fingers slowly relaxed, and the reaching arm fell down. Blood was still flowing from the victor's sliced ear, and as soon as he realized that the jargon-talker was beyond fighting back, he pulled the blade out of the stomach and sliced the ears off the jargon-talker's head while the man was still alive. Then he cut his throat to finish the job. He stood up, looked down contemptuously at the body, and spat on it.

Shouts of congratulations came from the other three Slavecatchers. Laughing and talking, they slapped the victor on the back. Gradually they calmed down a bit and talked with each other briefly.

Then all except the killer, the man with the sliced ear, began to gather sticks to build a fire. The body of their former companion was ignored. Striker asked himself again, What kind of men are these? He thought about the tales he had heard of Spaniards, and he recalled the behavior of the bad Frenchmen who had rebelled against their own leader and threatened to take over Kituwah.

These Slavecatchers, he thought, behaved like white men, but they were not white. Their skin was brown, like his. They wore moccasins and buckskin leggings and breechcloths. Sliced-Ear had a shaven head with a long, loose flowing scalp lock, and his chest and arms were covered with tattoos.

The language they spoke was yet a puzzle to Striker. The more he listened to them, and the more he thought about it, the more convinced was he that it was similar to the language of the French. Similar. Not the same. So these men who were not white men, behaved like white men and spoke a white man's language. At least it seemed so to Striker.

He put the question temporarily aside and assessed his own situation. The odds were certainly improving. The Slavecatchers had started out seven strong. Now there were but four of them. It was four against one, and his hands were tied. But if Woyi showed up, it would be four against two, and those odds were not at all frightening to Striker.

But how soon would Woyi show up? Where were these men taking Striker? How soon would they be there? And once they reached their destination, would there be more of them? Would Spaniards be there? The odds were not bad, but only if Woyi would hurry.

While Striker was thus deep in thought, the Slavecatchers stripped the body of the jargon-talker. One of them found his pack and emptied its contents out on the ground. They divided his belongings up among themselves, and then they ate. One of them stuck some dried meat into Striker's mouth, and though he was disgusted by his surroundings and by the company he was in, he was hungry, and he ate it to keep up his strength. He noticed that a chill was in the night air.

They woke him in the morning with a kick, and they gathered up their things. They left the body, and they left the smoldering remains of their fire. They loaded their belongings, including Striker, in the dugout, and they started once again traveling down the river.

They seemed to talk incessantly, and it seemed like meaningless banter, for one of them would say something, and the others would laugh, and the laughter was sniggering and snide and not at all joyful.

When they stopped again, it was just past midday, for Striker noticed that the Sun had just left her daughter's house to begin her slow descent to the western edge of the Sky Vault. They made another hasty and haphazard camp, but this time Sliced-Ear did untie the hands of Striker, and no one dared to challenge his right to do so.

Then Sliced-Ear made it clear by signs that he wanted Striker to gather wood and make a fire. Striker thought about fighting for his freedom or running, but his arms were numb from having been tied so long, and the four men were watching him closely. He hoped that they would get a little careless while he was still unbound.

But they did not. They sat close to him while they ate, and then, leaving the campsite a mess, as before, they once again tied his hands and resumed their journey.

When the Sun was low in the west, Striker wondered if they would stop once more to camp for the night, but it was just about then that he saw the village up ahead. He thought that it must be their destination, for they made no attempt to hide. They headed straight for it. As they drew closer, Striker realized that he had never before seen a village quite like this one.

There was a stockade fence, but not all the houses were inside the fence. Some were scattered here and there on the outside. On closer view he saw that the houses were not even all alike, and the fence was carelessly, sloppily constructed.

As the boat drew near the shore, Striker saw more clearly some of the people of the village. Their appearance was more or less like that of his captors. They seemed to be from several different tribes, and some of them wore bits and pieces of the white man's clothing. In fact, the whole village, if such it could be called, contained evidence of the presence of white men, or at least, their influence.

Iron pots were over cooking fires. There were a few horses and even some pigs. But mostly the evidence was in the weaponry carried by the men, and all the men that Striker could see were heavily armed. The whole appearance of the place was of a hastily constructed armed camp.

As the boat ran aground and his captors jumped out, a couple of other men ran up to meet it and help pull it ashore. They talked the same strange language as did his captors, and he could tell that at least some of what they were saying had to do with him. He imagined that some also had to do with the men who did not return.

They pulled Striker from the boat and shoved him toward the stockade fence. He noticed along the way women sitting beside hovels or stirring cooking pots. Some of them glanced up to look at him as he passed them by. They seemed slothful and lethargic. The men, other than those who walked along with him, were lounging lazily in front of the huts, some drinking from strange-looking containers.

They reached the fence, one much like that around Kituwah, except that the poles were thin and crooked and not set well in the ground. To compensate for that lack of stability, they had been lashed together, and the entire fence sagged and weaved its way around the enclosure.

Two armed men stood guard at the entryway, and Striker was pushed between them into the short and narrow passageway. He stopped a few steps in and looked back over his shoulder. Those who had brought him there had already turned to walk away. One of the guards spoke gruffly to him and gestured with a hand for him to get on inside. He walked on in.

There must have been a hundred there: men, women, even a few children. And then he realized that he had seen no children outside the wall. And inside there were no houses, not even the rude huts he had seen outside.

So the fence, he realized, did not surround the village, or camp, for defensive purposes. The camp was all outside, and the fence contained the captives, one hundred people bound for Spanish slavery. His heart sickened at the thought.

46

She sat in the saddle in front of him, and he controlled the big *sogwili* from behind her. She had never before been on the back of one of the white man's beasts, and it was a little frightening, but it was also exciting. Soon she got used to it, and she thought that she would actually have enjoyed it had it not been for the urgency of the mission they were on.

And the feel of the body of the man behind her, his arms coming around her to hold the lines that came from the animal's head—that was exciting, too. But when she tried to picture him in her mind, the face that she saw was that of the other man—the man they were going to rescue, the one who had rescued her and gotten himself captured in the process.

"Woyi," she said, "tell me about Striker."

"He's my friend," said Woyi. "He and I made Friendship."

She knew about the Making of Friends Ceremony, and she knew what it meant to the men who went through it together. They were bound to each other in a deep and abiding friendship that would last throughout their lives. They would laugh and play together, hunt and fight together. Either one would readily die for the other.

"He's a brave man and a good fighter," she said.

"He's the bravest and the best," said Woyi. "He saved my life on the battlefield."

"And he saved me from those men," she said.

"And got himself caught," said Woyi, and she couldn't help but notice a resentful edge to his voice as he said it. Clearly Woyi blamed her for the situation his friend was in.

"We'll find him," she said, but her statement seemed weak in the face of the quest they were on.

They rode on then in silence for a while. She had been hurt by Woyi's words, or at least by the tone with which they had been said. Perhaps she did, after all, feel responsible for Striker's predicament. Perhaps, she thought, Woyi was right, she was to blame. If it had not been for her, Striker would not be the captive of those strange and awful men. Then she noticed a faint odor in the air that seemed to be out of place. She stopped feeling sorry for herself and sniffed, trying to concentrate.

"Woyi," she said. "I smell smoke."

"I don't smell anything."

She scanned the trees along the river to their left, and then she found the smoke, a thin wisp rising out of the woods. She pointed.

"There," she said.

And Woyi saw it too. He turned the horse and headed toward the woods, but not directly for the smoke. If it was someone's camp, and they were there, he wanted to see them before they knew that anyone else was around. It might be Striker's captors or some other enemy. Woyi had to check his excitement and exercise caution. He knew that he had a tendency to be headstrong, but Striker's safety had to come first.

He pulled the horse up at the edge of the woods and shoved himself off the back end. Awiakta dismounted, and Woyi loosely tied the reins to a small tree. They were still some distance from the rising smoke.

Woyi made his way carefully along the edge of the treeline, and Awiakta was not far behind. He thought about telling her to wait with the horse, but he decided against that. Let her do what she will. He moved ahead, slowly, carefully, quietly. When he thought that he was very close to the spot where the smoke had come from, and was about ready to move into the woods, he hesitated and looked back over his shoulder, and she was nowhere in sight.

He felt a moment of panic, wondering if someone could have reached out from the woods and grabbed her, managing at the same time to keep her quiet. Then he heard her voice, and it was strong and clear and calm.

"Woyi, it's all right. There's no one here."

Relieved and angry at the same time, Woyi moved into the trees, and soon he found her standing beside the fire. It was an old fire. It had probably been left unattended, almost burned out, and it had flamed up again on its own.

He wondered who would leave a fire like that. But even more puzzling was the neglected body lying nearby.

"Well," said Awiakta, "no one alive is here. That's one of the men we were following."

He could tell from the condition of the body that it had been abandoned for some time, a day, maybe two days. Scavengers had been at work on it. It was a gruesome sight, and it was hard to tell just what had happened to the man, except for one thing. The ears had been cut off. Any other wounds, including any death wound, had been obliterated by the gnawing of the scavengers.

"What happened here? I wonder," he said.

"Could Striker have killed him?" she asked.

"Maybe," he said, "but I don't think so. Striker wouldn't have cut off the ears like that."

"And if Striker had fought with this man, the others would have fought him at the same time." She shook her head. "Maybe they fought among themselves."

"Why would they do that?" Woyi asked, incredulous.

"I don't know," she said, "but I've never known men like these. They act crazy."

"Would they kill one of their own and then just leave him like this?"

"They might," she said. "They're crazy."

"By the way," he said, "how did you get here ahead of me?"

"I came through the woods," she said, pointing, "that way."

He started to say something else, but she had already turned to look further around the camp. She had seen more than enough of the mangled body anyhow. She strolled around looking at blurry footprints, at places where people had sat. In her casual search, she ambled a little farther down toward the river.

Woyi continued to study the ghastly remains, not sure whether he was simply fascinated by the horror of it or whether he really thought that he might be able to learn something more from a prolonged study.

"Woyi," she called.

He straightened up and ran to her side. She was standing down by the edge of the water.

"What now?" he asked.

"Look. They had a boat here, and they dragged it out into the water."

He looked at the signs she pointed out, and he saw immediately that she was right, and his heart sank a little. They would move much faster in a boat. He looked up into the sky and saw that the Sun was well on her way to the far western edge of the Sky Vault.

"Let's go," he said. "We need to make a camp for the night, but I don't want to be too close to this place."

"No," she said. "Neither do I."

They rode until there was almost no more light, and then they found a spot and slept there beside the trees, on the prairie's edge. They didn't want to sleep down in the woods beside the river, not after what they had seen in the campsite they had found. For reasons of safety, they made no fire, even though the night was cool, and they went to sleep hungry that night.

With the early-morning light, they went down to the river's edge and caught some fish. Then they built a small fire there beside the river and cooked the fish and ate. Woyi felt much better then, and he also thought about the way he had behaved toward Awiakta the night before. And he knew that she hadn't deserved it.

"I was rude to you," he said. "I blamed you for what's happened to Striker, and I was wrong."

"It is my fault," said Awiakta. "He was captured saving me."

"But he made the choice to do what he did," said Woyi, "and if I had been there instead of him, I would have done the same thing. The blame is on those men who came into our land and captured you in the first place. Any man of the Real People who saw what we saw and failed to try to help you would be a coward, and Striker is no coward. The blame is not on you, and I was wrong."

She smiled softly, and looking at him sitting there across the fire from her, she suddenly wanted to move over to sit beside him and put her arms around him. She did not, of course. She only thought about it.

"I understand," she said. "You're worried about Striker, and I am too."

"I even wondered for a while if I should have let you come along with me," he said. "But if I had not brought you, I would have ridden right past that campsite last night. You found it. Not me. And you found the signs of the boat."

"Is it important?" she asked. "What we found there last night?"

"Yes. Of course. We know now for sure that we're on the right trail," said Woyi. "We also know that they're moving faster now, and we know that there is one less of them to deal with when we catch up with them."

She glanced across the fire into Woyi's face, and he was staring down at the flames, so he did not notice her glance. She noticed, though, that he was handsome, as handsome as the other. She had already entertained secret thoughts about Striker, for she had found him handsome, too, even in the brief time she had seen him, and he had rescued her from those horrible men. She did not even know Striker, of course, and she realized that, but it didn't seem to matter.

He was bold and brave and strong. He was a good fighter, and he was generous. He had thrown himself away for the sake of a woman he did not even know. What more, she asked herself, did a woman need to know about a man? Except perhaps—did he already have a wife?

Even so, he could have another. He could have two wives if he wanted them, and if he could support them both. But his first wife would have to agree, and, of course, she would always be first. A marriage with two wives was not always ideal for the second one.

"Woyi," she said, and he looked up almost startled. His mind had been somewhere far away.

"What?" he asked.

"Does Striker have a wife?"

"No," he said. "Why do you ask?"

"If he had a wife," she said, "she would be worrying about him. That's all."

But Woyi wondered if that had been all. Could this woman be thinking about Striker in that way? She hardly knew him. She didn't know him. She had only seen him and heard him speak two words or three. But then, she had seen him in action, and that action had all been taken for her sake. Perhaps she was thinking of Striker in that way.

Well, Woyi thought, she was a good woman, young and beautiful, brave and bright. She would make Striker a good wife, if Striker wanted her. He wondered if Striker would want her, and if they were to marry, what would life be like after that? How could Woyi and Striker continue to be inseparable friends, if Striker had a wife?

Woyi thought it strange that this question had never come into his mind before. Of course, one or both of them was bound to marry sooner or later. He had just somehow not thought of it as being soon.

Would Striker want to— He stole a glance at the woman sitting across the fire from him. Long sleek black hair falling down her back and shoulders; skin that looked smooth and clear and seemed to beg to be caressed; long, strong, lovely-looking legs. Ha. What a question. Of course he would.

Then Woyi realized that he had feelings for Awiakta too, and with that realization, he felt profound guilt. He swore to himself that he would keep those feelings to himself. If Striker should ever ask him how he felt about this woman, he would say that she is like a sister. Nothing more.

"And you?" she said.

"What?"

"Do you have a wife?"

He stood up suddenly and started walking toward the *sogwili*.

"No," he said. "I don't have a wife. We'd better be getting started."

"I'll put out the fire," she said, and while Woyi saddled up the horse, Awiakta threw dirt on the fire to smother it. But she watched him walking away, and she wondered as she watched just what she would do once they had rescued Striker. How would she feel seeing these two young men standing side by side?

Which one would she choose for herself—assuming, of course, that she had such a choice to make? She had to admit, she had no reason to believe that either one was interested in her that way.

47

Wild Man had gone into Itowah, and at a council meeting there, he had told them all the story of the invading Slavecatchers and their capture of a young woman of the Real People. He told them that the Slavecatchers had killed a Wolf Person at the pass in order to make their way back out of the country of the Real People. He told them about Striker and about Woyi, and he told them about the Howler with his company of Frenchmen and Senikas, waiting at the pass.

Much debate followed, and the council had to break up with no decision having been made and a promise to meet again the following night. At the second meeting, again following much debate, the people of Itowah agreed to allow the foreigners to come into their town.

"After all," someone said, "their leader is a Real Person, so it's really not at all like letting foreigners come in."

And so the Howler, followed by Owl and his Senikas and Tournier and his Frenchmen, went into Itowah. And there they ate and rested, and there they attended another council meeting. This time the Wild Man of Itowah made a different kind of plea.

"These Slavecatchers are the worst kind of men who live," he said. "As bad as the Spaniards are, these men are worse, for they prey on their own kind to serve the Spaniards' purposes.

"Seven of them came into our land. They captured one of our young women, and they got out again by killing a kinsman of mine who was helping to guard the pass.

"Striker, formerly of Stikoyi, now of New Town, is following them to rescue the woman, and now his friend Woyi is following them. Two men alone. These Slavecatchers have led them out of our country, and if we don't catch up with them soon to help our people—our people, three of them, all young people, will be killed or captured and sold as slaves to the hateful Spaniards.

"These men here, our guests, are going after them. Shall we sit home and do nothing while white men and Senikas go off to rescue our young people for us? I think not. I'm grateful for the help of our new friends, but I mean to go with them, and I want to know who will be going along with me."

So when the Howler once again rode out of Itowah and back onto the trail of the Slavecatchers, he rode at the head of a party of over fifty men. The twenty or so Real People from Itowah ran on foot behind the mounted men, but they would not be far behind.

At the end of their first day of travel, they stopped and camped, and though they were no longer inside their own country, the camp they made was a bold one, for they were fifty strong, and they feared no attack. They built four fires there for cooking, and they sat and talked in groups around the fires. Wild Man sought out the other leaders.

"How will we know that we're following the right trail?" he asked.

"Woyi is ahead of us," said Howler, "and he's riding on a *sogwili*, one *sogwili* alone. His trail is easy to follow. You didn't see it, because all of us had ridden over it by the time you came up behind. So far, he's moving along parallel to the river there."

Owl, the Senika, thought about what he had just heard. It didn't seem right to him that Wild Man, a war leader and a man of some reputation, should run behind the horses. He did not believe that any white man could keep up with the Real People on foot, but a Senika could—easily. He called one of his men and told him to give his mount up for Wild Man to ride.

The next morning the party was led off by the Howler, Owl, Tournier and Wild Man, riding side by side. At midday they followed the tracks of Woyi's horse to the edge of the woods. They dismounted there and soon discovered the campsite and the mutilated body. They saw the signs nearby that a boat had been launched, but they couldn't figure out the rest.

"Either Striker or Woyi must have killed this man," said Tournier.

"No," said the Howler, "I don't think so. Someone cut off this man's ears."

Tournier recalled having seen Woyi gouge out the eyes of the last corpse they had found, and he wondered what the difference was in the two mutilations, but he decided that it was not the time to pursue the matter. If the Howler was convinced that neither of those two young men had done the deed, so be it.

"So what has happened here?" he asked.

The Howler gave a shrug.

"This man is dead," said Wild Man. "We don't know how or why. The Slavecatchers had a boat here, and they left in it, I guess. I guess they still have the woman, or Striker and Woyi would be coming back, and we have not seen either of them."

"Let's go," said the Howler, and they mounted up again and continued to follow the trail left by Woyi's horse.

The council house was finished there at New Town, a solid, seven-sided structure, large enough for the entire population of the town to get inside and sit and hold their meetings. The benches weren't yet built, but the building itself was done. Some of the people slept in it at night. And the wall around the town was complete. Sturdy enough for men to climb up on and look out, it circled the entire town, and then its two ends overlapped for a distance, forming the long and narrow passageway through which anyone must enter. Oliga was pleased.

With the work on the townhouse and on the wall out of the way, the people finally had the time to work on their own homes. Ordinarily women built the houses, for women owned them, but there was nothing ordinary about the establishment of New Town. Everyone pitched in to get the job done.

But when Osa tried to work on her house, Whirlwind would scream, and her screaming distracted everyone.

"I never heard one that size with such a voice," Diguhsgi said.

"And look," said another woman. "There are no tears."

When anyone other than her mother tried to pick her up and calm her, she screamed louder than ever, until Osa at last gave in and took her up, and then she stopped—at once.

"She surely gets her way, doesn't she?" said someone.

"And so young," said another. "She'll grow up to be no good. She's spoiled already."

"And look at her brother, won't you? Such a good little boy."

Not far away, the Little Spaniard in his cradleboard was propped up against a tree, and from his upright position there, he calmly watched Guwisti working on her house.

"You know," a woman said, "old Uyona had the little girl to herself right after she was born."

"How long did she have it?" asked another.

"I don't know for sure, but it was quite a while, and no one else saw it at all during all that time. In fact, she kept it with her clear up until she died."

"Hush," said yet another woman. "It does no good to talk about such things."

"Well," said the other, "at least I'm not going to do any work on that woman's house, when she doesn't even work on it herself."

While all this talk was going on, Osa held her daughter in her arms. She sat on the ground leaning back against a tree, and she rocked a little, and she talked, her voice soft and low.

"They're talking about us, aren't they?" she said. "Well, we don't care. We don't care what they say or what they think. They can't hurt us. Not you or me or your brother. We have the strength of Asquani. Your father. Yes. We do."

She looked up to see Comes Back to Life walking toward her, and she stopped talking and waited for him to arrive. When he did, he dropped down in a squat and looked at the *usdi* in her arms.

"She looks healthy and happy," he said.

"Yes," said Osa. "She is."

"And her brother, too," he said.

"Yes. That's because of your wife. She, at least, is very good to us."

Comes Back to Life thought that he knew what Osa was talking about, but he didn't want to pursue the topic, at least not just then.

"Do you have everything you need?" he asked her.

"Yes."

"How is your house coming?"

Osa looked down, embarrassed.

"I haven't had much time," she said. "This one takes all my time."

Comes Back to Life knew exactly what Osa was talking about this time. There was no question. He also knew about the talk among the people regarding the nature and early days of little Whirlwind, and he knew all the implications of that talk. They believed that the old woman had been a witch, and they further believed that she had made this little one into a witch.

He didn't know whether to believe that or not. Perhaps it was all true. He did know that the old woman had helped him and his Guwisti, and he was not afraid of her or any of her work. And he was very much obligated to this woman and to her children, both of them. He smiled.

"I'll see that your house is built," he said.

So he worked with Guwist' to finish her house, and then right next to hers they built another, and that one belonged to Osa. There was some talk about the houses and their proximity to one another, but Guwisti and Comes Back to Life ignored it. The location of the two houses made perfect sense to both of them. He had taken on the responsibility of the care of Osa and her family, and Guwisti had taken on the Little Spaniard—most of the time. They should be close together.

Oliga worked sometimes with Tsiwon' on her house, but he had other things to do. New Town had been conceived as a defensive border town because of a weak spot they had discovered there, and as the War Chief of New Town, Olig' meant to see that the weak spot was properly taken care of. He checked the wall, and now and then he climbed up on a notched pole to look out one direction or the other.

Sometimes he went outside of town and climbed up on a hill to look around for as far as he could see. Inside the wall, he checked with all the men to make sure that their weapons were in order, that they had a good enough supply of arrows in case they were attacked.

He did this so often that it almost became a joke. Sometimes when they saw him coming, one of the men would shout, "Yes, Olig', I have plenty of arrows."

He did all this because he felt it needed to be done, but he also did it to keep himself busy. He did it to keep himself from thinking about the Howler and Striker and Woyi and the Frenchmen and Senikas who had gone out with them.

It had seemed such a simple problem when Woyi had first come back to the column to report the intrusion of seven strangers into their country. The Howler and Woyi had gone after them with the Frenchmen and the Senikas, but they had been gone so long. Why had they not returned?

Could the seven strangers be giving them so much trouble? It was hard to believe. Of course, the seven would be no problem at all in a fight, but they could have led the Howler and the others in a long chase. They might be good at evading their pursuers.

He told himself that must be the explanation, that there could be no other. But in truth he knew that there could be other reasons that the Howler had not returned. The seven could have been a part of a larger party of invaders, and they might have led the Howler's company into a trap.

Or the Senikas, or the Frenchmen, even, or the two of them working together as allies, might have turned on the Howler and Woyi and the Striker for some unknown reason. For all Olig' knew, the seven strangers might even have been Senikas or some other allies of the Senikas. He tried not to think these thoughts.

He wanted to trust the Frenchmen, and he wanted to believe that the new alliance with the Senikas was a good and lasting one. He also tried to convince himself that there was no better man to lead a war party than the Howler, and that there was no one who could trick the Howler into a trap.

He wanted to believe these things, and he tried to believe them, but mostly he tried not to think of them. For that reason he kept himself as busy as he could with other things.

He was working on his wife's house one afternoon, but then he stopped. She knew that he was about to leave. It was his pattern lately.

"Husband," she said, "do you have to go off somewhere? You never rest. Stay here with me, and let's just sit awhile together."

"No," he said. "There's too much to be done."

"The work's all going well," she said. "We can take a little time to rest."

"It's coming along," he said, "but I have other things to do. You rest."

48

The compound inside the flimsy wall was filthy and it stank. And the people in there were pitiful. They looked healthy enough, but they seemed so dejected. They wore long faces, and they just sat around doing nothing. Of course, there was not much they could do, but they didn't even talk to one another. They might at least talk, thought Striker.

He felt conspicuous standing there just inside the entry, and, sure enough, he noticed that several were staring at him from different directions. He looked around, trying to find a place to move to and sit. At last he decided to let them stare. They'd get tired of it soon enough. He walked a few steps to his left and sat down right there against the wall.

He studied this new situation in which he found himself, and he did not find it to be a hopeless one, in spite of the apparent attitude of his fellow captives. It seemed to Striker that there were at least as many captives as there were Slavecatchers. True, the captives were unarmed. True, a good many of them were women and some were children. Still, the numbers were not all that bad.

He wondered then why someone had not already led an attack against the Slavecatchers. Why did they just sit inside this wretched fence waiting to be taken away and. sold they-knew-not-where? There were problems to be re-solved, of course, but they not insurmountable.

There was the problem of the fence. Should the captives decide to just boldly and openly attack the Slavecatchers, they would have to run single-file through the narrow passageway, and the Slavecatchers would be able to pick them off easily one at a time. It was just the opposite of the defensive strategy of a walled town.

But if the captives were to get together and make some plans, there had to be a way to solve that problem. The fence was flimsy. Maybe they could tear it down. Or maybe they could find a way to get the Slavecatchers to come inside, and then they would be able to pick them off one at a time.

Or they could make their move at night. It would be a fairly easy matter, he thought, for two or three, maybe even four, to slip through the passageway and quickly and quietly throttle the two guards. The rest of the Slavecatchers would most likely be asleep, and the captives could begin killing them in their sleep one at a time and gathering weapons as they killed. Then when the rest of the camp awoke, as they were bound to do, at least some of the captives would have weapons, and then it would be a real fight. That was the best plan, he thought. That one should work.

Again he wondered why it had not been done already. It was not such a difficult plan to come up with. What was wrong with these captives? Soon he found the answer, for a young man walked close to him, and Striker spoke to him, using the trade language.

"Hello," he said. "Do you understand me?"

The man, young and burly, only glanced at Striker, then looked away. He had the appearance to Striker of a man who could fight with a bear with no weapons. If this man was too demoralized to fight for his freedom, then this bunch of captives was indeed a hopeless lot. Striker stood up and tried again.

"Do you speak the trade language?" he asked.

The man looked at him and shrugged, then walked away. Perhaps, Striker thought, that is the whole problem here. These people all speak different languages and therefore cannot communicate with one another. Then the problem becomes how to find a way of communicating with them, or, if that fails, of escaping on one's own.

He leaned back against the fence, trying to think what he would do next. He would not do as these others. He would not just lie around inside this fence waiting to see what the vile Slavecatchers had in mind for him. He would not acknowledge that he was totally helpless and completely in their control. Then he noticed the man to whom he had tried to speak.

He had walked off some distance and was gesturing toward Striker to come over to him. Puzzled, Striker got up and walked over to stand in front of the man. He opened his mouth as if to speak again, but the other stopped him with a gesture.

"Speak low," he said, and he was using the trade language. So he knew it after all. "If they hear us talking to one another, they come inside and beat us. Come with me."

He led Striker to the very center of the compound and sat down on the ground. They were completely surrounded there by the other captives, and, Striker realized, they were as far away from any part of the wall as they could possibly get. There wasn't much chance of their being overheard from outside. He sat down next to the man.

"I'm Striker," he said, his voice not much more than a whisper, "of the Chalakees."

"I'm called Breaks Their Heads," said the other. "I'm Apalachee."

"Are there other Chalakees in here?" Striker asked.

"I don't think so."

"Other Apalachees?"

"No."

"Do any of the others speak the trade language?"

"A few, but they're afraid to talk."

"Who are these Slavecatchers," Striker asked, "and what is the strange language that they speak?"

"They're renegades from several different tribes. They've allied themselves with the Spaniards, and because their languages are different, they speak among themselves in Spanish."

"I see," said Striker. "And how many of them are there?"

"About seventy-five, I think."

"If that includes the ones who captured me," said Striker, "there are now but seventy-two."

"You killed three of them?"

"I killed two. Two others fought each other, and one was killed."

"Ah."

"I want to break out of this place," said Striker.

"And so do I," said Breaks Their Heads, "but how?"

"How many of them stay awake at night?"

"Two guard the passageway here," said Breaks Their Heads. "Some stay awake late into the night drinking *ron*. That's all I know about."

"Drinking what?"

"It's a Spanish drink, a kind of crazy water. It makes them stupid after a while, and then they fall asleep."

"Only two guards awake," said Striker.

Breaks Their Heads shrugged, as if to say, That's all I know.

"Then you and I," said Striker, "can go into the passageway late at night and kill the two guards. If we're very quiet, we can grab them from behind before they know what's happening. We can strangle them or kill them with their own knives. Then we can take their weapons, and these others can follow us if they will."

"It might work," said Breaks Their Heads.

"It will work," said Striker. "Even if no one else follows us, and we can't escape, at least we'll die fighting. Will you go with me?"

"Yes," said Breaks Their Heads. "I will."

"Tonight?"

"Yes."

It was a dark night, and it was almost cold, and Striker listened to the voices of the carousing Slavecatchers on the other side of the wall late into the night. He asked himself over and over, When will they sleep? And now and then, he dozed himself. Breaks Their Heads sat not far from Striker. They did not speak to one another. They waited.

Then Striker came awake with a jerk of his head, and he realized that all around him was very quiet. He wondered how long he had slept. He sat still for a moment listening to the silence and making sure that he was well awake. Then he looked to his left to see if Breaks Their Heads was still nearby. He was, and he appeared to be asleep.

Striker stood up and walked the few steps to where Breaks Their Heads sat leaning back against the wall. He squatted down beside the other man and gently shook him by the shoulder. Breaks Their Heads quickly came awake. He looked at Striker, and Striker gave a nod. Both men stood.

They walked close along beside the wall, and when they entered the passageway, they moved very slowly and cautiously. About halfway through, they could see the two guards standing there just outside the entry, one on either side. Striker looked at Breaks Their Heads, and he pointed toward the guard on the right, indicating that Breaks Their Heads should take that one. Breaks Their Heads nodded his understanding. They moved a little closer.

Suddenly Breaks Their Heads jumped forward, flinging an arm around the neck of the guard ahead of him. Striker sprang at his own assigned target an instant later. His right arm encircled the throat of the guard, and he began to squeeze, to choke off the man's voice and breath and life. As he choked, out of the corner of his eye he saw Breaks Their Heads all of a sudden release the other man, and Breaks Their Heads and the man he had let go moved quickly over to stand one on each of his sides, grinning, and Striker felt the cold steel of two Spanish blades touch the flesh on either side of him just below his ribs, and he relaxed his grip on the man he was choking, and he stood there, captive still.

Then the full realization of the meaning of the seeming lethargy of the captives inside the wall came clearly into Striker's mind. They could make no plans in there, for they never knew to whom they might be speaking, captive or guard, and for that reason, they simply did not speak. But before he could give it any further thought, the man he had been choking turned and slapped him hard across the face, and Breaks Their Heads and the other man laughed out loud.

Then one took him by each arm, and they dragged him away from the wall, away from the filthy prison there. Would they kill him now? he wondered. They dragged him toward a fire, a large, roaring fire, more than anyone needed at a camp, a careless, wasteful fire. On the other side of the fire he could see a frame of poles, two uprights planted in the ground, two crosspieces, one just up off the ground, the other high overhead.

They pulled and pushed him around the fire to the frame, and there they held his hands in front of him and tied them tight, and one threw the other end of the long rope with which his hands were tied up and over the high crosspiece of the frame, and then they pulled. They pulled until his hands were up over his head, and still they pulled. They pulled until his arms were stretched out their full length, and then they pulled some more. He thought that they would pull until they had pulled him apart, but then they stopped and tied the rope.

Now what? he asked himself.

But his tormentors turned and walked away, seemingly unconcerned—all but one. Breaks Their Heads stepped just in front of him and looked at him and grinned.

"Now you see that it is pointless to try to escape," he said. "You see why no one tries."

"So will you kill me now?" asked Striker.

The other laughed.

"No," he said. "Of course not. You won't die. We won't even break any of your bones. You're much too valuable for that. In the morning, though, you'll wish that you had not tried to get away. And one of these days soon, you may even wish that we had killed you on this night."

Breaks Their Heads turned and walked away laughing to himself, and Striker was left alone. He was stretched so tight, the skin under his arms and on his sides felt as if it would rip, and the ropes were tearing at the skin around his wrists. They would let him hang there like that all night long. That much was clear to him. Then in the morning they would do something worse to him, but they wouldn't break his bones.

Then he realized that no one was watching him, and that they had not tied his feet or legs to the lower crosspiece of the frame. He found that he could step up on that pole and get a certain amount of relief from the stretching. It was hard to maintain his balance standing that way on the crosspiece, and it caused a strain on the muscles in the backs of his legs, but it was better than the stretching.

He decided that he had made a terrible mistake. When he had been choking the guard and felt the knife blades touching both his sides, he should have choked the man harder. He should have tried to kill the man before they could stop him. He should have fought them then and there to the death. He no longer saw any other hope. He saw no other way out. He resolved that the next chance he got, however slim, he would force a fight to the death.

49

The Sun was low in the western sky, and the men and horses had been going all day. Tournier wondered when the Howler would call a halt for the night. These Indians, he thought, seemed to be able to go on indefinitely. They didn't seem to need rest or food. He knew, though, that his Frenchmen would be complaining soon. Undoubtedly they were already grumbling low among themselves. And then, of course, there were the horses.

"My friend," he said at last to the Howler, "are we going to ride all night? These *sogwilis* at least must have some rest soon or they will give out on us."

"*Howa,*" said the Howler. "We'll stop just over there and make a camp for the night."

They stopped and dismounted at a place where the trees were thin, and the way down to the water was easy, and they turned the horses loose to graze on the prairie grass or wander at will to the water's edge to drink. Tournier assured the Howler that with the reins trailing on the ground the animals would not wander far. They gathered wood and built four small fires. That would do for their numbers.

They ate *gahawista*, the dried, parched corn, and dried meat, and like the horses they went to the edge of the water to drink. In a short while, most of the men had stretched out on the ground to sleep and a few had been assigned to watch.

Tournier had been right. The Frenchmen were groaning and grumbling among themselves.

"This is insane," said one. "This driving of us all day like so many cattle."

"When cattle are driven," said Étienne, "men must drive them."

"You know what I mean," said the other. "I would not even drive cattle so long in one day."

"The Indiens are not complaining," said Étienne. "Can a Frenchman not keep up with *les sauvages?*"

"They're not human," said the complainer. "That's like asking me to keep up on foot with a horse."

"If I were you," said Étienne, "I'd keep my voice low. Remember the fate of *monsieur le docteur* DuBois and his little band of traitors."

"Ah, I'm not going to mutiny," said the groaning one, "but I can talk, can't I?"

Off a ways from his men, Tournier noticed the Howler standing alone, leaning against a tree and staring into the distance ahead, almost as if he might actually be able to see something out there somewhere. Of course he could not. They had not seen anything ahead of them earlier, and now it was getting dark. The captain walked over to stand beside the Wolf Clan leader.

"What manner of men are these that we are pursuing?" he asked.

"Slavecatchers, they said," the Howler answered.

"But they are Indiens?"

"Yes."

"They capture their own kind to sell into slavery?"

"Yes. It seems so."

"To the Spaniards?"

"It must be."

"What are they called?"

"Slavecatchers."

"I don't understand," said Tournier. "What were they called before there were Spaniards here?"

"I don't know," said the Howler.

Tournier found it puzzling, but he supposed that the Howler did, too. Could there be a whole tribe of Indians allied to the Spaniards? That did not seem likely. All of the Indians he had met hated the Spaniards. If not a whole tribe, then what? Outlaws? Renegades? And the Spaniards—where were they? He had thought that they were well out of these parts, far south in the land they called Florida. Might they have come back? If so, that was a matter of grave concern, not only for all these Indians, but also for his own government.

"Well," he said, "another day might bring us all the answers. Right now I'm going to sleep."

"Howa," said the Howler. "I think I'll watch awhile."

The Howler was worried. He had no doubts about catching up with the Slavecatchers, but he wondered if he would catch them in time to save Striker and Woyi and the young woman he did not even know. He wanted to catch and kill the Slavecatchers, and he was confident that he would accomplish that. But he also wanted to save the three Real People. That was even more important than the other part of his mission.

Comes Back to Life was not sleeping. He lay awake thinking about his duty to New Town and the cycle of ceremonies that he would lead. Already they had missed the Ceremony of the Bush, because they had been busy building a town. They would start the cycle at New Town, then, with the Ceremony of the Great Moon, and it would be time for that one before long.

He turned and reached over toward his wife, and his arm went around the Little Spaniard, sleeping between them. The three of them were lying on a thick bear rug on the floor of Guwisti's new house. When she felt his arm on her, Guwisti put her hands on it and squeezed a little.

"I thought you were asleep." she said.

"No."

"Does it bother you very much," she asked, "having the little one here between us?"

"No," he said. "Of course not. His father was my best friend, and I'm now responsible for his family. I'm proud of you for helping so much with this one."

She smiled, but of course, he could not see the smile there in the darkness.

"I don't mind. I like it. I feel almost like he belongs to us," she said, "this Little Spaniard."

"Well, in a way, he does," said Comes Back to Life. "Are you sure, then, that you don't mind?"

"Oh, no," she said. "Why would I mind? He's a beautiful little boy."

"When first we talked of marriage," he said, "all this was not in our plans."

"No. We had no way of knowing. Neither of us."

"We haven't had much chance to be alone, you and I," he said, "and it's all my doing. I'm to blame, and now you're the one who's being kept busy with this little one that isn't even yours."

"I don't mind at all. I love the Little Spaniard as much as if he were yours and mine."

"Then everything is good," said Comes Back to Life. "Besides, he sleeps a lot, and so we still can—"

"I'm glad that you're awake," she said, "and I'm glad that we started talking about this matter."

"Oh?"

"Yes. I've been thinking about something," she said. "It's something I've been wanting to suggest, but it has never seemed to be the right time."

"Yes?" he said. "What is it?"

"It's not an easy thing for me to say to you."

"Whatever it is," he said, "you can say it to me. I'm your husband. We share everything, you and I."

"Well," she said, "Osa's house is just here beside mine. And her baby boy is sleeping here between us, and he seems like he's our own. Osa's husband was your best friend, and she and her little ones are your responsibility anyway. Osa has no man, and she has no family here among us. I like her almost like a sister."

"Go on," he said.

"With your new position, you have plenty. You can easily provide for all of us."

"Yes," he said. "That's true."

"You're an important man now," she said. "Perhaps you should have two wives."

Comes Back to Life was astonished. What Guwisti had just suggested was not all that unusual among the Real People, but he had never thought of having a wife other than Guwist'. Had the thought come into his mind, he would never have believed that she would be the one to suggest such a thing. He sat up and looked toward her, but he couldn't see her there in the darkness.

"You think that I should marry Osa?" he said.

"Yes. Of course."

"But I—I never thought of that."

"That's why I had to think of it for you," she said. "Well?"

"Well, I—"

"Don't you like her?"

"Yes. Of course I do, but I never thought of her—in that way."

"She's beautiful. Don't you think so?"

"Well, yes, but—"

"But what?"

"I wouldn't know how to ask her. She might not like the idea."

"Don't worry about that part," said Guwisti. "I'll ask her for you. That's the way it should be done anyway. That way, she'll know that I approve."

"I— Well, all right."

Guwisti snuggled down into the bear rug.

"Well," she said, "now that's settled, let's get some sleep."

But Comes Back to Life was wide awake, and he kept awake almost all that night, thinking about what his wife had said and wondering about what life might hold in store for him in his near future.

In the house of Tsiwon', Oliga was not resting well. He flopped from one side to the other. He tossed and turned and groaned out loud. He could not find a comfortable way to sleep it seemed. At last Tsiwon' sat up.

"Olig'," she said.

He sat up, startled.

"What?" he said. "What is it?"

"You're wide awake, and it isn't me that's keeping you awake. It's something else you're thinking about, something that's bothering you."

"I'm all right," he said. "I just can't seem to get to sleep tonight. That's all."

"No, that's not all," she said. "You've been like this for days now. Here tonight, ever since you came to bed, you've been rolling around. Once you almost hit me when you swung your arm, flopping over this direction."

"Oh. I didn't mean to. I'll go outside to sleep," he said. "That way I won't bother you."

"Sit still," she said sharply.

"What?"

"I don't want you to go outside. I want you to rest properly, right here beside me where you belong."

"Well, I'll try to be still," he said, and his voice was pouty, like that of a child who's just been chastised.

"Olig'," she said, "listen to me. I know what's bothering you, and I know the only thing that will make you relax. Tomorrow, first thing, you need to get some young men to agree to go with you and go out to look for Striker and the others."

"But can I leave New Town?" he asked. "So soon? The safety of New Town is my responsibility."

"Most of the work here is done now," she said, "and there are men enough here to leave in charge of New Town's defense and still take some out on the trail. Talk to them tomorrow and make your plans."

"The Howler is out there already with plenty of men," he said.

"Even so, you can't stop thinking about it."

Oliga thought for a moment in silence.

"Yes," he said. "You're right. I will do what you suggested, and I'll get started first thing in the morning."

She thought that she could hear the sense of relief in his voice, as well as a little excitement. She was glad to know that he still had some of that youthful exuberance in him. He lay back down, and Tsiwon' noticed that he was still, and very soon he was asleep. He slept well the rest of that night.

It was late, and they were about ready to stop for the night when they saw the smoke. It was smoke from several fires, and it was not far ahead.

"Look," said Awiakta.

"Yes," said Woyi. "I see it."

"A village?" she asked.

"Or a large camp."

"Is it the Slavecatchers, do you think?"

"I don't know," he said. "If it is, they've joined their friends, and there are many more of them for us to deal with than there were before."

"Let's get closer and see," she said.

"Wait. Let's decide first how best to do it."

She pointed south, to their right. They had reached a point where the prairie had narrowed to a small band of flatland between the tree-lined river and a low mountain range.

"We can ride over there," she said, "leave your *sogwili* at the base of the mountain and climb to the top to take a look."

"Well," he said. He hesitated, then added, "Yes."

At the top of the mountain they looked across the narrow band of prairie and over the tops of the trees to a kind of town. There were houses, and there was a fence, but the houses all seemed to be outside the fence, and the smoke they had seen came mostly from the houses. There was one large fire burning, a fire so large that it made no sense to either of the Real People.

"What do you think?" she said.

"I've never seen anything quite like it," he said, "and so I think it's the Slavecatchers' town. I've never seen anyone like them before, either."

"Then the ones that we've been following, and Striker," she said, "must be in there somewhere."

"I think so," he said.

"Should we find out for sure?"

"How?" he asked.

"I could get down close and look," she said.

"That's dangerous," he said. "I don't want you to do that. Striker wouldn't want you to do that, either. He's there because he was concerned about your safety."

"I can do it. I won't try anything, either. I'll just get a look and come back and tell you what I saw. I won't get caught."

"Ha," said Woyi. "They caught you once already."

"Yes. Near my own home where I felt safe. I wasn't watching. I thought that you men were doing your job."

Woyi felt the sting of that last statement. Still, he didn't like the idea of Awiakta putting herself in danger.

"I don't know," he said. "I think I should go and look while you wait here."

"I moved through the woods back there where we found that Slavecatcher's body," she said, "and you never knew what I was doing. Did you?"

50

It seemed to Woyi that she had been gone for a very long time. He chastised himself for having let her go, especially alone. But then, she was a very difficult person to try to control. When she had made up her mind, it seemed, there was just no changing it. She was headstrong, stubborn, even.

He tried to reassure himself, or perhaps to assuage his own conscience, by repeating what she herself had said. Earlier, she had indeed slipped into the woods just behind him and gone quietly through to the abandoned campsite. Surely she would be able to get close enough to the large camp below to find out what they needed to know without getting herself caught, without any of the Slavecatchers even suspecting that she was anywhere near.

Still he was worried, and he was feeling guilty. He did not want anything to happen to Awiakta. Her initial rescue was the thing that had set off this whole dangerous trek, and if anything should happen to her now, he thought, it all would have been for nothing.

But that wasn't all. He was worried about her because he liked her. He liked her more than he wanted to admit, even to himself. He tried not to think of her in that way, for such thoughts made him feel disloyal to Striker. Well, he couldn't control his thoughts, but he could certainly resolve to never let them be known and to never act on them.

At last, tired of his thoughts and tired of waiting, he decided that she had been gone way too long, and he was not going to just sit around and wait any longer. He would leave the horse there at the base of the mountain and go on foot across to the woods and then on up to the edge of the camp. He would find her and make sure that she was safe. He gathered his weapons and stepped toward the open land.

"Where are you going?" said Awiakta.

He flinched, startled by her sudden presence. She had done it to him again. "I didn't hear you come back," he said.

"They didn't hear me down there, either."

"Did you slip up behind me like that on purpose," he asked, "just to show me how good you are?"

"I came back the same way I left," she said, ignoring the accusation.

"What did you see?"

"It's the Slavecatchers, all right, and there are maybe seventy or eighty of them. They keep their captives inside the fence."

"Did you see Striker?"

"Yes," she said. "They have him tied to a frame of poles all alone. It's just beside the big fire. He seemed to be all right, but they're planning to do something to him, the way they have him tied up there."

"They must be waiting for morning," said Woyi.

"Yes. I think so."

"Then we should do something tonight," he said. "Now."

"But we should plan it carefully first," she said. "Even if we get him loose from there, they'll come after us. We have your *sogwili*, but there are three of us. And they have some *sogwilis* too."

"How many do they have?"

"Not many for such a large camp. I saw only six."

"Where are they?"

"They're enclosed in a circle of rope on the other side of the wall, between the camp and the river."

"Are there guards?"

"Just two, and they're standing at the entrance to the fence, guarding the captives. And the rest of the Slavecatchers are mostly asleep. A few of them are still walking around, but they're staggering. I don't know what's wrong with them. They seem to be sleepy or dizzy. I don't know."

They mounted up and rode east alongside the base of the mountain until they were well beyond the camp of the Slavecatchers. Then they turned north and rode to the river's edge. There they dismounted and led the horse. When they were close enough to see the wall and the six horses in the makeshift corral, they stopped. They didn't need to talk, for they had made their plans.

Awiakta waited with the horse while Woyi went silently forward to the rope corral. No one was in sight. No voices were to be heard. The huts were all on the west side of the big, wobbly circular fence. He eased himself in among the horses, and some of them stamped and snorted a little, and he stood still for a moment and waited to see if anyone had heard. But no one came.

He examined the enclosure. Short poles, not as high as his shoulders, had been stuck into the ground at intervals in a circle around the horses, and one long rope was strung from pole to pole. He noticed that the horses wore no *gayahulos* on their backs, but that the lines with which to guide them were still attached to their heads, and the other ends of those lines were wrapped around the long rope.

As quietly as he could, and looking up from time to time to make sure that no one was coming, Woyi got the long rope loose from the poles. He left the lines from the horses attached to the rope, however. Then he took both ends of the long rope in his hand. That way he could lead all six animals together. He did pull loose the lines of one horse, and that one he mounted. He turned to look back in the direction of Awiakta, and he waved.

She rode quietly up to his side. They glanced at one another, and they started to walk the horses around the wall to the west end where the houses all stood and where the big fire burned.

Striker's muscles ached. He wasn't sure just what the Slavecatchers had in mind to do to him, but he almost wished that the Sun would hurry up and crawl out from under the eastern edge of the Sky Vault to start the new day, and they would get on with it, whatever it might be.

He had no idea how much longer it would be before the Sun would emerge. He was sleepy, but he had not slept, standing up and stretched out the way he was. Most of the camp, it seemed, had gone to sleep. A number of the Slavecatchers had stayed up well into the night drinking the crazy water that Breaks Their Heads had told him about.

They had talked loud, laughed and almost gotten into fights with one another, and then, one by one, they had crawled into their filthy little huts or just rolled over on the ground where they were sitting and gone to sleep. Not even the two guards at the entrance to the compound seemed to be alert. They were sitting, leaning back against the rickety fence.

Suddenly the pounding of hooves and a loud, chilling turkey-gobble war whoop split the night air, and Striker knew that it was Woyi come at last. And then he saw Woyi. He was mounted, and he was riding hard around the enclosure, and there were other horses running, but as the image became clearer, Striker also saw that only one of the other horses had a rider.

Striker was still puzzling over the riderless horses, when Woyi rode up alongside him tied there to the frame, reached up with his knife and cut the rope which held Striker to the top crosspiece. Suddenly released, Striker almost fell. His wrists were still tied together, and his hands and arms were numb, but he was free at last from the frame. Woyi maneuvered ahead just a little, pulling one of the riderless horses up beside Striker.

"Get on," he cried.

Just then Breaks Their Heads came out of a nearby hut, a war club in his hand. He quickly took in the situation, raised his club and ran roaring toward Striker, who was just then swinging up onto the back of a horse. Awiakta saw the Slavecatcher coming. She kicked her heels into the sides of her mount and raced directly toward him.

Breaks Their Heads saw her just in time to know what was coming at him, but too late to make any defensive adjustments. He roared out his astonishment an instant before the big horse ran hard into him, knocking him flat and running over him. He screamed as he shielded his face and head with his arms, and the hard, sharp hooves stomped his ribs and his legs.

A few other Slavecatchers had come awake by this time, but as they came bewildered and fuzzy-headed out of their huts, they saw only the dust kicked up by the horses, and they saw Breaks Their Heads writhing in pain there on the ground. Then they noticed that their captive was gone. Breaks Their Heads, groaning, got up to his knees.

"Get the horses," he shouted. "Catch them! Hurry!"

Two of the more clear-headed men ran toward their makeshift corral around on the other side of the fence. A short while later they came walking back.

"Our horses are all gone," said one.

Breaks Their Heads cursed loudly in Spanish for a while. Then, slowly and painfully, he got to his feet.

"We'll wait until morning, then," he said. "They won't go far tonight anyway. Not in the dark. And then, even in the daytime, *caballos* have to stop and rest. We'll catch them. We'll get them back. There were only two of them. With the one they set free, there are only three."

They rode hard, putting distance between themselves and the Slavecatchers' camp. When Woyi felt that they had gotten a safe-enough distance away, he called a halt.

"This is far enough for now," he said.

Striker looked back, as if he wasn't quite sure about the judgment of his friend.

"They're on foot," said Woyi. "It's all right. Even if they're coming after us, they won't catch up with us very soon. We got away with all their horses."

Striker glanced back over his shoulder one more time. Then he smiled, threw a leg over the horse's back and slid down to the ground.

"I knew you were coming, Woyi," he said.

He held his still-bound wrists out toward Woyi, and Woyi cut the ropes. Striker rubbed his wrists to get the circulation back to normal.

"There," said Woyi. "Now you can ride better. Shall we chase these extra horses off or take them home with us?"

"I'm not going home," said Striker. "Not yet."

"Why not?" Woyi asked.

"I want to pay those Slavecatchers back for what they've done," said Striker, "and besides, they still have one hundred captives back there. I want to set them free."

Woyi thought for a moment.

"All right, then," he said. "Howler and some others are coming. I don't know how far back they are. Let's ride and meet them, and then all of us together can come back here and attack the Slavecatchers."

"*Howa,*" said Striker. "That's good."

Awiakta had been sitting quietly all this time. Deciding that she had been ignored long enough by these two friends, she slid down off the back of her mount, and for the first time since his rescue, Striker looked at her.

"I'm called Awiakta," she said. "Thank you for what you did for me. I'm glad to see you free and well."

"But you are—"

"Yes. I'm the one that you set free," she said. "I'm the reason that you were captured. Since you helped me, I thought that I should try to help you."

"And she really was a help," said Woyi.

He told Striker all about the way that Awiakta had found the evidence of the boat and how she had sneaked down alone to get a look at the Slavecatchers' town. He even told Striker that she had helped to make the plans to cut him loose.

Awiakta modestly looked at the ground, but she was glad that Woyi was bragging on her to Striker. Striker, after all, did not know her at all. He had seen her briefly, only as a captive, and he had set her free, and she had run. They had never before even spoken to each other, not really.

She wanted him to know her, and she wanted to know him better. And still she asked herself, Which of these two young men am I the most interested in? She knew the full meaning of their friendship, and she realized that there could be a danger if she tried to come between them in any way, if she did or said anything to set them up as rivals for her attention.

It wasn't a physical danger, of course, and it wasn't a danger to either one of the men. The danger was that, if she was not very careful, both of them might turn away from her. They had made Friendship before the people, and nothing could come between them. That was something that she had to accept and figure out how to deal with.

Somehow, she knew, she would have to get to know both of them better. She would have to decide which one she really wanted, and, of course, she would have to find out which one, if either, would really be interested in her.

If neither one showed any real interest, then she would simply have to decide which one to set her sights on and find some way of making him interested in her. But even that decision would not be an easy one for her to make, for she liked them both. She liked them very much.

51

S triker, Woyi and Awiakta rode a little farther that night, and then they stopped to make a camp and rest. Woyi had a little trail food left in his traveling pack, and he shared it with the other two. They built a small fire and then they ate.

"One of us should stay awake at night," said Striker, "in case the Slave-catchers are following us."

"I think you should sleep," said Woyi. "Both of you. I'll watch."

"All right," said Striker, "but don't watch all night. Wake one of us in a little while. We'll all take a turn."

"*Howa,*" said Woyi, and he turned to start a climb up the side of the mountain. They had made their camp at the base of the mountain, rather than beside the river. Anyone following them, they thought, would look beside the river first. "I'll be able to see farther from up there."

It was foolish to climb at night. Woyi knew that. But he went slow and picked his way carefully. He really would be able to see farther, but the real reason he had decided to go up was to leave the other two alone, to let them have some time together. He didn't want to be in the way of whatever might develop between them.

"You have a good friend in Woyi," Awiakta said.

"Yes," said Striker. "I know. We made Friendship together, he and I."

"Yes," she said. "I know. He told me. I think that he was angry with me for a while."

"Why?" Striker asked. "How could he be angry with you?"

"He blamed me for your capture."

"It was no more your fault than it was my own for deciding to try to rescue you," said Striker. "He shouldn't have felt that way. What did he say—"

"He didn't say anything like that," she said. "I felt it from the way he spoke to me, that's all. Later he got over it. He told me what he'd been thinking, and he said that he was wrong."

"Oh, well," said Striker, "then that's all right. I'm glad."

"He didn't want me to come along with him to find you, either," said Awiakta. "He wanted me to go back to meet the others from your town, the ones who are following him."

"You should have," said Striker. "It would have been safer for you."

"Are you not glad that I'm here?" she said, and she moved a little closer to him.

"Oh, well, I—don't mind. It's all right now, I guess. We should be safe from the Slavecatchers by now, and tomorrow we'll probably meet the Howler and the others. Then the Slavecatchers will be the ones who need to worry."

"I'm glad I stayed with Woyi," she said. "I hoped to see you again, so I could thank you, and—"

She put a hand on his shoulder, and he felt a thrill run through his body. But this woman had been alone with Woyi for some time, and Striker thought that he could see something in the way they looked at one another. She was tempting. She was very tempting, but Woyi was his friend.

"I'm very tired," he said.

"Of course you are," she said. "Lie down. I'll hold your head while you sleep."

When Woyi came back down, he saw them there. They were both asleep, Striker's head upon her breast. He felt a pang of jealousy, but he fought it back. Striker was his friend, and he knew that he should feel good for Striker's good fortune. He would not wake them, he decided. He could keep watch until morning. He was strong. Striker had been treated badly and needed his sleep. Besides, they looked too comfortable to bother.

He turned to go back up the mountainside, and his foot slipped on a loose rock. It wasn't much. He caught his balance quickly and started to move on. But it had made a little noise, and Striker raised his head.

"Woyi," he said.

"I didn't mean to wake you," Woyi said. "Go back to sleep."

"No," said Striker. "I slept well. I'm awake now, and it's my turn to watch."

Before Woyi could argue more, Striker was on his feet. Awiakta lifted up her head.

"I can watch," she said.

"Both of you sleep," said Striker, and he started walking west, back toward the Slavecatchers' camp. "I'll watch from over here."

Both Awiakta and Woyi looked after Striker until he disappeared in the darkness. Awiakta shrugged.

"Come on over here next to the fire," she said.

"I'll sleep here," said Woyi.

"Why? Are you afraid of me?"

"Of course not," he said. "That's a foolish question to ask me. Have we not been traveling together?"

"Are you mad at me again?"

"No," he said, but he said it angrily.

"You are mad at me again," she said. "I understood why you were mad at me before, but I thought that you had gotten over it."

"I'm not angry with you," he said. "It's just that—"

"What?" she said. "What is it? Come over here and sit beside me so we can talk."

He felt himself giving in. He didn't want to, but her voice was so soft and gentle and compelling. He walked over and sat on the ground, just to talk, he told himself.

"Striker is my friend," he said.

"I know that. I like him too. Is that a reason to be angry with me?"

"I saw you with him."

"While I was holding his head? I made him comfortable so he could sleep. That's all."

"You didn't—"

"No. We didn't. Come here now. You've been awake too long. Come here and sleep."

The Sun had crawled out from under the eastern edge of the Sky Vault before Striker walked back to the camp. When he got there, Woyi and Awiakta were already awake. The fire had been put out, and Woyi was busy gathering the horses.

"No one is in sight behind us yet," said Striker.

"Let's take the *sogwilis* to the river for a drink," said Woyi. "Then we should be on our way."

They walked, leading the horses across the narrow strip of prairie, then through the woods to the water's edge, and there they let them drink.

"You didn't come back and wake me so I could watch," Awiakta said to Striker. "I hope you slept enough last night."

"I slept well," he said.

Striker and Woyi were both quiet, saying no more than they had to say to one another. Awiakta, one the other hand, was lively and happy. She smiled and talked. They both liked her. She knew. She thought that she would be able to have either one of them. But which one did she want? That was her only problem.

"Let's go," said Striker, and they each mounted a horse and led the other four. They rode west.

Oliga left New Town at the head of twenty men, all armed and ready for a fight. He didn't know exactly where he was going. He only knew that men from New Town, in the company of French and Senika allies, had gone on a mission to rescue a young woman of the Real People, and they had not returned. He felt responsible, and he intended to find them. He would follow his own path from Kituwah back to the point where the others had left, and then he would track them. Somehow, he would find them.

"I've talked to the women of both clans," Guwisti said, "and everyone agrees that it would be a good thing to do."

Osa looked at the ground in front of her. It had been a complete surprise to her, the thing that Guwisti had just proposed. She had never thought of marrying again. Not once since the loss of her husband. She had thought only of her two children, and of the time she would rejoin Asquani in the land of the spirits. She had not thought of marrying, and even if she had, she would not have considered Comes Back to Life as one of her prospects.

She did not dislike Comes Back to Life, did not find him unattractive. She did not even hold against him the fact that he had killed her husband. That had been an unfortunate accident. She had simply never thought of Comes Back to Life in that way.

She had first known him as a rash young man, then as a friend of her husband, and more recently, her benefactor, and the husband of her friend. But it was her friend, Guwisti, who had made the proposal.

"Thank you," she said, "but I don't know. He might not want to do this. He has a wife already."

"He can have two wives," said Guwisti. "Many important men have two wives. I've already talked to him about this, but of course, if you don't like my husband—"

"Oh, I do," said Osa. "I like him very much. It's just that—I never thought of him—that way. I think of him as just your husband."

"Will you talk to him about this?" Guwisti asked.

Osa still hung her head. It would be nice, she thought, to be a wife again, even a second wife, and since the thought had been put into her head by Guwisti, Comes Back to Life would make a good husband. She imagined that any other unmarried woman would quickly agree to what had been proposed to her.

And would it be fair of her, she asked herself, to refuse this offer and still allow Comes Back to Life to provide a living for her and for her two little ones? It would not be fair, she thought. Did she need the living he provided? Of course she did.

And what about the attitudes of the other residents of New Town toward her and toward her daughter? Would that change if she became the wife of Comes Back to Life? She imagined that it would.

"I'll talk to him," she said.

The Sun was high overhead, visiting at her daughter's house, when Awiakta saw the riders coming toward them from the west.

"Look," she said.

They stopped the horses.

"Who is it?" she asked. "Can you tell?"

"Not yet," said Woyi.

They sat on their horses' backs and waited for the others to come near enough to recognize. Then Woyi spotted Jacques Tournier's funny hat.

"I see the Frenchman," he said. "It's our friends. Come on."

They raced ahead until they met the others. Then they all stopped and dismounted, and the Howler had them make a camp to rest and eat.

"You two young men have done very well," he said. "And is this the young woman you went to rescue?"

"Yes," said Striker. "This is Awiakta."

"She helped me to rescue Striker," said Woyi.

They told the whole story to the Howler and the others, how Striker had rescued Awiakta only to get himself captured, how Woyi had met Awiakta and the two of them together had followed Striker and his captors, how they had found the Slavecatchers' camp and rescued Striker.

"Do you think that any of them are chasing you?" the Howler asked.

"I think that some of them are probably on our trail," said Striker.

"But they're on foot," said Woyi, "and we were riding, so we outdistanced them."

"Then I think that we should make a surprise for them," said the Howler. He turned toward Owl, the Senika. "What do you think, my friend?"

"I think a surprise is a good idea," said Owl.

"While you are setting the trap," said Tournier, "I can ride up on top of that mountain and look to see how many of them are coming."

"Good," said the Howler.

"The mountain is steep and rocky," said Woyi, "and it's covered with thick brush. It won't be easy to ride a *sogwili* up there."

Tournier smiled.

"I'll find a way to get him up there, my friend," he said. "And I'll be back with the information well before they get here."

52

Tournier rode along the base of the mountain looking for a way up. What Woyi had said seemed to be generally true, but the Frenchman would not give up. There was always a way, he told himself, and he had to make good on his boast. At last he found a place that looked like a possibility. It wasn't really a path or trail, but he could make it one, he told himself. It would do.

He turned his mare directly toward the mountain and urged her forward and up. She dug her hooves into the steep earth and lunged and struggled, climbing toward the top. Tournier leaned low against her neck. About halfway up, he realized that she wasn't going to make it much farther carrying him on her back. He quickly dismounted and moved ahead of her, pulling on the reins, urging her on.

It was a hard climb, but at last they made it. Together they made it, and Tournier praised the mare and patted her and rubbed her. Then he walked with her along the ridge a ways, and then he climbed onto her back once more, and they continued moving east, the man watching the valley below.

At last he saw them. A band of perhaps twenty Indians trotting along the flat land of the valley floor headed west. Tournier reached into the saddlebag on his right side and withdrew from it a long spyglass to get a closer look. The men were heavily armed, and their faces were grim and determined. He had not seen the Slavecatchers, but he imagined that these were they.

He put away the spyglass, turned his mare and headed back to join the others.

The Howler put Owl and all the Senikas at the base of the mountain, hidden behind brush and boulders, and he sent all the Frenchmen to the woods across the clearing. He and the other Real People—Striker and Woyi and the Wild Man and others from Itowah—moved farther west, then waited just in the middle of the flat land, in plain view of anyone who might happen to come along.

If everything went according to the Howler's plan, the Slavecatchers would run right past the concealed Senikas and Frenchmen before they saw the Real People. Then it would be too late for them. They would already be caught in the trap.

Striker, Woyi, the Howler and Wild Man were mounted. Awiakta was also mounted and was waiting there with them, in spite of strong protests from both Striker and Woyi. Weapons had been provided for Striker and Awiakta. The other Real People were on foot, just behind the mounted ones.

Then they saw Tournier returning, and the Howler rode out alone to meet him.

"Twenty Indiens are coming," the Frenchman said. "I think they are the ones we wait for."

"Good," said the Howler. "We're ready for them now."

He told Tournier where his men were hidden, and gave the Frenchman his choice of joining them or the Real People. Tournier rode back with the Howler to wait with the line of mounted men and Awiakta.

They didn't have long to wait. The Slavecatchers came into view, and, as soon as they saw the Real People and the Frenchman waiting there, they stopped.

"Are those the Slavecatchers?" the Howler asked.

"They seem to be," said Awiakta. "They're still too far away for me to tell for sure."

"Come on," said the Howler, and he started his mount forward at a slow walk. The others moved along with him. The Slavecatchers stood waiting, tense, ready for anything. The riders drew closer, and Striker saw and recognized the one with the slit ear.

"These are they," he said.

Without another word, the Howler sent forth the shrill and eerie sound of the turkey, and all of the riders kicked their mounts into a run. The Slavecatchers braced themselves for the onslaught. There were twenty of them, and they were faced with six mounted attackers. They were not unfamiliar with horses. Still, the sight of a horse and rider racing straight toward a man on foot is intimidating, to say the least.

Then they saw the others coming, the ones on foot running behind the horses. They had set out, twenty of them, to catch up with two escaped captives and one other man, twenty against three. Suddenly they faced an equal number of warriors, six of them were mounted, and it was a small consolation that one was a woman.

Sliced-Ear and a few more boldly stood their ground. The others scattered, some running straight back in the direction from which they had come, others toward the trees along the riverbank, still others toward the mountain.

Striker aimed his horse at Sliced-Ear, but just as he would have crashed into him, Sliced-Ear stepped aside and swung his war club at Striker. It was a blunt club, meant for cracking skulls, and it caught Striker only a glancing blow along his thigh as he rode past his enemy.

Striker turned his mount. Sliced-Ear was waiting for him, braced for the attack. This time, as he rode alongside the Slavecatcher, Striker threw himself from his horse's back. With his left hand, he caught the right wrist of Sliced-Ear, and his right arm went around the other's head. His weight and his momentum bore them both to the ground.

The Howler dealt a blow to the head of another Slavecatcher as he rode by. The man was spun around by the force of the blow, but he was still on his feet. He dropped his weapon and stood on wobbly legs holding his head in both his hands. The Howler turned his mount, intending to ride back and finish off the man, but just then Awiakta stopped her horse beside the dazed Slavecatcher, and with her borrowed war club, crushed his skull.

Tournier cut one man's neck halfway through with a single swipe of his long steel sword. Woyi rode one down, the hooves of his mount trampling his foe into the ground. By this time the Real People on foot had arrived, and they swarmed over the remaining few.

Just then Sliced-Ear managed to heave Striker off and to the side, and the two men stood facing each other. Sliced-Ear tossed aside his war club and pulled out his steel-bladed Spanish knife. Striker recalled vividly having watched Sliced-Ear kill a man with that same blade. He balanced his war club and waited for Sliced-Ear to make a move.

Then Sliced-Ear lunged, and Striker jumped aside, just avoiding the deadly blade. At the same time, he swung his club with all his might, bringing it down on the right forearm of Sliced-Ear. He heard the sound of the bone as it cracked, and he heard the scream of pain that came from the mouth of Sliced-Ear.

Sliced-Ear stood staring ahead at Striker with wide, disbelieving eyes, his Spanish steel knife on the ground in front of him, his right arm hanging useless at his side. Striker stepped forward, shifting the war club to his left hand. He bent to pick up Sliced-Ear's knife and held it up before the face of the man to make sure that he knew what was about to happen. Then he lowered it, and with a short underhand thrust, drove it deep, just under the rib cage and up into Sliced-Ear's heart.

The once-dangerous Slavecatcher slumped and fell forward as his warm blood gushed forth onto the hand and arm of Striker. Striker stepped back and jerked the knife free at the same time, and the lifeless body crumpled there before him.

The Slavecatchers who had run toward the mountain were just about to reach their imagined safety, when Owl and all the other Senikas stood up to reveal themselves. All were armed with bows and arrows. The Slavecatchers saw them and stopped as the Senikas drew back their bows. The arrows flew. Some of the Slavecatchers managed to turn their backs to run before the arrows found their marks. Some did not. All of them dropped with Senika arrows in their backs or chests.

Across the way, the other group of fleeing Slavecatchers was surprised by gunfire from the French. The gunshots killed a few, but for the most part the Senika arrows had been much more deadly and accurate than the French guns. The Frenchmen, having discharged their firearms, rushed out of the woods to finish the job with swords and knives.

The few remaining Slavecatchers were the ones who had turned to run straight back the way they had come, and the horsemen ran them all down in short order.

The bloody business was done without a single casualty on the side of the Real People and their allies. They gathered together there in the middle of the valley floor, congratulating each other on a job well done, and Striker walked over to stand beside the Howler.

"We've killed twenty of them here today," he said.

"That's good," said the Howler, "and none of us are hurt."

"Yes," said Striker, "it is good, but there are eighty more Slavecatchers back at their camp, and they are holding one hundred captives there. Many of the captives are women and children."

"Well," said the Howler, "shall we go then and wipe out the rest of these ugly people?"

Comes Back to Life walked over to the house of Osa. He had tried to think just what words he would say to her, but he hadn't been able to come up with anything. He felt awkward and clumsy, but he had promised Guwisti that he would do this thing, and, he thought, since she had brought it up, it did seem the right and proper thing to do. He found Osa sitting just outside the doorway at the front of her house.

" *'Siyo,*" he said.

She knew why he was there. She was embarrassed. She ducked her head.

" *'Siyo,*" she said.

"Where is your little one?" he asked. It seemed a stupid way to start the conversation, but he had to say something, and besides, it was unusual to see her without little Whirlwind clinging to her.

"You mean Whirlwind?" she asked.

"Yes," he said. "Of course. The other is with Guwist'."

"She's inside sleeping," Osa said.

"I see."

The moment was even more awkward than Osa had expected, and she asked herself why she had allowed Guwisti to put this thing in motion. She had expected to feel awkward herself, but she had also expected Comes Back to Life to take charge of the situation. But he stood there, not knowing what to do or what to say, and she could sense his discomfort, and she decided that she would try to give him some relief.

"I know why you've come to see me," she said. "And I also know that it was not your own idea. You don't have to go through with this. You can go back home if you want to. It's all right. If Guwisti should ask you anything about it, you can tell her that you tried, and I said no."

"Are you saying no, then?" he asked. "Do you not want—"

"I don't want to be your wife because you pity me," she said, "or because you think you owe me something from the past. I don't hold anything against you, and I appreciate what you've been doing for me. You and Guwisti. That's enough."

He stood a moment and looked at her sitting there, her head modestly inclined, and he told himself that she was beautiful, and she was young still, and, of course, he did still feel a heavy sense of responsibility toward her and her two little ones, in spite of what she had just said. He always would.

"If you don't want me for a husband," he said, "I'll go, and of course I'll continue to provide for you and your little ones—but if we should marry, it would not be out of pity or out of my sense of obligation to you. It would be because I have strong feelings for you, and so does my wife. It would be because we both—all three of us, I mean—have strong feelings for your children, both of them, and already my wife and I feel like we four really are a family." He hesitated just a moment before going on. "And if we were to marry, you and I, it would also be because you are young and beautiful, and I find myself—attracted to you—very much."

Then for the first time, she looked up, and she saw his eyes, briefly, before she looked away again. He looked sincere. He seemed to mean what he was saying, and she felt a warmth that she had thought she would never feel again. But there was another matter, and she thought that she should mention it at least.

"You know," she said, "do you not, what the people are saying about my daughter?"

She paused, but Comes Back to Life did not immediately respond, and so she continued.

"They've been saying that Uyona made my baby into a witch," she said. "Uyona helped me with my babies, and in exchange she made me leave Whirlwind with her. She kept Whirlwind until she died, and then I took her back. Uyona even gave her name to her: Whirlwind. Because she is one of a pair of twins, and because the old woman kept her for a time, they're saying that my daughter is a little witch, and they're afraid of her. Did you know about all this?"

"I've heard some of that foolish talk," said Comes Back to Life.

"And you do not believe it? It doesn't worry you to take on such a child?"

"Whirlwind is a beautiful little baby girl," said Comes Back to Life. "That's all. How could I believe such stories about her? Some of the people say that Uyona was a witch, but I don't believe that talk, either. Uyona helped me and Guwisti with her predictions. I don't listen to the foolish talk of people who have nothing better to do with themselves than tell tales."

There really was nothing more to be said after that, for he had just said the one thing that was more important to her than anything else in the world.

"Sit down," she said. "I'll get you something to eat."

53

The company of the Howler was camped for the night, and guards were posted all around. Most of the others—Real People, Senikas and Frenchmen—were asleep, but the leaders, the Howler, Owl, the Wild Man of Itowah and Capitaine Jacques Tournier, sat together beside a small fire. Just a short distance away, Awiakta was in quiet conversation with both Striker and Woyi, the three of them sitting close together.

"Something interesting is going on over there with your three young people," said Owl, with a wise and sly smile on his face.

"Maybe," said the Howler. "I don't know. Those three have been through much together. They must have many things to talk about."

"Yes," said Owl. "I suppose they have."

But the smile lingered on his face.

"Will we arrive at the Slavecatchers' camp tomorrow?" Tournier asked.

"Striker said that we should," said the Howler. "But it will be late in the day."

"And will we attack as soon as we arrive?"

The Howler shrugged.

"We'll see when we get there," he said. "Right now, I think that probably we will."

"We'll be outnumbered in this fight," the Frenchman said.

"Yes," said the Howler. "So it seems. When we attack, we'll send in the men on *sogwilis* first. Some will ride straight to the wall and tear it down. Striker told me that it is not very strong, and there are one hundred captives in there. When they tear down the wall, the captives will be free, and they can help us in the fight.

"Other riders will set fire to the houses. The warriors on foot will come in right behind. Striker also told me that the Slavecatchers drink a strange drink. He called it 'crazy water,' and he said that it makes them foolish and sleepy. If we attack them late in the day when they've been drinking this crazy water for a while, maybe they won't be fighting back so well."

"Yes," said Tournier. "They must be drinking Spanish rum. Let's hope that their supply is holding up."

Back at New Town, the houses had all been built, and in his capacity as Peace Chief and ceremonial leader of the town, Comes Back to Life called all the people to the dance ground there beside their townhouse. Each woman who owned a house carried with her a small clay bowl. The sacred fire was burning on the altar.

When the people had all gathered, Comes Back to Life said a brief prayer, and then he had the women with the bowls all line up. Then they came to the sacred fire one at a time, and they took some fire into their bowls to take back to their homes and kindle their home fires there. It was just the same as that time long ago when the first fire of all fires had been brought to the people to use. Comes Back to Life did not bother to retell the tale on the occasion of the lighting of the home fires. Everyone knew it already.

Way back in the beginning of time, there was no fire on the earth, and the animals were cold. One day Thunder took pity on them, and he had his son, Lightning, strike a hollow sycamore tree and set it on fire, deep down inside its hollow trunk.

But the tree was on an island, and the animals looked across the water and saw the fire. They knew that it was good, and they wanted it, and so they had a council to decide what they should do.

The raven, because he could fly over the water, volunteered to go and get it, and so he flew across to the island, and he perched on top of the burning tree, but the flames from beneath him scorched him black.

"Ga ga," he shrieked, and he flew back across without bringing any fire.

Then Wahuhu, the little screech owl, said that he would go, and he flew over to the tree. He flew over the tree and looked down inside to see the fire, but a blast of hot air came out and burned his eyes. Nearly blind, he flew back across, squinting his reddened eyes.

So Uguku, the hooting owl, and Tskili, the horned owl, went together across the water to the burning tree, and the fire was so hot by then, and the smoke was so thick, that both of them were nearly blinded. Just as they were over the fire, a puff of wind sent ashes flying up into their faces, and they flew away rubbing their eyes, but they couldn't rub off the white circles the ashes made around their eyes.

After that the other birds were afraid to try, but little Uksuhi said that he would try. The little snake swam through the water to the island and crawled through the grass to the tree, and he saw a hole there in the trunk down close to the ground. He crawled on through.

But the fire was so hot, he couldn't stand it, and he raced around in circles looking for the hole he had come in through. At last he found it, and he raced back out and back through the grass to the water, and he swam back across to where the others waited. And they saw that he had been burned black.

Then Gulegi, the Climber, decided to go, and he swam across and crawled to the tree, and then he climbed up the side of the trunk. When he reached the top he looked over the edge, and the smoke was so thick that it choked him, and he lost his balance and fell over and down into the fire.

He climbed back out as fast as he could, but just like Uksuhi, he was burned completely black. The animals were dejected. The birds and the snakes had tried and failed, and everyone else was afraid. They held another council, but no one would volunteer to go across the water to get the fire.

Just when they were about to give it all up, Kananeski Amayehi, the water spider, spoke up.

"If no one else will try," she said, "I'll go and get the fire."

The others looked doubtful, but no one else was willing to try, and no one had any other ideas, so they didn't disagree. Then while they watched, the little spider began to spin a thread, but she did not spin it into a web. Instead she wove a *tustiga*, a little bowl, and put it on her back.

She walked across the water then, and through the grass until she came to the burning sycamore tree, and then she put one little burning coal into the bowl on her back. She walked back through the grass and back across the water, and the animals made a fire from the tiny coal.

They rode boldly toward the camp, making no attempt to keep their presence a secret from the enemy, not worrying about surprise. Even so, they were fairly close before any of the Slavecatchers noticed that anyone was coming. Perhaps in their drunkenness, some had seen or heard them and assumed that it was their own men coming back with the horses and captives.

Breaks Their Heads was drunk, along with many others, but Breaks Their Heads was drunk because he was so sore. He was bruised and cut all over his body from the trampling he had suffered, and some of his ribs were broken, he knew. He had thought that drunkenness would relieve his pain, and it had, at least a little.

When he first heard the horses, he thought what the others were thinking. He didn't even look up. He had more important things to worry about. He was out of *ron*, and he wanted some more. With a tremendous effort, because of the pain in his ribs and because of his drunken state, he got himself to his feet. He knew where he could get more *ron*. But just as he was about to head for his destination, he looked up in the direction of the approaching riders.

Something was wrong, but his brain was too fuzzy to figure it out at once, and the evening light was fading. There were too many horses. The Slavecatchers had lost only six. He wondered if the men who had gone out could have stolen some more. The riders came closer. He squinted into the twilight, trying to focus his eyes on someone, any one of the riders, to see if he would recognize him, and then he did.

It was Striker, the escaped captive, the man whose back he had meant to flay with the long Spanish whip. Breaks Their Heads thought, Why have they let him ride? They should have tied a rope around his neck and made him run behind the horses. He stared at Striker too long, for when he finally tore his eyes away to focus on another rider, he saw that it was none of his companions.

"To arms. To arms," he cried. "We're being attacked!"

Drunken Slavecatchers staggered out of huts with war clubs or knives or Spanish swords in their hands. A few of them had pistols. They began to gather there in the middle of their huts around Breaks Their Heads.

"Who are they?" one asked.

"How should I know?" said Breaks Their Heads. "Just get ready to kill them."

"How many of them are there?"

"I don't know. Twenty, maybe. Thirty."

Then they saw the others coming up behind on foot.

"Fifty or more. Get everyone out here. Hurry."

Then the riders were in the camp. The men with pistols fired them off and missed their targets, and then the weapons were useless. They threw them at their attackers.

Breaks Their Heads looked up to see a big horse rushing at him, and the memory of being trampled raced back through his mind. The man on the horse was a white man, and he was waving a sword, and Breaks Their Heads could tell that the white man was not Spanish. He turned to run, and he felt the slash of a steel blade across his back, and he knew that the cut was deep. He felt the touch of air on parts of him that had never felt the air before, and he staggered and fell.

Striker and Woyi had ridden straight to the entryway to the compound that held the captives, and each of them grabbed a piece of fence and pulled. Inside, the captives realized what was going on. Some of them rushed out through the passageway to take part in the fight. Others began pushing and pulling at sections of fence.

Four Frenchmen, acting on earlier orders from Tournier, rode straight to the big fire that was blazing there and grabbed pieces of burning wood. They touched flame to the huts nearby and tossed the torches onto the roofs of other huts. Soon nearly the whole camp was ablaze.

Even though the forces led by the Howler were outnumbered, it was more like a killing spree than a battle, for the Slavecatchers, most of them drunk, were in no shape to fight. Real People and Senikas bashed their heads, and Frenchmen stabbed and slashed them. Some of the former captives grabbed Slavecatchers from behind and choked them with their bare hands. Others grabbed up anything they could find to use as weapons: sticks of wood, pieces of rope, weapons that the dead had dropped. Then the slaughter was over, as suddenly as it had begun.

For a while there was loud rejoicing, and many of the former captives vented their long-held hatred of the Slavecatchers by abusing the bodies of their former tormentors. At last they tired and quieted down. The Howler suggested they all move west together, away from the filth and carnage, and make a camp for the night.

54

They salvaged some food from the Slavecatchers' camp, and the Howler and his followers had, of course, brought some provisions with them. Still, with the one hundred former captives in camp, the portions the next morning were small. Some of the men went out to hunt, and some of them came back successful.

They stayed in the camp all that day, and by the end of the day, everyone was well fed. But, of course, it was too late in the day to travel, and so they stayed a second night. The next morning they ate again, and then the Howler called them all together for a meeting.

It was determined that some of the freed captives, especially young men, and some groups all from the same area with young men among them, could find the way back home and should be able to take care of themselves along the way. But there were some women and children who would not be able to fend for themselves. Something would have to be done for them.

Following much discussion, it was discovered that some of the groups could take some of these to their homes along their own way home without too much trouble, and when at last only a few were left with no place to go, the Howler said that they could go to New Town. All was arranged, and that same morning, various individuals and groups started on their different ways.

Only when everyone was taken care of in one way or another did the Howler say that he and his followers were ready to depart.

———

Olig' and his band found themselves at Itowah. The trail they followed had led them there, and there they learned that the invaders who had started all the trouble had been Slavecatchers. They also learned that Striker had followed the Slavecatchers by himself, and that the Slavecatchers had killed a man of the Wolf Clan who had been guarding the pass near Itowah.

Then Howler and Woyi with the Frenchmen and the Senikas had come, and Woyi had gone on alone, impatient with the Howler's decision to wait a while at Itowah. Following a council at Itowah, the Howler's force had been increased by men led by the Wild Man of the Wolf Clan. They had all gone east.

This new information eased the mind of Olig' a little, for he estimated that now the Howler's force was about fifty strong, and he couldn't imagine a danger they might encounter that they couldn't handle. Even so, they had been gone for a long time, too long for the simple pursuit of the seven invaders, he thought. And there was still the problem of the young woman captive and of Striker and Woyi who had each gone out alone. He decided that he would continue east and search for them all.

In New Town, the talk was all about the coming wedding of Comes Back to Life and Osa. It was not malicious gossip, for the Real People were accustomed to such marriages. They were not common, not every man had more than one wife, but they did occur. And, of course, any marriage is a fit subject for talk.

"Our Peace Chief is getting a second wife," they said.

"How will his first wife like that, do you think?"

"Ha. She won't mind. Already she's keeping the child of Osa as if it were her own."

"I heard that it was she who proposed the match in the first place."

"Guwisti?"

"Yes. It was her idea."

"Well, Comes Back to Life is young. Maybe Guwisti wants to have some nights when she can sleep."

And they all laughed at that.

Then came the day of the wedding. A great feast was laid out at the expense of Comes Back to Life, and the people ate and danced and talked and laughed, and then they all got quiet when Comes Back to Life met Osa in the square. She handed him a basket filled with corn. He gave her venison in exchange.

Together they walked into her house. Guwisti stood by with both babies, and even little Whirlwind was well behaved.

As soon as the newly married couple had disappeared into the house, the joking and laughing continued, and the general festivities lasted well into the night. In another day or two, the news was old, the new relationship was known to all and there was no longer any reason to discuss it. The talk turned to the absent Olig' and the long-absent Howler, Woyi and Striker.

"What could have kept them out so long?"

"Might the hateful Spaniards be back in this country?"

"Could the Frenchmen and Senikas have turned on our people?"

That last question became the subject of long debates. Everyone knew what the Spaniards had been like, and the Frenchmen were white men too. The people recalled the incident at Kituwah when the Frenchmen had violated the sanctuary of the town by bringing in their weapons. They recalled their rule about keeping foreigners out of their land, and many said that it had been a bad mistake to break that rule and allow the Frenchmen in.

And the Senikas were long-time enemies of the Real People. It had been doubly foolish, some said, to let white men talk them into bringing in their old enemies. Perhaps the French and Senikas had been plotting together against the Real People all along.

Howler and Woyi had gone out on this mission with no one behind them except the French and Senikas. Some made up their minds that Howler and Woyi and probably Striker, too, were all already dead.

If that were the case, how would Olig' fare with his small band when he caught up with them? Then some said that Olig' would likely never find them, for the Frenchmen and Senikas had probably killed the three Real People and headed north immediately thereafter, for the safety of the Senika country.

"If they ever dare to come back this way," one man said, "we should kill them all."

But it was time for the Ceremony of the Great Moon, and it would be the first major ceremony to take place in New Town. The people of neighboring Coyatee had no one to lead the ceremonies for them, so they would be invited, and surely they would all attend. When the people saw Comes Back to Life busy preparing for the ceremony, their minds turned to that great event.

There was still some talk of Olig' and the others, of course, but it was not so much as before. Now there were other things to think about and other things to do.

And Guwisti and Osa were both busy with the preparations. As the wives of Comes Back to Life, they shared the responsibilities with him, and it was the first time for them both, for it was also the first time that Comes Back to Life would lead a major ceremony on his own.

For the first time since the loss of her first husband, Osa was happy and content. She found herself surprisingly comfortable with her new status, and she and Guwisti got along wonderfully with one another. They were like sisters, and they were like two mothers to the twin babies.

Even Whirlwind was not quite so possessive with her mother as she had been before, and would sometimes allow herself to be kept for short periods of time by Guwisti. Osa had noticed that the other residents of New Town were treating her with a new respect and some of the other women were even becoming her friends.

Oliga was following a trail that had been traveled recently by a number of men riding horses, so he was pretty sure that he was on the trail of the Howler. He did still wonder from time to time about the loyalty of the Frenchmen and the Senikas, but he tried not to think such thoughts.

Then he saw them, a larger force than he was expecting, and they were coming toward him. He recognized the Frenchman first, because of his hat and his other strange clothing, but then he recognized the Howler, and a moment later he could see both Woyi and Striker. He went forward to meet them, and when they came together, they stopped to make a camp.

"We were worried about you back at New Town," Oliga explained. "You'd been gone for so long."

"The Slavecatchers took Striker in a boat and got well ahead of us," said the Howler. "It just took us longer to catch up with them because of that."

"Took Striker?" Olig' said.

Then they had to tell the whole tale over again, how Striker had been captured rescuing the young woman, how Woyi and Awiakta had met and followed Striker, how the Slavecatchers had led them all to an entire village of Slavecatchers, and how the Howler and the rest had eventually wiped the Slavecatchers out.

"And all of this without losing anyone?" Oliga asked.

"We had not a single man," said Howler, "or woman, lost in the battles."

"You've done well," said Olig'. "The people at home will be very glad to hear about it all."

Then Olig' turned toward Awiakta.

"We'll have to take you home," he said. "Your parents must be worried about you."

"You and the rest can go straight back to New Town if you like," said Woyi. "Striker and I will take her home."

"And we might stay with her there," said Striker.

"You mean the two of you might not return at all to New Town?" Olig' asked.

"A man is supposed to live with his wife," said Woyi. "Awiakta is going to be our wife."

"Both of you will marry her?" said Oliga.

"Yes," said Striker.

"A woman can have two husbands," said Awiakta, "just as a man may have two wives."

"Well, yes," said Oliga. "Of course."

And it was true. She could. He'd heard of it before, but never in his life had he actually known of two men marrying the same woman, of a woman with two husbands. It was—to say the least—unusual. But Awiakta was right, it was not forbidden.

Well, he thought, those two young men are certainly carrying their friendship through all the way. He'd heard it said that when two men had gone through the Ceremony of Making Friends, nothing could come between them. They would be inseparable friends for life. They shared everything. He had never before thought of it in quite this way, though.

"Well," he said, "if we start back early in the morning, we should arrive at New Town in time for the Great Moon Ceremony. Comes Back to Life mentioned it to me before I left. He said that it was time for him to select his seven councillors. They should be counting the days by now."

"Ah," said Tournier, "so soon."

"Will you stay for the ceremony?" Olig' asked.

"I think that Owl and his people should be getting home," said the Frenchman, "and I and my men should accompany them. We've already delayed our return in order to go on this mission with you. Your Gola will be on us soon with cold weather, and we should make our trip before it's here. Thank you for the invitation, but we should move on."

"At least you should stop at New Town on your way," said Oliga, "and let us supply you for your trip."

Tournier glanced at Owl, and Owl nodded his assent.

"*Wado*, my friend," said Tournier. "We will."

All doubts about the Frenchmen and the Senikas at New Town were dispelled when the combined parties of the Howler and Oliga at last returned. They had made it back before the Great Moon Ceremony had begun, and so they were able to call a meeting in which they could relate the whole story to all of the people at once. The Howler told them all how both the French and the Senikas had fought for them and helped them wipe out the hateful Slave-catchers. Oliga stood up to speak right after that.

"Our friends have had a great victory," he said. "And in that fight our new friends and allies have been a great help. But in our celebration of that victory, we must not forget the danger that is still with us.

"The Ani-Asquani may no longer be in our country, or even in the country of our near neighbors, but we have just learned that they have some allies near enough to bother us. We must be always alert to dangers from outside."

They spread a great feast that night, and they ate and danced until well after dark. The next morning, everyone slept late, and the Sun was overhead at her daughter's house before Tournier and Owl led the Frenchmen and Senikas north.

Comes Back to Life had a meeting with his seven councillors, and they determined with him that the time of the Great Moon Ceremony was upon them. He told them to go out and select seven hunters, one from each clan, and send them out to hunt. And he told them to select seven women, one from each clan, to supervise the preparation of the food.

That night, while others slept, while Osa and Guwisti each went to bed alone, Comes Back to Life stayed up late studying the moon and stars.

He had come a long ways. Not much more than one year ago his life had seemed to be over. He had been miserable, and he had thought that the year ahead of him would be the longest year of his life—if he managed to live through it. He had lived through it, and it was over with, it seemed, quickly. In order to stay alive, he'd had to secure himself within the sacred confines of the mother town of Kituwah. Often he had thought that he might not last the year, but then he had actually fulfilled the prophecy of old Uyona. He had died and come back to life, and the life he had come back to was really an entirely new life to him, a life filled with wonder and joy, a life he had never even dreamed of before. He had two wives, two infants and a highly respected position in a new community. Everything about his new life was wonderful. Everything was new.

Glossary

Ado huna, the fourth in the annual cycle of ceremonies, it has been translated as both "friendship" and "propitiation."

Adutludodi, masks.

Ahuli, Drum, here a man's name.

Ama tsunegi, the ceremonial Black Drink, but since the names of things considered to be very sacred cannot be spoken, it was called the White Drink, or literally, White Water. The Ceremony of Ama Tsunegi is third in the annual cycle.

Ani-Gilahi, the Long-Hair Clan, or Long Hairs, or Long Hair People. One of the seven Cherokee clans.

Ani-Kutani, an ancient Cherokee priesthood, which, according to Cherokee oral tradition as recorded by James Mooney for the Bureau of American Ethnology, was eradicated by popular revolution after they had become tyrannical.

Ani-Sawahoni, Shawnees, or Shawnee People.

Ani-Senika, Senikas or Senika People.

Ani-Sinuhdo, the Ceremony of the First New Moon of Spring, the fifth in the annual cycle of ceremonies.

Ani-'Squan', Spaniards, see "Asquani" below.

Ani-Tsisqua, the Bird Clan, or Bird People. One of the seven Cherokee clans.

Ani-Waya, the Wolf Clan, literally, Wolves or Wolf People. One of the seven Cherokee clans.

Ani-Wodi, the Paint Clan, or Paint People. One of the seven Cherokee clans.

Ani-yunwi-ya, the Cherokees' designation for themselves, literally, the Real 'People or the Original People. After the Cherokees adopted the foreign word, "Cherokee," they began using "Ani-yunwi-ya" to mean "Indian." "Yunwi" is a person. "Ani" is a plural prefix. Thus, "Ani-yunwi" is people. "Ya" is a suffix meaning real or original. See below "Tsisquaya." ("Tsisqua" means bird.)

Apalachee, (not a Cherokee word), a southeastern Indian tribe.

Asquani, a Spaniard. Probably an early Cherokee attempt at pronouncing the Spanish word, "Espanol." The Cherokee language has no "p." The word, in spoken Cherokee, is often contracted to 'squani, or even to 'squan'. Here it is also a man's name.

Asquani-usdi-no, and Little Spaniard. "Asquani" (as above), "usdi" meaning little, "no" is the equivalent of "and."

Atja, speckled trout.

Awi, deer.

Awiakta, Deer Eye, here a woman's name.

Awi-ekwa, elk, literally, big deer.

Awohali, eagle.

Awohali-dihi, eagle-killer.

Calusa, (not a Cherokee word), a southeastern Indian tribe.

Catawba, (not a Cherokee word), a southeastern Indian tribe.

Chalakee, a Choctaw word for the Cherokees, meaning "Cave People." It was likely passed into the southeastern trade jargon and therefore picked up by all of the invading Europeans. Soon everyone was calling the "Real People" some version of the word "Chalakee." Even the "Real People" picked it up eventually, calling themselves "Tsalagi."

Cheraques, (not a Cherokee word), a French rendition of Chalakee. See above.

Coyatee, an ancient Cherokee town name.

Creek, an English designation for the people who call themselves Muskogee. A southeastern Indian tribe and confederacy of tribes.

Dalala, woodpecker.

Dawoja, red elm, or slippery elm.

Delaware, (not a Cherokee word), an eastern Indian tribe.

Diguhsgi, Spider, here a woman's name. (In Cherokee tales, the spider is a weaver.)

Dlayhga, bluejay.

Dojuhwa, a cardinal, or redbird.

Donah Gohuni, Ceremony of the Ripe Corn, the seventh and final ceremony in the annual cycle.

Duhdisdi, pheasant, or ruffled grouse.

Edohi, walker, also a man's name.

Ela talegi, the Bush Feast Ceremony, the first in the annual cycle of ceremonies.

Elikwa, Enough, or That's enough.

Elohi, Earth.

Etsi, Mother.

Gado dejado', What's your name? Literally, What are you called?

Gaduhuh Itsei, New Town. (The word order is "town new.")

Ga ga, kaw, the sound made by a crow.

Gago, who.

Gahawista, dried, parched corn.

Gano-luh'sguh, Whirlwind, here it's a baby girl's name.

Gano-luh'sguh-no, and Whirlwind. The "no" is the equivalent of "and."

Ganuhgwadliski nigalo itsei, common speedwell (Veronica officinalis).

Gatayusti, an ancient Cherokee gambling game, known today (if at all) by the more easily pronounced Creek word, "chunkey," the game involved tossing a stone disc and throwing a spear. When the disc stopped rolling and the spear point stabbed into the ground, the score was based on how close the two were to touching.

Gatlida, originally a projectile point, later also used for "bullet."

Gayahulo, a saddle.

Gogi, roughly, summer; it's actually half the year, the warm half.

Gola, roughly, winter, the cold half of the year.

Gowanigusti, name for an infant's disease, possibly worms, literally, something is causing something to eat them.

Guhli, raccoon.

Gulegi, a blacksnake, literally, Climber.

Guwisti, sifter or sieve, also a common name for a woman. Often contracted to Guwist'.

Hesdi, stop. (Sometimes "Hlesdi.")

Howa, okay.

Huhu, the yellow-breasted chat, or yellow mockingbird.

Ijodi, an ancient Cherokee town, sometimes spelled "Echota."

Itowah, an ancient Cherokee town name, also spelled Etowah.

Jisdu, rabbit. He's the Trickster in Cherokee animal tales.

Jisduh, crawdad.

Kananeski Amayehi, water spider.

Kanati, in Cherokee mythology, the First Man, the husband of Selu (see below), known as the Great Hunter. He may also be Thunder personified.

Kanesa-i galuhq'diyu, the sacred "ark" of the Cherokees, a wooden box carried into battle, inside were other sacred objects. Literally, box, seventh. The vast importance of the box is indicated by the attachment to its name of the sacred number seven.

Kanohena, a drink made from hominy corn, traditionally served to guests.

Kituwah, sometimes spelled "Keetoowah," it's the Mother Town of the Cherokees, the town from which all other towns developed.

Kog' contraction of Koga, crow.

Kutani, one of the ancient priests. (See above, *"Ani-Kutani."*)

Lolo, a locust or cicada, here a woman's name.

Mohawk, (not a Cherokee word), a member tribe of the Iroquois League. (See *"Senika"* below.)

Nihina, And you?

Nodu, blackjack.

Notsi, pine.

Nuh yunuwi, Stone Coat, a mythological character in Cherokee lore.

Nuwadi equa, the Great Moon Ceremony, the second in the ceremonial cycle.

Ofo, (not a Cherokee word), a southeastern Indian tribe.

Oliga, Red-Horse Fish, here a man's name. Often contracted to Olig'.

Osa, (not a Cherokee word), Spanish for "Bear." Here a woman's name.

Osi, a winter house, a small, dome-shaped structure beside the larger summer house.

Powhatans, (not a Cherokee word), a once-powerful confederacy of eastern Indian tribes, made famous by the tall tales of Captain John Smith.

Saloli, squirrel.

Saras, (not a Cherokee word), a southeastern Indian tribe.

Selu, corn, also, the Corn Mother, the First Woman of Cherokee mythology.

Selu tsunegi sdi sdi, the Ceremony of the New Green Corn, the sixth in the annual cycle, sometimes called the early or preliminary corn festival.

Senika, one of the northeastern Iroquoian tribes which formed the League of Five (later Six) Nations, also known as the Iroquois League. The other tribes were Mohawk, Oneida, Onondaga, Cayuga and later, Tuscarora. The more common spelling is "Seneca."

Seti, the black walnut.

Sogwili, horse, literally, according to Mooney, "he carries it on his back." Often contracted to "*sogwil'*."

Shadageya, (a Senika word) eagle, literally, Cloud Dweller.

'Siyo, a greeting, like "Hello." A contraction of "Osiyo."

Stikoyi, an ancient Cherokee town name.

Tilia, basswood.

Timucua, (not a Cherokee word), a southeastern Indian tribe.

Tohigwu, I'm fine.

Tohiju, How are you?

Tseg' Duni, a Cherokee attempt to pronounce the French name, Jacques Tournier.

Tsisquaya, a sparrow, literally, "Real Bird."

Tsiwon', a woman's name.

Tsiyu, a boat (canoe); also, contemporarily, an airplane.

Tskili, horned owl.

Tskwayi, great white heron.

Tsola gayunli, ancient or sacred tobacco.

Tsule-hisanuh-hi, Comes Back to Life, here a man's name.

Tsusga, white oak.

Tsusga Guhnage, black oak.

Tsuwa, Water Dog, here a man's name.

Tustiga, a kind of bowl woven by the water spider.

Uguku, hoot owl

Ujonati, rattlesnake.

Ukitena, a mythological creature, like a large rattlesnake but with antlers and wings, it could breath fire, kill with a look or with its breath. Often contracted to "uk'ten'."

Uksuhi, a small, black snake.

Ukusuhntsudi, Bent Bow Shape, a man's name.

Ulisi, Grandmother.

Ulunsuti, literally, "transparent," a powerful and dangerous divining crystal believed to come from the forehead of an Ukitena.

Unagina, chestnut.

Unali, friend.

Usdi, small; also an infant or a small child.

Uyona, Horn, here also a woman's name.

Wado, Thank you.

Waguli, whippoorwill.

Wahuhu, screech owl.

Walelu uhnaja luhgisgi, spotted touch-me-not.

Wanei, hickory.

Woyi, Pigeon, here a man's name.

Yansa, buffalo.

Yona Hawiya, Bear Meat, here a man's name.

Yoneg, a white person.

Made in the USA
Coppell, TX
04 November 2021

65197383R00206